ENDORSE.

Most books about the Shroud of Turin are purely scientific, but Guy Powell's novel is unique. His controversial approach brings the 2,000-year history of the shroud to life for Christians and those of any faith or no faith at all.

—*Myra Kahn Adams, executive director, SignFromGod.org and NationalShroudofTurinExhibit.org, author of Bible Study for Those Who Don't Read the Bible*

Guy Powell's *The Only Witness* masterfully weaves a myriad of true historical and scientific details regarding the Shroud of Turin into a fascinating novel about this treasured relic and the people who were involved with it. His storytelling breathes life into history and is a joy to read!

—*Theodora ("Teddi") A. Pappas, sindonologist and criminal defense attorney*

Kudos to Guy Powell who, in *The Only Witness*, has skillfully presented a most intriguing work of historical fiction regarding the putative burial cloth of Jesus Christ.

—*Jack Markwardt, historian and author of The Hidden History of the Shroud of Turin*

The missing element in Shroud studies has been a book like this.

—*David Rolfe, BAFTA-winning producer of The Silent Witness and Who Can He Be?*

THE ONLY WITNESS

THE ONLY WITNESS

A ~~The~~ History of the
SHROUD OF TURIN

GUY R. POWELL
Foreword by Joe Marino

REDEMPTION
PRESS

ISBN 13: 978-1-95130-46-2 (Paperback)
978-1-951310-45-9 (ePub)

LCCN: 2023900076

CONTENTS

FOREWORD

I'm honored that Guy Powell asked me to write the foreword for his book. He had posted a YouTube video about a novel he was writing on the Shroud of Turin, a subject I've been deeply immersed in for forty-five years. Over the course of those years, I've written two books and numerous articles and have presented at multiple international conferences. Additionally, I am in constant contact with other scientists and researchers all over the world. Guy had offered a free preview of the book, which I read. I proceeded to make some comments to him about the book, and we were soon emailing and talking on the phone about our mutual interest in the Shroud.

In this novel, Guy has tackled one of the most crucial aspects of the Shroud—its history. Although there are many clues in history that the Shroud existed in the time of Jesus, the historical record is sketchy, so the historical possibility of the cloth's early existence is of the utmost importance. Guy presents a plausible history of the Shroud, beginning with its apparent origins in Jerusalem in the first century AD. It can help to fill in some of the historical lacunae, which, in turn, can help strengthen its case for authenticity.

In telling the story, Guy combines actual historical figures along with fictional characters. There are maps and illustrations, as well as section headers with historical dates and locations. All of these resources help facilitate the readers' understanding of the material.

Guy also includes chapters on the "Shroud of Turin Research Project" (STURP), the 1997 fire in Turin—which some suspect to have been an arson attempt—and another chapter that postulates a likely reason that the 1988 carbon-14 dating test on the Shroud produced medieval dates of AD 1260–1390. That chapter also includes a speculative look at the possible future of Shroud research, providing insight into the valuable work of STURP—the group of mainly American scientists who were given access to the Shroud for five straight days, 120 hours, in 1978 for nondestructive multidisciplinary testing. Their valuable mission was to determine how the image had transferred to the cloth. They were not able to come up with a satisfactory answer. There was real blood on the cloth, and they concluded that the image was not the product of an artist.

The final chapter also informs the reader that Guy's future endeavors, which will include works on such Shroud-related topics as the Sudarium of Oviedo (believed by many to be the face cloth mentioned in John 20:7), the Crown of Thorns, and the True Cross.

While looking forward to more works from Guy, we can, in the meantime, enjoy his historical work about the enigmatic Shroud of Turin.

Joseph G. Marino
BA, Theological Studies, St. Louis University, 1985
Author of *Wrapped Up in the Shroud: Chronicle of a Passion* and
The 1988 C-14 Dating of the Shroud of Turin: A Stunning Exposé

ACKNOWLEDGMENTS

I want to acknowledge and thank a number of people who were instrumental in getting this book completed.

John Catton helped with the historical research. He was great to work with and had a lot of good insight as to the living conditions of people in ancient and medieval times.

Rhiannon Ewalt helped initially doing research and has now switched to being an enormous help in building out the social media presence for the book and assistance for the book launch and eventual promotion of the book once it's published.

Connor McMahon was also a great help in researching the history surrounding the book.

My brother Lloyd Powell was an inspiration getting the book off the ground and providing initial feedback to early versions of the manuscript.

Many others—too many to be named—went into getting this book out. I had a handful of beta readers who helped with general feedback. Many others provided specific insights on various questions.

Everyone at Redemption Press was incredibly helpful in pulling the book over the finish line. Wow, what a great team of professionals!

In addition, there are many Shroud experts, such as Joe Marino and Barrie Schwortz, who were incredibly helpful in providing inspiration.

Recently I've come to know Matt Collins, who has been a great help and inspiration as we spread the message about the Shroud.

Thank you to all of you!

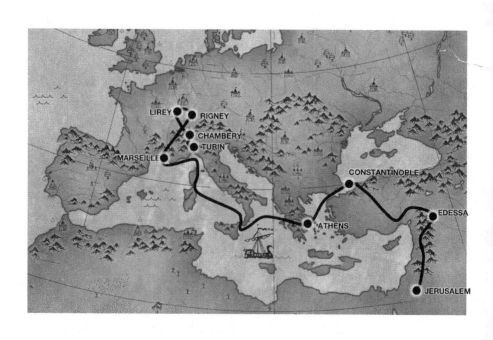

CHAPTER 1

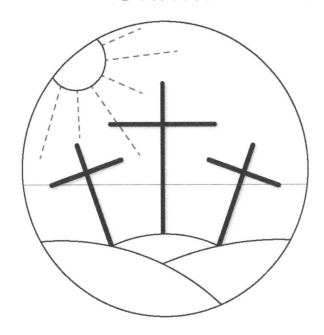

Genesis

Jerusalem, the center of the universe for Judaism, a backwater of the Roman Empire, was situated on the crossroads between the geopolitical powers of Egypt and Persia. Three decades before the Romans would obliterate it, the Jewish hierarchy was in league with their despotic oppressors to keep the peace. One man might have ended this peace. His death now would maintain the short-lived peace yet lead to cycles of war and peace for millennia to come.

JERUSALEM
LATE MORNING, FRIDAY, APRIL 3, AD 33

*J*oachim could hear the muffled voices but couldn't make out what they were saying. While he helped his mother outside to prepare the Seder meal, his father and Nicodemus[1] remained inside, talking quietly. It was clear his father, Jonai of Bethlehem, was concerned, but Nicodemus was persistent.

1 Nicodemus: See John 3:1–21, 7:50–52, and 19:38–42. Leading Pharisee, leader of the Jewish people, member of the Sanhedrin, and friend of Jesus.

Edom, who sat under Nicodemus as a student, came a few minutes later and was out of breath after having raced the entire route from Golgotha. It was a beautiful, sunny morning in the month of Aviv, the time of spring when green fruits and grains ripen for harvest.

"My sincere apologies for my tardiness. The streets were much more crowded than normal."

Nicodemus gave him a short stare, not happy with his tardiness.

Edom stood with his hands folded in front of him, saying nothing. There was something in the air.

Joachim couldn't put his finger on it—something different from the traditional excitement at Passover. They weren't talking about Passover but something else. Joachim was only twelve, but he had seen a lot in his life, or so he thought. "Mother, what are they talking about? I can't hear a word they're saying."

"Hush! It's none of your business." His mother kneaded dough for the Passover matzos underneath their makeshift rain and sun shelter in the court-yard outside their family home. He had helped his mother before, but today, the first day of Passover, the kneading went on longer than he expected. Maybe it was due to the cooler air making the unleavened dough thicker than the leavened dough.

His two sisters assembled the beets and maror to be prepared later in the day.

"Mother, tell me again the story why we eat maror twice for the Passover meal. Those herbs are so bitter."

"You must remember this. Our tradition starts with 'They embittered our lives with hard work.'" She continued reciting the story. "When you have your own family, you will teach them the Haggadah—the story of Passover."

The discussion continued as Joachim's sisters prepared the ingredients of the Passover meal.

Joachim hoped he could have greeted Nicodemus. He, too, wanted to learn from Nicodemus. "Mama, what do I need to do to sit at Nicodemus's feet so I can also learn the Torah?" Joachim's family was from the Levite tribe, but no one in his family was a rabbi. "Will Papa be able to ask him now? I want to be able to study under him. Mama, can't you talk to Papa?"

"No, this is Passover, but today is a very sad day. They have other concerns to worry about." Joachim's mother was certain it wouldn't be a good time to ask.

The discussion between Nicodemus and his father was interminable, and worse yet, they spoke softly so they couldn't be overheard. There were no grins or laughs—a stark contrast from the typical Passovers when the whole family gathered to walk through the story of Moses and the Exodus.

As his mother's strong arms kneaded the dough, Joachim took care of the fire in their oven. It wasn't difficult since the morning fire still glowed with some embers from the night before.

After removing the excess ash, he placed a mixture of straw, one piece of wood, and a slice of dung, and the fire quickly reached the temperature needed for a good baking fire. "Mother, the fire is ready, but the oven needs a few minutes to fully heat up."

Once the oven was warm enough, the first matzos were placed in the oven. It was only then that Joachim's father and Nicodemus came to some resolution. Breakfast had been over for an hour, but they still gathered around the table. A few pieces of leftover bread and some olives lay on the cutting board. Jonai reclined at one end of the triclinium, the platform where the family would lie and partake of their meals. Nicodemus was to his left, and Edom was to their right, standing.

When Edom left Golgotha, he had been given a small coin pouch from Joseph[2] for the purchase of the cloth, and now Edom gave it to Joachim's father. Though Edom was apprenticed to Nicodemus, he had also grown to respect and love Joseph, a wealthy man from the small village of Arimathea, just outside of Jerusalem.

"Joachim," his father called, speaking loud enough so that Joachim could hear him from outside. "Come here. I need you to run an errand, and you need to do it now, quickly!"

Joachim was just outside the doorway, stoking the oven fire but keeping his ears open to hear what he could.

"Joachim."

Joachim moved to the doorway, upon his father's beckoning.

"I want you to go to the cloth maker, Hagepeth son of Apollinara, next to the assistant rabbi's home. See if he has some new cloth. It must be white and clean. Here is some money. It should be enough. Now don't tell him anything about what it's for." He handed him the money pouch from Edom.

Joachim was surprised at how heavy it was. It was heavier than he expected. He had never been given this many coins before. "But, Papa, I don't know what it's for. Why do you need this cloth? Mama doesn't sew very well, and we have never needed white." He grabbed his shirt to expose the uneven stitching throughout. "Mama says it gets too dirty too fast."

"Look, Joachim. This is very important. You must go, and go quickly. It's already past breakfast, and it may be too late," his father demanded. "Oh, and

---

2 Joseph of Arimathea: See Matthew 27:57, Mark 15:43, Luke 23:50–52, and John 19:38. Member of the Sanhedrin. Arimathea, presumed to be just north of Jerusalem.

the cloth must be at least three feet wide and fourteen feet long. We can't use anything less. As soon as you've found it, come right back here. Then I will tell you what to do with it."

Joachim took the coins. He wanted to run down the street, but the streets were crowded with pilgrimaging Jews and their animals making their way to the temple. He didn't have his bearings correct and spun around. He hoped his father hadn't seen him running in the opposite direction in front of their home. He was swimming upstream against the traffic away from the direction of the temple. He knew his father wouldn't yell at him, but he also didn't want to disappoint him. From the tone in his father's voice, this errand was consequential.

He decided to turn right at the baker's, and then he ran up the hill until he came to the home of the assistant rabbi next to the city wall. The assistant rabbi's home wasn't like Joachim's. Jonai told his son that the assistant rabbi didn't need much space since he lived alone and didn't have the luxury of living with his larger family in a compound like theirs. There was room for little more than one stool and a small table. Apparently, the assistant rabbi hoped he'd live in his family's small compound when it came time to marry and have children.

Once past the rabbi's home, it wasn't much farther. The morning air was warming. As Joachim ran he could feel the sweat sticking to his shirt, but it wasn't warm enough to remove his shirt.

The city was beautiful this time of year. He was looking forward to the hard work of helping his father plant the wheat in the springtime. He was now twelve, and with that came new responsibility. Soon he might even be married, if his father and mother could make a suitable arrangement.

Joachim arrived and approached the entryway. Partially yelling and partially speaking, Joachim said, "Weaver Hagepeth, it is Joachim. My father, Jonai of Bethlehem, sent me. We need some nice white cloth. Are you there?" He felt a surge of Jews streaming past the weaver's compound.

"Yes, yes. I am here. Slow down. I'm coming," the weaver answered. "What do you need this for? Are you getting married?" Hagepeth smiled. "If not, I have some fine linen cloth that would be perfect for you. Why does your father need the cloth? He knows I don't often weave white cloth. What is he going to do with it? Is it a gift for his beautiful bride?"

His curiosity annoyed Joachim. He didn't know the answer. Trying to ignore the questions, Joachim noticed Hagepeth's young son peeing into a large jug. The collected urine would be used later for bleaching the materials to make a fine white for his richer patrons.

"No, no," Joachim interrupted. "I don't know what it's for, but he was exacting about the size. It must be white, made of fine linen or wool, and measure three feet by fourteen feet. How much would this be?"

"Wait, wait, my young one," Hagepeth said, slowing him down. "I must look to see what I have. I just wove a bolt of white cloth for the Jeremiah family." He searched through the pieces he had. "Ah, here they are. These are the only white pieces of material I have. Let's measure them to make sure they're long enough. If they aren't long enough, perhaps I sew them together for him? Otherwise, I have some cloth bleaching now. It will be ready in a few days. What does he want with this? Surely, he is not going to till the fields in it?" Hagepeth laughed at his own joke.

"I keep telling you, I don't know, but he said it was very important. Adon Hagepeth, please, I just want to get the cloth and bring it home," Joachim interrupted using the formal *Adon* appellation, starting to realize this may not be as easy as he thought.

"So why does your father send you out to find a cloth on a day such as this? There is a lot of stirring in the wind today and right in the middle of Passover. We must be careful and look in all directions before we venture out. No one can trust those Romans," he said in a hushed voice as he rearranged the rolls of cloth to remove the two white bolts of cotton. "Well, the first piece I have is maybe a bit too wide, four feet, but it is not long enough. It is only four and a half feet long, but it is a fine linen. Perhaps that will do? Do you want to take it with you? If it is too short, you can bring it back, as long as you don't drop it in the Jordan river on the way home." He chuckled. "Your father can always cut it down to the right width. Or I can. Do you have sharp shears at home?"

"But that isn't long enough. How long is the other piece?" Joachim probed, getting impatient.

"The other piece, I believe, is shorter. Let me measure." Hagepeth folded up the first piece and carefully placed it back on the pile of cloth, making certain to keep it clean. "Ah, here we go." He pulled out the second bolt of white linen and unrolled it on the only table in his home. "This one is just over ten feet long. Won't that do? Why does he need such a funny size? Come, I sew them together for him, and that will work. I will give him a good price."

"But the colors don't match well. This one is not as white as the other one." Jonai was certain his father didn't want two pieces sewn together. That just wouldn't make any sense.

"Now, why don't you run back home and see if your father would like to buy both pieces sewn together? I can easily sew them together, and he can have them before lunchtime," Hagepeth asserted, trying to make his sale for the day. "Listen, I know your father. This is what he would want you to do, and I will let him have the material for twelve drachmas. It is one of the best cloths I have made in many months."

Joachim was hesitant, realizing this was going to take some finesse. He had seen his father handle other merchants before, but this time he was alone, and he had never bought something this valuable. "Okay, I will run home and ask. Then I will come back. Twelve drachmas, though, may be too high. My father didn't give me that much money." Joachim wasn't going to let on that he had fifteen drachmas. He knew that his father never meant for him to spend it all for this cloth. From watching his father bargain, he knew he should counter with nine, maybe ten if it was a special cloth.

Joachim remembered another weaver over near the granary on the way back home. It was fifteen or twenty minutes by foot, with all the people in the streets. He decided his father would appreciate it if he went to the second weaver. It was over by the public toilets. With the swelling crowds from Passover, it would take a little bit longer to run there and back. *But what did Hagepeth the weaver mean by being careful? Is that why my father was so secretive with his friends, Nicodemus and Edom? They had always met with other friends and talked quietly, but they were never this uneasy. What were they afraid of?*

It hadn't rained in over two weeks, so there was little water flowing through the city's sewage system. Joachim hoped he could avoid walking past the public latrines, but in his haste, he couldn't remember the way to avoid them. The smell coming from the public latrines was atrocious. Only two people were using them, a woman and her young daughter. They held their noses while they sat. It was the worst he'd smelled in a long time. The buzzing of the flies was like the frenetic sound of a beehive. He ran past as quickly as he could and tried not to breathe, but it was impossible to escape the smell. He closed his eyes for a second as one of the latrine flies buzzed his face.

"Watch where you're goin'!" The sewer cleaner shouted as Joachim ran directly into him. His stench was putrid. The man had only one front tooth and sores all over his arms.

Joachim immediately pivoted on his left foot to avoid the man and put distance between them. He ran faster to separate himself from the sewer worker and the stench.

"Get. Get. Get!" the man yelled after him, knowing he had power over others conveyed upon him through his fetid stench.

After another few minutes, he came up to the door of the second weaver. "Hello, hello," he was out of breath, so his second hello was not very loud.

There was a girl of maybe five years in the street, and she replied. The fragrances from the spice vendor next door were intoxicating, especially after having breathed in the stench from the sewer cleaner.

"My uncle is not here. If you need to buy cloth, you must go over there, and he will come." She pointed to a door across the way, about three doors down, just on the other side of the spice vendor. "If you want, I can go get him. I am supposed to clean our home and not venture too far, especially today."

"No, I will go and ask," already walking in the direction that the girl pointed. She was very well dressed for such a young girl. Business must be good for this weaver. "Girl, what is your uncle's name?" He shouted from across the way, trying to be loud enough to be heard over the others in the street making their way to the temple.

"It is Rosanai," she said, loud enough for all to hear.

"Adon Rosanai, Adon Rosanai, it is me, Joachim. My father is Jonai of Bethlehem. I am looking for some nice white linen cloth for my father. Do you have any?" Joachim shouted into the doorway the girl had just pointed to. The memory of the sewer man's stench made him want to hold his nose. He was afraid the stench from the man and the latrines had seeped into his pores and was now radiating back into the air. He swallowed a few times, but his mouth was dry, and it didn't help to get rid of the memory of the smell. A slight breeze was blowing in the opposite direction, so the sweet fragrances from the spice vendor couldn't be sensed. A small ball of shorn wool rolled across the street, driven by the breeze.

"Yes, son, but I don't think I know you or your father. How is it that you come to me? Who is your father?"

Joachim looked inside, and there were four other men sitting and sipping posca, a sour vinegar and water drink flavored with spices. They all turned and looked him over. *Why are they looking at me so suspiciously?*

"Weaver Rosanai, I just came from Hagepeth the weaver, and he didn't have what my father needed. Do you know him? He is the weaver near the east wall. He had two nice pieces of cloth, but they needed to be sewn together. And their colors didn't match well."

"Yes, yes, but why do you come out today? It is not safe for anyone to be on the streets. There are a lot of serious things happening. Your father would be wise to try tomorrow."

"No, no, I need it today. This morning. What do you have? My father needs a cloth—a white cloth—at least three feet wide and fourteen feet long?" Joachim emphasized it had to be white.

Rosanai turned, thinking. *No, it couldn't be.* "That is a strange size. It is not often someone comes asking for that size of cloth. What do you need it for?"

Rosanai's eyes burned directly into Joachim's, and Joachim felt a chill of fear go up his spine. Neither of them said anything. Rosanai looked away and headed out the door.

"Come this way. I may have something for you." The weaver hurried across the street, darting back and forth to make his way through the throngs of Jews.

Joachim did his best to keep up. They arrived at the weaver's home. The home was quite clean, with planking on the floor and a nice table in the middle of the room. Behind the table were large and small jugs of dye, stained with a range of colors. Ruth, the girl he met earlier in the street, was inside.

"Ruth, go get—what was your name?" He turned to Joachim. "Yes, Joachim. Ruth, go tell your sister, Elizabeth, to fetch Joachim some posca. He looks like he ran here from a long way. I hope you like it with mint and coriander. Also, go tell her to bring a slice of citron."

Elizabeth returned with the cup of posca. Ruth stood behind her. "Don't worry, it's not too strong. It's Elizabeth's favorite. It has more vinegar than wine." Rosanai eyed Joachim, who he could tell was thankful to be receiving some much-needed liquid.

He drank it all down.

"So, what kind of cloth do you need in this unique size?" He said the word hinting that it wasn't that unique.

"My father said it must be white and of fine linen. He doesn't want wool unless it is the only thing available." As Joachim answered the weaver, he noticed Elizabeth for the first time. She was cute with long, wavy black hair, with most of it hidden behind her head covering. She carried a few beautiful pink rock roses. Joachim guessed she was eleven or twelve.

"Onka, I picked a few pink roses. Do you like them?" Elizabeth enjoyed collecting flowers. Although her uncle wasn't wealthy, they were better off than others, affording her the freedom to spend time with her flowers. "I'll be right back with more posca." She left the flowers and the citron on the table. Elizabeth, her sister Ruth, and their mother had lived with Rosanai ever since the girls' father drowned.

"Well, if it's white you're looking for, we may be out of luck. I only have a few small pieces in white. For the size you are looking for, I may not have anything. Last year I made this special cloth for the butcher's wife on the occasion of Purim, but when the day came, he got very sick and never picked it up. It was a very special cloth with a herringbone weave. It took me three long weeks to make it, and I have never been paid. If you want it, I will give it to you for a special price. Material of the size you want must always be special." Rosanai emphasized *always*, realizing he knew more than Joachim did about the purpose of this cloth. Joachim was not yet acquainted with death; he didn't understand the significance of his request.

"Let's look at this cloth. I think you will realize how beautiful it is once you see it."

Joachim still hadn't purchased the cloth. The time was just after noon. His stomach made its emptiness known, despite the memory of that putrid smell. He hoped his father would not be upset. There wasn't any other choice. Joachim had spent all morning searching.

"Ah, here it is. What do you think? It is slightly longer and wider than you asked. It should be perfect for what your father needs. It is more of a light tan-gray than white. What do you think?" Rosanai asked. "You know, in times like these, you mustn't be picky. Jewish custom doesn't mind if the color isn't white, it must simply be pure."

Now Joachim was confused. *Did he know what it was for? How could he? I don't even know. And what does Jewish custom have to do with it?*

"Please, I must get back to my friends." Rosanai tried to hurry the boy along. "They are waiting for me, and I don't want to be out today. It may not be safe."

Joachim wondered why he kept bringing up this concern for his safety.

Elizabeth turned to leave and then turned to smile back at Joachim.

"It is a beautiful cloth," Joachim said, as he watched Rosanai spread out the cloth on the table. "I have never seen a weave like this. What does it mean?"

"It is a very special weave. It takes over three days to set up the special tooling on the loom to make this weave. I learned how to make it from a guest of the royal palace. The governor had a guest from the South, from Nubia. He stayed for many months, and his servant came and requested it. When I told him no one in the city could make it for him, he went running back to the palace. He was a funny man. He was black, with fine tattoos on his face and arms. There may have been more, but I didn't see them. Anyway, the special guest—the prelate himself—came into my home the next day. Imagine that. All the way from far in the South. He showed me this special weave. Even his servant knew of this weave. He ordered his servant to stay behind and help me to set up the loom. He didn't speak much Greek—no Hebrew—but he did know some Latin. He was a very interesting man. He was captured many years before and put into slavery. I think he was much smarter than his master, but he never revealed it when his master was present.

Anyway, I only made one bolt of cloth for the prelate, and then he was off. I don't know if he ever returned to the city."

Now Rosanai looked deep in Joachim's eyes. "But I always kept in the back of my mind how special this weave was. I think I am the only weaver in all Jerusalem who knows how to make it," he said, staring out the door proudly, as if he invented it. "That was many years ago. I was younger then. Elizabeth was only a few years old.

"When the baker asked for something special, Elizabeth suggested I try to make something like what the Egyptian had asked for. I don't think they weave material like this very often either. It certainly makes an impression on everyone who sees it. I have only shown it to a few customers, but none of them ever wanted something this special. I think Elizabeth was hoping I would never show it to anyone, and I would give it to her. She is my sister's eldest daughter. She has become my princess. With my wife having passed away two years ago, I must now spend money very wisely." Rosanai could have spoken all day if allowed to continue, but now he wanted to get back to his wine and his friends.

"So, Joachim, son of Jonai of Bethlehem, what do you think? Is it good enough for you? I let you have it for fifteen drachmas. That is a fair price. Look, the sun is getting very high, and you must get back with this cloth to your father. What would you like to do?"

At that moment, Elizabeth came back in. Her smile was gone. Her magic cloth was about to be sold, and she knew no one could resist her uncle when it came to selling high-quality cloth.

"Okay, I will take it. But only if you let me bring it back if my father doesn't like it. I think it is perfect, although I am not exactly sure why he needs it. Why would he need something like this?"

Rosanai was stumped for words and didn't want to bring up death in front of Elizabeth. The death of her father was still a painful subject for both girls.

"Never you mind. Come take the cloth. Pay me fourteen drachmas and be on your way before it is time for the midday meal. That's one less than I really want."

Joachim hesitated and then relented. He had been gone an hour, and he needed to get back. He was certain his father never thought he would be gone this long. Joachim counted the drachmas out on the table, looked at Elizabeth and then Rosanai. Elizabeth looked disappointed, but Joachim knew he had to be off. "Thank you, Weaver Rosanai. My father will be most grateful."

Joachim now had to run back home. It was starting to get quite warm in the sun. It was after noon, and the city had come alive, bustling with even more Jewish worshipers with their sacrificial goats and lambs. Everyone was talking in hushed tones, in opposition to the vivid colors of the wild and cultivated flowers. It was springtime, and the bees buzzed from flower to flower. The birds flitted in the trees, building their nests, unaware of what was in store for the Jews in Jerusalem.

Joachim hoped his father would be happy with his purchase. After all, it was the only option.

"Why are you so late?" His father reprimanded, instantly seeing the cloth was not white. But before he said another word, he took a deep breath. "Was it difficult to find some cloth? Why did you spend so much time with old Hagepeth? Was he not there when you arrived? Let me see what you have brought."

Jonai picked up the cloth. "But it is not white. This is very strange. I have never seen anything like this before."

Joachim interrupted. "Yes, Father. It is very different. The style comes from a prelate in Egypt. Weaver Hagepeth didn't have any cloth of the size you required, so I went to Weaver Rosanai. I had to run all the way over past the temple to his shop near the bakery. It isn't far from the palace." He paused to catch his breath. "He—Rosanai—said he may not know you, but he wasn't sure. It sounded like he knew what it was for. He said this cloth is very special, unique for what you need it for. What was it—"

Jonai interrupted him before he could ask his question. "Good, good. You have done well. This is a perfect cloth. It will do very well." Jonai inspected it further. He was surprised at how fine the material was, especially with this unusual weave.

A sense of foreboding came over Joachim.

"I must run and take this cloth to Edom's father, Joseph. I hope it's not too late. I want you to stay near our home today. Do not wander very far. These may be dangerous times, especially as the hour of darkness appears." As Jonai said this, he hoped he hadn't let slip too much. No matter, he would be leaving shortly, and Joachim would be home together with his sister and his mother.

At that moment, Abigail, Joachim's mother, came in carrying water, onions, and oil for the noontime meal. "Jonai, aren't you going to stay and eat with us?" she asked. "You know how much I don't like it when you are not here to eat with us. I also have some fresh garam. I know you like it."

"Not today. I must help Edom and Nicodemus. Joachim just bought this cloth, and I must take it to them immediately. It is important they get the cloth before it's too late." And that was it. Jonai was off, out the door, walking swiftly up the alleyway toward the palace and the temple.

✝✝✝

"Papa, Papa, wait. I'll come with you." Joachim shouted after his father, who was already out the door. "I want you to speak to Nicodemus about—"

"No, Joachim, not today," he interrupted his son. "You stay here. I don't want you that close to—" Jonai did not want to disclose the heartrending task he had in front of him.

"But where are you going?"

"I go to Golgotha," his father finally relented. And he was off.

"But, Papa," Joachim pleaded. His father didn't listen and simply ignored the plea.

✝✝✝

At that time, Jerusalem was a bustling city of about 75,000. Jonai did not live close to the palace nor Golgotha. He was to meet Joseph at Golgotha, which was right outside the gates, and hand over the cloth. No one ventured near Golgotha for fear of the iron fist of the Romans and because the smell of suffering would turn even the most hardened man's stomach. Only the Roman soldiers enjoyed watching the dissidents and the scum of the earth suffer in their agony. It was a trying time with much talk about this King of the Jews, a controversy Jonai would have preferred avoiding altogether.

As he traveled, Jonai reflected. *I heard this man. Believed him. Saw the many loaves come out of nowhere. How could I refuse? "Blessed are those who are persecuted because of righteousness . . ."*

The streets were full of people and animals. He tried to walk hurriedly, but his pace was slow as he tried to avoid them and their animal's dung piles in the streets. Jonai had to reach Golgotha before it was too late. Near the temple, the money changers set up tables to change the heathen Roman money into Jewish currency.

"Excuse me, excuse me. Please let me through," Jonai said, making his way through the crowds of worshipers and animals around the tables. "I'm so sorry." He pushed a bit too hard, and one of the worshipers dropped his cage with the two doves he had for his family's sacrifice.

The man sneered at Jonai but let him pass. He said something, but it was not a language Jonai understood. The man was frustrated he had to change his money from his homeland so he could pay the half-shekel temple tribute. His facial expression changed when he realized the cage hadn't burst open and his doves were still safely in their cage. When he looked up, he said something again. It sounded like "*Chag Pesach sameach*," but with his accent, Jonai wasn't certain whether it was Happy Passover or not.

"Again, my apologies. Let me give you the half-shekel you'll need for the temple. There's no reason for you to spend time waiting for your turn with the money changer." Jonai felt sorry for the foreigner and gifted him the half-shekel.

"*Chag sameach.*"

Jonai bowed and turned to push his way further through the throng.

Finally, the street cleared just a little. He hadn't been in this much of a hurry in a long time. *It's critical I get there before . . .* His thoughts trailed off as he began to think the unthinkable. *This great man, was He truly the Messiah? The Son of God would be dead, and I'm carrying His burial cloth. The cloth wasn't exactly what I wanted, but it was all Joachim could find this day. And besides, it had been Nicodemus that had simply expected me to help. What was I to do?* In his mind's voice, he spoke these last five words in staccato.

Golgotha certainly wasn't a place that anyone visited frequently, if ever. Known as the place of the skull, it could have been a pretty knoll in the springtime if it were covered with grass and wildflowers. Yet with its reputation for suffering, it was shaped like a rounded bare skull, remarkable for its resemblance to that of the most enduring shapes of a man after death.

Golgotha was all the more chilling because it was where many criminals and political prisoners were crucified. It was here that they suffered excruciating pain as their lives drained out of them, hanging from a cross hoping each breath would be their last. Many of the criminals' bodies were simply removed from the cross and thrown to the side to make way for the next. If no one claimed them, they could lie there for days, their stomachs bloating up. Uncollected bodies were taken to the Southeastern Hill, the garbage dump for all of Jerusalem.

The crucified didn't have to be fully dead for the buzzards to inflict their final indignity, pecking at their bodies and their eyes. If that wasn't enough, if they weren't dead before about three in the afternoon, the Romans would break their legs so they could be done with their duties before sunset. Jonai wasn't sure which death was worse.

As he traveled, Jonai's thoughts turned to Joachim. *Even my father never let me come to Golgotha. I will never bring my son.*

While Joachim had been busy searching for the cloth, Jonai had been collecting tools that would be needed for taking Jesus down from the cross. He shuddered as he thought of the task. If his pliers were necessary to detach Him from the cross, he would never use them again.

Jonai's pack was heavier than he expected. He rested just a second. Leaning against a wall, he took a hurried swallow of posca. He breathed in the fresh air and the scent of flowers, which contrasted with his thoughts of death and excruciating pain. In his pack, Jonai carried the burial cloth and another smaller one. The smaller cloth was white and made of linen. He made certain he had two small coins in his money purse—two widow's mites. The water for the cleansing of the body weighed down his pack the most. *Or maybe the weight of the events of the day was a heavier burden than the weight of the bags.* As Jonai approached the site of Jesus's death, he felt older and nearer to death.

Who was this man being sentenced to death? Why do they call Him King of the Jews? There are rumors He worked miracles. I wasn't so sure, but I didn't need to see the miracles to become a believer. I heard His message, and I was turned into a believer. When Jesus spoke, I was overcome by His message. I was with Him when He taught the Beatitudes. It was a beautiful day then, just as it is now, but the darkness of His impending death blotted out today's bright sun.

Jonai rested a second time. A soft breeze helped to cool him in the afternoon sun before he continued his journey.

Just a few more minutes, and he turned the corner around the northern wall. He could hear the wailing of the women coming from above. It took another minute to reach the base of the three crosses and the women. It wasn't a site he wanted to see . . . three men dangling from crosses, their lives escaping from them.

Nicodemus was there. Had the end already come?

One of the guards was confused. He was examining his spear for some reason and discussing it with the other guards. Something was different, but Jonai was unable to make it out.

Clouds darkened the sky as they gathered directly overhead. He was supposed to meet Edom, Nicodemus, and Joseph and hand over the cloth. Joseph was nowhere to be found. As Jonai walked up to Nicodemus, he noticed the man's eyes were teared up. This man had clearly been affected by this Messiah ben David, the King of the Jews. "Nico, I am so sorry."

"Jonai, thank you." Nicodemus paused to swallow. His throat was swollen from the emotions. "Thank you. I see you brought the cloth. It is perfect. Joseph has just . . . just left to plead for permission from Pontius Pilate to take the body. He will . . . he will be back shortly." Nicodemus stuttered as tears welled up in his eyes, moistening his cheeks.

"Nicodemus, Nicodemus. I will help you. Just say what you need me to do, and it is done."

"Is it getting darker?" Mary[3] cried as she noticed the graying skies. "Why is it so dark?"

"I see it too. I see it too." He tried to say the words in a soothing way, even repeating them softer and more slowly. Jonai didn't know her well. He hoped his words might reassure her, but they didn't. The darkness merely added bewilderment to the grief. *How could any words soothe a mother's pain watching her son suffer in such an odious way?*

Joseph returned and informed them Pilate[4] had given him permission to take Jesus's body. There was a commotion about twenty feet beyond the group of Christ-followers. The Roman soldiers were arguing over the purple robe. "Split it in four!" The oldest soldier took another swig of wine as he packed his share of the garment into his pack. "We'll cast lots for the last rag."

"It wasn't easy, but Pilate's wife, Procula,[5] persuaded him we could take the body once Jesus was dead," Joseph said.

The words struck Jonai like a bolt of lightning. The first pang of grief was stronger than he had ever experienced. *How could our Messiah be dead? Dead at the hands of the Romans and the Sanhedrin.*

"We will lay Him in my family tomb," Joseph said.

Nico looked away from the Romans in disgust. He loathed what they did to Him. He was a member of the Sanhedrin, but he would never return. "Yes, yes, Mary, He has truly suffered for us . . . for all of us," Nico murmured, saying another prayer to himself. "He suffered for us." The anger again welled up within him. He prayed. This time he steeled himself to teach all he learned from his friend. He would turn the other cheek. He would teach any who would listen. His anger slowly dissipated, lingering in the base of his skull.

"Nico, Jonai, help me."

They removed the staves holding the cross upright, and they and others standing nearby received the weight of both the body and the cross as it began to lean forward. They laid the cross down carefully, and emotion welled up within all of them.

Three of the guards were already making their way down the hill back to their lairs. They were no longer laughing and shouting, as they were when they led Jesus up the hill. There was only silence. One had a piece of purple cloth in his arms. Another had Jesus's undergarment.

As they lay the cross down, blood and water seeped from the wound made by the guard's spear.

---

3 Mary: Jesus's mother.
4 Pontius Pilate: Fifth governor of Judea under Emperor Tiberius from AD 26 to 36.
5 Procula: Wife of Pontius Pilate. Born AD 6, died AD 81.

"Edom, give me the cup, quickly."

It took a second for Edom to retrieve the cup from the supper the night before.

Joseph took the cup and tried to capture the discharging mortal blood and liquid. Once he had captured the blood, he didn't know what to do with it. It wasn't much, but Jewish custom dictated it needed to be preserved. Only a bit more seeped out, and this, too, Joseph was able to capture. When they turned the body again, the seeping stopped.

"Edom, take this. Don't let any of it spill." Joseph handed him the cup with the few drops he was able to capture.

At that moment, the women were busy whispering, even arguing. Mary, Jesus's mother, was about to begin washing her son's emaciated body when one of the other women stopped her. "He died violently, and we must obey our custom," whispered one.

"He should not be cleansed," whispered another. "Jonai has brought the sovev, the burial cloth, and he must be buried with it. We cannot cleanse . . . the body." She gasped that she so readily switched from *Him* to *the body*. "We mustn't disturb His fluids of life."

"Yes, but I must," retorted Mary. "My son. I just can't bear—" Mary choked back the emotions welling up within her. "I can't bear to see Him like this."

Jesus was still attached to the cross. They didn't know how they would remove the nails from the cross when Jonai retrieved his pliers and a mallet. Nico took the pliers and mallet from Jonai. It was hard work. Although Jesus was now dead, they couldn't bear to be the cause of any more suffering. It was hardly possible. As gently as they could, they removed the long nails from his feet—eight inches long and a quarter-inch in diameter.

To remove the nail from Jesus's feet, Joseph lifted one side of the cross while Nico hammered against the nail protruding through to the back of the center beam. The banging caused the women to start sobbing again.

Jonai tried to watch but was unable to. Finally, the nail was back out of the wood. It now needed to be removed from the bone. It stuck to Jesus's flesh. Pieces of his bone were visible. Jonai did everything possible not to vomit but was unable to stop the involuntary response. As it was pulled through the bone, the nail's sound stabbed them all in the heart. The Messiah, now dead, was before them. A broken body. And now the sounds. He was glad he made his son stay home. *This is not something for a twelve-year-old boy. This is not something for a twenty-nine-year-old man.*

"Leave the spikes in his hands! There is too much blood." Joseph didn't want any more of Jesus's life to spill out. "He should suffer no more." Joseph looked at the others, and they, too, weren't able to keep their emotions back. "We can't inflict more suffering on this man."

The two nails were relatively easy to remove from the crossbeam. The nail holes in the crossbeam of the cross were well worn, so there was little resistance as they were pulled out of the wood.

The last Roman guard, standing and watching the effort to care for the body, grunted as he took the spikes from these Jews. "Pull those spikes out of his wrists! Now!" The guard commanded. No one moved. The guard stooped down and yanked the nails from Jesus's hands. He then pulled out a tattered brown rag to wipe the blood from the nails, which would be used many more times.

"Stop. Stop. Don't take that away!" Joseph objected to disturbing the body. No more of His life blood should be lost.

The Roman spit in disgust. "Give me the last spike from his feet." He picked up the goatskin bag of posca Mary had brought for Jesus and drank from it. He sneered this time, proud that he could inflict one more spiteful act against this criminal's friends.

Joseph stood and took a few coins from his pocket and handed them to the guard. "Take this and leave this man in peace."

The guard scoffed, then walked off. His business was very profitable that day.

Joseph, Nico, and Edom carefully laid Jesus and the cross back on the ground. They folded Jesus's arms over His stomach and took a short break. Although the sun was hidden behind the dark clouds, the men had begun sweating from shifting the weight of the cross and Jesus's body.

A drop of sweat touched Joseph's lips, and he could taste the salt. It would soon be getting dark, and they wanted to make sure they were able to lay Jesus's body in the tomb before it got too late.

Another of Joseph's companions, Jehohanan, walked up the hill carrying a stretcher on his back. It was made of two long, wooden poles with six crossbars.

Jonai had met Jehohanan a few times before, and they were more than just acquaintances. They greeted each other with a simple, imperceptible glance, as grief filled the air.

Jehohanan laid the stretcher next to the body.

The four men lifted Jesus's broken body onto the stretcher. His rib cage was distended, having been pulled apart as his weight slowly led to his suffocation.

What was it like? Was the pain from the scourging worse than the pain from the spikes? Or was it the fear of death through agonizingly slow suffocation?

"Careful, careful!" Joseph implored as they initially struggled with the weight of the body. "We will carry him to my family tomb. It is new and, so far, unused. There we can lay Him to rest until the body is ready."

Dusk approached as they struggled down the hill to the freshly hewn tomb. As they reached the garden in front of the tomb outside the Damascus gate, they noticed there was still dust from the work the stone carvers had recently completed. Mary, Jesus's mother, grabbed a torch that was left for them and proceeded inside the tomb.

"Lay him here," Joseph said, trying to make His lifeless body comfortable for the depths of the afterlife.

Mary took the small linen cloth from Jonai. "Let's clean His back first." She folded the cloth and made a cushion with which to rest her son's head. She placed it over His forehead and face as the others helped roll Jesus onto His stomach.

There were so many wounds from the scourging. They were everywhere. Bits of ripped-out bone protruded through some of them.

"Careful, careful. There must be no impurity," Joseph said in a soft, distraught voice, his prudence leaking through his sadness.

Nicodemus stopped him and pulled a clean cloth from his pouch. The image of the beaten and disfigured face was something he would never get out of his mind.

They were ready to place the body onto the burial Shroud. Joseph looked around for the cloth. "Nico, Jonai, where is the burial cloth?"

Nico produced the cloth, and he and Jonai unfurled it inside the tomb.

Jesus was taller than most, and His body when laid out was quite long.

Joseph was glad he had specified a long cloth to Jonai. They rolled Him over for the last time onto His back and lifted Him onto the burial cloth. Now that the body wouldn't be jostled, they could be more circumspect about the preparation procedures.

"Jonai, do you have the mites for the eyes?" Nico asked.

Jonai took them out of his change purse and handed them over. Nico put them over the eyes to keep the eyelids closed. They weren't worth much, just a small fraction of a drachma, just the right size for their purpose now. It was painful to look at Jesus's body. He had been a handsome man, pleasant to look on, but in His death, it was unbearable to look upon him. It took all his might to stave off pangs of pain, imagining what this man suffered for us. *How much did He suffer?*

Strange. His blood was not clotting. Nicodemus had prepared other bodies, but for some reason, this man's blood, Jesus's blood, stayed liquid even now.

As they were preparing Jesus for His rest in the tomb, he also noticed the clear liquid. *Where was this water coming from? Was this the water that had confused the guard?* Nicodemus continued spreading more spices and oils on the body. They were made up of an earthy mixture of myrrh and aloes. Nicodemus looked up and said another prayer. He and Joseph grabbed the end of the Shroud and pulled it over his friend's body. They both tried to avoid looking into the man's face but couldn't. His deathful image was branded into their souls.

With the cloth covering the mangled body, all the small blood stains from the whippings slowly seeped into the burial cloth. The blood kept oozing out. In the pale light from the torch and the setting sun, the many small blood stains disfigured the cloth with an irregular, mottled pattern of red spots and blemishes. Large blotches emerged around his head, chest, and hands.

When Nicodemus was taking one last look, the women came into the tomb and brought with them flowers to lay next to the body and inside the cloth. There were a few different kinds, including some beautiful white chrysanthemums. Joseph would have recognized them in the daylight, but in the dimming sunlight and flickering of the torches, it was difficult to see what they had brought inside the tomb. *At the end of Shiva, the seven days of Passover, I will remember to ask Mary what flowers they had cut from the garden,* he thought to himself as he carefully completed his work.

They said a prayer, and Nicodemus placed a tiny prayer box on Jesus's forehead. Mary had given it to him earlier for Jesus. It had been in their family for quite some time, and she wanted to make certain their family prayers would be heard. This prayer box, a small metal box, about a quarter inch on each side, was made of silver and was connected to a leather band. He was able to wrap the band around Jesus's hair and make a small, simple knot.

Oh, how we loved this man. How will we continue without Him? Joseph thought, his grief piercing his heart. Jesus had been so much more than a friend. Jesus loved him like no other, and Joseph loved Him back. Not even the love he had for his wife and his own son compared to the love he had for Jesus. The Messiah. His Messiah. *How was this possible?* He tried not to cry, but he could feel the pressure building in the back of his eyes and forehead.

The massive stone meant to seal the mouth of the tomb was specially cut by the stoneworkers and was heavier than Joseph thought it would be. Grave robbers would have trouble rolling the stone away if they ventured to rob the tomb and steal the body. He was exhausted mentally, emotionally, and physically.

All four men pushed with all their remaining strength. It didn't budge. The stoneworkers had tried to level the threshold in front of the tomb, but with the weight of the stone, any slight incline seemed like a mountain.

Finally, with a large collective breath, the stone gave way, and they were able to roll it into place. It took them fifteen minutes to roll the stone just four feet. Exhausted and panting, sweat poured down their foreheads.

The sun had set, and the light from the torches flickered in their eyes. They all sat and rested in the garden and drank the rest of the posca from what Jonai had brought to Golgotha. The anxiety from the day drained from their bodies. Nicodemus led them in a short prayer. Their exhaustion brought a sense of calmness, yet they also each felt a sense of foreboding.

With Jesus gone, what will happen next? With Jesus gone, how can we remain as Jews? With Jesus gone, how will we know what to do? With Jesus gone, how will we know what to teach?

They opened their eyes and looked up. Each of them planned on returning to the tomb at first light after the Sabbath. A few yards away, the Roman guards laughed and played dice. Their drunken laughs punctuated the silence of the evening. There was no other sound to be heard.

Each stood and walked away, not wanting or able to speak. Thoughts swirled in their heads.

What will happen now? Is this how we, too, will die? Will the Romans and the Sanhedrin conspire against us as well? Will we, too, be crucified?

Behind the Roman guards was a man dressed in black, standing in the shadows. No one noticed him.

✝✝✝

GOLGOTHA, JERUSALEM
LATE MORNING, SUNDAY, APRIL 5, AD 33

Rumors spread quickly throughout all Jerusalem that the body of the crucified Jew was missing. It was stolen. It was no longer in the tomb.

Joseph of Arimathea heard them as well as he sat alone eating his morning meal. *How could that be? Why would someone take that body? His feet and wrists were, were . . . indescribable.* He couldn't erase the image of Jesus's disfigured body from his mind. And the face. The face. *Did the disciples come and steal the body? But the tomb was guarded. I saw for myself. I made sure of it.* Grief pierced his heart again, this time blunted with confusion.

Joseph ran for about five minutes before reaching his tomb. It was true. The stone was rolled away. "Who could have rolled the stone away?" Joseph asked, but no one responded.

The centurion reprimanded two guards while eight others stood behind him, all at attention. These two would suffer ignominy among the Roman army. They may not survive long either. *Who would want them in their unit?*

Pilate gave explicit instructions to guard the tomb, and these two failed. Did they fall asleep? The centurion would have to report, and he, too, would suffer the consequences—maybe more so since he would be blamed for not assigning more of his troops to guard the tomb.

Joseph entered the tomb, and the cloths they had so carefully wrapped the body in were lying to one side, neatly folded. The cup sat right next to the cloths, just where he left it. The blood was now dried. The earthy fragrance of the burial spices hung in the air, triggering the horrific images of the last few days. *Did the disciples do this? Where did my loving friend go? Is this what was meant in Genesis when it was said about Enoch that God took him?* Joseph gathered up the cloths, the cup, and the crown of thorns and walked slowly back to his friend's home where he was staying in the outskirts of Jerusalem.

The next morning, the rumors continued and grew louder: *It was said that Mary Magdalene[6] had seen Jesus near the tomb—alive! She had been at Jesus's side, traveling everywhere He went, hearing everything He taught. And now she saw Him alive? How was this possible? He was dead. He was definitely dead. No man could have survived that level of scourging. Yet he returned?*

Joseph was confused. He went to the disciples to inquire, but they weren't sure what happened either. *What was happening? Had Jesus truly risen from the dead?* What Jesus taught him to pray, he couldn't. It was no use. He couldn't concentrate. His mind darted everywhere, and memories flashed before him. He tried again and then again. The image of Jesus's face kept welling up inside him. The grief was overwhelming. He couldn't hold it back.

✝✝✝

The members of the Jewish ruling council, the Sanhedrin, were dumbfounded. Annas[7], a Sadducee, turned and faced his fellow Sadducees. "There is no afterlife. There is no resurrection. Those guards were drunk, and those Christ-followers bribed them. They stole the body." Annas sat down on his throne in the Chamber of Hewn Stone, the council chamber for the Sanhedrin, and thought a few minutes.

Others stood in the middle of the hall. The rest of the Sanhedrin sat in small groups on the raised floors surrounding the walls of the chamber. They all whispered among themselves, each reevaluating their beliefs and what they had learned over the decades of their lives.

---

6 Mary Magdalene: See Mark 15:40, John 20:11–18, and Luke 8:1–3, among others. Christ-follower and friend of Jesus.

7 Annas: High Priest from AD 6 to 15. Appointed high priest of the Jewish people, president of the Sanhedrin. Died circa AD 40.

"Chief of the Guard, take this money and give it to those Romans guarding the tomb, those sons of perverse women. They are to say that the disciples of Jesus stole the body. You will handle this personally. Do not fail. Now go. Go!" Annas removed his purse, and, with his nose up and looking in the opposite direction, held it out for the chief of the guard. The guard took it without touching the fingers of the high priest.

The chief of the guard marched out of the hall. "It cannot be true," Annas spoke in punctuated staccato. "We will not let it be true." Caiaphas[8] and Annas looked at each other. Annas could feel the blood raging in his skull, his heart beating and adrenaline fueling the shaking of his hands.

Caiaphas supervised the removal of the torn curtain across the entry of the council chamber. He tried to calm his father-in-law. "What does a pig know about noodle pudding? Those Christ-followers have no culture." Caiaphas looked directly at Annas. "Doubt can be a valuable weapon. Whether anyone believes the guards, a bribe or no bribe, the doubt will last an eternity."

The whispering among the others slowly started back. They all feared retribution from the Romans. *How will they respond? Will the strain of the tax burden on the Jews climb even higher?*

✝✝✝

JERUSALEM
MIDAFTERNOON, SUNDAY, APRIL 5, AD 33

Pilate was livid. He feared that the Jews and the Christ-followers would clash, unsettling the peace. Pilate's breathing was heavy, and his nostrils flared. He would take the blame from Tiberius Caesar[9] for any uprising and be lucky to keep his head. He doubled the guards throughout the city. No soldier was given any rest. *How could his men have been so foolish to have let someone roll away the stone? The strongest army in the world outsmarted by a few simple Jews! They weren't even Jews. They were Christ-followers. I should never have had Him* . . . Pilate was disgusted.

"Those guards will be flogged to within an inch of their lives!" He screamed so loud those in the courtyard outside the Antonia Fortress heard him. Even the Sanhedrin next door heard him. Everyone in the fortress was aware of those fools who had been guarding the tomb. "Find that damned body and find those Jews involved in this. Find them!"

Activity in the Antonia Fortress was frenetic. There was no one who wasn't on edge.

---

8 Caiaphas: See John 18:13. High priest from AD 18–36 and son-in-law of Annas. Died AD 36.
9 Tiberius Caesar Augustus: Second Roman emperor. Ruled from AD 14 to 37. Born 42 BC, died AD 37.

"Tiberius Caesar cannot find out about this. If necessary, we will double the taxes until the body is found. That will provide the right incentive for these swine eating their own dung and drinking their own urine."

✝✝✝

The chief of the guard, Azaaih, returned to the temple from his mission. "Your Most High, we paid the guards as instructed. They, too, had concluded the Christ-followers came in the night and stole the body." Azaaih glowered. "As expected, the two guards in question were drunk and had fallen asleep. They were already drinking this morning. They will be flogged by nightfall."

"Did they take the money, and can it be traced back to us?" Annas was interrupted before he got an answer.

The temple guard announced the arrival of the Roman legionnaire. "Caiaphas, Annas." The guard did not recognize their titles. "You have been summoned at once to see the praefectus, Pontius Pilate." There was a short pause. "At once," the legionnaire ordered. These priests were given no choice.

✝✝✝

"Abigail. Abigail! The body, it's gone. It's gone!" Jonai couldn't contain himself. "We put the body in the tomb. I was there. The Sanhedrin say it was stolen, but why? Why! Who would steal it?"

Abigail hadn't yet become a strong follower of Jesus. She went along with whatever her husband said, but this was the first time she'd ever seen her husband like this. "Jonai, what are they saying? What does Nicodemus, your friend, say? He's a member of the Sanhedrin. He must know?"

"He has been mostly in hiding. He, too, is at risk for having been at Jesus's side too often. The Sanhedrin is closing ranks, and Saul,[10] under Gamaliel's[11] direction, is threatening anyone who might be a Christ-follower."

"And Barnabas?[12] What does he say? Or is he in hiding with Peter[13] and the other disciples?"

"I've not seen either of them. At dusk, I will go to the tomb and see for myself. They say the stone was rolled away. It would have been impossible for any one man to move it. We could barely move it."

10 Saul of Tarsus: A Roman citizen. Persecutor of early Christians. Later known as the apostle Paul of Tarsus. Taught by Gamaliel. Born circa 5 AD, died circa 65 AD.
11 Gamaliel: Rabban Gamaliel I, renowned Jewish scholar and teacher. Died AD 52.
12 Barnabas: See Acts 4:36–37. An apostle from Cypress.
13 Peter: An apostle and one of the twelve disciples. Generally thought of as the first pope. Died AD 67 in Rome upon being crucified upside down under Emperor Nero.

"Papa, I will go with you. I want to see it too." Joachim had been listening to his animated father.

"No. Don't go. I don't want you hurt, either of you." He looked at his son. "What would your mother do without you?"

The Christ-followers were only now becoming aware of reports of Jesus's missing body. It was an affront to the Romans and the Jewish hierarchy. The news flowed throughout Jerusalem like a tsunami. *Would the Romans and the Jews exact their retribution?*

Anyone connected to Jesus feared for their lives. All the Christ-followers did their best to stay in their homes. They didn't dare be caught out in the open. No one had been arrested. Yet. There were rumors flying throughout the city that arrests were imminent. Whether gentile or Jew, everyone in Jerusalem was asking who took the body.

Joseph was the first to be arrested. Many more arrests would follow. When the Jewish guards came, they were led by Annas, former high priest of Judea, and the scholar, Gamaliel, the elder.

Joseph was brought to a cell and locked in. The door was sealed, and a guard was posted. Joseph warned them. "You can't keep me here. Jesus will set me free. After what you have done, you must repent. The wickedness you perpetrated on that man will haunt you forever. It will destroy you!" He shouted from his cell, but there was only silence in return. He was totally alone.

In the darkness and solitude of the cell, Joseph found it much easier to pray. His fear of being arrested—or worse—no longer haunted him. He prayed only for forgiveness that he would be absolved for not having done more to stand up against the Sanhedrin. He no longer feared them. He no longer feared crucifixion. *I should have risked my life for Jesus. I could have prevented it.* Joseph continued praying. "Please forgive me. Please forgive me. Please."

It was midnight, and he felt cool air enter through the door and into the room. A cool breeze would have been welcomed on any other night. But on this night, the cool air was bone-chilling.

"Wha—Did someone kiss me? Who's there?"

The room started to shake. The whole jailhouse shook.

"Who's there? What is happening?"

There stood an apparition; no, it was a person.

"Could it be?" Joseph thought. "Is it . . . is it you?"

"It is me. I am Jesus. You begged for my body from Pilate. You wrapped me and placed me in your tomb. I have just left the disciples, and now I come to you. You must leave this place."

"Are you a phantom? How is this possible?" Joseph was trembling. Then Jesus and Joseph were suddenly in front of the tomb.

"You placed a napkin to rest my face and then prepared my body," Jesus said. "You laid me to rest. Do not be afraid." Jesus looked deep into Joseph's eyes, just as He had done when they first met. "You must now go. Go to your home in Arimathea and remain there for forty days. Do not leave your house, for I must go see my brothers in Galilee."

Joseph ran back to his place of lodging to collect his belongings, the bloodstained cloths, the crown, and the cup. He was filled with belief and disbelief. Jesus, no less, freed him. Jesus appeared to him!

"Charinus,[14] Lenthius[15], wake up. We must go. Now. To Arimathea. Hurry." Joseph woke his sons, and they gathered all that they needed. "We'll leave the rest of our family here. We will leave immediately, before second watch." It was a long day's walk, but they could make it. Starting in the middle of the night, they should make it before dusk that day. "I saw Jesus. He told me what to do. We must go. Now!"

✝✝✝

Arimathea
Midafternoon, Wednesday, April 18, AD 35

"Father, the tensions in Jerusalem have continued to fester. They have only gotten worse over the two years since Jesus was crucified. You may no longer be safe, even though you are far away here in Arimathea," Joseph's two sons reported after having just returned from their annual pilgrimage to the Holy City.

After two years, Joseph's life had settled down to a routine. His testimony about Jesus to the Sanhedrin over a year before had been masterful, but no one on the council was swayed. He was released, admonished not to speak of this peasant blasphemer—a lowly carpenter—anymore. What could a carpenter have known of the law?

"Father, if you don't cut back on your Jesus teaching, they will come to arrest you." Charinus was always the first to speak. "We must move farther away so that Pilate and the Sanhedrin do not come to arrest you again, or much worse."

"But I must, and I will continue teaching and preaching and spreading the word of Jesus. Jesus has saved me more than once, and he will save you too," Joseph replied. "I am not afraid of what might happen to me."

He would never forget the face and the image of Jesus. *Could that happen to me?* "Jesus suffered for us. He died for us. I don't know if I could withstand

---

14 Charinus: Son of Joseph of Arimathea.
15 Lenthius: Son of Joseph of Arimathea.

what he went through. Every day I pray that I will not fear. I will not fear!" Joseph repeated his prayers. He said them softly, and every movement in the room stilled. Joseph was not the only one to have seen the image on the cloth. His two sons also saw the image on the cloth. The blood. Everything.

There was silence in the room for several minutes. Everyone could feel the pain embodied in the image down to their bones.

✝✝✝

Four men and a boy rode up to their home.

"Father, what do we do now?" Joachim whispered to his father.

Jonai and Barnabas had been selected to help in this task for the Christ movement. Barnabas, originally from Cyprus, was one of Jesus's closest followers. After being part of the burial of Jesus Christ, Jonai had become one of the strongest members of this new Jewish sect. In the years since Jesus's crucifixion, his new friend Barnabas had been instructing him on everything he could about Jesus and his teachings.

"We wait. Don't make a sound." His father put his hand to his lips to make certain his son understood the whispered command. Joachim was also learning what Jesus meant to him, to the Jews, and to the world.

Barnabas got down from his wagon and entered the room, having just arrived from Jerusalem. He wondered about the strange silence but broke in, "Peace be with you." Barnabas and Joseph learned the teachings from their friend and had become fast friends and fellow evangelists of the word.

"Barnabas." Joseph greeted him with a big smile.

"Joseph, your sons and I have spent most of Holy Week together. It was a wonderful celebration of Passover." The discussion continued for a few minutes, remembering the beauty of spring, but mostly it was about remembering the good times they had with Jesus.

Barnabas got down to the purpose of his visit. "Joseph, we all—you and I—must continue spreading the word. There are so many beginning to follow Jesus, but we must also protect the cup and the cloths. They are the only things we have left from Jesus." Barnabas paused.

"Peter and James,"[16] Barnabas's voice was less excited. He lowered his voice and spoke in a deeper tenor. "And I believe it is now time to do something about the cloths, the cup, and the crown of thorns. The time has come to move them away from the vicinity of Jerusalem. Any day they could come and seize them or destroy them."

---

16 James: Apostle and half-brother of Jesus.

Joseph worked for two months, sewing a protective leather valise for each of them. "Yes, they may be taken at any time. And to lose these precious reminders." He paused, the image coming back to him. "These reminders of what Jesus gave us and sacrificed for us."

"Peter, James, and I have spoken, and we believe we must separate these beloved elements. It's all we have left from Him. They can't wind up in the hands of the Sanhedrin or the Romans." Barnabas spoke with authority, invoking the authority given to Peter by Jesus. He was on a mission sent from Peter and James—the leaders of the recent Christian movement. "We want to separate them so that these elements of our Lord can avoid possible destruction at the hands of our and Jesus's enemies."

Barnabas continued. "We have decided only Peter, James, and I will know where they go. It must be kept secret. Outside are four men, and they have been instructed to take the items. Do not speak to them. Do not let them know what is inside, for they don't know what they are transporting. They only know that they are of some value. I have brought some leather valises that should suffice to protect them."

"But can they be trusted? They are carrying all that we have of Jesus." As he protested, Joseph also realized this was the right course of action.

"Yes, they have walked with Jesus and are now with us." Barnabas calmly responded. He brought with him a sack, an ordinary-looking linen sack, and within were four leather cases. All were sewn together of well-worn leather. They looked as if they could contain only worthless items. "Let us see if these will work."

As the four leather valises were unpacked, Joseph sent his two eldest sons to retrieve the four relics. Charinus carried the two cloths, and Lenthius carried the crown and the cup. As they both returned from the relics' hiding place, Barnabas knelt and said a prayer before all that remained of their friend and teacher. There was no body and no grave that they could go to kneel and pray with their friend. Only these four elements remained.

He took the folded leather satchel holding the face cloth, removed the cloth, unfolded it, and viewed the stains. He refolded it and placed it back into the satchel and placed the satchel into the valise he had brought for it. It barely fit, but Barnabas was eventually able to slide it in.

With Joseph's help, Barnabas removed the Shroud from the second satchel and began to unfold it. He gave one end to Charinus, and they tried to keep it from touching the ground. Barnabas was finally able to step back and view this miraculous image. This was the first time he was able to view this miraculous cloth. It was also his last.

No one who saw the Shroud could understand its creation, but they knew that God's hands were at work. Neither could anyone reconcile the awe of God's handiwork with the anguish in the face of their former friend and mentor.

Barnabas tried to study the image, but the emotions were simply too strong. He was able to hold back the tears, but his lower lip began to quiver. Within a minute, he nodded, and Joseph and Charinus carefully and reverently refolded the cloth and slid it into the leather satchel. They folded it so that the image of Jesus's face was displayed on top, as protector of the entire piece.

As Joseph handed the satchel to Barnabas, he tried to keep the tears from flowing. He had been unable to hold back the tears ever since that day—the day of Christ's suffering and death. Any thought of that fateful day brought tears to his eyes.

The same procedure was repeated for the cup and the crown. The red stains of blood were evident in each piece. Inside the cup was also a lighter stain of the water from Jesus's side. Each piece was removed, inspected by Barnabas, returned to the leather pouches, and placed inside the valises Barnabas had brought. He didn't take note that the blood was still red. It hadn't turned brown.

"I trust you in caring for these reminders of the Messiah's time with us." In a much softer voice, he commanded, "Care for these. Care for them with your lives. They are everything."

Joseph and his two sons stood and looked on in silence, realizing this would be the last time they would ever be in the remaining physical presence of the Son of God. Barnabas nodded in respect to Joseph. Each man stood motionless, bowing their heads, and praying a long prayer to themselves.

Then Barnabas stood and said the Lord's Prayer out loud. He turned and brought the first valise out to one of the four men.

Joseph and his two sons returned to their seats at the table and silently watched, realizing their work guarding and caring for these remains of the Messiah was now coming to an end.

As Barnabas returned for the next valise, the first wagon could be heard driving off into the distance. Barnabas waited until the wagon could no longer be heard before he brought the next valise to its courier.

Jonai, with his son, was the third courier to receive a valise. Barnabas had recruited them for this task only two weeks before. They would do anything to help and support the burgeoning flock of Christ-followers.

When Barnabas returned the third time, Jonai nodded and jumped down from his wagon while Joachim remained, holding the reins of the donkeys. The first two wagons had already disappeared, each taking separate paths out of Arimathea.

Barnabas said little to Joachim, working to minimize the time his transporters were in Arimathea. He was afraid a Jewish spy might learn of the locations of these valuable reminders of Christ on earth.

Barnabas nodded, and Jonai placed the valise in the wagon with other supplies so that it wouldn't stand out as the true purpose of the journey. Jonai remounted the wagon, and within a few minutes, they were out of sight.

The last valise with the Shroud was given to the man on horseback. He had a long ride ahead of him that only a horseman could accomplish in a short amount of time.

"Brother Barnabas," Joseph said. "A weight has been lifted from me. Tell brothers Peter and James our family was blessed and honored to be able to care for what we had left of our Lord."

✝✝✝

The Roman road from Arimathea to Chalcedon was narrow and not often traveled. It only had room for one wagon. If another wagon appeared, one of the wagons would drive off to the side while the other passed. This was where trouble happened as the sides of the roads were not even. They were designed to let rainwater drain off the main stone path. With the weight of the wagon's cargo on uneven pavement, the strain on the wooden axles was the highest.

"Joachim, jump down and let this wagon pass." Jonai led the way and jumped down as Joachim moved to the nose of the donkey to grab its rein and direct it off to the side. "Let's rest here a few minutes." Jonai enjoyed the frequent breaks with his son. During these breaks, he was able to impart many of the teachings from Barnabas of what it meant to be a Christ-follower.

"Joachim, what is the greatest love a man can have?"

"The love of your parents. The love of your wife?" Joachim had been contemplating whether to inform his father of his desires about the girl Elizabeth he had met a few years earlier.

"Those are very important, yes. But Barnabas taught—Jesus taught—there is no greater love than to lay down your life for another." Jonai let that sink in a few minutes. He enjoyed teaching his family what Barnabas had taught him.

"Do you remember Stephen? How Saul incited the crowd? We were there. Stephen, too, loved us. He laid down his life for us." Jonai paused and thought further.

"Joachim, when Jesus died on the cross, He died for all of us. For you, for me, and for that girl I've been watching you sneak off to visit." His father grinned. He knew he would have to start finding a bride for his son. He had already been gathering a dowry. Now he and his mother needed to find the girl that would also have great love for his son.

"Papa, I want to tell you something." Joachim grinned too. His visits to Elizabeth weren't secret anymore. "Papa, I would like to marry Elizabeth. She is only a year younger, and she would make a perfect wife for me." Joachim made his declaration with great confidence—the confidence he had learned from his father.

Jonai had been seventeen when he told his parents he wanted to marry. Joachim was fifteen.

His father looked at his son and could see the burgeoning man in him. When he thought back to how he told his parents he wanted to marry Abigail, he was not as confident and forthright as his son. "You make me very proud, my son. Very proud. You will make a wonderful family with this woman." Jonai thought about the joy he had building his family with Abigail.

"We will begin the negotiations with her uncle, Rosanai, upon our return. If things go well, we can have the wedding after the harvest in the fall."

✝✝✝

CHALCEDON IN GALILEE
LATE MORNING, THURSDAY, APRIL 19, AD 35

Jonai and his son drove their wagon slowly up to the home. Jonai dismounted and approached the door.

Joachim did the same, tied the donkeys to the post, proceeded to gather the valise, and followed his father two paces behind.

"Crispus, Crispus." Banging on the door. "Brother Crispus. I bring a package from Barnabas." Jonai stood before the door. Joachim stood behind him.

Crispus came to the door. It was a Thursday, and he had just finished feeding his flocks of goats and sheep. His wife and daughter followed him out the door. "Brother Jonai, Barnabas said you would be arriving today or tomorrow. I'm glad you are on time. Please come in and join us for our midday meal." Crispus motioned to the door, his wife and daughter stood to the side.

"I'm sorry, brother. Barnabas specifically asked us to return to Jerusalem immediately. I cannot stay." Jonai turned to Joachim, took the valise, and handed it to Crispus. "I give you this package from Barnabas." He then nodded to Crispus, "Peace be with you, brother."

"Peace be with you," Crispus responded. The whole episode took less than two minutes.

Jonai and Joachim were off.

Crispus whispered to his wife, "If Jonai had known the value of the package he had delivered, perhaps he would have lingered longer. At least to water his donkey and share a meal."

"Perhaps they knew," she replied.

Later that evening after their daughter, Atara, was in bed asleep, Crispus and his wife unpacked the valise and removed the leather pouch and its contents. It was a simple wooden goblet. Nothing special, yet the red stains of dried blood were unmistakable. It was Christ's blood. "I've never seen dried blood like this. Why is it so red?" Crispus looked at his wife. Something didn't make sense. *Was Christ's blood different than man's?*

Crispus was not present when Jesus suffered his humiliation and crucifixion, but he knew how gruesome the Romans could be. Since that day, he had held only smaller gatherings, converting many, perhaps thousands, over the last two years, to this new Jewish sect. He used the same method Jesus had taught them as he sent seventy of them out into the countryside to meet the people and be with them. Crispus told people of the wonder of not just following the law but believing and acting in the way. The way of Jesus.

"This is the chalice used during Jesus's last meal," Crispus explained to his wife. "It is also the chalice Joseph of Arimathea used to collect Jesus's blood as he suffered on the cross. This is the blood of Jesus, the Messiah. I, too, may suffer the same fate, although I hope and pray God has other plans for me. I pray God will give me the strength and courage to spread the word here in Galilee and elsewhere if necessary."

His wife looked over at their sleeping daughter. In her sleep, she was the most beautiful thing. She looked at her and then down at the goblet. It was just a plain wooden goblet, similar to the ones they themselves used every day for their meals. She studied it further. There were no markings—nothing to make it stand out. Just the red stains of dried blood. Red, not brown. "Put it back. Atara might awake. Where shall we keep it? I'm sure Barnabas will come for it at some point, and it must not get lost or damaged."

Crispus placed it into the leather pouch and then back into the valise. "I will dig a hole in the floor and bury it in the corner." They both looked over where Atara was sleeping on her bed mat and then to the western corner.

"The western corner is the best since it never gets wet with the heavy rains. It will stay safe there and will stay dry until Barnabas comes." Crispus paused, then spoke further. "Although it will be out of sight, we must tell Atara what it is and how important it is. She is never to play with it or touch it. She must simply ignore it. Do you think she is old enough to understand?"

She gave a look of uncertainty. "She must," she answered. "She must be. She knows how important Jesus and His teachings are. She will understand. She must. We will pray for it to be so."

There was a knock at the door. Both lost a heartbeat.

"Brother Crispus, Brother Crispus, it is I, Yoash. I wanted to tell you about Elishua of Dan." It was their friend and mentee, Yoash. "We invited them for dinner last night, and they were very receptive to the word. I want you to meet them as soon as possible. They want to join our flock."

Mark[17] spent most of the morning speaking with a small Jewish community he had found favor with just north of the city. After having awoken before dawn, he made his weekly trek there. A few weeks prior, the planting season had concluded. The hustle and bustle of the season had now subsided. There were about fifteen members of the community, and many of them he had become close friends with. Today they were all present.

This morning Mark recounted his time when he was sent out by Jesus as part of the seventy. It was a wondrous mission. They were sent two by two on a mission to spread the word. If they were welcomed as friends, they would stay, heal the sick, and tell of the word.

Mark had been sent with Parmenas, the Cypriot.[18] This morning he recounted the story of being rejected by the second town they visited. As they exited, they followed Jesus's instruction. They brushed off the dust from their clothes and clapped their sandals together to purge the dust that had accumulated. This story reminded him of the tribulations he and this community would need to endure so they could persevere in their quest to spread the word of Jesus. Commitment to Christ did not mean a road free from obstacles. Each obstacle must be recognized as a small step to ultimate salvation upon completion of life's journey.

Mark had received the package from Barnabas's rider almost a week before, yet he hadn't opened it. He knew what it contained but considered the cloth both a blessing and a curse. Often when he thought of the cloth, he saw it as a reminder of his friend, and he took that time to cherish the memories of their time together. It made his faith stronger and reminded him Jesus was able to conquer sin and death.

---

17 Mark: Author of the book of Mark, disciple of Peter. Born AD 12, died AD 68.
18 Parmenas the Cypriot: Believed to be the bishop of Soli of Cilicia. Martyred AD 98.

He had so many joys when he was with Jesus, but he also wondered if Jesus had to die to fulfill Isaiah's prophecies. *Could his life have meant as much had He escaped the persecution and the crucifixion? Or did He have to die? Did He have to be crucified for His word to be branded into our souls?*

Mark also didn't want the cloth to be proof of Jesus being both man and God. The cloth could easily become an idol, just as the golden calf was for the Israelites in the wilderness. The new Christ-followers needed to believe in the redeeming power He gave freely without price. Following Jesus was not a perfunctory act of discipline. Instead, it was a belief system that must become part of every Christ-follower's inner being.

There was no place to hide the valise, so Mark hid it in plain sight, piled up inside a bed mat and laid on top of the pile of other bed mats. It was there that was the driest when it would rain. Tonight though, he would open it and see what it contained. He understood it to be the face cloth, but it was time to make sure. As he understood it, the Shroud went to Peter. But with the rising tension between the Christ-followers, the Jews—primarily the Sanhedrin—and the Romans, it was possible Jesus's burial cloth would be taken. With Peter constantly under threat of arrest, it was surprising he could continue walking freely and preach.

Mark wanted to continue writing his thoughts and memories from his time with Jesus. He had made great progress, yet there was much to do.

"Brother Machlah, come in," Mark said as he greeted him at the door. "You know you don't have to knock anymore. You are always welcome in my home."

"I'm glad we're able to start earlier today. It will be easier to see the manuscripts as we work. Last week it had become too dark to work effectively by lamplight," Machlah said, as he moved to the table. "I worked since last time to make four new fresh papyri, so we should have enough to finish the story of Jesus's Sermon on the Mount. I remember it so vividly. I was only a boy handing out fish and loaves of bread. There were so many people, and yet there was more than enough food."

"Brother Machlah, let's begin there. First, let us begin with some bread and wine to sustain us and give us strength for the afternoon," Mark answered, excited about getting his Jesus stories on paper. "Before we begin, let us look at something else to inspire us." Mark walked over, retrieved the valise, and set it on their writing table. He opened the valise and unfolded the face cloth.

"This is Jesus's face cloth with his blood. There is so little we have left of Him." Mark stilled the tears welling up in his eyes.

Machlah examined the cloth and tried to understand the butterfly shape of the stains. If this was Jesus's burial face cloth, then He bled copiously from his face and head. There was so much blood.

"Today, we will write about Jesus's death," Mark announced, with all the memories coming back to him about those fateful few days immediately before and after Jesus's death. "Please sit. Sit. We will start."

And when the sixth hour was come, there was darkness over the whole land until the ninth hour.

✝✝✝

JERUSALEM
LATE MORNING, THURSDAY, APRIL 19, AD 35

"Brother Peter, Brother James, I come from Arimathea, from Joseph and Barnabas," Uzziah said quietly as he entered Peter's temporary home. He had ridden straight from Arimathea.

James was also present, awaiting Uzziah's arrival. This was their temporary living quarters, as they rotated to a new home every day.

The Sanhedrin, the Jewish ruling tribunal, was still seeking retribution against the Christ-followers but hadn't arrested them yet, although they had tried several times.

Uzziah was out of breath but not overly tired from having ridden the night. He was unaware of what he was carrying. He assumed it was something valuable. Otherwise, he would not have been requested to ride through the night.

"Take a seat. Rest a moment. We will share breakfast together. Bless you that you have arrived safely." Peter motioned to the chairs and table in the lower part of the room. "Come, I want to hear about your trip. Did you have any troubles," Peter said, taking the valise from Uzziah and placing it at the end of the table. Peter and Uzziah sat across from each other at the other end of the table.

Uzziah had never been in Peter's presence before. It was like Peter was an old friend. James was the last to sit and took his seat next to Uzziah.

"The trip was uneventful. Just arduous to complete in one night. There was no one else on the road." Uzziah continued to recount his night ride. They shared some bread with garam and a few olives together. The conversation continued about Passover and the politics of Tiberius and Jerusalem. Pilate was able to keep the peace despite the fact that his guards lost the body. His threats to the Jews and the Sanhedrin were effective, although no one was ever able to produce the body of Jesus.

"Pilate will continue as governor. He suffered a setback with the death of Jesus, but Tiberius didn't care as long as the Jews—and us—keep paying our taxes." Peter lamented about how much his flock had to pay in taxes to the Roman authorities.

When they were done with their meal, Uzziah got up to leave and travel back to his home in Galilee. Peter and Barnabas had made the right choice with Uzziah. They purposely chose riders from different parts of Judea but not from Jerusalem itself.

"Travel safely and farewell. Peace be with you." Peter said a short prayer, and Uzziah was off.

James and Peter returned inside. Peter walked over to the pouch, picked it up, and held it to his breast. He looked up to God and then down to the floor, except his eyes were closed. Finally, he opened the pouch and, with James's help, took the cloth and unfolded it. It was just as he had imagined it. The last time he had seen the cloth, it was lying in the tomb. They had been the first disciples to reach the tomb upon learning that it was empty. Peter didn't notice the image then, but he had heard from Joseph about it. Now to see Jesus's graven image, it was simultaneously breathtaking and overwhelming. Both James and Peter said nothing as they viewed the image. After a few minutes, they refolded the cloth and placed it back into the valise.

Peter grabbed both of James's hands, and they said a prayer together. They ended with the prayer their friend taught them: ". . . lead us not into temptation. But deliver us from evil. Amen."

It was several more minutes before either one of them could speak. James broke the silence. "Peter, you should keep this cloth. Take it with you wherever you go. You must preserve it as lasting evidence of God's miracles done on this earth by the Messiah, Jesus Christ."

Peter was silent but nodded to James in agreement. "I only hope I can protect it from the Sanhedrin and Saul. They have become much more militant after the murder of Stephen. I will pray to God, and it will be so."

Yechezkel was exhausted. He had ridden four days straight, directly from Arimathea to Bithynia. His horse was also fully drained from the weeklong trek through northern Israel, Syria, and finally Anatolia. He was curious about what he was carrying but was given strict instructions not to open the valise. Yechezkel was born a Jew but now followed the teachings of Jesus Christ. It was Andrew, one of Jesus's twelve, who was now in Bithynia spreading Jesus's teachings throughout Asia Minor.

Andrew had just completed his afternoon preaching and communing. As he was leaving his friend's home, making his way back to his own home, he was accompanied by two of his followers. Archelaos and Ethycos were two of his earliest converts, and now they were well on their way to becoming great teachers of the word with the church in Bithynia. Some day they would also become part of the episcopate.

"Brother Archelaos, you were very helpful today and have learned very well the teachings of Jesus. You have become invaluable to Jesus and his teachings here. I hope someday you will take over my work here in Bithynia. Ethycos, you too will soon lead your own church, but I think you will need to do that when you go back to your home in Mysia. I would like that to happen soon as I want to evangelize in Byzantium and build the church there."

The conversation continued as they reached Andrew's home. Yechezkel was outside watering and feeding his horse when the three turned the corner just to the south of their home. Andrew immediately recognized him as the courier bringing the valuable package mentioned by Barnabas. Brother Barnabas's letter from Jerusalem had arrived a few days earlier telling that someone would bring the crown of thorns worn by Jesus at his death.

"Brother Yechezkel, is that you?" Andrew looked at Yechezkel and smiled. Yechezkel nodded. "We've been waiting for you. We're so glad you arrived safely."

"I rode straight through from Judea. It took almost a week." They greeted each other with a hug. Archelaos and Ethycos hugged the rider as well.

"Please join us for our supper. We have just completed another blessed day teaching a new group of followers. Archelaos and Ethycos have become fully versed in the word and will soon take over my work throughout all of Bithynia." Andrew beamed with pride and excitement. "Tell us of your journey and give us news of Barnabas and Peter."

Yechezkel retrieved the leather valise from his horse and walked inside with Andrew and his two mentees. As soon as they were inside, he handed the package to Andrew, who immediately opened it. Being this far away from the Sanhedrin in Jerusalem, he didn't worry about the tensions that were ever present there. There was no evidence of the contentious relationship between the Jews, Romans, and Christ-followers here in Bithynia. The Romans simply considered it a backwater frontier of the empire, just like any city that was not Rome.

The others watched as Andrew carefully unpacked the valise and removed a strange-looking crown. It had one larger stain and red, dried blood on many of the inner tips of the one- to two-inch-long thorns. They were a deep red. It was the blood of Jesus.

"The suffering that Jesus endured for us," Andrew said as he carefully laid the crown back onto the table. "The Romans are experts in their craft."

The others bowed their heads, each whispering a silent prayer that they would not have to put their convictions to the same test as Jesus. They prayed that if they had to, their faith would be strong enough to bring them through the ordeal and then to heaven to their friend Jesus.

✝✝✝

EDESSA, OSRHOENE
LATE MORNING, THURSDAY, EARLY SEPTEMBER, AD 36

"Has Peter responded yet? You must send someone after our messenger," King Abgar[19] roared. His leprosy continued to get worse. None of the salves worked to alleviate the itching. "When is he expected back? I gave him two horses, so there should be no reason for him not to have returned yet."

"Your Majesty, it has only been three weeks." His proconsul, Soghomon, answered. "Mesrop is our best rider. He will surely arrive soon."

Soghomon tried to think of a way to distract the king. "Since Jesus's death, I have heard his followers are in hiding. They fear the Sadducees and Annas. How blessed are we that you have been a follower of Jesus? What did his letter say? 'Blessed are you who hast believed in me without having seen me. For it is written concerning me that they who have seen me will not believe in me and that they who have not seen me will believe and be saved.'" Soghomon looked directly at the king. "Your Highness, you are saved."

"Get me my leech! They must have more salve for this incessant itch. It is interminable!" Abgar interrupted. He grimaced, but the pain and the itching were ceaseless. "There must be something they can do."

The royal physician returned for the third time that morning, having become an expert in leechcraft concerning ailments of the skin. He, too, was frustrated with his inability to cure his royal patient. He only had treatments to relieve the itch and the dryness. "Your Highness, we have developed a new mixture. I've added an extra dose of rose water and gall. Relief from the itching should come quickly."

"Your Highness." Alexandr, legate of the Imperial Guard, bowed and then entered the king's private chambers. "Your Highness, Mesrop has returned."

Mesrop bowed deeper than Alexandr and entered behind him. Another man entered along with Mesrop. "Your Highness. I have a gift from Apostle Simon Peter, son of Jonah," Mesrop began. "Peter sends his greetings from Jerusalem. They are traveling about the city very carefully so as not to be

---

19 King Abgar V: King of Osrhoene, follower of Christ. Died AD 50.

arrested and persecuted by the Romans or the Sanhedrin. He sends his blessings. Thaddeus joins me, Apostle Judas-Thaddeus. He is one of the twelve and will also tell you news of the goings-on in Jerusalem."

Joy came over Abgar's face, finally able to ignore the pangs of pain and itching. "Mesrop, Thaddeus, come, come, tell me more about your travels. Tell me the news of Jerusalem."

Mesrop proceeded to apprise him of his time in Jerusalem. "It is very dangerous for the followers of Jesus. Peter and the others go out every day, avoiding the Jewish guards. It has become exceptionally dangerous for them. They stay every night in a different home. There is peace, an uneasy peace. Pontius Pilate fears every day that there will be riots and Rome will blame him. Annas sends spies everywhere to track the Christ-followers, yet every day more and more men, having heard of the miracles and the word, follow Peter and the others."

"Yes, yes, Thaddeus, what news is there of the movement? Tell me." Abgar was fully engrossed in the details of his rider's travels. "Continue, continue." He was able to stop the relentless desire to scratch while he listened. The pain and itching subsided enough to where he could sit back in his chair.

"Peter sends his regrets for not being able to come himself. He sends a special gift for your safekeeping. It is a marvelous gift with the face of Jesus upon it." Mesrop removed the large leather valise strapped over his shoulder and unbound the leather straps and cover flap. Mesrop took the cloth out and handed it to the king. It was folded such that a faint image of the face of a man was exposed. A gruesome, expressionless face was imprinted on the cloth in an unusual brown and tan style.

"Peter trusts you implicitly, and because it is not safe for the cloth in Jerusalem, he beseeches you to safeguard this with the vast weight of your kingdom."

Immediately Abgar fell to his knees and prayed. "It is the face of Jesus. My God, my God. The Son of Man is here." Abgar completely ignored the pain and itching, as he communed with God for several minutes. He finally looked up at Soghomon, and waved his arm. "Leave me. Leave me. I wish to be alone with Thaddeus. Do not disturb me anymore today."

His counselors and rider left him, walking backward a few steps, then turning and exiting the royal chambers.

Abgar viewed the face of a man's image on the cloth. "It is the Shroud, His burial Shroud." He couldn't stop staring. Thoughts of his allegiance to Jesus and everything He preached welled up within him. "Thaddeus, pray with me."

After a time of prayer, Abgar shouted at his attendants. "Get me the letter from Jesus. Bring me the letter! Bring it to me immediately!"

Only a few years earlier, he received a writing from Jesus. It was sent in response to his request of Jesus to come to Edessa.

Soghomon returned with the letter and handed it to King Abgar.

"Thaddeus, read the letter to me. Please. Tell me about this man."

"Blessed are you who hast believed in me without having seen me. For it is written . . ." Thaddeus read the letter aloud and then began to tell of the many miracles and the teachings he experienced.

Abgar fixated on every word of Thaddeus, now fully engrossed in the stories of Jesus. The itching and burning and pain finally subsided. "Thaddeus, your presence has cured me. The burning and itching are gone. I invite you to preach to all my subjects to rid our kingdom of all their false gods so we can worship the one true God."

✝✝✝

CHALCEDON IN GALILEE
EVENING, WEDNESDAY, SEPTEMBER 19, AD 36

"Crispus. Why do you need to go this late at night? It isn't safe. It's already dark, and our son needs to be in bed." Crispus's wife, Selah, was not accustomed to not having her husband home and in bed with her and her son. They lived in Chalcedon, in Galilee, a day's walk from Jerusalem . . . not far enough not to be found by Saul and Gamaliel or the Romans.

Joachim knocked on the door. It was time for Crispus to go. Crispus opened the door and then closed it quickly once Joachim had entered.

"I must go. Jonai and his son bring news from Jerusalem. They are the ones who brought the cup. A few others will be meeting as well. Peter has sent word from Jerusalem. The Sanhedrin is still searching out our fellow Christ-followers. There are rumors Stephen was stoned to death. They say Gamaliel had his lackey Saul seek him out and then incite the crowds to do his dirty work. I will—" Crispus put his finger to his mouth. "Shh," he whispered.

The marching of a half dozen Roman guards could be heard.

"Blow out the lamps."

They all stood in silence. It was ten minutes before the guards passed, right in front of their door. The guards turned the corner, and they could no longer be heard.

"I will return by third watch." Crispus kissed Selah on the forehead and then looked over at his son. "I will knock three times when I return. Don't let anyone else in." Crispus and Joachim exited from the small home.

"Crispus, I will stay behind and watch over your home while you're gone," Joachim said.

Crispus looked at him and could see how the fifteen-year-old boy was becoming a man.

"Stay out of sight, over there behind the olive press." Crispus nodded in the direction of the press. It was dark, but in the moonlight, the stone wheel of the press could be seen. Crispus turned and looked both ways and made his way to meet the other Christ-followers. Two barely noticeable strands of smoke made their way up through the chimney into the clear, moonlit night.

As soon as Crispus and Joachim exited the house, Selah locked the door and the window shutter. She removed her cloak and crawled onto the bed mats with her son. The bed was already warm from his body but cold for her feet. It took only a minute, and she had her cloak situated to keep them both warm. Her son woke up as she worked to stay silent. "Shh. Father will be back soon. He'll be back soon."

✝✝✝

"Check around back. Do not let anyone escape out a rear window or door," Eliphelet commanded two of his men. "You two, stay with me in the front. This Crispus, like Stephen, was a key follower of Jesus and was rumored to have been with Jesus from very early in his ministry." Eliphelet had been with Saul at the stoning of Stephen and was now out to target other Jesus-followers.

"Break the door in," he commanded his men. It was approaching second watch and he was expecting Crispus would have already bedded down for the night.

"Over there. Get him!" Eliphelet saw Joachim hiding by the press. Joachim tried to run, but there was no place to go. He was trapped by the wall of Crispus's small family compound. Two of Eliphelet's men caught him and dragged him to Eliphelet in the front of the house.

"I recognize you. You were there with Stephen. You refused to pick up a stone when we punished Stephen. You were with an older man. Where is he? Is he here? Who was that?" Eliphelet's demeanor changed as he thought he could wipe out even more of these Christ-followers. "Was that your father? Is he here too? He is a coward! Where is he?"

Joachim spit in front of him, disgusted by what they did to his friend Stephen. "My father is no coward!" Joachim tried to break free, but the men's grips were too experienced. He had to stand there and suffer from this man's hate for Christ-followers.

Two other men barged into the home, shouting. "Crispus. Crispus."

Eliphelet followed immediately behind them. "Where is he? Where is he?"

Crispus's wife and son slowly awakened, scrambled to their feet, and pressed themselves against the wall.

The guards grabbed them and threw them to the floor, realizing that Crispus was not there.

"Where is he? Crispus?" Eliphelet growled at the woman. "Where did he go? Bring them outside."

His two men from behind the house now entered.

"Burn everything. Burn it all." He should have been disappointed in not finding his quarry but would enjoy watching the woman and son suffer the pain of witnessing their home being consumed in fire.

The first soldier took his torch and leaned over to the bed mats. They caught fire instantly, and the second soldier watched.

Eliphelet exited the home, knowing his men knew how to destroy the living quarters.

An oil lamp burned and added fuel to the expanding flames. One of the soldiers kicked an oil jug in the direction of the burning bed mats. Oil seeped into the ground, not catching fire, as the guards kicked over two other jugs, mixing wheat and oil into the fiery mass. Embers rose from the bed mats and caught the roof on fire, forcing the soldiers out of the home. One soldier carried out a jug of wine, taking a big celebratory swig. A second soldier forced the door off its hinges and threw it onto the flames.

Joachim tried to escape and freed his one hand to strike his captor, but he wasn't quick enough.

One of the soldiers grabbed his dagger and thrust it into Joachim's side.

Joachim turned just in time to see the soldier pull the dagger out of him, his blood dripping from it. The soldier grinned at him, his teeth bare, the smell of wine on his breath.

Joachim fell to one knee, then fell prone to the ground. He looked up and saw his father's face in the moon. He could feel the life draining from him. His eyes closed, and he could see the face of Elizabeth, his bride-to-be. "No greater love."

"No! No!" Selah's screams pierced the night. "No!" She watched the life's energy drain out of Joachim as the fire grew in power. She was devastated as the blood soaked the ground. She turned and watched as everything she owned went up in smoke. Her heart broke at the destruction of the one thing that meant more than anything—the cup with Jesus's blood.

"Have some wine. He won't be drinking any this evening." The two soldiers laughed.

Eliphelet looked on but didn't partake. He was enjoying the sobbing of the mother with her boy in her arms, watching the flames consume the roof.

Selah looked on in horror, knowing that the cup, the wooden cup of the Messiah, would be destroyed.

CHAPTER 2

Edessa and the Mandylion

Edessa was the capital of the kingdom of Osrhoene, formerly a Syrian city in northern Mesopotamia. Now named Şanlı Urfa, it is situated in modern-day eastern Turkey. In AD 214, it was swallowed up by the Roman Empire as part of the eastern frontier between the Roman Empire and the Sassanid Empire.

EDESSA, OSRHOENE
LATE MORNING, THURSDAY, EARLY SEPTEMBER, AD 525

*H*alf a millennium following the resurrection, Christendom was a fully thriving religion. It spread throughout most of the Roman Empire after its acceptance by Emperor Constantine at his deathbed conversion in AD 337. Christianity was no longer a Jewish sect. Instead, it had supplanted Roman and Greek pagan worship to become one of the dominant world religions. King Abgar V of Osrhoene was the first major power to convert to Christianity and to convert his kingdom. Five hundred years later Christianity was the primary religion in Edessa.

The water came out of nowhere. It hit everyone, whether Christian, Jew, or Zoroastrian. It rose twenty feet in just a few minutes. Thirty days of incessant rain had finally beaten the city.

Anahit's mudbrick home surrendered to the conquering flood, the small home now caving in. Anahit and her daughter, Milena, had to get to higher ground. As they tried to cross what used to be the street in front of their home, a floating log hit Milena in the small of her back, and she lost the grip of her mother's hand.

Her mother was stunned as the powerful current dragged her daughter away. Anahit was frantic, yet she couldn't catch up. "Milena!" All she could see was the girl's long blond hair floating in the water. "Milena. Milena!" her mother cried. "Milena!" The sound of her wailing after watching her daughter being carried away was chilling.

The rain came down even harder. The torrents drowned out Anahit's cries, but her screams didn't stop. Her throat became sore from her terrified shrieking. She continued to look for her daughter, but couldn't see anything. The water had swallowed the girl.

Anahit tried to run, but the water was too deep. *Thump.* Another floating timber hit Anahit, and she nearly lost her balance.

Milena was nowhere to be seen in the surging water. All Anahit could see was debris and raging water. Even though she loved bathing in ponds near the Daisan River, she had never learned how to swim. She lifted her feet and let the currents take her to somehow stay close to her missing daughter.

Another log bumped her. This one had a sharp point and drew blood. When it hit her back, she felt her teeth clang together. The timbers were the remains of homes higher up in the street that had just collapsed.

Pangs of guilt consumed Anahit's thoughts as she realized she and Milena should have escaped much earlier to avoid the rising waters. A wave hit her face, and the brown water sloshed in her mouth.

"Milena. Milena!" Even with the pain in her throat from her hoarse voice she couldn't stop screaming. The futility matched her desperation.

✝✝✝

Davit turned when he thought he heard a woman's cries above the din of the rain. He stood at the entrance to the palace chapel, on a hill above the rest of the city, so he could see what was happening below. After a minute, his scans revealed a woman below, but he couldn't quite discern her dilemma.

His assistant, Selewkus, turned and saw the woman as well. She was walking and floating in the churning water. She needed help looking for something, but the two men were bewildered as to what it was. They were almost too far away to be able to help. Behind her was a partially disintegrated row of houses, the wooden roof beams carried away by the waters.

"Selewkus, go quickly. See if you can offer help. That woman may drown in the speeding water. Take one of your men with you."

Bishop Asclepius[1] was already inside when the first shrieks of the woman were heard by Davit and Selewkus. He didn't hear the shrieks as he removed his soaking wet cloak. He wanted to remove his waterlogged boots and sit in front of the fire, but he needed to first inspect the chapel for rain damage. His cold feet would have to wait.

With so many buildings succumbing to the rains, the bishop was worried about all the governor's properties, especially the governor's private chapel. Even his chambers had a pot to collect rainwater that leaked through the ceiling. The bishop began inspecting the ceiling but didn't see anything amiss.

Davit and the bishop both vied for the approval of the governor. Davit had the governor's ear concerning the administration of the province. The governor looked to the bishop for matters relating to the church and the practice of their faith.

The bishop never made it known, but he despised Davit, the eunuch. He was jealous of Davit's devotion in having sacrificed his genitals for Christ. And the bishop envied Davit's unlimited access to the governor's court. Every time Davit spoke, his high voice reminded Bishop Asclepius of the counselor's relationship to the governor and his ultimate power in the former Osrhoenian capital.

Having progressed through the ranks of the church hierarchy, the bishop knew how to hide his true feelings for the counselor. Today they needed to inspect the chapel to make certain it wouldn't follow the same fate as many of the homes in the city. If it was damaged, they'd need to remove the church treasures—the brass and gold fixtures and relics—to a safer location. Though it wasn't clear where safety from the floods and the rains might be.

"These are Noahan rains," Davit said out loud to Bishop Asclepius, suppressing his concern about the woman and refocusing on their inspection of the chapel. "Will they never end?"

The rain was incessant. For over three weeks, the rains came and came and came. The Daisan River, a small river during normal times, swelled and swelled.

"Bishop, should we have built an ark?" He grinned, turning back to his friend.

---

1 Bishop Asclepius: Bishop of Edessa from AD 522 to 526.

Selewkus and the two guards turned the corner and found the woman. She was now about a hundred yards from her home, walking, floating, and bobbing with the fast-flowing water.

"Help me. Help me! My daughter. My daughter! I can't find her!" They could barely hear her desperate pleas above the roar of the rushing water and pelting rain. Her voice was gravelly, and each time she screamed, the pain in her voice equaled the guilt she felt about her lost daughter. "Milena!"

When they heard the woman's shouts, the three men deduced exactly what happened. "Woman, is Milena your daughter?"

She didn't respond. Anahit kept moving as fast as she could.

The three men caught up and then passed her. Selewkus led the two guards and the woman, imagining what it would be like had he lost his daughter to the flood. They were drenched, and the rain continued to pummel them.

A lightning bolt hit the palace a few hundred yards off and exploded in their ears.

"My daughter, Milena. Please, we must find her. Please!" Anahit screamed behind them. Her voice was so hoarse the men could hardly understand her. She was frantic. Her drenched clothes hung from her shoulders and weighed her down. Her tears of guilt and fear were just as heavy.

The men tried to move as fast as they could, sometimes letting the flow take them. Other times their legs bogged down, tangled in debris and mud. The water raged as it spewed down the inclined narrow streets. Debris from the mudbrick houses filled the water.

It was hard to keep the water out of their mouths as they searched. They were able to walk in areas with shallow water, but it was much more dangerous in the deeper water. Large roof timbers passed them or bumped them and nearly knocked them off balance. Their water-soaked clothes stuck to their skin and made it hard to advance. When the water was too deep, they progressed with the flow of the water. Sometimes wooden dishes and goblets floated alongside them.

The brown, dirty water splashed into their eyes, making it hard to see. The turbulent water was muddy, and nothing could be identified once it was below the surface.

Selewkus's foot caught on something, and he went down face first. The current pushed his face down farther into the water. Another timber jutted out into the street lodged against what used to be a rock wall. Struggling, he freed his foot as he held onto the wall to steady himself against the torrent.

✝✝✝

"This flood is as bad as the floods that washed away the old Church of Saint Thomas," Bishop Asclepius said, as he inspected the chapel and grounds. He was a stout man and enjoyed his wine and sweets, causing him to huff and puff as they trekked through all the palace grounds. "I remember the original church was built to commemorate Saint Thomas's visit to Edessa. He later went to spread the word in India." The bishop continued inspecting more of the damage. His huffing and puffing began to subside. "I hope our chapel doesn't wash away like that."

Davit had to think a moment. He remembered hearing of Saint Thomas evangelizing in Edessa. "I think that was over four hundred fifty years ago, a few years after Abgar V died. I don't think they ever met, though." Davit noticed some water dripping in through the roof. "Let's hope this church is a little bit more stable."

They moved from the narthex into the nave. Bishop Asclepius and Davit were now in the chapel's sanctuary, named after King Abgar V, king of Osrhoene, the earliest royal follower of Jesus. Under Emperor Justinian, the Abgar dynasty had been swallowed into the Roman Empire. Under Justinian, the palace was used as the governor's residence, and the royal chapel had become the church of the governor. Under Justinian, Edessa was a small city on the frontier to the Sassanid Empire.

After the first week of rain, on the advice of his weather prognosticators, the governor had retreated to Antioch. It was one of the few times the weather prognosticators were correct in their forecasts. It was now the third week of unrelenting torrents of rain, exactly as they had predicted.

In his absence, the governor left Davit, his chief counsel, in charge. Davit could only watch as the waters washed away large swaths of the city's poorest homes. The rain was so strong, it was beginning to damage everything, including the palace and the governor's chapel. There wasn't much he could do except to watch and pray as the water destroyed more and more of the city.

He was glad he had ordered Selewkus to go rescue the woman. It was the only thing making sense amidst the damage inflicted on the city from the rain.

Both men were led through the palace buildings by the chief of the guard. Most of the buildings were connected by various hallways, but they had to enter the chapel from the outside because the chief of the guard didn't have possession of the hallway entry key.

"Here is where the most damage has taken place," the chief of the guard said, pointing to the panel above the chapel antechamber. In the mosaic above the wooden doors was a mosaic of Jesus with the words, "All ye will see God," above His head. Below it, the words, "God the Father is with you." They were also the words from Jesus's letter to King Abgar centuries earlier. They were the only words the king would read from his singular correspondence with the Messiah.

The chapel was about twenty feet wide by forty feet deep and could accommodate about thirty worshipers. The room had a high ceiling, about eighteen feet high, with long windows that stretched up more than twice the height of a man. During Mass, the smoke from the censor could be seen wafting up past the windows to an upper row of colorful mosaics, which depicted scenes of Christ teaching his disciples and giving his Sermon on the Mount.

The north-side wall above the altar had an image of King Abgar receiving the Mandylion. The king was shown with a gaunt face, wearing his crown and royal robes. The Mandylion was a cloth about thirty inches square with the tortured face of Jesus suffering the passion and wearing the crown of thorns.

The south side had an image of Abgar, strong and regal, riding on horseback and carrying a golden cross into battle. On his breast was an image of the Mandylion.

The archway above the door from the antechamber had partially given way and revealed a large crack in the facade. The facade was made up of a four-foot-by-four-foot mosaic of Jesus holding up two fingers of his right hand, blessing all those who enter.

Each of the three genuflected as they entered. The crack emerged from the right corner of the doorframe and reached all the way to the ceiling. It had split, and a large, triangular, four-foot section of the mosaic remained in place. The downward pointing end protruded out about two inches. At the ceiling, the triangle was over two feet wide. "This is the largest part of the damage. We'll need to shore up the archway as soon as possible to avoid further damage." The chief of the guard pointed to the crack on the top of the triangle. "So far, the roof seems to be intact."

All three men continued inspecting the room when a large thunderclap exploded overhead. Each of them instinctively ducked. It was so loud it caused the building to shake. The archway shifted further, causing the triangular wedge to crash down between them onto the stone floor in a cloud of dust. They should have feared for the ceiling to also cave in, but none of them moved. The three of them looked at each other, startled and thankful they weren't standing under the mosaic, as mosaic tiles rained down around them.

"Bishop, do you see what I see?" Davit pointed to where the triangular piece came from. His curiosity caused him to furrow his brow.

The bishop turned and focused his gaze where the governor's counselor was pointing. "Is that an eye?"

"It looks like a wooden box or something." The chief of the guard's thoughts were now fixated on uncovering this strange wooden object. He moved a bit to the left to get a better view, craning his neck to quench his curiosity. "It's an eye painted on a box?" The chief of the guard uttered the words more as a question than a statement of fact. The damage inspection would have to wait. "There was always lore there was a cloth, the Mandylion, hidden somewhere in the city. I had always thought of it as a foolish legend."

"I had heard it was hidden above the eastern gate," Davit said, scrutinizing the eye. He grabbed a torch to improve the light and pointed it up as high as he could. Part of a face appeared.

The bishop could barely hold back his excitement.

Davit took charge. "Go and get some of your men. We must uncover what's underneath. Have them bring a ladder and some masonry tools."

✝✝✝

Battling the cold, fierce water sapped all their energy. They were exhausted. "Milena! Milena!" Each of them screamed, hoping the girl would respond.

Anahit was filled with guilt and shame that she had lost her daughter in the water. Adrenaline pumped through her veins. She couldn't concentrate on anything but the face of her daughter when her hand had slipped out of hers. "Milena!" Her increasing desperation burned hotter and hotter into her conscience.

"Look there. There!" One of the guards pointed ahead at something floating in the water, being pushed under by the current. It looked like a sack of some kind. No. It was blond hair, caught on something.

Selewkus reached her first.

Then Anahit. "No. Noo!" Her screams arced across the water. The pain in her voice was excruciating. She wailed further. "Noo. Milena. No!" She remembered the pain of losing her husband. Now this.

Anahit grabbed Milena's lifeless body, her hair still entangled in the tree branches. Despite her efforts, she was unable to lift her daughter's face above the water, and her frenzy caused the water to splash about.

Selewkus and Anahit worked to free the girl's hair. He could only think of his daughter and worked gently so that he would not pull out a clump of hair from her scalp. He had to concentrate hard to separate thoughts of his own daughter. *What if this had happened to her?*

The other two men rushed to their aid. They tried to block the rushing water so the mother and the lifeless body of her daughter could resist the power of the flow. Finally, Selewkus broke the branch off the tree, and Milena's body was separated from its captor.

"Her hair, her beautiful hair. Why did this have to happen to her?" Anahit tried to smooth her hair as she had done so many times in the past. "Why?" The tears returned. They were tears of despair. The full recognition of the death of her daughter weighed her down and almost pulled her under.

All four plodded through the flow to where they could stand on solid ground. Anahit's tears dissolved in the streaming rain. She tried to remove the branch, but it was too entangled in the long blond hair. The girl's hair would only be able to be combed after the branch was cut out. She brushed her hair trying to give life back to her daughter, but it could never return to what it once was. She could only think of how she used to brush her hair. She had been the most beautiful girl in all of Edessa.

✝✝✝

The chief of the guard returned after about thirty minutes. Davit and the bishop investigated other cracks in the wall and roof of the chapel. Water had already begun trickling in behind the altar.

Over the course of an hour, the stonemason removed much of the mosaic, keeping it intact with little additional damage. It revealed a box with a painted image of the bearded face of Christ.

The work was interrupted when Selewkus and the two soldiers returned to the chapel. "Chief Counsel, I'm sorry to say we found the woman and her daughter."

"The girl—Milena—didn't survive." Selewkus thought of his own daughter as he revealed the result of their search. The bishop and Davit each genuflected. The bishop responded with a short prayer.

"We were able to locate her body. She was a few hundred yards away. Her hair was caught on a tree limb next to what used to be the bakery. She was face down in the water." Selewkus shook his head. "She had no chance."

The joy of finding the box with Christ's face painted on it was lost in the memory of the screams of anguish from the girl's mother. There were words—widow and orphan—for those who lost their spouse or parents, but there was no word for a parent who lost a child. Language couldn't fathom the pain suffered by a parent of a dead child.

"Bishop, I fear the girl won't be the only one needing your prayers in the next few days." Chief Council Davit caught the eye of the bishop. He could father no children but could sense the pain in the screams of the woman and in the voice of his aide, Selewkus. His excitement at finding the box was now dashed at the thought of more storm victims. He suddenly felt the weight of being in charge. He was responsible for finding a way to minimize damage and death to the city, but there was little he could do.

Rain pelted against the roof tiles overhead. Off in the distance, rolling thunder echoed through the sky. There was nothing anyone could do to stop the rain or avoid the extent of the damages the rain brought.

Suddenly, they heard a small crash in the corner. The chapel roof near the altar gave way, and water began streaming in.

"Hurry, hurry, before more of the roof caves in. Quickly." Davit glared up at the stonemason, imploring him to continue but worried about what would happen next.

Another thunderclap rumbled. This one was even closer than the last.

The stonemason continued to painstakingly remove more of the mosaic. The pieces were placed on the floor, along with many other individually colored tile pieces that no longer matched their original location in the image. The stonemason worked diligently until he freed the box and slid it out of its niche from within the wall. He stepped down the ladder and handed it to the chief of the guard, who proceeded to open it.

Inside was a cloth with an image of a distorted face with two closed eyes.

"Unfold it," Davit and the bishop said simultaneously.

"Don't let it touch the ground. Don't let it touch the ground," Davit continued. "Hurry before any more of the roof gives way. This could be the cloth given to King Abgar by Jesus. Careful. Careful!"

"No, wait. Not here. We can do that in the palace. The roof might cave in any moment." The bishop was just as eager as Davit but didn't want to risk any damage to the cloth.

"No, now, here, the palace may be no safer," Davit responded.

The bishop relented, despising Davit's high voice that was even higher now with all the excitement.

Selewkus, the stonemason, and the chief of the guard unfolded the cloth. It was about fourteen feet long and four feet high and didn't fit in the antechamber. They had to move to stretch it through the doorway into the chapel.

The stonemason remained in the chapel and held one end, and the chief of the guard held the other in the antechamber.

Right under the doorway was the face and the two faint eyes they had first seen.

"It is the Mandylion," Bishop Asclepius exclaimed. "It is. It did . . . it does exist." The bishop's eyes widened. A broad smile came to his mouth. He had often heard the rumors and whispers about the cloth, but now it was true. "The legend is true."

CHAPTER 3

The Siege of Edessa

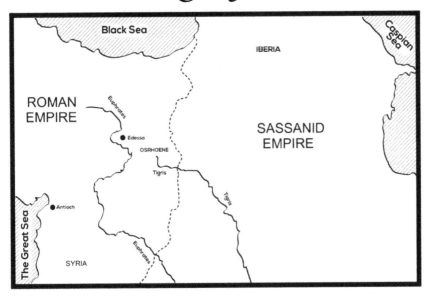

All was not well for the Roman Empire. Rome attempted to increase its power and was in need of money and men to wage war. Rome found it easier to pay off its rivals than to fight a battle to a conclusion. In the late AD 400s and early 500s, the Sassanids had expansion ambitions and waged war on their eastern frontier with the Roman Empire. In the 500s, Khosrow I,[1] king of kings of the Sassanid Empire, brought many reforms to the empire, including a centralized method of tax collection. The approach significantly improved finances and provided the means to expand the empire.

In AD 532, Rome and Khosrow signed a Perpetual Peace Treaty, with Rome paying 11,000 pounds of gold. Eight years later, after the disintegration of the treaty, Khosrow moved east, extending the Sassanid Empire all the way to Antioch. He then moved north, invaded Lazic on the Black Sea, and waged war on Edessa.

---

1 Khosrow I: Third son of Khavad, king of kings of the Sassanid Empire, Anushirawan, The Immortal Soul from AD 531–579. Born circa AD 501, died AD 570.

OUTSIDE THE WALLS OF EDESSA, OSRHOENE
AFTERNOON, SATURDAY, EARLY SEPTEMBER, SECOND WEEK OF THE
SIEGE, AD 544

"Your Highness, King of Kings of Sassania. Before you beat me with the next round of backgammon, we have a special presentation for you. It is the completion of an extraordinary tapestry woven in traditional style with a scene of your great victory over Antioch and Apamea." Gazri, Khosrow's chief counselor, spoke in a grand, booming voice so that he could be heard outside of King Khosrow's tent. If it had been any louder, the people in the walled city of Edessa, just under a mile away, would have been able to hear. Everyone needed to know this tapestry represented the greatness of Khosrow and his personal leadership in the defeat of the Roman Empire at Antioch.

"It is a small piece but has been completed in your honor as you lay siege to your next conquest. Edessa and then Lazic will fall just as did Antioch." Gazri admired the beauty of the hand-woven wool tapestry embellished with gold and silver threads and adorned with the spoils—rubies, diamonds, and emeralds—taken from the Antiochian palace. The pictured Antiochian Cathedral was just like he remembered it, with its burnt-sienna-colored dome roof and the Orontes River surrounding the palace grounds.

"The tapestry is small compared to others but will make a fine memorialization of this battle against Justinian's[2] lackeys and his God. We designed it to match the themes found in the Baharestan carpet in the Great Audience Hall of the palace. Each of these carpets illustrate beauty inspired by God."

The Baharestan carpet was enormous. It was ninety feet long and ninety feet wide, woven of fine gold and silver silk threads by the best Persian artisans. Rare gems were embedded throughout the carpet, depicting a utopian garden. The reflection of the gems glinted into the eyes of the observer, imparting the fantasy of being with Ahura Mazda,[3] lord of wisdom and creator, as he admired his earthly creation.

Khosrow and his counselor were biding their time while their men completed the siegeworks against the capital city of the former kingdom of Osrhoene, the city of Edessa. They had already been encamped several weeks. The time was nearing when the siegeworks would be ready for their intended purpose. Khosrow was ecstatic at the coming conquest of this frontier city, which would expand his Sassanid Empire westward.

Gazri held a different relationship with Khosrow compared to others. He

---

2 Justinian the Great: Last Roman emperor and first Byzantine emperor from AD 527 to 565. Born AD 482, died AD 565.
3 Ahura Mazda: Lord of wisdom, creator, and highest deity of Zoroastrianism.

was Khosrow's chief counselor, and he also managed the kingdom's treasury. He helped grow the treasury for Khosrow's father, Khavad I,[4] and now for Khosrow. Because of Gazri's financial savvy, he enjoyed the ear of the son in both matters of state and war. His management of the treasury provided Khavad and Khosrow with the money to hire the Huns to help wage war and finance the expansion of the Sassanid Empire.

"Gazri, my friend. It is beautiful. I can see myself in heaven with our god Ahura smiling down over our victory against Justinian." Khosrow continued gazing at the tapestry. "This tapestry reminds me of the time we spent in the Great Sea at Antioch. Those Edessans have their cloth with their god painted on it. I have this wonderful Baharestan tapestry. If it's not too late in the fall, once we've conquered Edessa and Lazic, I wish to bathe in the Black Sea just like we did in the Great Sea after we won the battle in Antioch."

Khosrow was in good spirits. A smile came to his face. He could feel the warmth of the afternoon as he remembered sunbathing in the waters of the Great Sea. "Perhaps we can hold some more chariot races where the blue Justinian faction loses to us again."

Khosrow and his counselor laughed aloud, remembering how their chariot races in Apamea ridiculed the Roman army. "I was glad to take their tributes, but it was better to beat them in battle and at the races." They both continued laughing. "We will earn even more money once these Edessans give in."

"Put down a new wager. I will take your money this time. You know I only let you win the last game." Gazri smiled at his opponent at backgammon.

Khosrow focused his attention back on their backgammon game.

Gazri only allowed himself a few wins against the king of kings. He considered himself a friend to the king but never tested the limits of their friendship. It was much better to have his king in good spirits than to win a few skirmishes on the backgammon board.

"What I like about this game is that it teaches the subtle and random nuances of fate." Khosrow recounted how his father related the game of backgammon to life and religion.

The small hand-carved ivory pieces tinkled together as Gazri cleared the board for their next game.

"Although there is a skill in playing this game, the result of winning or losing is often decided by fate."

Each of the hand-carved ivory stones sounded a percussive musical note as they were gathered and placed in their starting positions.

---

4 Khavad I: King of kings of the Sassanid Empire from AD 488 to 496 and AD 498–531. Born AD 473, died AD 531.

"My father taught me that even the best players will lose once in a while." Khosrow leaned back on his leather cushion. It felt cool through the layers of his robe. "The best players will win more often than not because the randomness of the die will even out over time. That's when skill makes the difference, and our skill is what won us the battle at Antioch and will win here in Edessa," Khosrow said smiling. "Bring me more bread!"

Upon Kosrow's demand, the cupbearer clapped his hands, sending a servant scurrying out of the tent.

In addition to the presentation of the Antioch tapestry, the talks about strategy against Justinian, the tactics to win the battle, and the negotiations against Edessa had made Kosrow hungry. He was ready for his favorite indulgence. "Bring more dates as well."

Gazri watched as a second servant followed the first with this new request.

Khosrow lamented he could never eat enough of them. "The best dates come from the Mesopotamian Valley. Egyptian dates are good, but those grown close to home are the best."

"Ahura Mazda will be pleased once we have defeated these swine here and in Lazic," Gazri said, certain of the strength of their god over all other gods. Ahura Mazda was the creator of the universe. His strength and compassion had been revealed by the prophet Zoroaster. "Your good deeds will do much to spread the faith around the world." Gazri used a deferential voice.

Khosrow smiled and recollected when his father and the chief priest had taught him about their religion, Zoroastrianism, and their god, Ahura Mazda.

"As I was growing up, my father would teach me about—" Khosrow's mood changed when he realized how late it was as his chief negotiator, Zaberganes,[5] entered the tent. Backgammon had simply been a diversion. He anxiously awaited news of the talks with the Edessan peace delegation. His hunger for Mesopotamian dates disappeared.

Zaberganes strode into the tent and stood at attention, realizing he had interrupted the king midsentence. "Your Majesty. My apologies. I bring news of the negotiations."

Khosrow was tired of his chief negotiator not bringing good news. A partial sneer came to his right lip. He noticed Zaberganes's left hand twitching. It wasn't going to be good news.

"Yes, go on." Khosrow's mood changed. The fond recollections of his successes in Antioch and Apamea were replaced by frustration and impatience. His eyes narrowed and his focus went directly on Zaberganes. The sneer became more pronounced. His frustration caused his hunger to return with a

---

5 Zaberganes: Persian diplomat and Khosrow's chief negotiator with the Edessans.

vengeance. Without looking away he demanded, "Where are my dates?"

The servant had still not brought a fresh plate. The servant who had brought the bread dashed out of the tent to help hurry the dates along. Khosrow's order demanded strict obeisance from all those present.

"Where are my dates?" this time even louder.

His cupbearer ran out of the room after both of the absent servants.

Zaberganes stiffened his stance. "Stephanus[6] brings you greetings and best wishes. He sends you condolences on the death of your father." Aside from his twitching hand, Zaberganes still hadn't moved since he had interrupted Khosrow. "He wishes to meet you when negotiations are concluded to reminisce about the times decades ago when he treated your father."

Zaberganes was always able to convey his message to the king with deferential confidence. "The talks have stalled. They believe they will withstand your attacks and are not budging in their position."

"Did you tell them they can buy their peace?" Khosrow boomed. "That they will either save their precious city now, or, in a few days when we have breached the walls, we will take everything, including their lives. They will not hold." Khosrow made a fist, strode to Zaberganes and looked him directly in his eyes. He was only inches away. Khosrow's breath was putrid smelling, like a mix of garlic, onions, and rotting fish.

Zaberganes didn't move. He'd been approached like this in the past and knew not to back down. "Yes, Your Highness. As you instructed, I told them there would be dire consequences and that they must hand over all the wealth within the city walls. They need to deliberate most carefully to avoid the fate of the Antiochians." Zaberganes, though the inferior, spoke with authority. "When I convey your next instructions, Stephanus and their chief negotiator, Martinus,[7] will take your demands back to Prince Peranius.[8]

Counselor Gazri stood without saying a word.

Khosrow knew they had the upper hand, even though they didn't win their first skirmish with these sons of Edessan whores. "We are making great progress on our siegeworks. It will only be a few more days. They cannot hold out that long."

Although the Roman army was clever at hindering their efforts, it was only a matter of time.

"It was my engineers that swayed the battle at Antioch. They will not fail this time either."

6 Stephanus: Physician (leech) and negotiator for Prince Peranius. Previously physician to the Sassanid King Khavad I, father of Khosrow I.

7 Martinus: Chief negotiator for Edessa. Mentioned by Procopius.

8 Prince Peranius of Iberia: General of the army for the defense of Edessa. Died from falling from a horse while hunting. Died circa AD 545.

"Justinian will not be able to hold this fortress here and win in Lazic." Gazri worked to enhance his power with the son, who was even more powerful than the father. "Perhaps we negotiate for a monetary settlement now to finance the war in the north and then return and take the whole city after our victory in Lazic."

Khosrow grinned with complete satisfaction. "My father taught me how to play backgammon and chess, but it was I that introduced both games to teach strategy to all my lieutenants." He went over the calculations in his mind. He could feel the moves needed to checkmate the Edessans. He could smell the success in this battle, and the battle hadn't even started.

He moved around to the table where they had just played backgammon. "Now, each of my officers is skilled in the subtleties of the games. In chess the ultimate prize is to capture their king, their so-called emperor, Justinian. But that is a long way off. As they bleed themselves dry in the west, and as we milk them of their gold in the east, they will become weaker . . . maybe enough for them to lose their king to me." He picked up one of the ivory pieces and stared off in the direction of Edessa. After a moment he turned to Gazri. "Edessa is simply a piece on the chessboard, perhaps no more than the stature of a bishop."

Khosrow became more determined than ever. "No, we will—"

General Azarethes,[9] general of the army attacking Edessa, entered the tent, disturbing the discussion the treasurer held sway over.

With no expression on his face, Gazri nodded at his peer, belying the disdain he had for the interruption.

"Your Highness, the Romans are strengthening their resolve with a surprise attack. We will be putting it down shortly but will delay our siegeworks by a day. They are running out of men and equipment. It won't be long now. We suggest surrounding the city and executing a full assault on the Great Gate."

Khosrow smiled. Each update reported by Azarethes meant they were closer to removing this pawn from the chessboard.

His general stood with confidence. He would succeed at any given task. He didn't stand at attention like Zaberganes. He stood with his feet wide, his thumbs in his belt. Khosrow couldn't win without this man. The general wasn't royalty. Instead, he was the son of Khavad's most trusted military genius.

"Your Highness, Edessa is critical to Justinian. It has been renamed in his honor to Justinianopolis." The general continued, "If we win here, we will break

---

9 General Azarethes: Commander of the Sassanian army during the siege of Edessa under Khosrow I.

the spirit and pride of the Romans, and it will only help strengthen our battles in the north in Lazic. We will prove that our god is stronger than their Christ."

Gazri concealed his annoyance while the arrogant general spoke. He breathed in deeply, without making a sound. He didn't want either the general or the king to notice his contempt. "General Azarethes, wouldn't it be better to let them drain their supplies further by waiting? Afterall, they haven't been able to resupply since we surrounded the city. Let them expend—"

"Continue all efforts to take this city and kick those Roman negotiators out," Khosrow said as he stood up, his focus now fully on the general. His resolve strengthened by the treasurer's words. "We are not yet ready to settle, not when we have the upper hand. If they don't want to deliver their commanders, we will not relent." He took a deep breath. "I can smell the fear in their army's men."

Gazri hid his smile. There was no hint of an attack order.

Khosrow turned and walked out of his tent. Looking out over the encampment, he took pride in the beautiful sight. Fires burned and men worked, preparing for the imminent offensive. He breathed in the spicy scent of onions and cumin being cooked for his men. His conscripts fought well alongside his regular troops and the Hun mercenaries. In the next days and weeks, they would be tested again.

The fortress was just under a half mile away—in full sight of the king's view when he stood outside his tent. Off to his right, out of sight of the city, were neat piles of newly made arrows, spears, and ladders. To his left, forty or more men sharpened their swordsmanship and marksmanship.

General Azarethes stood behind him.

Khosrow grinned as he watched the progress of the siegeworks growing against the fortress walls.

There were also two Cilicians, large screens made of goats-hair, hiding the progress of the ramp below and protecting the men behind it building the siegeworks. It had been only two weeks, and victory was only a few more weeks off.

"Tell those Roman envoys that if they don't want to lose everything—" Khosrow interrupted himself. "No. Tell them if they don't deliver the heads of Peter[10] and Peranius, they will lose everything." He pondered a few more minutes, enjoying the words he chose to issue his threats. "Repeat that they will lose everything. I will turn Edessa into a pasture for sheep!" Khosrow laughed with resolve, anticipating his quick success.

---

10 Peter: Roman general who defended Edessa under Prince Peranius. Mentioned by Procopius.

EDESSA, OSRHOENE
SUNRISE, MONDAY, LATE SEPTEMBER, FIFTH WEEK OF THE SIEGE,
AD 544

Inside the walls of the city of Edessa, the Romans didn't stand idly by. They weren't going down without a fight. Plus, they had the power of the cloth—not painted by human hands—discovered twenty years earlier in the wall of the king's chapel.

Prince Peranius of Iberia and general of the army for the defense of Edessa stood at the entry to the failed tunnel. They had to stop work on the tunnel under the siegeworks because they were afraid the Sassanids would discover it. "We will begin again tomorrow. We will not allow this siegeworks to succeed. The power of God is with us." Peranius turned from his engineer and his men and walked in the direction of the southern wall.

The chief engineer and his lieutenant continued to stand at attention until their commander was out of sight. In these battles, it was the cunning of the engineers that swayed the outcome.

"We begin at second watch." The engineer had to coordinate the tunneling effort with the protection of his men. He was surprised the Sassanids hadn't fully comprehended what his plans were.

The Sassanids had successfully built a strong ramp, but he was able to conceal his own efforts to destroy it. If successful, he would be able to weaken the ramp enough so that it would collapse under its own weight. It would be even more successful if the ramp collapsed and took some of the Sassanids with it. And most successful would be to destroy not only the Sassanid attackers but also their builders and engineers. The loss of engineers would be a serious blow to any advantage the Sassanid army might have. In this fight, engineers were invaluable to the success of the Sassanian siegeworks.

"Get some rest now. There will be no sleep tonight." As the engineer spoke those words, a stranger, dressed completely in black, entered the periphery of his vision. Or was it a shadow? "Optio, is that person working with you?"

The man disappeared behind the armory.

The optio, an officer reporting directly to the engineer, didn't respond. The optio commanded the men working under the engineer. Although they'd worked together over the last five years, the engineer still called him by his rank, Optio.

This man in black didn't fit in at all. He didn't seem unfriendly, but they couldn't take any chances.

"Never mind. It—" The engineer didn't finish his sentence. He thought he had seen a man dressed like that before. *Was it in Belisarius, in Italy?* But he couldn't make the connection. *Was he a spy?* "Optio, send two of your men after him."

†††

Peranius strode up to the top of the fortress wall and peered out. The centurion of the wall stood at attention behind him. Peranius was careful not to expose himself but did see off in the distance what looked to be their delegation returning from their negotiation with Khosrow. They were being chased off, not given the respect of equals but, rather, treated as a group of sheep being chased by a wolf.

Peranius started to seethe. His head filled with blood. His ears turned red and burned. He clenched his fists in anger. "We will not let that scum desecrate the walls of this city. We have more than just our lives to protect. We must defend our Christian heritage."

The image of Jesus's face from the Mandylion came to him. What he saw, though, was a folded cloth—a cloth, a washcloth, believed to display the image of the face of Jesus imprinted on it as Jesus wiped his face. *But it was odd that the cloth also showed his neck. How could a man wipe his face and neck at the same time with a single cloth?* He took a deep breath and drank in the confidence he felt in himself and his men. "We will survive this onslaught." The image of the face of the scourged man resolved to accept the fate of crucifixion was all he needed to remain steadfast against these Sassanids.

"We must hold the city to continue to tie down the Sassanids here so that the battle at Lazic can be won." Peranius now watched his men and the townspeople below gathering materials to increase the height of the wall. The townspeople made bricks and let them dry in the sun before they were fired. The bishop stood over them, as he held the sacred Mandylion and prayed.

The Mandylion had never been seen by the townspeople, but at this moment, it was brought out to provide divine support for their efforts to defend the city. Peranius held the top two corners of the cloth, and the sun caught the full face of the image. Although he wouldn't take up arms, he would support the men with prayers like David did for his army against the Philistines. Each brick and slab of mortar would increase the height of the wall to defend against the ever-present, ever-growing siegeworks.

After morning Mass, the bishop and his priests moved to the square in front of the cathedral and set up a small table. From there, their prayers were spoken in a regular, musical cadence. The prayers continued all day and ended after dusk. They helped to blunt the fear and anxiety for what would come next. At the end of each prayer, the workers responded in unison, "Amen." Every available tool and defense, both earthly and godly, was marshaled to hold back the Sassanids.

Speaking to no one but loud enough to be heard by those attending him, Peranius said, "We cannot let them gain access to Pontus Euxinus—the Black Sea—where they can threaten the Roman Empire throughout the region. Access to the sea would give them a waterway to threaten Constantinople directly." Peranius thought back on his arrival in Edessa, traveling from Constantinople to Lazic by water and then to Edessa on horseback. The Sassanids weren't great navy men, but under Khosrow and his father, Khavad, before him, they had proven themselves to be resourceful foes over each of the last few decades. "Gaining access to the sea would be a serious strategic blow to the entire Roman Empire."

Peranius returned to the engineer, who was conferring with his men. "Engineer," he called out. "How many feet per day can you achieve? This ramp is getting closer, and we must be ready for them."

The engineer had been involved with other sieges, both attacking from the outside and defending from the inside. "We can build seven feet per week." It was the materials and logistics that would make the difference. "We have the townspeople making bricks, and if the sun holds throughout the day and the ovens at night, those bricks will be strong enough to provide a proper defense."

He was able to feign confidence for the townspeople, even though the weather had otherwise not cooperated. The intermittent clouds slowed the drying of the bricks. "Our concern will be how to strengthen the extended wall to avoid a cave-in. For that, we will need more timbers to keep it from caving in. For the ovens, we'll need more wood. If the wall falls in, we will be able to rebuild it. If it falls out onto the Sassanid ramp, they will use those bricks to their advantage."

"Take what you need from the homes. As much as you need," Peranius instructed his engineer. "None need be spared."

The engineer paused for just a few seconds and looked around at the homes facing him. "We hope to recover some of the timbers used by the Sassanids in their ramp for the tunnel works. If that's possible, it will lengthen the time for our defenses and improve the negotiating position of our peace envoys. We must more than match their progress." He stooped down to the ground and grabbed a handful of cold damp dirt. "We will not let them breach this wall." He stood and held the moist earth for a moment. Then he squeezed it in his hand and let it fall to the ground. The engineer spoke with undeniable confidence. "The weather is the only risk. Rain for us also slows the Sassanids. What matters for us are the clouds. If we have clouds but not rain, the Sassanids might gain the advantage. The bricks must dry in the sun."

Peranius's eyes locked with the engineer's. In that instant they both silently acknowledged the risks, not letting on to anyone around them.

✝✝✝

"Your Highness, we are close to winning in the north. A few thousand more men would make all the difference." Gazri hoped his counsel would lead to both victory in the north and south, plus money in the empire's coffers.

Khosrow was standing outside of his tent, staring at the siegeworks. There was something different from the day before. The wall extension had caved in. The hastily built extension to the wall in front and above the siegeworks had collapsed. The intermittent clouds hadn't allowed the bricks to fully harden, so they cracked and disintegrated. *Was it possible?* If this were true, they would only be a few days away from routing the Edessans. Khosrow chuckled as he thought of the commanders and engineers he was fighting against . . . Peranius and Peter. Their failed attempt to extend the height of their wall was laughable.

Khosrow took a date from his hand and put it in his mouth, its sweetness matching his mood. He wished his father could be here to enjoy the spectacle. "Unfortunately, they may be able to reuse some of the bricks. But then—"

Something from the siegeworks caught his eye. "Gazri!" His tone made it obvious that he was commanding him to come to his side. His smile was gone. "Is that smoke?"

There were small fires all around the siegeworks. The Cilicians were suddenly toppled by stone projectiles launched from the Edessan ballistas.

Khosrow became frantic. The Romans were shooting burning arrows at his men. Within seconds his euphoria turned into bewilderment and then into loathing. Enraged, he ran to the enormous mound of earth, trees, and stone that used to be a ramp. Arrows and burning coals landed all around, but there was something else wrong.

Gazri was never too far from Khosrow's side. He was just inside the tent and started running, trying to catch up to the Sassanian king of kings. With the Cilicians smashed, the Sassanid engineers and workmen were exposed. Panic set in. Smoke and fires were everywhere. More was coming from the mound, but it didn't fit. At first, it wasn't clear if it was from the Edessans dropping burning embers and shooting burning arrows onto the ramp to impede building progress or if it came from another source . . . inside the ramp!

The fire inside and under the mound continued to gain strength, and it was clear the smoke was not only from around the ramp but from the ramp itself. The barrage of arrows left men screaming in pain.

"General, get more water and dirt. We must put this fire out immediately. Now!" Khosrow screamed. His rage burned even deeper within him, matching the intensity of the fires.

The Edessan engineers were successful in hiding their midnight attack preparations on the siege ramp. In the night they had gathered dried timbers from the town's houses, soaked the timbers with cedar oil, and then coated them with bitumen and sulfur. Through a tunnel, they were carried in, placed under the siegeworks, and set ablaze. The saturated logs, once lit, burned in a juggernaut of never-ending fire.

"The fires will not go out. More water. More water!" Azarethes barked in vain.

The mound collapsed in one area, and three men were swallowed up. Their water fell in with them, completely useless.

As the Sassanids put water over one fire, another fire extended its tentacles to another spot right next to it. "It's bitumen and cedar oil mixed with sulfur." The general yelled orders louder and faster through his coughing. His mind raced. He could see no way to regain the upper hand in this battle. His lieutenants were running just as fast as their men, but the fires kept on moving. The smoke was intense. They couldn't help their coughing either.

The louder they barked their orders, the more they coughed. "Don't use water. Use earth." Water made the fires worse causing the burning oil mixture to flow and ignite the next timber. Instead of dousing the fire, water helped carry the flames to the rest of the support beams installed by the Sassanids. "Use earth, not water!" But the orders were lost in the coughing and the mayhem. Khosrow's men threw more water on the fires.

Men with arrows in them tried to crawl to safety but were trapped by the flames. Their screams of agony and death drowned out the orders of their commanders.

"You damned Peranius. We will kill—" Khosrow started coughing. He was at the edge of the siegeworks coughing up an awful tasting black phlegm. It caused him to double over and start wheezing. "We will kill all of you for this. This will not stand." He coughed again. The fumes were overtaking him, especially the sulfur. "General, we will order a counterattack immediately. This cannot stand." Khosrow could see weeks of his efforts go up in smoke. He doubled over again, coughing and sulfur burning his throat. He could hardly breathe.

General Azarethes waved to one of his lieutenants to help the king move away from the ramp and the unbearable smoke. Sulfur and bitumen burned his nostrils and throat.

Within an hour, the entire siegeworks were covered in thick black smoke from the burning, fresh timbers supporting the ramp and the oil-soaked timbers below.

There was a roar from inside the city walls. The Edessans were cheering their success against the siegeworks. "Those cursed Edessans!"

The Sassanids hadn't prepared for a fire of this magnitude. There wasn't enough water or dirt to contain it.

By afternoon, the ramp was useless. The foundation had been badly burned by the fire, and most of the timbers had been reduced to ash. A large portion of the ramp had collapsed. The part left standing couldn't be trusted to support a sieging army.

General Azarethes summoned his lieutenants. He wheezed, "How many ladders are complete?"

His underlings began to answer, but he didn't wait.

"Get . . ." he wheezed again. His throat burned. "Get the engineers building ladders through the night. We'll need everyone they can muster. The winner of the battle will be the one who reacts the swiftest." He coughed again, but this time there was blood in his mouth. "Prepare immediately for an attack at dawn. We will scale the walls!" His heart pounded beneath his armor. Furious about the attack on the ramp, the general screamed his orders, repeating them louder each time, despite the burning pain in his throat.

His lieutenants quickly moved to organize the attacking force and the ladders. The ladder attack had been successful in Antioch, and they would use it here. His army was ready, but it was the first few men who had the least chance of surviving.

He loved the give and take of battle, and if a few men died, what did it matter? A fall from a ladder would maim or cripple. An arrow in the shoulder or leg was a slow, more certain death. Death wouldn't come instantly, but it would come within a few hours . . . or within a few excruciating days. Only victory was important.

As Azarethes's lieutenants prepared a main thrust against the Great Gate, there was also a plan underway for another simultaneous ladder attack to the west wall.

"We will use the ladders to divert attention from the attack at the gate and split our forces here and here." Azarethes ran his fingers across a diagram of the city-fortress. "This two-pronged attack should split their defenses so we can achieve success with one. Entering through the Great Gate will be our primary objective."

"My lord, we've noticed some new activity. They are preparing a counter-attack in retaliation for our destruction of their siegeworks," Peranius's chief adjutant explained as Peranius surveyed the defenses.

"We have wetted the gate planking all night, and it should now be impervious to flame." Peranius banged on the gate. It was a soft thump, not a crisp thud. "Our engineers have succeeded. The barbarian from the east is awakened." Peranius could see Khosrow's forces gathering in the gray pre-dawn mist.

The next few hours would determine the success of all their past efforts. It all led up to this.

"The captured rainwaters have made the difference in our ability to be ready for a flaming attack on the gate." The engineer prided himself on the success of his planning.

Massive hundred-gallon water jugs were placed on the wall, ready to be emptied should the need arise.

The adjutant paused while Peranius inspected the additional rainwater held in reserve at the foot of the wall to the side of the gate. The adjutant spoke with confidence. "Strengthening timbers have also been placed. They were moved from the failed wall fortifications and should be able to withstand the pressure of an attack on the gate."

The sun was a few minutes away as the dark blue-gray of the sky brightened to a lighter blue and fiery orange. The calm of the dawn was nowhere to be found, frenetic activity was everywhere. Brickmaking was replaced by arrow and spear making, and pots of boiling water were prepared for the wounded. Peranius knew his men and the townsfolk were ready for what the Sassanids had in store for them.

"We are also prepared to counteract a potential ladder attack. The towns-people have been heating olive oil since the fourth watch, and it is ready to repel anyone who ascends up the walls." The chief adjutant fought back the flow of adrenaline that came from apprehension as well as lack of sleep. He hadn't slept in over forty-eight hours and wouldn't sleep for the rest of this day.

The image of Jesus's face from the Mandylion came to Peranius. It gave him a sense of calm and confidence in whatever would come from the day's outcome. "Who is that man over there?" Peranius caught a glimpse of a man dressed in black.

The adjutant looked in that direction, but the man was gone.

"Is he a Sassanid spy? Have your men find him immediately." Peranius was now worried the Sassanids had slipped a spy into the city. "Do not let that man escape the walls of this city. He can't be allowed to inform Khosrow of our defenses!"

His adjutant commandeered two men, and the three of them ran off to pursue the mystery man.

"Bishop, you are up early." Peranius greeted the clergyman as he turned from inspecting the gate. "Can we count on your prayers for us this morning?"

The bishop was about ten yards from the gate, trying to stay out of the way of Peranius's men's work. "You can. We will need God's blessings over all our efforts today."

Father Sarkis, the bishop's chief assistant, was behind him carrying a beautifully engraved wooden case containing the Mandylion. Another priest and two acolytes were just a few more steps behind.

"Khosrow is activating his forces for an attack, and we must keep this fortress and the Mandylion out of the hands of the Sassanids." Peranius informed the bishop of his expectations for the day.

At that moment, Stephanus, their chief negotiator, appeared and nodded to them both. "We shall be praying all day. The cloth is our divine protection against all foes. No one can conquer us! These Sassanids are waging war against our God, and He will not let us lose."

The bishop removed a leather valise from the beautifully decorated wooden box held by Father Sarkis. He placed it on the table that had been set up by the young acolytes. "Would you like to see the image of the Son of Man? You will not be hindered in your efforts today. Jesus, God, and the Holy Spirit will be with us. I will make certain . . . we will make certain of that." The bishop removed the folded cloth from the leather valise, and the gray-brown face of Jesus stared up at both of them.

Stephanus and Peranius kneeled and kissed the lips of the image of the face of the Son of God.

The bishop put his hand on the shoulder of the men now empowered by God to defend the lives of everyone inside the city walls. As they prayed, they were not distracted by the commotion and activities all around. They had prayed many times in preparation for battle and had learned to focus on their prayer regardless of what was going on around them. After a minute, Stephanus and Peranius rose and strode off.

The bishop moved around behind the table, and the two priests moved to either side of the bishop. They brought small pillows, and each of them kneeled and prayed. "In Nomine Patris . . ."

It would be a long day of prayer.

Two acolytes stood behind them as if on guard.

"This Azarethes is a cunning general. With the loss of their siegeworks, they will come at us with aggression. It will be in a way we least expect." Stephanus related his impressions of the Sassanid general, based on the short interactions they had during the failed negotiations. "At each turn in the negotiations, he would respond with some new unrelated demand. His method was designed to keep his interlocutor off balance. This new attack will be executed in the same way." Stephanus thought a few moments before adding, "If we can hold them off now, we may be able to convince them to turn their attentions elsewhere."

The pair advanced in the direction of the Great Gate to inspect the fortifications. The Holy Spirit made certain they had chosen their defenses wisely.

✝✝✝

"Father Sarkis. Father, come quickly. Sarah is giving birth. It is very early. Two months!" Narek was out of breath. He had run a few hundred yards to where the bishop and Father Sarkis had set up their table for prayers. He was too old to be on the walls yet still able to provide supplies and water to the soldiers. It was his daughter giving birth.

"Please. Hurry."

Father Sarkis stood and looked at the bishop, then at Narek. "Yes, of course." What he feared, he imagined was also in the minds of Sarah's father and the bishop. Last rites for men dying in battle were difficult because of the number, but last rites for a baby lost at birth were the most painful for any clergyman. No one wanted to face a mother who had just lost her child. This would be the first casualty of many for the day.

As Father Sarkis approached Sarah's home, he could hear her sobs from the street.

The midwife stood at the door, trying to hold back tears. As many births as she had assisted, some babies just couldn't be saved. "Father, the baby lived for just a few minutes, then couldn't catch her breath. She was too young. Too young." She looked at the priest, took a long breath, and exhaled. "The anxiety of the coming battle, and her husband on the gate, must have precipitated the birth."

It was just as Father Sarkis had known all along. What was going to be a joyous day two months hence, turned into a sad day today. Kings and emperors had their games, and the peasants suffered. It never changed. "Thank you, sister. I know you did your best." Father Sarkis entered the small home and saw the mother sobbing, clutching her daughter. The tiny bundle was wrapped in cloth. "Has anyone gone for the father?"

"I will go. He is defending the west gate." The grandfather took one last look, turned, and quickly headed to the west gate. He tried to hold back the tears.

Father Sarkis looked down, attempting to remain emotionless for the sake of the mother. "Will you pray with me?" He reached his hand out, and Sarah took it and held it. The sadness emanating from the grieving mother was overwhelming. No words came to him other than the Lord's Prayer, "In Nomine Patris . . ." The words were reassuring, and his soft, calming voice helped to reduce her sobbing. Father Sarkis continued to console the woman, and her weeping finally abated.

She wasn't ready to relinquish the tiny body. Her eyes were now calmer and her breathing more regular. She dozed off, resting after the hours of tortured childbirth. Her grip on the priest's hand loosened, and he placed her hand back around the baby's body.

The midwife and priest exited to the street. The midwife dealt the next blow. "It was a painful birth, and the placenta tore. I don't expect her to last more than a few days."

"She won't be the only death. We will have a busy few days as this new battle unfolds." Father Sarkis looked into the eyes of the midwife, then back through the door at the grieved mother and lifeless child. Anxiety and sadness pulsated in his mind. Even with the knowledge and hope of a life in heaven, he was not prepared for what would come this day.

Sarah's eyes were closed. She was fully spent. Her grip on her daughter remained tight even in her sleep. "I must return to our prayer vigil."

✝✝✝

"Your Highness, we were unable to find the Sassanid spy." Peranius's adjutant was out of breath. He interrupted the conversation between the prince and his negotiator. "I have four men continuing the search. Shall they continue, or should they reinforce the West Gate? What are your orders?"

Peranius looked at Stephanus, then at the adjutant. "Have two men continue the search. Have the others return to their posts. The Sassanids are amassing their men to attack, and we'll need all the men we can to hold them back." Peranius turned back to Stephanus. "If we hold them off today, perhaps we can negotiate a settlement here and in Lazic. We can't allow them access to the sea."

The first glint of sun broke over the horizon as the Sassanids completed their attack formations. The cover of darkness had only partially masked their intentions. As they had done for the last three days, they worked through the night, launching an hourly salvo of burning arrows into the fortress. A few minor fires distracted the defenders. The recent rains provided them ample water to douse them soon after they started. What was a detriment to their defenses against the siege ramp was now a benefit to the imminent attack. At a minimum, the salvos disrupted the sleep of the Edessans, so that when the final attack did come, the Roman army would be fighting with limited sleep.

"Are the ladders ready?" Azarethes inquired of his lieutenants, agitated at not seeing any smoke. The fire arrow barrage had failed. There was no smoke coming from the city. *Would nothing work against this cursed city?*

Khosrow and Gazri stood at the entry to the king's royal tent.

General Azarethes approached the king and his companion. "Your Highness. We are ready to commence. Awaiting your signal."

Khosrow looked directly at his general, then at the city. It was a beautiful sight. The city would fit well into his empire. He steeled his gaze, removed his dagger from its hilt, and stabbed it into the table. "Go. Go. Go!" The king repeated, each time louder, showing his impatience and frustration with the Edessans.

The Great Gate faced the east, with the sun shining in the eyes of the defenders.

General Azarethes was proud and confident everything was in his favor. There was no hesitation in his swagger. Now his men only had to succeed with their assault on Edessa.

Azarethes's men had positioned themselves in perfect ranks facing the walled city. They were out of arrow range and stood at attention. Not a sound was made. In the gray light and the morning mist, the ladders couldn't be seen by the defenders, nor the battering ram poised to attack the Great Gate.

It was just before dawn and the gray sky began hinting a fiery orange and dark blue. Azarethes stood at the front of his men on his horse, a black stallion coated in armor. He surveyed the city for the last time. "Charge!"

At his command, the left columns split off and ran with ladders in hand to the west wall. The right columns ran, followed by their battering ram and fire pots to the eastern wall and Great Gate.

Two additional brigades appeared out of the woods, each with five ballistas. One moved left and the other right. In the west, ballistas began pounding the walls ahead of the ladders. In the east, the ballistas pounded the gate. The ballista barrage lasted thirty minutes. After the ballista barrage, in coordinated fashion, the left column advanced to the walls with their ladders. The walls were instantly covered with men, ladder after ladder with no room in between. Arrows hissed overhead.

The day advanced, but nothing went right for the Sassanids. The walls stood firm against the ballistas. When the men reached the top of the walls, they were sprayed with burning oil. No matter how many ladders were stacked against the wall, they were all pushed back. Very few of the defenders were injured or killed in the melee.

Khosrow's men who made it to the top of the ladders were pushed back and fell to their dooms. If they didn't die right away, the Edessans pummeled them with arrows.

Countless waves of attacks were advanced. All were repulsed. The Sassanian army sustained heavy losses.

The attack on the gate was also not successful. At one point, the gate was about to give way, but it magically strengthened. Azarethes's men were able to start the gate ablaze three times, but the defenders were able to squelch the fires each time. Pots of water had been perfectly placed so they could quickly douse the flames.

Every tactic was used against the gate, but each one failed woefully. The battering ram couldn't penetrate the thick walls. The attack continued for nine hours straight, wave after wave, but all attacks were rebuffed. Divine providence was on the side of the Edessans.

Could the rumors have been true? Did their God truly protect this fortress? How could the attack have failed? Khosrow was deflated. He was mounted on a white stallion and pushing his men to fight, but it was ineffectual. In an act of futile defiance, he grabbed a spear and threw it against the gate.

After the success in Antioch, he was bewildered at the steadfastness of the Edessans. "General! Pull the men back. We will begin to rebuild the ramp while we negotiate a settlement."

Khosrow turned to Gazri, who had remained by his side during the whole battle. "Gazri, what would be the pecuniary value to us for us to abandon this place. Five hundred, six hundred? Stephanus offered two centenaria—two hundred pounds of gold—but we should not accept any less than five." Khosrow spoke of his former friend, Stephanus, who had led the Edessan negotiating entourage a few weeks before.

Gazri smiled with delight at the thought of that amount of money. Five centenaria of gold. Azarethes prided himself in the number of men under his command. Gazri prided himself in more tangible possessions. This amount of gold would require a large contingent to transport back to Ctesiphon, to the royal treasury. "Let us continue our aggressions until they send out their Stephanus. We can settle on five hundred."

General Azarethes ordered his men back from the Great Gate, and they retreated about four hundred yards to avoid any harassment from the defenders manning the wall.

Inside a cheer went up, guttural and exuberant.

Azarethes clenched his teeth and yelled back. "This battle is not over!"

The Edessans had won. This battle.

Once Azarethes's men had retreated out of arrow range, it didn't take long for Stephanus and a small entourage to appear at the Great Gate. Khosrow recognized Stephanus and ordered they be given safe passage to his tent. It took about ten minutes for them to arrive.

"Stephanus, I will be forever grateful for what you did for my father. I remember your visits from when I was a boy and how you cured my father. Who knows? Had you not done that, perhaps you would be negotiating with my uncle Jamasp[11] at this very moment." Now, Khosrow wanted to pursue the battle at Lazic. Edessa was tiring him, and his efforts against this small fortress were only delaying his bath in the Black Sea.

The two continued to exchange pleasantries, and then finally Stephanus got to the point of his visit. "Your Highness. As you can see, we are very capable of defending our small city. We no longer wish to be a burden to you and wish to make you an offer to abandon the city. Besides, there isn't that much in the treasury, since most was removed prior to your visit."

The smell of the bitumen, cedar, and sulfur hung over the area. All of this was a simple negotiating ploy. They were able to settle on five centenaria of gold. Neither of them wished to be in the other's presence much longer. It simply came down to a number, and five was it. One for each finger on a man's hand. One for each toe on a man's foot.

Once the deal was concluded, it didn't take long for the Sassanids to retreat from Edessa. With fifty men, Gazri brought the booty back to Ctesiphon, where he would catalog it and secure it safely in the vaults of the capital of the Sassanid Empire. He enjoyed the trek back to the capital and would return to join Khosrow in Lazic to swim in the Black Sea.

Khosrow and General Azarethes made plans for their siege against Lazic. They were disappointed they couldn't add the city of Edessa to their empire, but the five centenaria was a good sum to assuage their regret.

Within a week, Khosrow, the general, and his men began their four-hundred-mile march north to Lazic, where their next conquest lay. Khosrow dreamed of his bath in the Black Sea.

---

11 Jamasp I: Younger brother of Khavad I, king of kings of the Sassanid Empire from AD 496 to 498. Died between AD 530 and AD 540.

CHAPTER 4

The Shroud is Secreted from Edessa to Constantinople

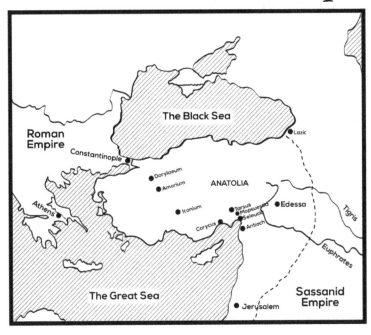

The Dark Ages period was so named not because of a lack of light but because there was little written about these times. This is also true for the Shroud. Major events were documented, such as the on and off war between Rome and the Sassanids in the early AD 600s led by Khosrow. In AD 590, Khosrow II became king of Sassania. After a few years, he lost the throne to rebellion by one of his top generals, Bahram Chobin,[1] but Emperor Maurice of Rome reinstalled him, which bought his allegiance. With turmoil in Rome, his allegiance was short-lived. In AD 602, Emperor Maurice was overthrown, and Khosrow sensed an opportunity to expand the Sassanid Empire. He sent his armies to the south, east, and north, threatening the cities along the frontier, including Edessa.

---

1 Bahram Chobin: Nobleman, general, and political leader of the late Sassanian Empire. Reigned from AD 590–591. Died AD 591.

EDESSA, OSRHOENE
AFTERNOON, SUNDAY, OCTOBER 10, AD 602

*T*hey had been with the archbishop five minutes, and the reason for their visit hadn't been revealed. When he needed to give bad news, he always delayed. The news he was about to impart must be unpleasant because they'd never had to wait this long before.

"God bless you, Your Excellency," Tigran said, responding to the loud sneezes of his superior, Archbishop Severus.[2] They were standing in the archbishop's chambers. Tigran had been saying this for many years, but now it was the official response to a sneeze, sanctioned by Pope Gregory two years earlier.

The fire roared, but it didn't seem warm. It was cold outside. The uncertainty of the news from the archbishop intensified the cold. After the ravages of the Justinian plague—named after him because he too contracted it—every sneeze seemed to foreshadow the awful illness.

Severus had one of the deepest sneezes that anyone anywhere in the building could hear—some even in the courtyard. His suffering wasn't a result of the plague but rather from the pollen in the air of early fall.

"God bless you, Your Excellency," Arakel echoed Father Tigran. Arakel, a transitional deacon, was well on his way to becoming a new priest. Just one more year of training, and he would be prepared to take his vows for ordination. He had wanted to be a priest since he was eight years old.

"I pray the plague is not returning. I don't think I could suffer the pain of watching so many more people die. I lost so many friends." Tigran genuflected as he recalled living through two returning bouts of the plague, remembering the swollen, red eyes, red noses, and horrendous deep coughs that all portended a certain death. Only a few survived. Even the young weren't spared.

"It's my eyes, my eyes," Archbishop Severus whispered under his breath, trying not to scratch them because it only made things worse. "It's the same every fall since I was a youth." Rubbing his eyes brought temporary relief from the itching, but it soon returned worse than before.

"I have a special—" Severus held back a sneeze, "A special mission for you. This is one of utmost import." He couldn't take it any longer and rubbed one eye and then the other. "Aahh."

Severus walked back behind his desk and pulled out a small drawer on the bottom left. The drawer itself was well hidden. It was only known to those often in the archbishop's chambers. "Here are the keys to the treasury. Go

---

2 Archbishop Severus: Archbishop of Edessa from AD 578 to 602/603. Stoned to death by Narses, AD 602/603.

down to the vault and retrieve the Mandylion and bring it to me." He handed the keys over to Tigran, who then clutched them tightly in his left hand.

"Arakel, go fetch some donkeys and a wagon. Make preparations and gather supplies for you and Tigran for a journey. It could last several weeks, maybe more." Severus debated as to whether to provide them with the full details of his upcoming mission. "Also, bring used clothing with you from the dispensary. Make certain they are not too well off but not too poor either. You will be traveling under the guise of a special journey."

Arakel could feel the confusion on his face. *What are we now about to do? This is a very unusual request.*

"Tigran, bring the cloth right away. Arakel, prepare for travel at daybreak tomorrow." Severus contemplated further. Tigran and Arakel were silent, knowing Severus preferred silence unless he asked a specific question of his underlings.

"Your Excellency," Tigran couldn't wait any longer. He interrupted the silence after about a minute. His impatience exceeded the cold in the room, breaking with Severus's desire for silence. "With Narses's[3] troops now entering the city, how do you see us venturing outside of the city walls? They will be interrogating all travelers. Will we need permission?" When he contemplated the politics unfolding between Emperor Phocas[4] and General Narses, he lowered his voice. "With the tensions in Constantinople and General Narses aligning with the Sassanids against the emperor, how will we be safe to travel?"

Severus didn't initially respond to the question. Finally, after another long minute, he responded, "Arakel, when you bring the clothes, bring a few blankets as well. Maybe six or eight. Tell no one! Tigran, your question is a good one. I will tell you more in the morning. No one must know about this mission. With the extra clothes and blankets, you will be able to easily conceal your true cargo. You will be bringing gifts and donations to the poor in Seleucia and then to Constantinople. Arakel, you may go." Severus waved his hand and signaled for him to leave his chambers. There would be no more questions permitted.

Severus waited for Arakel to be out of earshot behind the closed door. "Tigran, you will be transporting the Mandylion out of Edessa. As your cover, you will be bringing clothes for the poor. That should allow you free passage as you travel west to Constantinople. I am drafting a letter for you to bring

---

3 General Narses: Eunuch. Gave military aid to King Khosrow II of Sassania. Burned alive circa AD 604–605 by Emperor Phocas.
4 Emperor Florias Phocas: Roman emperor from AD 602 to 610. Born AD 547, executed by Heraclius, AD 610.

to Archbishop Cyriacus,[5] our patriarch in Constantinople. There are rumors Narses is bargaining for protection from the Sassanids, with Khosrow[6]—" He paused with loathing in his expression. "Against Rome." He shook his head. "I fear the cloth will be traded, ransomed in exchange for that protection. This cloth must never leave the hands of Christians." The emphasis on *never* made clear how much of his being had been put into the protection of the cloth.

"The king of kings of Sassania is nothing against the true might of the Roman Empire." The revulsion was in his voice.

It was the first time Tigran understood exactly where Severus stood in his politics. Tigran was relieved and glad he supported Rome.

Severus believed in the Roman Empire. He supported Emperor Phocas, and he believed Constantinople was the center of the world's political and military power, and, most of all, the center of Christianity. "The Sassanids may never get this cloth."

"Tigran, many things have changed since we paid off the Sassanids decades ago," Severus spoke in a very soft voice.

Tigran had to take a step in closer and lean in to hear. The scented perfume couldn't cover up the body odor of his superior.

"Now we are fighting more internally than against external forces. This fool Narses will be the downfall of Edessa, if not Rome. No one can trust him. You will bring the Mandylion to Constantinople."

"Constantinople! Why Constantinople? The Mandylion should stay here. Edessa is safe. Just like the Mandylion saved Edessa from the Sassanids fifty years ago, it will save us now. We were able to hold the Sassanids and Khosrow off before. There's no need—"

Severus interrupted him, raising his hand.

"No. I've spent the last two decades of my life protecting it. With Narses taking over the city and making deals with Khosrow, we need to get it out of Edessa. It will be safe in Constantinople. Archbishop Cyriacus will protect it. It will be up to him now. And you must bring it safely to him." Severus paused a moment. It was a big risk. The cloth had protected the city all these years. "You must."

EDESSA, OSRHOENE
MORNING, BEFORE SUNRISE, MONDAY, OCTOBER 11, AD 602

"The bishop has been acting strangely. He is deeply troubled about the rift between Phocas in Constantinople and Narses in Edessa." Tigran helped Arakel load the wagon. "He is very concerned about Narses's negotiations with the Sassanids."

Constantinople was many months off and winter was coming. Although he didn't want to be in the middle of a battle for the Empire, Tigran also didn't want to leave his home in Edessa. If they survived the trek through the front lines and made it to Constantinople, they would be safer there with the cloth.

Arakel worked to make a knot in the line holding the pyramid of clothes and rags on the wagon. On top of the pyramid were several sheepskins to keep the rains off their cargo. Two donkeys were in front of the pyramid, and in front of them was a stack of hay. "These politics, I certainly don't understand."

Shoushanik, Arakel's wife, was there. She did all she could to help, loading on clothes and helping with the lines, but she was unable to keep the tears from her eyes.

"There's politics everywhere, even in the church. The longer you're in the ministry, the more politics you'll see. Our biggest issue is disagreements that Christ was both divine and human. Not just human, or not just divine." Tigran pulled on the lines one more time, testing whether they were properly tied down. "Our biggest failing is the money tied to prestige in the church."

Tigran had joined the church because his father was a priest and his father before him. He belonged to a long line of religious men. Over the years, he realized there were priests who helped the poor and taught the poor. Then there were bishops. Many paid their way in. They waged politics with and against the aristocracy. Political bonds were forged and broken every day so that the bishops could enrich themselves. Many were trying to leave a legacy for their families and their names. Only a few were in it for the sole benefit of the church.

Severus was one of the few. Nevertheless, he too had to wage political war, expending capital to grow his power base. He was appointed bishop of Edessa and then archbishop. His appointment was granted not because of a payoff but because he was the best to promote the church and its parishioners.

"I trust Severus's understanding of imperial politics. We can't let the Mandylion fall into the hands of Narses or the Sassanids." Arakel spoke while testing the lines.

"For the moment, none of that matters, especially to us." Tigran thought of their discussion from the previous day and changed the subject. "What matters is that upon our return, you will be ready to be ordained a priest."

Tigran continued from where they had left off the day before this trip was even known to them. "As we studied the words of Luke from the Last Supper, we just need to know—more than know, believe—that Christ is both divine and human. That the bread and the wine are truly the body and the blood of Christ." Tigran inspected the sheepskins to make certain the rains couldn't penetrate down to the Mandylion at the bottom of the pile. "This talk about divine or not divine, human or not human, is all just dancing on the head of a pin. Ignore everything else. Christ is both human and divine."

"Yes, of course. That is what I believe. That is what I was always taught." Arakel believed deeply that Jesus was God incarnate, but Tigran was still left to explain how the bread became divine during the Eucharist. "This is my body," Arakel repeated Jesus's words from the story of the Last Supper. "This cup is the New Testament in my blood."

Severus approached them as the first glimmer of sunlight came across the horizon. "This is the most beautiful time . . . of . . . of . . . day." Severus sneezed again, louder than ever.

"God bless you, Your Excellency," Tigran and Arakel both responded in unison to Severus's sneeze. "We pray you feel much better upon our return."

Shoushanik was silent and bowed her head to the archbishop. She contemplated what it would be like without her Arakel.

"Tigran, I have written a letter of introduction to Archbishop Cyriacus II. He will tell you what to do. You are to go initially to Seleucia, then through Seleucia directly to Constantinople. The guise of clothes for the poor should be sufficient to gain you safe passage through any of the factions vying for power. While you are traveling, only think of and speak of it as a cloth. Never mention that it is the Mandylion. Never. Is that understood?"

Tigran and Arakel were silent, their thoughts racing. They both nodded their obeisance. It would not be an easy or short trek to Constantinople. Neither one of them was happy at the thought of being away from their families for months.

Severus imagined the doubts they had in their minds and the sacrifice they would be making. "There is nothing more important for you than to bring the Mand—" Severus turned and looked at Tigran and then at Arakel before continuing, "this cloth safely to Cyriacus." Severus needed to affirm the importance of this mission to safely bring the cloth to Constantinople, out of the hands of Narses and possibly those of the Sassanids. "It means everything to us, the church, and our mission here on earth." He paused. "Your life and your afterlife are depending on you. You must not fail."

The three went silent.

Severus paced slowly around the wagon, inspecting the clothes, rags, and blankets. "Where is it?"

The cloth was near the bottom of the pile. Arakel reached in and lifted up a few cloths to reveal the distinctive herringbone weave of the Mandylion. "I added a few additional blankets since winter is now coming upon us."

Tigran watched Severus reach his hand out. He put his hand on the cloth and knelt down on one knee.

Tigran and Arakel joined him.

Severus prayed out loud.

"In Nomine Patris et Filii et Spiritus Sancti. Holy Father, provide travel mercies on these two valiant men of faith. Help them to accomplish their mission." The prayer continued for another minute. Finally, Severus rose. All three men had solemn expressions on their faces. This mission would be the most important of their lives.

As he rose, Severus sneezed again. When he looked up, he noticed a man dressed in black. "Tigran, do you see that man over there. I've noticed him a few times. Do you know him?"

The man disappeared into the darkness. The sun was now directly in their faces, making it difficult to see as the man hid in the shadows.

Severus handed Tigran a map and two letters. "Thank you, Your Excellency."

Tigran studied the simple map. It wasn't a map; rather, it was more a list of towns indicating the path they would travel. "You have Mopsuestia, Tarsus, Seleucia, then lastly Iconium." Tigran continued looking at the map. He'd heard of these towns and cities. He never dreamed he would travel to them. His sense of foreboding at having to pass through the Narses lines and to be away from home for a long time was assuaged by excitement and curiosity of seeing new places.

Arakel looked over Tigran's shoulder but couldn't quite see the list very clearly.

"Then you have Laodicea, Amorium, Dorylaeum, Nicaea, and Nicomedia."

There was quiet as the distances sunk in.

"Your Excellency, this will require several months to travel there and back. And we will be traveling in the winter." There was a hint of objection in Tigran's voice, but he did his best to quell it. He had been getting close, very close, to a woman in the convent named Mari. With this mission, their relationship would be put on hold for many months or possibly even a whole year. They wanted to marry and were planning their wedding in the next few months.

Mari was not present. They didn't want their relationship to be known for fear it would affect her standing in the convent. Once the relationship was made known, she would be forced to leave the convent.

"I recommend you return home only in the spring when the weather begins to improve. There are two letters. One a letter of introduction for Archbishop Cyriacus. The other a letter of introduction as you reach each church along the way." Severus then handed Tigran a small bag of silver and bronze coins. "You will need to acquire feed and supplies along the way. This should suffice for the trip and the return." The bag had double what was required. Severus looked into the sun. The colors in the clear sky were turning a perfect blue. "You must guard this cloth with your lives," Severus whispered.

Shoushanik was unable to hear but imagined what he was saying. She couldn't focus, worried Arakel wouldn't be by her side the next few months, maybe longer.

Tigran fully understood what they were being entrusted with. He believed Arakel did as well.

"Do not tell anyone of your final destination until you are close. No one."

Arakel and Tigran looked at each other. The seriousness of their mission was now sinking in. Neither of them was certain if Narses's military would inspect the pile of clothes, detain them, or simply kill them to take the money and burn the worthless rags.

A wave of apprehension rolled over Tigran as he contemplated failing Severus, not being able to protect the cloth, or being killed. They had no choice but to travel out of the city and through the Narses's lines.

When they were done, Severus took one last look and strode away. He didn't linger to see them off.

As soon as Severus left, Shoushi approached Arakel. "How long will you be gone?" She had a secret to tell him.

"We hoped it would be only a few weeks, but it will more likely be several months." Arakel was incensed. His eyes widened. It was the first time he let his emotions be known.

Shoushi looked into his eyes. "We'll be going to Seleucia. Severus gave us a list of towns to stop in, however it remains to be seen what happens once we leave Edessa."

Shoushi looked at him and then leaned in so only he could hear. "When you return, I will have a surprise for you." She smiled with love in her eyes, grabbed his hand, and put it to her belly.

Arakel smiled with a broad grin. It would be their first.

Tigran watched and recognized what was meant. He was jealous and happy for his friend and the couple—and the baby.

Severus didn't tell them he would assign four other men on horseback from the palace guard to safeguard them throughout their journey. They were to remain undetected by the two clergy. Severus didn't want to trust the safety of the Man-dylion to only two clergy. As much as he believed in their ability to accomplish their mission, he didn't want to leave its success to chance. Four of the best palace guards would be a good safety net. They, too, would be disguised *and* armed.

There would also be another.

SOUTHEASTERN ANATOLIA

MORNING, BEFORE SUNRISE, FRIDAY, OCTOBER 15, AD 602

Tigran and Arakel reached the outskirts of Seleucia within a week. As instructed, they passed through Mopsuestia and Tarsus. At every turn they expected to see Narses's men, but they were nowhere to be found. Each night they stayed off to the side of the road so as not to be noticed. They approached Mopsuestia and Tarsus carefully and only stayed long enough to replenish supplies. These first few days gave them the confidence they needed to feel like they would be able to accomplish their mission and deliver the clothes and blankets as directed.

"Read from the letter of Paul[7] to Timothy[8] again." Tigran was able to secure one of the papyri from the small Edessa church library to accompany them on their journey. "We have many weeks to learn this book." Tigran had memorized most of Paul's epistle to the Corinthians. That was years ago, and he used his knowledge to teach Arakel all the messages from Paul. "It's not necessary for you to memorize the book, but memorization will be helpful in your ministry. Plus, you may not have access to the written word. It was many years after my first appointment before my church was able to afford a few writings from the Bible."

Tigran enjoyed teaching. His biggest joy was teaching the peasants simple math, reading, and the words of the Bible. He would show them the magnificent drawings accompanying the papyri and spend hours explaining

---

7 Paul of Tarsus: Apostle, formerly Saul. Studied under Gamaliel. Died circa AD 64–68.
8 Timothy: Paul's companion and missionary partner. Died circa AD 97.

every nuance in each one. He could teach anyone anything. He hated, though, that the more he taught the boys, the better soldiers they would make. Boys with a good working knowledge of math and reading made the best soldiers. And good soldiers were fodder for the aristocracy to lavish their innocent blood on petty ambitions of glory and conquest.

"Paul, an apostle of Christ Jesus . . ." Arakel read the words excitedly at first but then began to drone on. It was the fourth time he was reading from Paul's epistle to Timothy. This letter was written to Timothy to help better spread Christ's teachings.

Tigran used this book to teach Arakel. The sun was warm in their faces, negating the cool breezes. There was rain in the morning, but that had passed. It brought a cool breeze along with it. Before they could continue, they needed to make certain the cloth wouldn't become wet. It required some repositioning of many of the top blankets to keep the cloth untouched. "And for this purpose, I (sic) was . . ." Tigran had trouble keeping awake. The riding was monotonous, and the rote memorization was just as tedious. "Tigran, Apostle Paul of Tarsus wrote just under half of the New Testament. Have you read all of his letters? Does the archbishop have a complete set of them?"

"I have read them and memorized them. It is a task I recommend for every priest. Not only does it show devotion, but it also provides the ability to apply his teachings to any and every situation."

Arakel went back to his memorization, and Tigran leaned back. He fought hard not to let sleep overcome him but dozed on and off. At one point, Tigran awoke thinking he heard something. He felt like they were being followed but was never able to see anything. Yet he knew something, or someone, was there.

The four guards were there. They were excellent at their craft, stalking their prey without being detected. They spread out, one on each side of the clergymen and two behind, ready in case they were needed.

Tigran woke and stretched his arms. The day was much warmer, especially for this late in the year. "You will enjoy Seleucia. I've been there only once before. This time I'd like to spend an extra day or two." A lone mosquito started buzzing around his head, and he tried to shoo it off. "I hope we can visit and pray in the cave where Saint Thecla[9] lived. Some say she lived there for over seventy years."

Having slept most of the day, Tigran was now fully awake. "Saint Thecla was a neighbor to Onesiphorus,[10] and she would sit at her window while Paul

9 Saint Thecla: Born in Iconium, became a follower of Paul. Died first century AD. Entombed in Seleucia.
10 Onesiphorus: Mentioned in 2 Timothy. Thought to be one of the seventy disciples chosen by Jesus.

preached and built the early Christian church in Seleucia. Paul's preaching yielded many converts, including Thecla. She was so beautiful; however, Paul recognized and feared her beauty. He wouldn't baptize her for fear she would be tempted by the desires of the flesh."

Tigran thought of his Mari, with her cute nose and her dimpled chin.

Arakel thought of Shoushanik.

It was the first time both of them had thoughts of home and the ones they left behind. Arakel wondered how big the baby bump was and whether she could feel any kicking. "Do you think Thecla was ever baptized? Maybe not by Paul but maybe someone else? She must have been since she became beatified." Arakel answered his own question as his mind focused back on their trek and the possibility of visiting Thecla's cave.

Tigran continued, "According to legend her conversion was so complete, she was later able to escape martyrdom three times—once by fire, once by a lion, and once in the arena against the beasts. Each time God intervened—once by rain to quench the fire, once by the kindness of a lion, and once by lightning to kill the beasts in the arena."

"Do you think miracles can happen today? To you? Or to me?" Arakel never imagined he could be beatified. That he could be part of one of God's miracles. He just wanted to be ordained. It was what he dreamed of his whole life, and now this trip would delay that by months or possibly longer.

"That's up to God. Only God can grant a miracle, and prayer is the way you can ask for His intervention. Prayer can lead to miracles, and that's where we'll go. We'll go to the small cave where Thecla lived out her life, albeit in celibacy, staying true to her conversion." He hoped he wouldn't have to live in celibacy. He couldn't imagine not being able to return to be with Mari. He hoped their marriage wasn't going to be delayed, that they would be able to marry directly upon his return. *Will this be my sacrifice? To possibly never consummate our love?* "Arakel, when you join the priesthood, although you won't need to be celibate, you will need to make a similar sacrifice. What will yours be?"

Both Tigran and Arakel became silent as they weighed their own sacrifices. The question stabbed both of them in their hearts. Would they be Christians in name only, or would they truly give up everything for Jesus to spread His word? The rustling of the leaves and the clopping of the donkeys was all that could be heard as they both fell deep in thought. Arakel thought of his wife, now with child in her belly. *Will I return to witness his birth? Or will it be a girl?*

For Arakel, the question demanded even more thought and prayer. *Will I ever be forgiven for my sins? Am I the greatest sinner? Will God be able to forgive me for the sins I am guilty of? Do I truly believe? Will I be able to sacrifice enough to make up for my sins? I understand what sacrifice means in the Bible and what it meant to Jesus, but can I, too, sacrifice everything like Jesus?*

"So read the first chapter again, then tell me what you think." While teaching, Tigran learned just as much if not more than his student. It was the reason why Tigran so enjoyed working with the transitional deacons. Even more than working with the peasant children.

The mosquito returned, this time with a few of his brothers and sisters buzzing around both of them. Shooing them off was futile. The mosquitos finally relented after they had fed on their share of blood.

The rest of the afternoon passed quickly as Arakel studied and memorized the book from Paul. "He was here. Paul was here, so close to us. He may have even traveled this very road." Arakel said after reading out loud from the letter to Timothy. "His message is clear. There are false prophets everywhere." Arakel contemplated for a few moments. "Do you think there are false prophets today?"

"You are getting better at bringing everything together. You will make a fine priest very soon. I just hope this trip doesn't delay you on your path to ordination." The discussion continued for quite some time. "One thing we must remember. Before Saul[11] was blinded by the light, he was on a crusade to root out all of Christianity. Yet Jesus was able to convert him. Through Jesus's intervention, Paul became one of the most influential teachers of the word in all of early Christendom."

A few minutes passed. "Paul was a learned Jew and had studied under Gamaliel,[12] a Pharisee and one of the leading Jewish authorities. I think these teachings gave Paul—Saul at the time—the inspiration, eloquence, and logic to write all that he wrote. Because of his clear writings and his strong will, he was able to rein in the false prophets and keep the early church on the path set by Jesus. Jesus was the message, but Paul built the early church. Paul was the perfect person to choose." Tigran always smiled in awe at what Jesus did both before he died and then afterward. "Paul was able to bridge the old ways of Judaism to the new ways of Christ."

"If you were to assemble a compilation of all the writings, which would you choose?" Arakel admired his companion and mentor and was grateful that he imparted his wisdom during these long and lonely days. "I think all of the writings of Paul would be interesting, especially his letter to the Ephesians."

Tigran stopped the cart and hopped down. They were about to cross a small bridge. The meadow on the opposite side was a bright green in the dawn

---

11 Paul of Tarsus: Apostle, formerly Saul. Studied under Gamaliel. Died circa AD 64–68.
12 Gamaliel the Elder: Rabban Gamaliel I. Died AD 52. Renowned Jewish scholar.

sun. The leaves were turning a vibrant orange, with dew glistening on them.

Tigran shooed another mosquito away. "Don't forget the Gospels and the second book of Luke, of course."

"How much of the Old Testament would you include?" Arakel thought, answering his own question. "Definitely, Isaiah. It is amazing that he prophesied so much about Jesus, his life, and his suffering" There was silence. "'He was pierced for our transgressions; he was bruised for our iniquities.'"

The two rode for a few more hours. Conversation waxed and waned. Most focused on Paul, contrasting with Peter. Just before dusk, they stopped and built a fire, ate some bread, and went to sleep. They were both resigned to spending the next few months away from their families. The pain of separation was always in the background. The conversation and the training kept both their minds off their families and homes.

As the monotony of their journey advanced, both prayed for a safe and speedy return to their loved ones, but it wasn't clear if their prayers would be answered. They were on a mission, in the name of the church. It meant sacrificing their simple lives with the women they each loved to protect one of the most valuable relics of Jesus Christ from the heathen Sassanids from the East.

They both fell asleep quickly, but on this night Arakel was unable to sleep soundly. In the middle of the fourth watch, he sat up and saw Tigran sleeping next to him. "Who are you? Who are you?"

Tigran awoke and looked at his friend and mentee. He had heard of people talking in their sleep but had never experienced it.

"Who are you?"

"I am Tigran, Tigran."

"No, no, nooo." Arakel was confused. "Where is Serli? Where is Serli?" Confusion filled his expression. "Noo." Arakel leaned back, and a restless sleep overcame him.

Tigran took note and decided to ask his companion about Serli. *Who is Serli? It's not his wife?*

They continued on their trek the next day. The conversation was similar, but Tigran waited for the right time to ask his question. He was excited to uncover Serli's identity. It would be a change of pace from reading and discussing Paul's letters, but asking at exactly the right time was important.

Just after noon, the two men saw a monk up ahead, running away out of the forest along the roadway and waving his arms. A second monk came after him doing the same thing. Both were dressed in black frocks, the tops of their heads shaved in honor of Saint Paul.

"What is going on?" Tigran asked Arakel, before it became obvious.

"They're running from bees. They're running from bees!"

There was a small pond up ahead. Both monks jumped in.

Tigran pulled up on the reins, and the donkeys and wagon came to a stop. They waited a few minutes for the swarm of bees to disperse, and then they pulled forward with a quickened pace.

Both monks emerged out of the water and began laughing.

"I must have gotten stung ten times. How 'bout you? The worst is on my face and hands." Brother Darga was the first to speak, standing in four-foot-deep water.

"Most of mine are on my hands." Brother Eren started to look at small red spots that would soon form into welts. He had already removed his frock. His underwear covered his loins and stretched down to his knees. They were dripping wet in the shallow water.

"I must have fifteen or twenty. It will be an itchy next few days." He chuckled at their booty, a beehive filled with honey and wax.

"Are you both alright?" Tigran shouted out to them. Arakel and Tigran remained in their wagon in case the bees hadn't fully retreated from the stream. "Did you have a run-in with some bees?"

"Yes, and we were able to steal away with a good two or three pounds of honey and wax." Brother Darga emerged from the water. He was also undressed to his underwear, holding his frock in one hand and the beehive in the other. His spindly legs showed from his knees on down. "We'll dry off in the sun here." He held up their prize, the hive. It was soaking wet. Drowned bees were everywhere, on the hive and floating in the water. "Where do you hail from?"

"We're on our way to Iconium, coming out of Seleucia." This was the second pair of monks they encountered along the way. These were more remarkable than the first.

"We're part of the monastery in Corycus, just outside of Seleucia." Brother Darga was the junior of the two and was fully open to talking with the other men of the cloth. "Every once in a while, we venture out to capture some fresh honey from those prickly bees. We've been making mead from the likes of this honey and would be glad to share if you're up to ferrying us to the next town over."

"I am one of the best cooks in Corycus and will make you a fine meal of saffron and fish," Brother Eren chimed in, glad to have some new visitors. "What are you going to do with all those clothes and blankets?"

Tigran and Arakel were glad to have two new companions and a diversion from the monotony of their trip and from Severus's instructions. "Some good mead and fresh honey would be a bit better than the dried fish and bread we've been eating. We will come with you, but only one night. We need to deliver these clothes to Iconium and then be off."

Arakel whispered so the two monks couldn't hear. "Are you certain this is safe. We have our mission to accomplish."

"We need to eat and sleep somewhere, and what better company than two brothers of the cloth . . . with some fresh honey." Tigran smiled, excited for the change for the first time since leaving Edessa.

CENTRAL ANATOLIA
LATE MORNING, FRIDAY, NOVEMBER 12, AD 602

Since they left Corycus and the two monks, Tigran and Arakel were fully settled into the daily routine . . . learning and memorizing the Scriptures, talking about any subject that came up, and dozing on and off.

They were both half asleep when they were surprised by a group of soldiers. "Get out of the wagon. Now!" The first tirone, the lowest rank in the Roman army, ripped the sleeve on Tigran's arm as he forced compliance with his order. Along with seven milites, there were three newly recruited tirones under the tutelage of Decanus Alba. Alba had ten men under his command, seven regulars—milites—and three new recruits, the tirones. It was a perfect tent group of men in the Roman military structure.

Since the encounter with the two monks outside of Seleucia four weeks ago, this was the first time Tigran and Arakel had any interaction with anyone along the way.

The three tirones still in training hadn't yet been promoted to milite and were fixated with showing they were just as capable as the milites.

Neither Arakel nor Tigran gave any resistance, their heads bowed as they landed on the ground. "Where are you going?" Their eyes darted back and forth between themselves and the men in this ten-man Roman tent group. They both feared for their lives and for their cargo. The three tirones looked for approval from their group leader, Alba, to make certain they were being harsh enough on the two.

"Easy, boys. Easy. We don't want to upset these fine clergymen." Although suspicious of the two clergy, Alba dissuaded his recruits from their exuberance. "Fathers, where are you headed on this fine day?" Alba was dressed in his uniform and rode a fine dark brown horse.

Tigran gained the courage to look up and face the decanus.

Alba dismounted and strode over to the two clergymen. Alba was losing his patience at the display of the bravado of the three tirones.

The seven milites stood back and enjoyed the spectacle. They had already proven themselves in battle and didn't want to waste their energy on two unarmed clergy.

"We are providing clothes and blankets for the poor." Tigran looked directly at Alba.

Arakel still hadn't looked up. The truth was easy to blurt out. There was no hesitation.

"We are being sent from Amorium to Dorylaeum. I have a letter from the bishop." Although Severus hadn't instructed them to do so, Tigran asked each bishop in each city they entered for a letter of introduction to the next city on their journey. Bishop Sabrisho in Seleucia mentioned that Narses might not appreciate the politics of Severus. If this were true, then Severus's letter might not lead to a friendly encounter. These additional letters would be more helpful in avoiding any trouble with any Narses troops they might encounter. He handed the letter to Decanus Alba.

"What's in this pile of clothes?" the second tirone demanded, stabbing into the pile with his spear. He jabbed like he was practicing his hand-to-hand combat. "Aee-yahh."

Tigran's heart beat out of his chest, but he tried not to show his dread at the potential damage to the Mandylion as the tirone stabbed the pile again. He watched as it leaned to the left and then came tumbling down with a few more stabs.

"How do we know these men are friendly with Phocas and not Narses? Perhaps they have some hidden money that might help convince us of their loyalties?"

The tirone's statement piqued Alba's interest. "Let's see if they're hiding anything of value in this pile of clothes."

The no man's land between Edessa in the east and Constantinople in the west had no specific border. Only the organized units of Phocas's men provided any sense of order in the frontier with Narses. Travelers could be escaping Narses in Edessa, or about to spy on Phocas, or it could be the opposite.

"Bring over a torch. Perhaps these men have some money or wine hidden under this pile that we could coax out of them," Decanus Alba said, wanting to test their reaction.

A tirone opened the tent group's fire pouch and blew on the saved embers until a small flame ignited. One of the first lessons when joining the Roman army was to learn how to carry their own portable fires. Instead of starting a fire when needed, the fire pouch carried a glowing mushroom or ember from the fire of the previous day.

The other two tirones brought over torches dipped in oil, and there was soon fire. Within a few short minutes they were ready to set ablaze the pile of clothes. "Remove those sheepskins and light the pile!"

"No! Decanus, I beg of you. These clothes and blankets are meant only for the poor in Dorylaeum. Please, if you destroy them, many women and children will freeze this winter." Tigran did his best to dissuade them, but the fire had already started. His mind raced, desperately trying to find a way to save the Mandylion, as he watched a few of the top blankets burn. The small bit of hay for the donkeys ignited instantly, but its flames fizzled as the pile of clothes refused to stay lit.

Arakel bolted forward to save the pile, but the first tirone used his spear to hold him back. "Don't burn these clothes. We beg of you. Don't!"

Tigran frantically tried to persuade them. "There is no wine or mead in our cart. We are clergy and don't drink. Please let us put the fire out. If they're burned, they'll be no good for the poor in Dorylaeum." He too was blocked by one of the tirones.

As the clothes slowly caught fire, an optio road up on a chestnut brown steed. As deputy centurion, he was sent to check on Decanus Alba's tent group and then report back to the centurion. The optio had several decani under his charge. Both the optio and his horse were fully armored and ready for battle. "Put that fire out! These men have done nothing. Do you want to upset the church? It would be a sin against our fellow men and against God. Put that fire out!" He yanked on the reins, turning his horse and eliciting a loud neighing. "Put that fire out! Now!"

Arakel lurched forward and pushed the spear aside. He sneered at the tirone.

Tigran joined him, and they quickly pulled the top burning and smoldering blankets off the pile and stamped on them until the fire and smoke subsided. Tigran avoided glancing at Arakel for fear of giving away their primary cargo.

"Enough, you fools!" cried the optio, waving his arm. He whipped the tirone near him with his reins to make certain he immediately complied with his order. He shook his head in disgust.

Alba handed the bishop's letter to the optio. "They are providing clothes and blankets for the poor in Dorylaeum." Alba's voice was firm but showed deference to his superior.

The optio glanced at it, and handed the letter back to Alba, who handed it back to Tigran. "Leave these men be. They are providing clothes and blankets for the poor." The optio looked back at Tigran. "My new recruits are a bit youthful having just been recruited by Phocas to fight the traitor Narses.

Forgive them m' Lord."

"Back in line, boys!" The optio looked at Tigran and nodded. He kicked his heals against the sides of his horse and bounded off to check on the next tent group under his charge.

"Bless you, Optio," Tigran said, his heart still pounding, his blessing not heard by the optio. Both he and Arakel now stood beside the wagon. Tigran said a quick prayer and both said "amen" in unison. They rearranged the clothes back into a neat pyramid and secured the lines holding them down, relieved that the pile of clothes—and their prize—had mostly survived.

"These burned blankets could possibly be salvaged if the undamaged parts were woven together." Arakel inspected the damage to the blankets now on the ground. They were too valuable to simply discard. When they reached Dorylaeum, they would work to repair them.

Tigran and Arakel looked on as the group of ten soldiers marched off, the decanus in the lead and the optio further off in the distance. Tigran and Arakel watched in silence until the soldiers were out of sight.

Tigran's heart beat quickly but less violently than a few moments before, and his fear subsided. If these soldiers were any indication, they were now past the edge of Narses's territory and fully in Emperor Phocas's territory.

"Do you see that man hiding in the tree line?" Arakel hopped up on the wagon. "I noticed him once before in Seleucia but have yet to see him clearly. He seems to be shadowing us."

Tigran looked around but saw nothing. He followed Arakel and jumped up on the wagon. "If you see him again point him out to me. We'll need to determine if he is friend or foe." Tigran arranged his cloak and took the reins. "Let's go."

"Let's uncover the cloth tonight to see if there was any damage. I don't want to arrive in Constantinople and find a hole ripped into it from some foolish soldier."

Thirty minutes passed without a word. Tigran's heart no longer throbbed out of control, no longer bursting through his neck. He wiped the dried sweat from his brow. This was the closest they'd been to losing everything. Their mission would have been a failure if the optio hadn't arrived in time. *Would the Romans have killed us after the clothes and blankets had burned? Would they have let us live? If we lived but the cloth was destroyed, how could we return to Severus? To Mari? To Shoushi?*

WESTERN ANATOLIA
LATE AFTERNOON, SUNDAY, MAY 15, AD 603

Autumn had turned to winter and now to spring. It had been an exceptionally cold winter and very late spring, slowing their progress immensely. They were only able to travel when the weather cooperated, and those days were few and far between.

"What do you think will happen now that Phocas is firmly in power in Constantinople? With Narses murdering Severus, do you think Phocas can defend against Narses? Do you think Narses will ally with the Sassanids and Khosrow II? I don't want anything to do with Khosrow." Arakel was filled with questions, and they were right in the middle of it. With Severus dead, their protector was no longer. They needed to make it to Constantinople and then—somehow—back home. "How do I get back to Shoushi? How?" Arakel regretted being on this trek. He wasn't yet ordained and was months away from getting back to his Shoushi.

Tigran took a few minutes to respond. He didn't want to encounter any more Roman soldiers on the border from either side, friend or foe. "My concern is whether we can ever return to Edessa." Tigran thought of Mari, hoping she was unharmed. He thought about some of their last moments together, feeding soup to the poor. It was their passion to help others. Even when helping the downtrodden, Mari was able to bring a smile to all of them. He missed serving with her, laughing with her, and talking with her.

"We were blessed that Father Maximilian, Vicar of Nicomedia, allowed us to overwinter and provided us food and lodging for the last few months. Although it was a challenge to survive there in the winter, it was better to be among friends than to be traveling along an open highway." Both men had grown up in Edessa, and both desperately wanted to see their families again soon. The longing for home grew stronger as they neared their final destination. Their journey would be almost a year long by the time they returned . . . if they ever could return.

"Let us break here before we cross this stream." Tigran pulled up on the donkeys and dismounted from the wagon.

Arakel got down and unhitched the donkeys to let them drink from the fresh, cool water.

"This reminds me of the book of John and his reference to the living water. Do you remember?"

Arakel recited the passage. "Yes, the story of the woman at the well and the living water, chapter seven. 'He that believeth in me, as the Scripture hath said, out of his belly shall flow rivers of living water.'"

"This stream, any stream, reminds me of that verse so often. When you

look at the stream, you can't actually see the water. You can see the floating
leaves, the twigs, or even the reflection of the sun, but you can't see the crys-
tal-clear water. You can't see it, but you can feel it in your hands and in your
stomach when you drink it. It is like faith. You can't see faith, but you know it's
there. You can feel it in your heart and in your soul." Tigran was exhausted after
a day of riding. The fear of what was ahead and the longing for home, this day
especially, tired him. After only a minute, he leaned back and dozed off.

Arakel eventually succumbed and dozed off himself.

The hush of the winds and the burbling of the stream eased them through
their light slumber.

Arakel's demon returned. "Serli, Serli, where are you? Serli!"

It was loud, and Tigran awoke.

Arakel, asleep, jerked and turned. He breathed deeply and then stilled.
His sleep was penetrated by the piercing outcries for Serli. Tigran recognized
the cry from his mentee. As they got further from Edessa, Arakel's cries in his
sleep became more frequent.

One of the donkeys brayed and woke Arakel from his drowse. Arakel
brushed the leaves and debris from his hair and frock. It only took another
few minutes, and they were on the march again, across the stream and back
on the road to Constantinople.

"We're less than a day away from Constantinople." Tigran watched the
rhythm of the donkeys as they trudged along. He could see how the muscles
of each hind leg lifted and tensed and then relaxed. "Archbishop Cyriacus,
I believe he's the second with that name, will certainly be interested in the
gift we have for him from Severus." His melancholy was replaced with joyful
anticipation. The short afternoon nap had completely changed his demeanor.
"Cyriacus will be ecstatic with the gift we are bringing from Severus. There is
nothing more valuable than this cloth."

"I hope he can keep it safe. There is nothing safe with Phocas usurping the
throne by beheading Emperor Maurice[13] and his son, Emperor Theodisius.[14] And
Severus is now dead, killed at the hands of Narses." Arakel looked back at what
they had been carrying. He didn't care about the politics unfolding around him.
Arakel thought about their mission, his longing for home and his delayed ordination. "We haven't made one donation to the poor. We haven't converted anyone.
We haven't preached one sermon. We haven't heard confession. These clothes
have been good camouflage for the Mand . . . the cloth, but now I hope we can
finally distribute them and then return back to Edessa and do the work of God."

13 Emperor Maurice: Roman emperor from AD 582 to 602. Beheaded by Phocas.
14 Emperor Theodisius: Co-Roman emperor from AD 585 to 602. Beheaded by Phocas.

Arakel thought further about his family in Edessa. *I should have already been ordained, and it could still be another few months, possibly years before it could take place. And my child. My new child? Was it born? Did it survive childbirth? Did Shoushi?*

"When we arrive in Constantinople, I will see about your ordination. Perhaps Archbishop Cyriacus can do it." Tigran looked over at his mentee. Arakel looked back at Tigran with a pensive smile. He wasn't hopeful.

"Arakel, I've heard it twice now. In your dreams. In your sleep, you had a dream or nightmare about someone named Serli. Who is Serli?" Tigran stated the question uncertain as to how his friend and mentee would respond. He had waited weeks to ask, but it was finally time. They were close to their goal and just about to reach Constantinople. It had gone through his mind many times, and finally he just blurted it out.

"I don't like to speak about her." Arakel demurred, partially stunned his mentor would know to ask the question. His immediate response was to breathe in and straighten his back. His breathe was louder than he expected, and he hoped Tigran didn't hear it, but Tigran wouldn't let go.

"This is one of your demons. You must speak about it in order to be free from it so that you can truly be at peace with Jesus Christ. Who is Serli?"

"I will not speak of her. Do you hear? Never!" Arakel didn't mean for it to come out as loudly or as forceful as it did, but it did. He wished he could take it back. It just wasn't something he wanted to discuss, not even with his friend and mentor, not even with his wife.

Tigran never heard his mentee so adamant. *What was he not saying? What happened to this woman?* He decided not to press the issue, not at this time. There would be many more months to find out more. There had been many times in the past when his parishioners would come to him when they had to speak about difficult topics. He wanted to be there and ready when Arakel was ready.

They both heard some noise from up ahead. It sounded like soldiers marching.

The noise grew stronger. Then they saw the army contingent. "Tigran, can you tell if they are Phocas's or Narses's troops?" All of their eyes were fixed on the men as they were now also seen. "We've come so far . . ." Their last encounter was a disaster. *Will they recognize that we're not from western Anatolia? Will they think we were spies? Will they recognize that our accents are from Edessa and Narses, not from Constantinople or Anatolia?*

"We're so close. They must be Phocas's men." Tigran breathed in. His heart started pounding again. Adrenaline spiked in his veins. He had to do all he could to control his nerves. There was much more at stake than just his life. It was the life of his friend and the survival of the cloth. Severus, though dead, had given him a mission, and he had come too far to fail now.

The centurion dismounted. He had a fine stallion with magnificent chocolate brown fur. It glistened in the orange glow of the setting sun.

"What have we here?" he barked, as four milites came running behind him, spears drawn. These men were well-trained soldiers and ready to take on Narses's army if it came to that. "It is not safe for you on the roads. That Narses pig is coming, and we have been sent to escort him to Phocas." The threat was clear. Get off the roads or else.

Three more milites approached the wagon. One sneered at Tigran, baring his missing teeth. The single remaining tooth was black with decay. Each milite sweated under the weight of their chain-mail armor and uniforms. They were ready for battle if it came to that. Tigran received the message loud and clear. He was relieved they weren't in the mood for accosting non-militants.

"My lord, we are on a mission from the bishop of Nicaea to deliver these clothes to the poor in Constantinople." Tigran didn't look up to catch the centurion's eyes. He'd learned that lesson long ago when his father was beaten by Sassanid soldiers. According to his father, eye contact signals resistance and arrogance—something soldiers despise when confronting an uncertain threat. He kept his head down and showed deference and obeisance.

Two of the milites rummaged through the pile of clothing and blankets, one taking a blanket and throwing it over his shoulders. Another, a bit older than the others, approached Arakel. His teeth, just like the other two milites, were mostly black and half missing.

Arakel had to turn away at the smell of his breath . . . a mixture of tooth rot and alcohol. Arakel said nothing, as he moved down from his perch. Tigran did the same, and they both tried not to breathe in the stench, but it was unavoidable.

These milites weren't as abrasive as Arakel and Tigran's previous encounter, yet they caused more anxiety in the men. They both feared for their lives and for the safety of the cloth. Nabbing a single blanket was nothing, but they feared the milites would confiscate all the clothes and blankets and distribute them among the soldiers.

"Leave them be, men. Leave them be." The deep voice of the centurion slowed the advance of the men.

"There are rumors some of that eunuch's forces are trying to infiltrate the city, all the way to Constantinople. Narses is a damned eunuch, governor of Edessa, conspiring with Khosrow and challenging the Roman Emperor." The centurion waved to his milites, and they threw the clothes and blankets to the ground.

Tigran and Arakel's fear subsided as they realized that with the centurion present, they weren't going to be harmed. Yet Tigran's heart didn't stop pounding, and he felt pressure in his face and neck.

"Yours is the third we've encountered this morning," the centurion said.

Third what? Tigran handed a letter from the bishop of Nicaea to one of the milites who gave it to the centurion.

"Sir, we have seen no one."

After a moment, the centurion handed the letter back to the milite. The centurion didn't read it. The milite couldn't.

Tigran and Arakel both hoped this would be the last encounter with Phocas's troops. With control of the empire at stake, the sooner they got away from the frontier between the two factions, the safer they and the cloth would be.

"We found nothing. Nor did we find any wine." The milite scoffed and threw the blanket off his shoulders. It was too hot to carry it, and there was no room in his pack.

"Return to the line. These two are nothing." One of the milites spat in Arakel's direction.

Arakel exhaled as the milites moved back to their marching formation and resumed their march. Within five minutes, they were out of sight.

Tigran's face, neck and ears were a bright crimson red. He could smell his own sweat. It would be an hour before his nerves would return to normal.

"Let us break for the day. We must not be far now." Arakel and Tigran loaded the clothes back onto their wagon. Thankfully, the Mandylion hadn't been disturbed.

Tigran detected movement in the wood off to their left.

Arakel noticed it too. "Are we being followed?"

"I think I saw what you saw."

Both watched carefully for any new disturbance. There was nothing.

They took their time as they looked for a place to overnight.

In the meantime, four other tent groups passed, each group comprised of eight soldiers and led by a decanus on horseback. All marched in perfect order.

"Quick, move the wagon off the road. Give these soldiers a wide berth," Tigran ordered.

Arakel moved quickly forward to the donkeys, grabbed their reins, and walked them off to the side in the direction of the disturbance. He saw nothing as he looked off into the wood. They were now fifty paces off the road. The last of the four groups passed. The traffic on the road indicated their proximity to Constantinople. It also indicated how much care Phocas took to make certain Narses would not be able to threaten his empire.

✝✝✝

Encounters with others on the road were frequent. They were close to their destination, Constantinople, the capital of all Rome, the hub of all commerce. It was the center of trade routes that spanned the globe, all the way even to China. Wealth could be seen everywhere . . . in nearby villages, in lords' manors, and in the dress and decorated horses of those they met.

"This road will lead us to a ferry for us to cross the Bosporus," Tigran said to his travel companion. Within a mile they were in view of the docks.

They weren't the only ones looking to cross. At least three other transport wagons were waiting to cross. Each carried something for sale in the city . . . local produce or trade from Egypt. One was well guarded and full of silks out of China.

It looked like a full centuria guarded the crossing. Of the hundred men, about twenty of them worked to repair the roadway that had washed out in a recent storm. The rest practiced their fighting skills. With Narses close, they were taking no chances.

Arakel and Tigran rode up to the port and noticed a handful of empty docks for ships that had already sailed. Some ships were for fishing and others for transport, straight across the Bosporus or out to the sea to the Propontis.

"There she is." The smell of the sea filled Tigran's lungs.

Both smiled. Their goal was in sight. The view of Constantinople was spectacular, with columns and arches everywhere. Arakel tried to count them but failed three times.

They could see the beautiful, rounded dome of the Hagia Sophia. Only the Hippodrome was larger. "I've never seen anything so grand. God has showered this city with many blessings to build something so magnificent." Arakel's smile was as large as the city across the Bosporus.

Tigran stood on his toes to try and see more. "One last step, and we're there. We will soon be home, you with your wife and me with Mari. My only regret is that we didn't marry before we left."

Finding a ship to take them across wasn't simple. "If you're goin' to the Sophia, you'll want to disembark at the Harbor of Sophia on the south of the peninsula," the man on the dock interjected. He spoke their language but was barely understandable. He had one leg and only two fingers on one hand. A wooden crutch lay on the ground next to him. His ploy was always effective, especially among the Christians. "Be a good Christian and give me a few coins."

He knew he would get sympathy if their destination was the Holy Sophia. The Sophia Cathedral was the pilgrimage destination for all Christians in Constantinople, and Tigran and Arakel were dressed as priests on a pilgrimage. "Lost these three to fightin' under General Germanus.[15] M' leg, too." An appeal to their patriotism often increased his take. "The other pigs—those Sassanids— didn't fare so well. M' name is Petronas, but everyone here calls me Petro. It's what my decanus named me when I first joined his unit. Don't know why."

†††

Tigran tried to hide his money pouch as he searched for some small nummis for the man. "Here are two coins. What is a good price to cross?"

"Aye, you have a nice wagon and two donkeys. That, of course, is a bit more. You'll have to travel with one of the larger ferries. The one you'll need is the Justy. You'll recognize it." He slurred a few of his words, making his drunk and hungover demeanor more obvious.

As he handed over the coins Tigran smelled the old wine and realized his coins would go for alcohol, not food.

"My good friend Michael, he fared better than I in Lazic. He only lost a finger. He'll get you across. He'll return before noon at that slip over there." The former milite pointed off to the left. "It'll be another hour or so. For another coin, I'll make sure you're the next one."

"You didn't mention the price." Tigran was impatient to get the details of the crossing.

"You'll need a folli and a decki." The old man had a serious expression on his face, using the vernacular for the forty nummi follis and the ten nummi decanummium.

"That price seems fair. Is there any special price for a good Christian having traveled far?" Tigran asked but received no answer. He wasn't a good negotiator, especially considering the suffering this veteran had endured.

The man grinned and said nothing.

Tigran retrieved another nummi and handed it to the battle-scarred veteran of Lazic. "Arakel, that gives us an hour." The scent of the bread continued to overwhelm their nostrils. "Shall we purchase some fresh bread?"

"We'll also need some feed for the donkeys. Perhaps a carrot or two," Arakel said, feeling almost intoxicated as he breathed in the salt sea air and the aroma of fresh bread from a nearby bakery. He was now as happy as he had been throughout the whole journey. He wished Shoushi could be with him to take in the view of the Constantinople skyline.

---

15 General Germanus: Commander in the Byzantine army, serving under Phocas. Died AD 603.

They sat for just under an hour, waiting for the Justy ferry and enjoying their freshly baked bread. A few other ships arrived while they waited. "I've been timing the ships as they cross the Bosporus. It looks like it takes just under an hour to cross."

The dome of the Holy Sophia stood out so clearly in the midday air. "After we cross, we could be at the cathedral in less than an hour." As the Justy pulled into the slip, Arakel felt like he was only six years old, waiting for his father to come home from his daily chores at their small church. "My father would spend most of his days giving alms to the poor. When I was a young boy, right before Easter, he would bring a fresh lamb, slaughtered by one of the parishioners especially for us. The man was a lord with hundreds of acres." Arakel's heart began to race. "My mother and father would spend all day Saturday preparing it. My sister and I would help. My mother, she would have my sister and me knead the dough or keep the fire going, and then we would share it with many of the others in the parish for Easter Sunday meal. There was nothing better."

Tigran thought as well about his childhood. "Yes, this is a wonderful day. God has blessed us more than we deserve. I can only imagine what it would have been like to be in Jesus's presence. Something like the way I feel today."

They walked together to the wagon and prepared for the journey across the eastern end of the Propontis, the sea at the foot of Constantinople that separated the Bosporus and the eastern end of the Mediterranean.

The Justy was now against its slip. One man jumped out while the other barked commands.

"That must be Michael there." Tigran nodded in the captain's direction and walked over. "Your man said you can take us to the Sophia Harbor?" Tigran spoke louder to overcome the din of the comings and goings at the port.

Captain Michael jumped off his ship onto the dock and looked at the two of them and at their wagon. "Aye. We'll load you up right away."

"Boys, take care of these two. I'll be right back." The captain left the Justy and walked over to his friend, Petro, while the two shipmates worked to board the two donkeys and wagon.

Tigran and Arakel boarded the Justy and looked out across the water at the opposing skyline from their new vantage point. They watched as the captain helped Petro to his feet, and then led him to the baker to get some fresh bread.

CONSTANTINOPLE
EARLY AFTERNOON, WEDNESDAY, MAY 18, AD 603

There were many more Roman soldiers in the city. Some marched in formation and patrolled the streets around the city and others seemed to be doing nothing.

"Constantinople is much larger than home." Arakel's face beamed, stating the obvious and glad to be back in the presence of so many people. "There are so many odors. Some good—" They both held their breath as they rode past a public toilet. "Some bad. One minute you smell the worst of the city and the next the best." After a minute, the smell of the toilets was gone, and the smell of a kitchen again filled the air. "The city reminds me of mornings in Edessa when the cooks began preparing food, and the wonderful fragrances of cumin, oregano, and allspice filled the air. I remember my mother made this most wonderful soup every Sunday."

Tigran thought of his favorite dish. "My favorite was a delicious mix of pork—the worst cuts because we couldn't afford any better. My mother would use a mallet to soften it and then pound the spices into the meat."

They both could see the cathedral dome only a few hundred yards away. "In a few minutes, we'll be there. We should first inquire about the archbishop." Tigran whipped the reins to encourage the donkeys to quicken their pace. Mari's image with her eyes looking directly at him was as close as ever.

Arakel looked up at the sun and the blue sky and soaked in the rays. It was so warm, just like sleeping in front of the fire with his wife. He would soon be able to return to his family.

They both thought about their meeting with Archbishop Cyriacus, as they pulled up to the main entrance to the Holy Sophia. They saw a man with a frock standing at a table to the side of the main doors providing soup to a line of twenty or so women and children. It wasn't different from the many other churches they'd visited on their journey, except this church was many times larger. Standing outside the church made them feel like ants approaching a large boulder. Close up, it was much more massive than it looked from the other side of the Bosporus. It looked like they would need an hour just to walk around it.

"Father, where can we find His Excellency, Archbishop Cyriacus?"

The man looked up from his work. He was much younger than they thought. They breathed in the aroma from the spiced soup.

"I am Philippicus, only a transitional deacon. I haven't yet been ordained." The young man said, correcting Father Tigran.

Arakel's mind raced. *Maybe I could become ordained here in Constantinople. That would be a wonderful gift for Shoushi.*

"I have a letter and gifts for him. We have traveled far to bring them." Tigran avoided giving away where they came from, although a more mature person might recognize their accents. He wasn't yet sure if he could trust the man with the knowledge of what he was about to deliver as a gift to Cyriacus. He'd kept the existence of the cloth secret for so long, he wasn't yet ready to trust anyone with their true objectives for their trek to Constantinople . . . not until he was in the presence of Archbishop Cyriacus himself.

"He is at the palace with Emperor Phocas preparing for the arrival of Narses. He won't be here for several hours."

Arakel thought and responded before Tigran was able to. "Where can we leave our wagon and donkeys? Perhaps we can assist you while we wait?"

The young deacon pointed to the north corner of the church, just a few yards away. "There is a hitching post there with a trough. It will be in our sight from here. I would welcome your help."

The afternoon passed slowly for Tigran and Arakel. In between ladling soup for the poor, their thoughts leapt from Severus to Mari and Shoushi and everywhere in between. Arakel enjoyed serving every ladle of soup as he thought about home in Edessa.

Tigran did most of the talking. Both men were impatient to hand over the cloth. It was late afternoon before all the poor had been fed.

"His Excellency should be returning soon. He usually joins all of us for evening dinner and vespers." Philippicus broke the short silence as the three of them worked to break down the makeshift table and serving supplies. "We'll store everything outside the kitchen. There is a storage room there." Philippicus began loading the supplies onto a small two-wheeled cart. "You'll want to bring your wagon."

Arakel walked over to the hitching post and untied the donkeys. He patted both, and they each responded with a snort. One of them brayed. The other pointed his ears at Arakel. "It's been a long journey, but you'll both get a break from the travel." He announced to both donkeys as they returned to the table where Philippicus and Tigran were organizing everything.

"What do you have with you?" Philippicus was now fast becoming one of their friends. "We could have used these clothes and blankets this winter. There were days and nights that were exceptionally bitter this past winter." Philippicus was dressed in a traditional frock. He didn't have much else. "The May weather has been beautiful, so most of our parishioners don't need much now. But these will be invaluable to have for harvest season." He was surprised to see the number of used clothes and blankets. "Why would you travel this far to provide clothes to the poor?" Philippicus turned and faced Tigran with a quizzical expression on his face. "You certainly didn't travel as far as you did just to bring these clothes and blankets. What are you doing here?"

†††

They entered the kitchen, and Philippicus introduced Tigran and Arakel to Father Stylian, one of the four priests serving in the cathedral.

"This Sunday, I hope you'll join us for Mass. We have three, with the first beginning at dawn." Father Stylian gripped the forearms of Tigran and Arakel with both of his hands. "You have arrived at a momentous time, with Narses arriving tomorrow." Stylian smiled. "It's not clear whether he will be embraced or disgraced."

Tigran was surprised by the arrogance of the statement, realizing Stylian was no fan of Narses and would rather be part of the politics, as opposed to separate from it. Father Stylian was one of two aides of the archbishop and privy to most of the archbishop's consultations. Their position and inside knowledge allowed them to hold power over all others in the cathedral staff.

"They are waiting to meet His Excellency," Philippicus replied, inviting them to sit, and then sat down next to them to partake of their meal. They were in the dining hall along with another fifteen clergy and other workers from the cathedral. The hall had two long wooden tables with benches on both sides. A special place was reserved at the head of the table for Archbishop Cyriacus. Stylian took his seat directly to the right of the archbishop's chair. Everyone else squeezed in to provide room for the two guests.

Stylian looked at the two guests with a quizzical look in his eye. He continued to express his opinion of the situation. "His Excellency has just concluded his conference with Emperor Florias Phocas and is taking his meal in his chambers. I think he's not going to be happy with what he heard. What I understand is that Phocas has not forgiven Narses for aligning with the Sassanids." Stylian spoke in a tone indicating he, and only he, was privy to certain discussions with the archbishop. "We've been paying tribute to them for so many years, and Narses aligns with them to defend his position in Edessa." There was disdain in his voice. "I think he'll be escorted to the dungeons and locked up. I just hope it won't lead to an insurrection with his troops. That will only lead to wounded and disfigured to be cared for."

Stylian muttered but could still be heard. "This war has been going on for so long."

Father Licinius walked in and greeted the newcomers at the end of the meal. He was the chief aide to the archbishop and senior to Father Stylian. "Philippicus, bring Father Tigran and Deacon Arakel. His Excellency will see them now. He has just finished his meal." Licinius was ever terse and to the point. He was taller than Philippicus and stood with a very stiff back, which added almost an inch to his height and a foot to his conceit. After all, he was a priest at the greatest cathedral in the world. His directions were always carried out to the letter. He countenanced nothing less.

Licinius looked up and down at Tigran, inspecting this supposed priest from the backwaters of the realm. Tigran obviously knew nothing of the ways of Constantinople, the foremost city of all Rome. He finally spoke to Tigran with disdain. "What reason do you have to speak with the archbishop? He's not accustomed to meeting with just anyone who shows up at his doorstep." Licinius spoke with the perfect polished accent of Roman aristocracy.

Tigran, Arakel, and Philippicus stood and turned toward Father Licinius, but Licinius partially blocked their way. He used his body to reinforce his inquisition.

Tigran glared back at him, not budging either. He would allow nothing to dissuade him from completing this mission that had consumed over six months of his life.

Licinius wasn't about to let these inferiors have an audience with the archbishop without first vetting the two backwater clergy.

Tigran used silence as his argument and said nothing. It was the easiest way to counteract an inflated ego.

After half a minute, Licinius relented and bowed slightly, realizing Tigran was not about to reveal his purpose to anyone other than the archbishop.

Father Licinius acquired his demeanor from his mentor, the archbishop. His condescension to strangers without known pedigree mimicked exactly the behavior of the archbishop.

Until now, in all their travels, Tigran and Arakel had been fully welcomed into the church family at all of their stops. Although Tigran had letters from Archbishop Severus and each of the bishops, they were never necessary to gain an audience with any of the bishops. He wasn't going to use them here either with this self-important aide to the archbishop.

"Come in," the archbishop commanded, rather than welcomed, from behind the door. His Excellency stood and offered his hand, palm down.

Tigran knelt and kissed the ring and then stood and backed away so Arakel could do the same.

Father Licinius moved to stand behind His Excellency.

The archbishop was at least a foot shorter than the other three, and standing made him uncomfortable in the middle of the three taller men. To regain his height advantage, he quickly moved to a chair in front of his desk and sat down. The chair was slightly taller than the other chairs, so the archbishop had to hop up on it.

Tigran noticed the hop and was momentarily perplexed. He forced back a smile when he realized the situation. The archbishop's feet barely reached the floor.

The archbishop waved for Tigran to take a seat and face him. The visitor's chair was not as grand, purposefully meant for a visit with an underling. It also had much shorter legs than usual, so the backs of his thighs were above the seat cushion. In this configuration, the archbishop gained a height advantage and looked down at his interlocutor.

After about a minute, the archbishop broke the awkward silence. "What are you here for?" The archbishop breathed in, and Tigran and Arakel's pungent odor began to envelop the room. The two had not bathed for weeks. The archbishop and Licinius put a hand to their faces to try and avoid breathing in the odiferous air.

Tigran paused and looked at Father Licinius, then back at the archbishop. "Your Excellency, I would prefer we speak in private."

Licinius glared, his eyebrows raised. "How dare you! Your Excellency, we have no idea who these men are!" Licinius protested the affront.

The archbishop turned his head toward his chief aide, then looked back at Tigran. "You come here unannounced and ask to be alone in my presence. How do I know you're not a Narses follower sent here to kill me." This time he sneered at the intruder. After all, he was the archbishop, patriarch of Constantinople, the greatest city on earth.

Tigran didn't budge. He just continued looking straight at the archbishop. Arakel's mind raced. He'd never seen Tigran so unflappable. He wanted to get this meeting over with, so they could return to Edessa.

The silence in the room was deafening, but Tigran was not about to be bested. He had learned from Severus that silence can be a strong weapon, especially in countering inflated egos. It raised his stature to that of an equal, regardless of title.

The archbishop also didn't budge. It was two minutes before Tigran decided to back down from his request. "My apologies. We have strict instructions from Archbishop Severus to provide his gift to you and only you." Tigran showed a modicum of deference to the archbishop and patriarch of Constantinople. He finally reached into the chest pocket inside his tunic and retrieved the letter from Severus. He looked up at Licinius, then back at the archbishop, and handed it to the archbishop. The archbishop didn't open the letter. He handed it instead to Father Licinius as if it were beneath him.

"Your Excellency. We have been on a mission, a secret mission, from His Excellency, Archbishop Severus from Edessa." He let this sink in a few moments.

Licinius read through the letter. "The Mandylion?" He didn't mean to say this out loud, but it came out audibly enough to be heard by everyone in the room.

The archbishop remained motionless, the quiet persisting in the air along with the smell of the unbathed visitors.

Licinius inspected the seal from Severus, and it appeared correct. "Your Excellency, his bona fides seem genuine." He handed the letter back to the archbishop.

Cyriacus had not yet deigned to speak to this underling.

He finally looked down and read the letter. Stunned, his eyes widened and he took in a short, punctuated breath. *These two men carried one of the greatest treasures of Christendom. It was here? Now?*

The archbishop's demeanor changed slightly. "We must keep this secret. Until the dispute between Phocas and Narses has been resolved, no one can know what you have brought with you. Where is it? Bring it to me immediately." He paused. "No. Wait." Cyriacus didn't want anyone other than the four to know anything about the cloth. "Wait until everyone has retired. Father Licinius, go with them and stay by their sides. Don't let that cloth out of your sight. Then bring me the cloth at second watch. Fetch the keys to the treasury. We'll keep it there."

"Yes. Your Excellency," Licinius bowed. No other words were spoken. He was as perfunctory as ever but now treated both the priest and the deacon with more respect, yet not quite as equals.

✝✝✝

CONSTANTINOPLE
LATE EVENING, SATURDAY, MAY 18, AD 603

It was well after dark, and finally they were able to unpack their wagon of clothes and blankets. The donkeys were washed down and led to a stall. The larger more mature donkey, Arakel's favorite, had developed an open wound on the back of its neck.

Philippicus volunteered to treat it. "It will heal quickly. I have a special salve my father and I used on our own donkeys as we were growing up. He shouldn't have any problems."

Arakel breathed in. These two donkeys had been with them for many months, with many more to come. Arakel patted the donkey on its neck and rubbed its back, glad to be able to help his animal friend.

"Brother Philippicus, help provide sleeping arrangements for Father Tigran and Deacon Arakel," Licinius commanded. "They will be joining the archbishop in a few hours to finish their meeting."

It was the first time Arakel had been formally addressed in many months. He so wanted to be Father Arakel.

"Shall I show you to your quarters?" Philippicus was getting curious and wanted to learn more, but no one was giving any hints.

Arakel and Tigran took advantage of their temporary quarters. They were both exhausted and fell asleep for a few hours while they waited to be taken back to Archbishop Cyriacus to hand over the cloth.

For Arakel, the end was in sight, and his mind drifted in and out, causing his sleep to be restless. Tigran slept lightly, disturbed by the tossing and turning of his mentee and friend.

"Serli, Serli! Please God, where is she? Where? Serli!" She was nowhere in sight.

The loud voice from Arakel's nightmare woke Tigran.

"Serli. God, where is she? No!" Tigran noticed tears in Arakel's eyes.

"Arakel, wake up. Wake up." Tigran wasn't going to let this nightmare continue. He shook his friend.

Arakel woke with a start. "Hmm?" He was no longer in the cold stream water looking for Serli. Instead, he was in a dark room. The only light came from the nearly full moon. He looked around. "What are you—"

Tigran shook him again to help clear the fog of waking in the middle of a nightmare.

"Arakel, you must tell me. Your dream of Serli is overcoming you. This is a night of joy, and you are suffering." Tigran was adamant. This secret was no longer going to consume his friend. "You will tell me now about Serli. Is she your sister? Your girlfriend? Who is she? Where is she? What happened to her?"

Arakel was exhausted. He had hidden it for so long. He couldn't hide it any longer. Tigran's questions forced a confession. "I killed her. I killed her!" It came spilling out. "I killed her."

There was silence amid the shock while Tigran tried to think of an appropriate response, not wanting to blurt out something he would regret. He debated whether to wait or to see if Arakel would reveal more. Thirty seconds passed, then sixty. Arakel volunteered nothing more.

"Tell me. Confess it to me. How did she die? I've known you for many years now. You did not kill her. I know you. That is impossible."

The story came gushing out. "We were playing together—my sister and I—in a stream. I knew how to swim, but she hadn't quite learned yet. I was eight; she five. It was so hot, and I really wanted to swim. She did too. My father had warned me not to swim alone with her, but I—we—went anyway. We both stepped into the stream. I loved the feeling of holding my breath under the water. I could hold my breath for many seconds, maybe even a minute." Arakel paused. He could see the bright sun rippling through the slight waves above, just as if he was there in the stream right then.

Tigran reached out and put his hand on his friend's shoulder.

"When I came up out of the water, she was nowhere to be seen. I thought she was doing exactly as I had done. I went under again and came back up after another thirty seconds, and she was gone. She was gone! The water wasn't moving that fast, but I couldn't find her. I looked and looked. I couldn't find her!" Arakel fell silent. He remembered telling his father. "I never found her."

Tigran tried to console his friend. There is no touching in the confessional, but here he could gently squeeze his friend's shoulder.

Arakel continued his story of Serli. "I ran back home to tell my mother, and when we returned back to the stream. We searched and searched. She was gone. Gone." Again, came silence. "My father never forgave me. He hated me. He could never look at me. It was the reason I wanted to become a priest. If I can't be forgiven, then at least I can forgive others."

"You didn't kill her. You were only eight. You were not responsible. I know God will forgive you." Tigran had heard many confessions, but to hear one from a close friend, especially a revelation of such consequence, caused tears to well up in his eyes. He tried to hold them back.

Arakel laid back, his eyes closed and his mind racing. He had finally given up his demon. Never before had he confessed his sin to anyone.

Tigran looked over. In the darkness of the moonlight, he could see the pain of his friend. "Yes, God can and will forgive you."

They laid in silence, neither sleeping, both with their eyes closed. Tigran thought of the apostle Matthew, "'For if you forgive men their trespasses, your heavenly Father will also forgive you. But if you forgive not men their trespasses, neither will your Father forgive your trespasses.' Arakel, you must forgive yourself and then God will forgive you. His love for you is unbounded. He will forgive you!"

Licinius knocked on the door. Arakel's confession of Serli's death led to a calmness for him. All his tension had drained away. He could feel both Tigran's love and God's love flowing over him, as the water did when he had entered into the stream.

Tigran was focused on how he could help his friend. He no longer had to teach him about becoming a priest. Instead, he needed to teach him how to forgive himself—one of the hardest teachings of any priest.

The three made their way back to the archbishop with the Mandylion.

It was wrapped in a thin cotton cloth and folded like a simple carpet. There was no gold-and silver-plated box . . . nothing fancy and altogether ordinary.

"This was a perfect disguise. You are to be commended that you were able to safely bring this valuable relic so far without damage, especially amid the political machinations between Narses and Phocas. I do want to hear about your exploits." Licinius now respected them as equals. The arrogance was gone.

"Licinius, clear my desk, so we can examine the cloth," Cyriacus commanded. That kind of work was beneath him.

Tigran looked over at the archbishop, who nodded for him to unfold the cloth. It only took a moment. Only half the cloth could fit on the desk at one time. Jesus's distorted face was there, as if sleeping. His eyes were closed.

The archbishop genuflected. He was now truly in the presence of what remained of God on earth. The archbishop had heard of the Mandylion of Edessa. It was thought to be a washcloth, but this wasn't a washcloth. It was Jesus's burial Shroud. This cloth, known as the Mandylion, was simply the Shroud folded to reveal only His face and neck. It was the exposed face and neck of the Son of God. Once unfolded, the rest of His torso and back of His body were revealed.

This is Jesus's burial Shroud! The archbishop's whole body shuddered, as he imagined the pain Jesus endured for himself and for everyone. Wounds and blood were everywhere all over the image of His body.

"The blood. There are so many bloodstains. Bright red. Are they from the whippings?" The archbishop winced as he took in the many marks from the three-pronged flagellum used on Jesus's back. "There are tens of them, maybe a hundred," he whispered. "How he suffered for us." He knelt and prayed, putting his hand on the cloth, and all of those present followed suit.

Arakel finally realized why he had sacrificed six months of his life to transport this relic of Jesus Christ—a reminder of God's presence here on earth.

Cyriacus prayed to himself for several minutes before looking up. Tears were in his eyes, as he thought about the agony Jesus had endured. "Licinius, bring the candle here. I need more light to see the face." The archbishop's sight had faded with age. "Careful, careful. You're dripping wax onto the cloth." He was mesmerized by what he was seeing: the arms folded across His waist, the blood from His side, the blood at His feet and wrists. The Gospels were here, alive and in front of him.

After thirty minutes, the archbishop was done. His imagination of Jesus's suffering overcame him. He started to speak but had trouble getting the words out. "Father Licinius . . . Father Licinius, Father Tigran, Deacon

Arakel. Speak to no one about this. No one. This cloth must remain a secret."
Another minute passed, and Cyriacus began to think more clearly.

"Father Licinius, take the Shroud to the treasury. Hide it there."

✝✝✝

Other events took place that night, at the other end of the city, which
sealed the destiny for both Phocas and Narses. Phocas won. Narses lost and
was executed that night . . . burned alive. Phocas was not going to suffer a
traitor. Instead, the traitor was going to suffer. Narses's men were arrested.
He'd deal with Khosrow and the Sassanids later. After all, he was the emperor
of all of Rome, including Edessa and Osrhoene.

CHAPTER 5

The Shroud in Constantinople

After three hundred years hidden away in the treasury of the Hagia Sophia, the Shroud was rediscovered and its significance recognized. Archdeacon Gregory Referendarius and Archbishop Theophylactus exhibited the Shroud for the people of the city of Constantinople.

THE HAGIA SOPHIA, CONSTANTINOPLE
MORNING MASS, 6:00 A.M., EASTER SUNDAY, APRIL 5, AD 944

"Julian, sit still. Be reverent. Sit still!" his sister Joannina implored in a strong but whispered voice, but it was no use. They were the same words she had heard many times from her parents only a few years before. Julian didn't even know what reverent meant.

They were in church at morning Mass. He was only six years old, and he wanted to be outside, running through the grass and riding their pony. They stood in their row about halfway down the main hall of the cathedral. Julian was hungry, and there was nothing he, or his sister, could do about it.

Every time the family went to early Mass, none of them had the energy early in the morning to prepare anything to eat, other than some dried bread from the day before. The Theophanus family had one servant, Martina, and she didn't normally work Sundays, especially not on Easter Sunday. But today was an exception because Julian's mother was pregnant with his brother . . . or at least he hoped it was a brother. He'd find out in another four or five months when the baby was born.

The family had one horse and one pony for him, his older sister, his baby sister, and his two parents.

The whole family stood together when they came to Mass. Father stood on the aisle, then mother with the baby, then Joannina, and lastly Julian. He preferred standing on the end, so his father wouldn't be able to discipline him. He was supposed to behave, but that was boring. If he stood next to his father, his father had a way of twisting his ear to gain compliance. Although if the rivalry between Julian and his sister escalated too much, he would have to stand in front of his father.

For those times when he had to stand by his father, he liked standing on top of his shoes. It was Julian's favorite spot. He'd stand on his father's feet and hold both of his father's hands for balance and so his ears couldn't be twisted.

"Leave me alone!" Julian said in response to his sister's call to be reverent. He said it loud enough that their parents must have heard, but they didn't shift their gaze. They were focused on the altar and the archdeacon. Julian looked down and found a beetle to play with. He used his toes to change the direction of the beetle as it tried to scurry off.

"My fellow believers. Today I want to tell you a story of Constantinople. Constantinople is the jewel of the Roman Empire. It is the capital of the wealthiest empire in all the world. The artwork we have is second to none in its beauty and elegance. Its importance stems from Emperor Constantine.[1] He was the first Christian emperor, and he helped spread our great religion throughout all of Rome. In his honor, the name of the city was changed from Byzantium to Constantinople. He was instrumental in building the wonders of this city. We have the marvelous Hippodrome, the Blachernae Palace, this cathedral, and innumerable monuments and spires not found anywhere else in the world. But this you all know." The archdeacon was building up to his high point.

"All these works are the works of man, by our hands. Many are divinely

---

1 Emperor Constantine I: Known as Constantine the Great. First Christian Roman emperor. Moved the capital city of the Roman Empire to Byzantium. Born AD 272. Emperor from AD 306 to 337. Died AD 337.

inspired, but still, they are works of man. Just like this great city and this great empire, we hope they will last forever, but we know they won't.

"We have, however, in our possession, the possession of this church and the holy Roman Empire, a work not of man but of God." He waved his arm to the displayed cloth. "It is the holy Shroud. The burial cloth of Jesus Christ." He paused, hearing gasps throughout the sanctuary. Everyone whispered among themselves.

Julian heard the hushed speaking and suddenly looked up, but he wasn't tall enough to see. He looked down again, in time to see the beetle escaping.

"You can see the image of a face and also the figure of the whole body." Gregory Referendarius,[2] archdeacon of the Hagia Sophia, continued his homily once the whispering died down to a soft murmur. "It is a miraculously rendered—not drawn or painted—but miraculously rendered likeness of the tortured body of Jesus."

There was a hush in the sanctuary. Gregory waited for that to sink in, not sure if the parishioners understood its true meaning. "I have never seen anything like this. It has been in the church vaults for several hundred years with no identification."

Julian had to stretch his leg to recapture the beetle.

"Based on the records we have, we believe it was brought to us—to Archbishop Cyriacus II—over three centuries ago."

"Stop it, or I'll tell Mommy." This was louder than a whisper, and Julian's mother looked over and put her finger to her lips. "Shhh."

Julian glanced over to his mother. The silence of the two siblings would last only a few seconds. A minute if she was lucky. His father continued to focus on the Shroud.

"It came from Edessa, where it was known as the Mandylion." Most of the parishioners had never heard the term. For those who had, only a very few believed it existed. "The Mandylion was supposed to be a facecloth used by Jesus that depicted his facial image. This is not that. This is his whole body, both the front and the back. Life-sized."

The archdeacon paused again. He was like a great conductor who had complete control over his orchestra. His conducting allowed the give and take of attentive silence mixed with controlled confusion, which helped his message sink in. "Today, I submit to you we need to protect it by building a protective case, decorated with the finest gold and silver smithed by our finest artisans. This is the most valuable relic from Jesus Christ. There is nothing more

2 Archdeacon Gregory Referendarius: Archdeacon of the Hagia Sophia, Constantinople. Known from his sermon of August 15, AD 944.

valuable." It was a solicitation of funds disguised as a homily, even if it was for a worthy cause. "This is something we must protect and cherish for all eternity."

Julian's father looked over at his wife and grinned. He had been commissioned to complete several gold-working tasks for the archdeacon and the church, and he was certain to be involved in this project. "This will be a very lucrative project," he whispered in his wife's ear. She could barely hear it over the din in the church, as the congregation reacted. "I will stop in and visit with him on the morrow."

✝✝✝

ARCHDEACON GREGORY REFERENDARIUS'S CHAMBERS, NEAR THE HAGIA SOPHIA (CHURCH OF THE HOLY WISDOM), CONSTANTINOPLE

MORNING, MONDAY, APRIL 8, AD 944

Archdeacon Referendarius and Archbishop Theophylactus[3] sat together in Referendarius's chambers discussing what to do with this newly found relic. It had only been discovered a few weeks earlier. The solicitation of funds the day before had increased the donations at the plate. Direct solicitations would be made of the aristocracy, and he was confident this project would soon be able to begin.

"There is only a record of two visitors from Edessa in AD 603. It must have come at that time. It's the only thing that makes sense. Then for three hundred years, it was hidden away in the cathedral's treasury. I wonder if that's what happened. If so, it would have been received by Cyriacus II. That was the time of the burning alive of Narses." Referendarius presented what he was able to surmise from his research the last few weeks. "There is much more to learn, and I am piecing the history together. The church had to be very circumspect in her political dealings. She had to chart a political stance somewhere between Emperor Maurice, Emperor Phocas, and Governor Narses. Cyriacus II, the ecumenical patriarch of Constantinople of the church in the west, died only a few years later. He was friendly to Pope Gregory[4] in Rome but not a friend. He wanted to conceal from Phocas and from Pope Gregory that the burial Shroud of Jesus Christ was in Constantinople and not in Edessa, nor in Rome."

"No need to poke the sleeping dragon, like Saint George," Archbishop Theophylactus chimed in, smiling at the coup perpetrated against Rome. He loved Rome but loved Constantinople, the center of the empire, more and believed it should also be the true center of the church. "Given your homily, Pope

---

3 Archbishop Theophylactus: Archbishop of Constantinople from AD 933 to 956. Died from falling from one of his own horses, AD 956.
4 Pope Gregory I: Pope from AD 540 to 604. Died AD 604.

Marinus[5] will be sending an envoy to request to move the Shroud to Rome." The archbishop smiled a very broad smile, followed by a bellowing laugh.

Father Alexius, the archdeacon's assistant, entered upon overhearing the laughter. "Your Excellencies, Julius Theophanus would like a word."

"Our goldsmith? Excellent." Referendarius bellowed, his mood matching that of the archbishop's. "He will be perfect for the design of the case we'll build for the Shroud." Both clerics rose and greeted the goldsmith. Theophanus bowed to each and kissed their rings.

"I am off." Theophylactus took a step to the door and stopped. "I will be meeting with Emperor Romanus.[6] He will want to take possession of the cloth. That will be more appropriate since we won't be able to protect it as well as he. We will present it as a gift." Before the archbishop left, he turned and looked at Theophanus. "The emperor will be supplying a large portion of the gold and silver required for the case. Brother Theophanus, think big."

The Shroud was spread out over two long tables in the archdeacon's chambers. Julius Theophanus looked on in awe, amazed to be in the presence of such an invaluable relic. "Archdeacon, I have never seen something like this. The archbishop was correct. This will require big thinking."

✝✝✝

CONSTANTINOPLE
MORNING, SATURDAY, AUGUST 1, AD 944

"Come quickly, quickly! Your wife. Your wife. She needs you." Martina's agitation was evident. It was the same level of excitement she had about the birth of her employer's third child, except this wasn't joy. This was fear. It was too early. According to the midwife, Gayane, Julius's wife, wasn't due for at least another five or six weeks.

Julius's gold- and silversmithing shop was three doors down from their home. He had expanded to this location to make room for his artisans to complete the work on the case for the Shroud. The project had been commissioned three months prior, within a few weeks of the display at the Hagia Sophia.

One of his artisans and junior partner, Vardan, was eight years younger and had been with Julius since the death of the master goldsmith, Euphrosyni, over fifteen years ago. Julius and Vardan had both learned gold- and silversmithing under Euphrosyni, until he unexpectedly died. Julius,

---

5 Pope Marinus II: Pope from AD 942 to 946. Resided in Rome. Died AD 946.

6 Emperor Romanus I Lecapenus of Byzantium (Rome): Reigned from AD 920 to 944. Deposed AD 944. Armenian peasant with the name of Theophylact the Unbearable. Saved the life of Emperor Basil I. Born circa AD 870, died AD 948.

through his family connections and family money, was able to take over the Euphrosyni business. Since then, Julius had been able to expand the business to include Vardan and one other junior artisan. Julius now also brought on two new junior artisans, making a team of five, to aid with the design and fabrication of the case for the holy Shroud. He hoped he could use this project to win other projects and keep all of them in his employ.

"I will take over the melting of the gold. You go. Go!" Vardan strode over to Julius and started pushing him away from his work area. "Go!"

"You, take over the bellows from me here while I continue . . ." was the last Julius heard from Vardan as he bounded out of the shop.

†††

Julius could hear his wife, Gayane, breathing heavily as he entered his modest home. The door to their bedchambers was partially open, and he listened to the calming words of the midwife as she wiped Gayane's brow with a cold, damp cloth.

Martina entered the bedchamber and finished placing the tapestries over the windows and door to darken the room and help relax the mother.

Julius was concerned. *Is my wife about to give birth? Five to six weeks early?*

"It's too early. Too early!" Gayane sobbed and screamed out the words. Another grunt came as the next contraction enveloped her. "No!"

The midwife closed the door as soon as she saw Julius looking in. He wasn't allowed in. It would have been bad luck for him, a man, to see his wife give birth.

This would be his sixth experience with childbirth. Julius's thoughts raced back to his two dead children. A girl, older than Joannina, died at childbirth with the umbilical cord wrapped around her neck. And a boy, their fourth child, had died of dysentery when he was about eleven months. Neither had caused his wife to go into labor this early.

Julius started pacing, frustrated he could not help. There was nothing he could do. He sweated from the heat and his growing worry.

"Is there anything I can do for you?" The priest entered the Theophanus home amid all the commotion. He would start his prayer vigil as soon as he could. He had prayed to himself the whole way from the church. A woman giving birth this early usually led to the death of the child and possibly the mother.

Julius looked at the priest in silence, both of them knowing the consequences of early labor. His two oldest children sat in silence; his youngest had fallen asleep. He could only stare at them and then back to his friend and religious leader. There was no emotion in his face, but fear ruled his heart. He thought of how devastated his wife was upon the death of their fifth child. The sixth child was to be their last. They had tried using cedar oil to corrupt the sperm, but it had failed.

"I wanted another child. She was against it. And now this. It's my fault. It's my . . ." His voice trailed off, speaking to no one in particular. *Did the cedar oil cause this?*

"Errrrrh," another series of moans and cries came. "Nooo!" The wails were louder than before.

"Drink this, drink this. It should help to calm you and ease the contractions. Yes, drink, slowly, slowly, yes." The midwife's voice brought calmness in the darkened room. She had two goals: to ease the birth, should it happen, and to help Gayane in case the birth could be delayed.

Another two hours passed, punctuated by deep cries. The children sat quietly while the baby napped. Julius paced back and forth, afraid his wife of ten years wouldn't survive, while the priest prayed and genuflected.

There was a pause in the cries, and they subsided to soft moans. After a third hour, they ceased altogether. The priest noticed it first but continued his prayers. Julius noticed it but didn't say anything. He didn't want to disturb the quiet. Another thirty minutes passed, and the bedchamber door opened. Gayane was asleep, exhausted from her labors. The two oldest children sat motionless. They hadn't moved since their father had arrived. Only the youngest, the one-year-old baby's soft breathing could be heard. Julius's fear was replaced with calm.

"The tea worked. We tried several combinations, and it was the last with chamomile and rue herb that seem to have paused the contractions and delivery. Perhaps it will last a few days, maybe a few weeks." The midwife shut the door and went back to tending her patient.

Quiet elation pierced the air. Julius took a deep breath, uncertain of what would happen next. He closed his eyes and prayed the pause would last more than a few weeks. The priest made his way over to Julius, put his hand on his shoulder, and whispered a blessing. The men and three children waited another two hours. No sound came from the bedchamber.

✝✝✝

THE HAGIA SOPHIA, CONSTANTINOPLE
MORNING, SATURDAY, AUGUST 15, AD 944

It required five bishops to properly carry the Shroud. They proceeded up the stairway to the city wall. They sweated in the summer heat, but no one complained.

"God bless this city, God protect this city, God bless Emperor Romanus." The archdeacon led the cortege on the right, the archbishop on the left. It was four months since the pronouncement of the existence of the Shroud. They were to parade the Shroud around the city, up along the city walls and then finally to the Blachernae Palace where it would be received by the emperor.

The crowd numbered in the tens of thousands. Hushed commotion followed the procession as the holy Shroud was carried along. Men, women, and children all joined in the prayers and blessings. Anything that could help protect their lives and livelihoods was well appreciated, and this cloth of Jesus—the holy Shroud—would help. Although the crowds surrounding the walls couldn't see the detail of the cloth, they were able to make out an ominous image of the Messiah. They could also see that the cloth was of an extraordinary length, at almost fourteen feet.

The entourage dressed in their finest ceremonial attire, and it was heavy in the heat of the August sun. "My brothers, today will be a day written about many times." The archdeacon aimed to inspire the bishops who were to carry the relic, but they didn't require any additional inspiration. Being close to Jesus's burial cloth left each of them with a strange warming of their hearts.

Following them were the envoys from Pope Marinus II, the hundred and twenty-seventh pope after Saint Peter, the rock of the church. The pope was disappointed that Rome would not be the recipient of such a tribute. No emperor, nor pope, would let such a valuable relic out of their possession, regardless of the entreaties of the pope. "Jesus is with us today. 'For where two or three gather in my name, there am I with them.'" The archdeacon recited the verse from Matthew by heart. "Today we're thousands, tens of thousands."

Over an hour passed before the procession climbed down from the southern end of the city walls on the Propontis. "Even the gulls are venerating Jesus Christ today." The archbishop looked out at a larger-than-usual congregation of birds circling and cawing overhead.

The view of ships in the harbor was astounding. There were countless ships and galleys of all sizes . . . trading ships, military ships, and royal ships. Unfurled flags of every color splattered across the masts and waved back and forth in the breezes. Never had there been so many large vessels from contingents all over the realm. The sun was bright and the water a deep cerulean blue. "The salt sea air is so refreshing. Invigorating." The archbishop was ebullient. The connection to the Aegean and the Mediterranean made Constantinople a perfect capital for a thriving empire. "This cloth will secure the realm for a thousand years."

Julian stood by his father, holding onto his jacket. He sensed the joy and excitement of his father, but he was ready to leave. "Father, can we go home now?"

His father tried to ignore his pleadings but decided it was time to intervene. Julian and his sister were certainly tired. They too were privileged to process with the cloth, albeit next to the wall, close to other mid-level dignitaries.

"Julian, I will carry you, and then I will carry your sister. It will be a long day, but this will be a day you will never forget. Never ever." His father used a voice that calmed his sister and him. Julian's mother, baby sister, and servant were also tired but weren't going to leave this important celebration. This was the first time they had all been out with their mother since the near childbirth two weeks before. Since then, his mother had been resting in bed, lying horizontal so as not to put undue pressure on her or the baby. She almost didn't come but felt this event was something she couldn't miss.

"I have a litter reserved for the next leg of the celebration." His father's litter was rented, along with the six bearers to carry the whole family. It wasn't the best litter, yet it did have some creature comforts, including a few cushions as well as four ornate, brass-covered posts that held up a dark green canopy to protect from the hot sun. His father would be on horseback. The servant would walk behind them.

"We will be in the presence of the emperor, and you will need to obey everything I tell you." Julian's father did his best to distract them from their weariness and thirst. "Come. When we reach our litter, I will give you some wine and a slice of orange.

"Julian, if you were to join the Imperial Guard, you could possibly follow in the emperor's footsteps. The emperor was born an Armenian peasant, and after having saved the life of Emperor Basil,[7] he rose in prominence all the way to admiral of the fleet."

Julius continued to try and distract his son from the heat and his obvious boredom. "You could also join the military and move quickly up the ranks. What do you think of that?" Julian didn't answer. The heat was too much, and they needed to make their way to the palace.

The trip to the palace took just under an hour. The route was lined by a centuria of the royal guard. They were decked out in their finest uniforms, their standards flowing in the breeze coming off the sea. The feathers on their helmets were a dazzling white and stood in stunning contrast to the gold and

---

7 Emperor Basil I the Macedonian: Reigned from AD 867 to 886. Born AD 811, died AD 886.

red tunics. "Julian, would you like to join the royal guard, or would you like to be a goldsmith like your father?" His father pointed to the finely bedecked milites and centurions. "I could talk with my friends and make certain you were well placed."

"If I joined the royal guard, would I learn how to use a sword and a bow and arrow?" Julian's imagination was piqued by his father. He looked over at the uniformed men lining the streets and standing at attention. Julian stabbed the air as if attacking a foe.

"See there on the left, there's the standard from where my brother served. Your uncle didn't survive the war with Bulgaria, but he served very proudly." A note of sadness touched Julian's father's voice. "My brother wanted to serve, even when he and I were your age." He paused and genuflected. "He's now with God and Jesus in heaven."

Julian continued stabbing the air and swinging his imaginary sword while they walked. When they reached the litter, he and his sister drank some posca to relieve their thirst while his father arranged slices of orange. Julian grabbed one and bit out the meat in one bite. His sister grabbed another. His mother sat on the litter and then lay down. She was exhausted. Julian took another orange slice and bit off a small piece, the juice squirting onto his jacket.

His father handed him a handkerchief. "I, too, when I was your age, could never eat an orange without some squirting onto my clothes." Julian's father looked proudly on his son, the thoughts of his dead brother now passed.

The hour to the Blachernae Palace passed quickly. The heat was exhausting, and everyone except his father slept in the litter as soon as they started processing to the palace. In their sleep, all three of the children perspired, with visible drops of sweat forming on their foreheads. Their clothes were drenched. Julian's very pregnant mother slept on and off, waking several times due to the oven in her belly.

When they arrived at the palace, they waited in line with about fifty dignitaries in front of them. Although they were invited, they weren't of the same stature, so they needed to wait as each of the higher dignitaries unloaded and the celebrants made their way into the palace. Julian's father expected they would be toward the end of the line, but he didn't expect there would be that many to wait for. The wait lasted over an hour.

"Wake up, wake up. Look Joannina. See the servants and their fans. They'll keep us cool once we're inside." Julian woke up first before his sister and wanted to run to the fans. The emperor's servants waved enormous palm fronds slowly up and down to provide air flow on the steps and throughout the palace. Within a few minutes, the Theophanus family was finally inside out of the sun. The enormous fans provided a noticeable breeze and kept the air flowing.

"Julian, look over there by the emperor's throne. He has two tiger cubs!" Julian's sister noticed them first. The tiger cubs ignored the heat, both of them biting and rolling over each other and entertaining everyone.

More than fifty people, all dressed in their finery, squeezed into the confined space in the palace. Each was grateful for the fans that made the heat more bearable. Every color of fine silk could be found, including sparkling gold and silver.

"Let's move to the back where we are out of the way. We won't be part of the formal greeting of the emperor," Gayane said, moving slowly to find a chair to sit down on.

Julian and Joannina sat on cushions on the floor, legs crossed. They could see the tiger cubs, just barely. Julian got up once to move closer, but his father remanded him back to his seat on the floor.

"Brother Theophanus, at last, I've found you. I've been searching for you everywhere in the palace. I'm glad you're here. I want you and your family to be recognized by the emperor." The archdeacon was dressed in a gold-embroidered, dark blue silk chasuble, with a perfectly pressed pure white frock underneath. It was magnificent. "Come this way. The emperor must greet the man who will design the case that will reside in the throne room, next to the throne of mercy. The case for the holy Shroud will be the most magnificent work of art of any in the realm."

Julius smiled. His family would prosper well this year.

✝✝✝

The two children curtseyed perfectly before the emperor, although the tiger cubs kept their attention throughout the family's audience with him. The cubs were restrained by iron chain leashes, yet there was nothing halting their entertaining antics. Like Joannina and Julian, the cubs were boy and girl.

After their short audience with Emperor Romanus, the Theophanus family made their way back to the fans. "I am so proud of you. You both bowed and curtseyed exactly how your mother taught you." Julius Theophanus was ecstatic. He held his head up higher than normal and bowed deeper than normal. His thoughts were to his designs and the work he and his artisans were to complete. When the designs and goldsmithing for the case for the Shroud were finished, he was certain the emperor would have him design and fabricate other works. He leaned over to his wife, who was standing silently and obeisantly next to him. "We must tithe even more to the church on Sunday. We must show our appreciation of what the archdeacon has done for us. Without his recommendation, we would never be part of this magnificent project."

Gayane felt a slight pressure in her abdomen. Then a strong pressure. It was obvious what it was. The activity and heat of the day had brought on a contraction. These were stronger than the last time. Since the last false labor, she had been extremely cautious of too much exertion.

But for this event, Julius insisted. After all, they may never get an audience with the emperor again.

"My dear Julius. I am sorry. We must go home immediately. It may be time. These don't feel like false contractions."

CHAPTER 6

The Sack of Constantinople

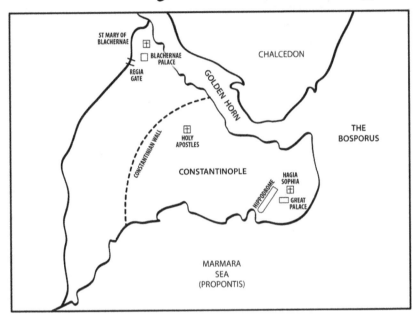

The first three crusades beginning in AD 1095 were organized to win the Holy Land back for Christianity, after having lost them first to the Seljuk Turks and then to the Muslims. Jerusalem changed hands but could not defend itself and fell each time to the conquering forces. By fighting in a crusade, Christians received indulgences for their sins. Financed by the Venetians, the Fourth Crusade was called together by Pope Innocent III[1] in AD 1202 to attack the Holy Land from the south through Egypt.

The Venetians financed the world. It didn't matter whether it concerned business or faith, they wouldn't do anything without a way for them to make a profit, and they demanded to be repaid in full. When internal squabbling over money led to leadership chaos, the original objective of the reconquest of Jerusalem and the Holy Land shifted. To repay those debts, Christians marched on Christians, first in Zara, now modern-day Croatia, and then in Constantinople.

---

1 Pope Innocent III: Pope from AD 1198 to 1216. Resided in Rome during the Fourth Crusade. Born circa AD 1160, died AD 1216.

THE SOUTHEASTERN SHORE OF THE BOSPORUS
EARLY EVENING BEFORE DUSK, JULY 10, AD 1203

"But I don't understand. Why aren't we marching on Jerusalem and Alexandria?" Estienne stoked the fire; each thrust punctuated his frustration. "These Muslim swine must pay for their insult to Jerusalem." He thrust again at the fire, showing his agitation. One of the logs went rolling, and he had to push it back. "Why are we going first to Constantinople after wasting our time in Zara? We killed fellow Catholics!" Estienne was not happy. He joined the Fourth Crusade to reestablish Christianity in Jerusalem and expel the Muslims, not to fight other Christians.

He looked out over the dark blue water at the wide expanse of Constantinople on the other side of the Bosporus. Fires and pillars of smoke dotted the city. "We must fight with all our forces united against the enemies in Jerusalem. We've been sitting here for two weeks, and now we're about to march on our friends and allies?" Estienne was young and had been in battle a few times aiding his master, Robert de Clari,[2] knight of Picardy.

"It's all about the money, the lucre. It always is," Robert de Clari responded. "If we don't take Constantinople, we won't be paid, and I, for one, didn't sign up to fight for free. And besides, Alexios[3] must pay as he agreed." The smell of the fires, the remains of the roasted meat, and the wine were intoxicating. De Clari sat next to his aide enjoying the afterglow of too much wine mixed with his fill of venison. De Clari spoke in a calm voice, thinking of his home in Picardy. A few months ago, they had won against Zara, one thousand miles to the north, but instead of marching on to Jerusalem, they would soon be marching on to Constantinople.

"We didn't win in Chalcedon, and now some of the men are going back home. And we must cross the Bosporus to invade Constantinople. What are we doing here?" Estienne's frustration and dejection were obvious. He'd never spoken like that before to His Lordship, his frustration boiling over that they wouldn't be fighting to recapture Jerusalem.

"They'll be here. They'll be here. Stop that nonsense. I will not have it. Now go fetch me some more drink and my writing box. I wish to add an entry to my diary. Also, I am still sore from the work of the last few days. Bring me something to put my feet up on." De Clari purposely distracted his aide from his whining. He, too, had the same concerns, but lamenting over them wasn't going to change anything.

---

2 Robert de Clari: Knight of Picardy under Count Peter of Amiens circa AD 1170–1216.
3 Alexios III Angelos: Byzantine emperor from AD 1195 to 1203. Born circa AD 1153, died AD 1211.

The entire armada of ships—galleys, transport ships, and more—was visible in the waters of the Bosporus the next morning. The number of ships from Venice and elsewhere was stunning. Fluttering flags of all colors adorned the tall masts. If a man had a large enough stride, he could run from one deck to the next, all the way across the Bosporus.

De Clari was ready for the coming fight. He too was frustrated they would no longer be liberating Jerusalem, but at least with success in Constantinople, they would be paid, and he could return home. "Constantinople thinks it is impregnable, but we will not let their treachery stand." The galleys were all well-armed and well-manned. The high masts and flag poles stood tall like a forest.

Estienne's demeanor changed as hundreds of ships stretched across the Bosporus to the end of the horizon. The sight of the sheer number of ships was awe-inspiring. "Once we've taken what we need from Alexios in Constantinople, we'll be on our way to Jerusalem. The enormous quantity of ships will also scare the Muslims into submission."

"Everyone needs to form up. We'll begin loading the transports tonight at dusk." Robert de Clari looked down at his aide, glad he was no longer complaining about their impending battle on Constantinople. "It will be a glorious battle. God will be on our side." De Clari tried to assuage his own frustrations over the direction of the crusade. He knew Jerusalem was in their plans no more. Not this crusade. *After we take what we want from Constantinople, there will be no assault on Jerusalem nor on Alexandria. We will be going home. I will be going home.*

✝✝✝

SAINT MARY OF BLACHERNAE CHURCH, CONSTANTINOPLE
MORNING, JULY 10, AD 1203

"Father, European invaders are amassing across the Bosporus in Chalcedon, where I grew up. What do we do?" Arcadius was nervous. His eyes darted around the sanctuary. He wondered if the church would be destroyed in the battle. He was a transitional deacon and had never been in a war. He wanted to care for people, not kill them. He so hungered to be a priest, and now this war and the one before it. It would be a few years until his ordination with Father Christos as his mentor. He was ready to give his life to his Lord and God.

"Arcadius, things will get worse, much worse, and it may last a long time. We'll need to be ready to help the injured and wounded. There will be many. We can use the sanctuary for space. We'll need to be prepared with boiling water and medicines and tools for surgery." Father Christos was surprised the battle for Constantinople would be this soon, if ever. "You need not worry. This army lost to the Chalcedons. Why would they think they would fare better here? This city is the most protected in the world."

Father Christos tried to allay the fears of his subordinate. "This battle should never begin. We should be fighting the real enemies—the Muslims in Jerusalem—not fellow Christians in Constantinople." As he said this, his mind raced forward. "Why are Christians battling Christians?" He said half out loud, half mumbling, not wanting to reveal his true emotions to his subordinate.

Arcadius was nervous enough. *Were they here to get their vengeance for what was done to the Catholics twenty years before, or was it just for the money?*

"Who are the real enemies?" Arcadius was perplexed. "What do you mean?"

"Arcadius, you were only a boy, but twenty years ago, the people were loyal to the emperor and our church." Christos emphasized *our church.* "They massacred thousands of followers of the western church . . . the Catholics. They drove them off, raped their women, and stole their property. That slaughter was a stain on us. Christian was fighting Christian. I only hope and pray the men—the Christians across the Bosporus—will seek compassion, not vengeance." Father Christos looked around and hoped this church wouldn't be destroyed. This was his church. It was hallowed ground, but bloodlust was blind.

"The real enemies are the enemies of Jesus Christ . . . those wishing to bring down the church." Christos spoke to himself and to Arcadius. His memories of his last hospital work came welling forth. Father Christos turned away from his protégé, and he almost vomited. He turned back to Arcadius, then turned away again. This time the spasms came twice. He was able to hold back his breakfast. The sound of sawing bone and the smell of death came back to him from the depths of his memories of the battles of the First Crusade. Death everywhere. The spasms returned.

"Father, are you okay?" Arcadius handed him a kerchief to wipe his mouth.

"Yes, yes." He held back a cough and could feel the blood filling his head and neck. He sat down and gathered his composure. The urge to dry heave had stopped, but he had an awful taste in his mouth. His face grew hot, as he tried unsuccessfully to suppress the memories.

"Begin collecting water and fill everything you can. Then bring any and all clothes. We'll need them to stem the bleeding. There will be a lot of blood." Father Christos's mind raced, as he focused on what was ahead. "We'll need to organize the nuns as well. Everyone will be needed." Father Christos looked around. He was certain there would be more required.

"Don't worry, Arcadius. God is on our side." His own words rang hollow as the urge to dry heave came back. His head filled again with blood. It felt like it would explode. He leaned over; saliva dripped from his open mouth. He couldn't staunch the need to vomit. This time it came gushing out.

✝✝✝

Saint Mary of Blachernae Church, Constantinople
Sunrise, July 18, AD 1203

"Arcadius, thank God, our casualties are very low."

The battle had lasted about a week. Father Christos's preparations had paid off. Of the wounded, only a handful needed an amputation. A few that might have needed one didn't survive. Most had simple wounds.

One young soldier lost a leg after it had been crushed by a hurtling projectile that had careened over the wall in the dark. The ballistas had hit their mark. Ballistas could hurl their hundred-pound projectiles hundreds of yards at speeds that devastated anything but the thickest of walls. The soldier was knocked unconscious by the blow. If he awoke, it would be to a lost leg.

Memories of his previous encounter with those wounded in battle during the First Crusade returned, allowing him to help the leeches in their gruesome work. Memories of the moans and cries of pain and the smell of blood, urine, vomit, and sweat came welling back. He worked hard to care for the wounded soldiers and to keep from vomiting. The taste of his own stomach acid persisted.

Christos and Arcadius made their rounds to the patients. Standing over a soldier who had lost his leg, Arcadius could only manage to say, "Bless you, my son. Bless you." *Did Christ fail this man? If both sides are fighting in the name of Christ, which side will God save?*

The Crusaders were now inside the walls of the city, roaming the streets. They were hungry to be paid and hungry to wreak vengeance for the deaths of their countrymen twenty years before. They would exact their payments with gold, silver, and art . . . and women.

They marched right in with little resistance. The southern walls weren't built to repel an invasion from the water. None of the defenders thought they would simply scale the walls from ship-borne siege towers, yet the attackers were able to find this one weakness and exploit it. The guardians of the city were devastated—gobsmacked. The richest and most protected city on earth fell to the pilgrims, the crusaders.

"My leg! My leg!" The boy woke up and saw his leg. He screamed, and then the pain hit him. "Ahhh! My knee, Father, my knee." His knee was gone, and he suffered phantom pain where the projectile had crushed his leg. He reached out and grabbed Father Christos's hand and squeezed harder than he ever squeezed. "Father!" His eyes welled up, and tears streamed down his temples and cheeks. The pain overcame him, and he wailed again.

"My son, let me pray for you?" Father Christos stroked the boy's blood-stained hair with his other hand. Father Christos silently cried inside, wondering what life would be like without his left leg.

"Father, how will I live with only one leg?" The boy could barely get the words out between the pangs of pain. Images of what life would be like with only one leg came to him, and he began to whimper.

"You have sacrificed much in honor of the realm. It will not go unnoticed by God and the empire." Father Christos knew these words to be true but understood they meant nothing in comparison to the lifelong loss of a leg. Christos had seen many men after the First Crusade missing a leg or arm, or more. All required extra care from their families and the church.

Christos took a short breath, inhaling the smell of vomit. He had to look away. The smell of blood, alcohol, and death overcame him. He was unable to hold back the urge to dry heave.

"God, bless this boy. Bless him." As much as he tried to focus on his prayer, his prayers were interrupted by his spasms.

Arcadius wiped drool from the boy's mouth, then shooed a fly about to land on the boy's forehead. He was silent, as he shooed more flies away. Guilt welled up within him. *Why wasn't I wounded? How would I have taken on that pain? Would I have had the courage to repel the invaders from the gates? Is that what Christ did for us, for me on the cross?*

With the battle over, the memory of the sound of sawing bone was all that remained. It was something he'd never forget. *How could I learn to try and say comforting words when words were as empty as a missing leg?* He had memorized every word Christos had said to the wounded and repeated them, but they didn't help. His mind bolted between thoughts of guilt and disgust for what man could do to man.

"Arcadius, help that man. He needs some wine." Christos noticed one of the men under his care reach out. The man had his eyes covered with a bandage over them.

Arcadius turned and saw the man on the bench behind him, trying to reach for a drink. One of his arms was also wounded. Arcadius looked closer and saw the bandages where his hand was supposed to be. His hand was gone.

"Let me help you." Arcadius poured the wine into a cup and held it to his lips.

"Thank you, Father. Will you pray for my family? I'm not sure they survived. I saw our home destroyed by the trebuchets."

Arcadius began to pray. It was more mumbled than spoken. He had trouble forming his words, so glad yet ashamed he was untouched by the fighting.

"Where was your home, my son? Arcadius finally asked with a bit more fortitude. "I can go for you and inquire about your family. Do you have any children there?" Arcadius longed to be out in the fresh air. "Perhaps I could go and visit them and give them news." Arcadius, however, wanted to avoid having the soldier's family visit their father here in the makeshift hospital. It was no place for family.

Father Christos watched approvingly, thinking he would like to help Arcadius find the soldier's home and see about his family. The horrid stench of sweat, blood, and death overpowered the normal aroma of incense he had enjoyed in the sanctuary only a few short days ago. Sounds of sawing bone, screaming, and moaning had replaced the sounds of chants and prayers.

†††

SAINT MARY OF BLACHERNAE CHURCH, CONSTANTINOPLE
AFTERNOON, JULY 22, AD 1203

A few days had passed, and the influx of wounded soldiers had ceased. The fighting was over. The wounded were on their way to recovering, and only the worst remained in the temporary hospital. The last two days had no more deaths.

A commotion at the entrance to the church startled Father Christos. The commotion was loud enough that a hush came over the sanctuary. Even the moans of pain were interrupted. With the fighting over, no more wounded were expected.

"Where is the priest of this church?" Robert de Clari asked the first nun he saw. He was well outfitted with his sword in his hilt. With the sun shining in from outside, large dark, red stains could be seen on the stone floor. The crusader handed his helmet over to his aide, Estienne. His tunic was stained and partially torn from the battle.

The nun tending a soldier near the narthex nodded in the direction of the priest.

"I am Father Christos." Christos stood up, glanced down at the boy he was ministering to and gave him a comforting smile. He turned to the westerner.

"I am told you have a cloth, a relic, that you display on Good Fridays," Robert de Clari stated in a commanding tone. There was nothing in his manner that meant he would be disobeyed. "It has the face of the Son of God on it. You are to take me to it at once." It was only an hour or two past sunrise, and the cool, fresh breeze from the sea followed him in through the door.

Arcadius turned and moved to Father Christos's side. Christos hesitated a moment.

"I assure you, I am not here to steal it from you."

Father Christos stared into the crusader's eyes. His duty was here with his patients, but he also didn't want to make a disturbance that would reduce the calm that was now returning. With sheer exhaustion from the last ten days of endless care for the wounded and dying, he had no will left to deny the request. "I will take you there." He was numb to everything, and this request simply added to his indifference.

"Arcadius, fetch the keys to the treasury." Father Christos said these words without taking his gaze off the French knight. Arcadius moved quickly to the priest's quarters, where the keys were kept. He returned within a few minutes.

Father Christos paused a few moments and looked over the sanctuary. The nuns had resumed their care of the men. "Come this way." Christos directed the two to the rear of the church.

Robert de Clari and Estienne began speaking between themselves.

Christos could not make out what they were saying. He assumed it was French or possibly Italian.

Arcadius returned and met them at the gate to the treasury.

The three men waited while the iron gate was opened. The door behind the gate hadn't been opened in over a month, and Estienne stepped in to assist Arcadius. The smell of mildew mixed with incense floated through the cool air from behind the gate. It was a pleasant change from the stench of pain and death above in the sanctuary. Behind the door was darkness. No one brought a candle, yet even in the dark, Christos knew where the cloth was stored.

Arcadius's and Christos's eyes adjusted to the dark. Christos unlocked the gilded wooden case and handed Arcadius the keys. Next to the case was a contraption used during the services to display the cloth at full length. He opened the case and began to remove the leather valise. The beauty of the case could not be appreciated in the dark. It was hand carved, gilded in gold and silver, and adorned with gems from three centuries before.

The valise was larger than de Clari had expected. He was expecting a small cloth, a face cloth, but this valise held something much larger.

Christos handed the valise to Arcadius. "Come this way. You'll want to see this in the proper light." Father Christos led the way to the altar, where the sun's rays illuminated the area. The sun was sinking in the sky yet streamed in bright enough so they could avoid taking it outside. "We will display this icon again for Good Friday."

Father Christos removed the cloth from the valise. It was folded so that a face—a graven image—could be seen.

The ghostly face was very different than de Clari was expecting. In his mind's eye, he was expecting a painted face, like a portrait, but this was nothing like that. There was no color, just shadowy red-brown areas of dark and light. The cloth wasn't just woven. It had a chevron type of weave, one not found in his hometown.

Christos didn't volunteer to unfold the cloth. Being in the presence of the divine cloth was a welcome comfort to what was going on in the rest of the church.

De Clari had no idea there was much more to be seen. He knelt and prayed. Christos knelt next to him, realizing they were both connected by God but separated on opposite sides of politics.

"In Nomine Patri . . ." Father Christos began to pray. Estienne and Arcadius knelt as well.

✝✝✝

Saint Mary of Blachernae Church, Constantinople
8:00 a.m., Wednesday, April 16, AD 1204

Daily Mass was held in the sanctuary. Today very few were in attendance. Although the second battle for Constantinople was over, parishioners feared returning to worship. Triumphant western crusaders roamed throughout the city and oftentimes terrorized the inhabitants. On the northern side of the sanctuary, there were still eleven suffering Roman soldiers being cared for by the nuns, lying out of the way of the worshipers.

The second battle for Constantinople was far more devastating than the first, only eight months before. This time the treachery of the shifting politics between Constantinople, Rome, Venice, and all the other great peoples of Europe made no sense for either side. Supposed allies became bitter enemies. The crusaders were out for blood and money, and they were successful. Christ was absent from both sides fighting in the name of Christ.

Once the fighting was over, the bloodlust and vengeance of the conquerors—the supposed Christian crusaders—were on full display as they took everything as their payment. At first, it was taken from the royals. Then it was pillaged from the nobles and private possessions. Finally, they started plundering the treasuries of the churches.

"Arcadius, take the Holy Week vestments and store them in my quarters. For evening Mass, replace them with the regular altar vestments." Father Christos was at the altar consuming the remains of the Communion wine and bread. Neither had yet noticed that five Danish soldiers had entered the sanctuary. Two of the Danes went to the altar; three went to the nuns.

Arcadius and Father Christos turned and took a step in the direction of the nuns, but their way was blocked. One soldier hit Father Christos in the stomach with the hilt of his sword. He fell to his knees. Arcadius was thrown to the floor.

"We're not here for you, Father. We have other things in mind." The soldier laughed and looked over at the nuns.

"How dare—" This time Father Christos was hit over the head. He was on his knees, his forehead bleeding. The nuns screamed in resistance. The three soldiers each had one nun in their hands. The nuns put up a fight, but they were no match for these much stronger, hardened men.

There was nothing Arcadius or Christos could do to intervene.

One of the nuns yelped.

From his knees, Christos looked directly at the soldier standing over him. "Sir, you are a Christian, or are you not? Leave these women alone!"

The soldier struck Christos again for his insolence. This time Christos fell on his side, numb from the blow.

The Dane smiled waiting his turn with the women.

The outsized doors to the narthex banged open, and a stream of light came in, illuminating the sanctuary turned hospital. A bird flew out, not wanting to see what would come next.

Twelve men and their commander entered, their clothes soiled from the battles here in Constantinople and in Zara. They were part of the French contingent commanded by and totally loyal to Burgundian Othon de la Roche.[4] Now that Constantinople was conquered, they were ready to move farther south to fight the Muslims and free Jerusalem. Instead, they would be going home, whatever that meant.

Some were happy to be done, some were afraid to miss the adrenaline of the fighting, and others were disappointed they didn't accomplish their mission of freeing Jerusalem. Although their ambitions were to go to Jerusalem, their march on the south was now a distant fantasy. They were loyal to their Burgundian nobleman and would follow him wherever he took them . . . as long as they were paid.

De la Roche's first lieutenant, Guilleaume, nodded toward the nuns. He

---

4 Othon de la Roche: Burgundian nobleman. Eventual duke of Athens from AD 1204 to 1225. Died circa AD 1234.

and four of his men made their way to them and the three Danish soldiers. Guilleaume had been with de la Roche over twenty years and had saved his life on a few occasions. De la Roche trusted him with his life.

"We don't want no trouble, but we do want these women!" one of the Danish soldiers barked in a statement of bravado, not yet ready to back off his conquest of the nuns.

Guilleaume took out his sword, as did the four French soldiers as they approached the Danes. Two additional French soldiers followed. The Danes didn't back down.

"Enough!" de la Roche commanded, and the three soldiers near the women let go of their grips on the nuns. One of the nuns spat on the Dane after he let her go. Christos was still on the floor recovering from the blow to his head. Arcadius stood and sneered at his Danish captor.

"You shall leave us now," de la Roche commanded. All his men held their swords, ready to take charge of the Danes. "You will let these women go!"

The nuns clustered together to escape their former captors.

The five Danes were well outnumbered by the twelve Frenchmen. They slowly bowed to the nobleman and backed out of the sanctuary the way they came in. One of them took a swig of their wine and gestured to spit in the direction of the French soldiers but decided against it. They would seek to satisfy their lust elsewhere.

One of the French soldiers called out to the two clergymen. "Priest." Two of them moved to surround Father Christos and Arcadius in front of the altar. The Communion serving dishes were still in disarray. This year was different from prior years. Holy Week would have meant using the pewter and bronze Communion implements. With the conquest of the city by the crusaders, nothing of value was revealed. The looting was underway throughout the city. Father Christos stood with Arcadius at his side grabbing his arm to help him to his feet. The two soldiers blocked a potential retreat for the two clergymen.

A second pair of the French contingent walked over to the nuns. The nuns stood and faced them, not sure of their fates. The soldiers surrounded them. Was one enemy simply replaced by a second?

"We are here to help safeguard the treasures of the church," de la Roche announced. He was one of the first of the French crusaders to enter the city during the second conquest, and he was collecting his due. "Father, we wish to catalog and protect the church treasures. You will help my men bring them to my quarters. Show me to the treasury at once."

"We are perfectly capable of . . ." Father Christos began to respond but backed off as one of de la Roche's men moved to threaten him. De la Roche simply looked on. His expression of confidence and inevitability didn't waver. He was in charge.

From his encounter with the Danes, Christos could still taste the blood from inside his mouth. He looked at the small group of men. There was little he could do. "You will be excommunicated for—" His protest elicited a strike to his cheek, and he fell to the floor a second time. De la Roche looked down at the clergyman, glad his man interrupted this insolence before more drastic measures were needed.

"I apologize for the overreaction of my man. They're all very exhausted, and I have them working this day. Let me help you up." De la Roche stepped forward and helped the priest to his feet. He brushed off Christos's tunic as he stood facing him. "Since we are not marching on Jerusalem or Alexandria, we wanted to make certain our efforts are not in vain."

"The pope, Pope Innocent III, has declared the destruction or looting of religious valuables an offense to God, sir." Father Christos knew his protests would be ignored but said it anyway.

"Yes, of course, that is why we have come to protect them. Just like we protected the nuns from harm." De la Roche smiled. "You certainly don't want the Danes or the Italians to take them." The soldier in front of Christos stepped back. Guilleaume and the other French soldiers joined them at the altar.

Although this knight was different from the Danes, the threat to the clergymen and the nuns was clear. "Take us to the treasury. Now."

Arcadius and Father Christos pointed to a door behind the altar.

Two men helped the two clergymen through the door followed by de la Roche and Guilleaume.

"Move." One of the soldiers gave the younger priest a slight push to accelerate the pace.

"Break down the gate." De la Roche didn't have any patience to find the key. He stood outside the door, waving his men inside. "Take it all. Leave nothing behind."

Father Christos and Arcadius watched in horror as each piece was taken. Their whole lives had been dedicated to the protection of the treasures. They were incensed as the French showed no reverence to what was taken. All of it was treated as a simple exchange of money. The last to be removed was the gilded wooden case that held the holy Shroud of our Savior.

Christos thought quickly. "My lord, let us come with you to care for the—" He was struck again as he tried to plead to protect the treasures. Both clergymen were thrown to the ground, this time with more force than from the Danes.

Christos and Arcadius could already sense the loss of their connection to the holy Shroud. Each felt a shiver as the blood drained from their heads. *I failed you! We failed. I can't simply let it out of our purview. It's been a part of my life for almost twenty years.*

Father Christos looked on with pleading eyes as the last of the treasures were carted off, the loss of each treasure adding more to his emptiness. "My lord, I beg of you. Take us with you to help you keep these treasures safe."

The men finished their task of bringing the treasures into the protection of the Burgundian noble. The church treasury was bare. De la Roche followed his men back into the sanctuary, proud of his work. He stopped and stared at the two clergymen and paused a moment. "Bring them." His command echoed through the sanctuary. "It will be good to have them. They will show how we are protecting these holy relics and treasures from the looters. Boniface,[5] leader of the Fourth Crusade, will have nothing to complain about."

†††

Danish Encampment outside the City Wall, Constantinople
1:30 a.m., Friday, April 18, AD 1204

"I'm not going to let those Frenchies take my women and my payments," Steinbiorn said, sharpening his sword. He was one of the five Danes in the Blachernae church. "That money and those women were ours. I didn't come here to not get my share of gold and silver. No good Dane returns home without any treasure to show for their efforts."

The Danes had each stewed that whole night in their resentment of the French for taking their payments and for taking their pleasures with those nuns.

"Is there a plan?" Sigmund whispered. He scratched his arm. The air was damp and cool. He stirred the fire to get some heat and suddenly turned his head to avoid the waft of smoke blowing into his face.

Steinbiorn handed him the sharpening stone.

"Wake up, Roald. We leave in five minutes." The fog of the wine earlier that night had worn off. Steinbiorn was thinking clearly and took charge of the small contingent. He had gotten a few hours of sleep and was now eager to exact vengeance on those French. He was the more senior of the three and gave the orders. Each of them had done well in the fight in Zara, but there was little in payments for their services.

Roald had been wounded in his left arm, but it was now fully healed. It hadn't detracted from his courage during the siege of Constantinople.

Roald began stirring the fire as Steinbiorn explained his plan. He and

---

5 Boniface I: Ninth marquess of Montferrat AD 1192. Leader of the Fourth Crusade from AD 1201 to 1204. King of Thessalonica from AD 1205 to 1207.

Sigmund listened intently. The Blachernae Palace, where de la Roche and his men were encamped, was only a few hundred yards away inside the gate. It was right next to the Saint Mary's Church of Blachernae. "We'll enter the city through the Regia Gate. That will allow us to approach the palace from the south. That way, we'll have cover right up until we reach it. If the gates aren't open, we'll have to scale the wall, but that shouldn't be difficult. There won't be any guards to worry about.

"At this hour, the guards at the palace will be asleep, as we saw last night and the night before. We'll slit their throats and then make our way inside. From there, we'll need to find the treasures they took from us. They're most likely in a vault in the cellar. Absolute silence will be critical to success."

It took them about a half hour to prepare, and the three were on their way. After a few minutes' walk from their encampment, they reached the Regia Gate. Only one torch remained lit. The others had died out and hadn't been relit. The gate was open and unmanned. None of the crusader factions felt it was their duty to guard the city, so it remained open to any and to all.

"Quickly. Move quickly."

A man stood directly inside the gate, next to the wall and partially hidden behind one of the homes. He was dressed in black, and in the darkness, almost invisible.

As they passed the man, the sacks they had intended to use for their loot slipped through Roald's belt and fell to the ground. They lay there just inside the gate, Roald unaware he lost them.

The man dressed in black looked on with no emotion in his face.

✝✝✝

OTHON DE LA ROCHE'S QUARTERS, BLACHERNAE PALACE,
CONSTANTINOPLE
2:30 A.M., FRIDAY, APRIL 18, AD 1204

As on the previous night when Steinbiorn surveyed the palace, there were only three guards, all asleep. Roald approached the first one, sleeping outside the palace, and dispatched him with a quick thrust. Roald wiped the blood off his knife, while blood spurted out of the guard's neck with each of the few remaining beats of his heart.

Steinbiorn and Sigmund did the same with their quarries. There would be no resistance from the guards. Inside the palace, Steinbiorn and his two compatriots found de la Roche's men sleeping on the floor. Empty clay wine jugs and sacks were strewn everywhere, and everyone slept. A woman stirred, her leg sticking out from under her man's cloak. The man she was with snored the loudest. De la Roche's men had enjoyed themselves with mead from the palace cellars and companions from the brothels in Constantinople.

"The three guards won't be waking at all tonight," Steinbiorn said. Revenge tasted sweeter with the three dead.

Roald fell in behind him, his knife ready for another neck to filet.

Roald tapped Steinbiorn's shoulder and pointed to his right to the frock of a priest. "It's that priest from the church. What's he doing here?" The priest was asleep on the floor, leaning up against a feather-filled cushion from the sleeping quarters.

The other two stopped and turned in the direction Roald was looking. They made their way over to the priest, not making a sound.

"Don't kill him. He'll know where the treasures are." Steinbiorn didn't want the murder of a priest on his conscience.

Their plan was to take the treasures while the French were asleep. They didn't want to risk one of them waking the others and then being outnumbered by the larger French contingent.

Roald and Sigmund moved more quickly. They both reached the priest at the same time. Sigmund pounced on top of him while Roald grabbed his neck and put his hand over the man's mouth. They did all they could to keep him quiet, so as not to wake any of the others. He choked the priest—not enough to kill him, yet enough to make certain he would be quiet.

The woman with the leg sticking out under the cloak stirred, not realizing the slight commotion was from the impending attack. She rolled over and went back to sleep.

✝✝✝

Roald showed Arcadius his knife. In the darkness, the priest could barely make it out but recognized it for what it was. Fear surged to his face as the adrenaline coursed through his veins. His wide-open eyes gave away the terror in his heart. He wanted to cough but tried to hold it back. Finally, he coughed, but with Roald's hand over his mouth, it was well muffled.

Sigmund shifted his weight to where his knee was, focusing his weight directly on Arcadius's chest. It caused the blood to rush to Arcadius's head. "Don't move. If you make a sound, you'll meet your fate."

Roald pressed the tip of his blade into Arcadius's cheek, and a drop of blood emerged.

Arcadius could smell the putrid breath and body odor of the Dane, but nodded his assent.

"If you help us, nothing will happen to you. You will take us to where the stolen gold and silver are stored." Steinbiorn watched as Roald and Sigmund forced the man to his feet. The strength in the young priest was no match for the seasoned soldiers.

Arcadius reluctantly complied.

"This way." As they moved, Sigmund held the priest's shoulder with his left hand and the dagger in his right. Roald tied a leather strap around Arcadius's neck to prevent him from running. It acted as a choker in case he decided to alert the others.

Arcadius knew that with these men, the church's treasures would be melted down and sold. At least with de la Roche, they might be saved intact. At least de la Roche promised he would keep them for what they were. Arcadius's first thought was to make a sound to save the gold and silver, but Sigmund had his dagger out and pressed against his rib, which dissuaded him from resisting.

They made their way to the cellar where the former resident kept his mead and wine. Before they went down the stairs, Steinbiorn grabbed a candle and lit it in the fireplace. He held his hand around the flame to minimize the light that penetrated the dark room.

Blood from Arcadius's cheek dripped down his neck.

"Where is the key? Who has it?" Sigmund pressed harder on the dagger.

"Guilleaume. Guilleaume has it." Arcadius squeezed the words out, the choker making it difficult to speak. He glanced in Guilleaume's direction, then realized he had given de la Roche's first lieutenant a death sentence.

Steinbiorn moved quickly to Guilleaume, put his hand over his mouth, and sliced open his neck in one single motion. The first lieutenant's death took only a second. There was a slight gurgling sound as the air left his lungs for the last time. Steinbiorn found the key on a leather strap around the man's neck and cut it loose

"Move! Quickly!" Sigmund said under his breath. He let go of his grip, as the stairwell wasn't wide enough for him to hold Arcadius while they descended. The candle barely lit the way. As they descended the dark spiral staircase, Arcadius mis-stepped and had to regain his balance. The choker jerked tighter around his neck and caused him to gag.

They reached the locked gate to the cellar at the bottom of the stair. Steinbiorn handed the key to Arcadius. Sigmund turned and pressed his dagger into the neck of the priest. Arcadius opened the gate. The candle flickered, and the church ware of gold and silver pieces could be seen on a table. Sigmund and Steinbiorn smiled, ecstatic with their find. Roald loosened his grip on the choker.

Arcadius glared at him in both rage and fear.

Sigmund picked up the gold Communion goblet from the Blachernae Church. It was a beautiful piece of art, etched with Jesus on the cross on one side and Mary holding baby Jesus on the other.

At that moment, Roald realized he no longer had the sack tied under his belt. They had nothing to use to carry the treasure out of the palace.

There was an open chest on the floor behind the table, and draped over the side of the chest was a folded cloth . . . the holy Shroud.

"Take the cloth and put all you can carry into it. Rip it in half if you must," Roald commanded.

Arcadius breathed in. He couldn't believe his eyes and ears. The cloth was the most valuable item in the cellar, and they were going to rip it in half. In the dim light of the candle, the cloth didn't appear to be anything special.

"Leave the cloth in one piece. I beg of you. It is a very special cloth and has been with the church for hundreds of years." Arcadius now lied without giving up the cloth's true identity. "It was given by Pope Sylvester[6] to Constantine himself. It holds a very special meaning." It was all he could come up with. "Take my cloak if you'd like. It will hold more."

Roald unfolded the cloth and saw stains on it. "It looks like you priests have spilled wine on here many times. It can't be that special." Roald took out his knife, preparing to cut the cloth in half.

"No!" Arcadius shouted, and they all froze, afraid the French would awake.

Sigmund moved to quiet the priest. Arcadius struggled from Sigmund's grip and removed his cloak. Steinbiorn moved up the stairs and listened for any sounds, before returning after about thirty seconds. "It's all quiet." He slapped Arcadius across his face with the back of his hand, and he fell to the damp floor. Steinbiorn leaned over the priest and whispered forcefully, "Don't make another sound."

"Leave the cloth in one piece. Take it and everything else. Maybe we can sell it. There must be some value in it if this fool is so adamant about it." Sigmund took the cloak and threw it to Roald.

He pressed his dagger into the side of Arcadius, who was on his knees on the floor. He drew blood—enough to get his point across without killing him. The blade pierced the skin but not past the outside of the rib cage.

Arcadius wrenched his back away from Sigmund, but now the blood flowed more. He grabbed his side to staunch the flow and fell prostrate on the stone floor. The cold and damp of the stones and the shock of the wound caused him to shiver.

"We must go. Now! Tie 'em up." Sigmund took the choker and wound it tight around Arcadius's mouth. Then he took Arcadius's leather belt and tied

---

6 Pope Sylvester I: AD 285–335, pope from AD 314 to 334.

his hands behind his back. The blood continued to flow.

Roald grabbed the makeshift sack and slung it over his shoulder. As he left, he kicked Arcadius across the face and knocked him out cold. They didn't want to kill him unless they had to. He'd be out for at least twenty or thirty minutes. Steinbiorn put out the torch so they could escape in darkness.

✝✝✝

"Father Christos. Father Christos, wake up! Wake up!" The man in black whispered. Christos was asleep, alone on the floor. "Wake up!" It was finally enough to awaken Christos. The man in black stood still, not showing himself.

Christos looked around but saw no one. The man in black hid behind a large wardrobe next to the corner of the room. Christos looked around and got up to see who had aroused him from his sleep. He tried to be quiet but made some noise when he tripped on another of de la Roche's men, Edward, sleeping a few feet away.

It was the end of the third watch. Edward awoke. The fire was out, and he would normally have been awakened long before to have taken over the next watch. He looked up with a jolt, realizing something was wrong. The fire was out, and it shouldn't be. He didn't want to be disciplined, nor did he want his friend to be disciplined for having slept through his watch. Normally the watch would have ended well before the fire went out, so that a few new logs could be added to keep it going.

Father Christos also noticed the fire was out. Normally the night guard would have kept it going, but not tonight. *Who was it that awakened me? Called my name?*

Christos fumbled around in the dark and realized Arcadius was missing. "Arcadius, where are you?" Christos whispered and then saw something from the corner of his eye. He also heard what sounded like scraping metal-on-metal coming from the direction of the cellar. "Arcadius." This woke Lehan, another of the Frenchmen. He was sleeping right next to the fire and should have been on watch like Edward.

Steinbiorn heard the voice and panicked, drawing his sword.

Christos saw the three men. "What's going on here?"

Lehan stood and moved toward Christos and the voices. He wasn't awake enough yet to think clearly. He never fully awakened from his stupor. Sigmund stabbed him with his dagger, and he fell to the floor. The three Danes began to run.

"Get up! Get up!" Christos yelled to anyone who could hear. Something was wrong, but in the darkness, it wasn't certain. Other men awoke and started to react to the unfolding calamity. The women woke and covered themselves, eyes wide open.

With his sword drawn, Lehan's best friend, Artus, moved quickly to the palace entrance. Another joined him. The Danes were trapped.

Steinbiorn turned and ran now in the other direction. There was another exit in the back.

Christos didn't have a sword. He picked up a spent torch from the night before and threw it at the Danes. It glanced off the back of Sigmund, but did not inflict any damage. It didn't slow the three.

Unable to find Arcadius, Christos was frantic. "Get up! Everyone! Get up!"

Edward saw the retreating men and ran directly toward them, blade in hand. He was faster than all of them and tackled Roald, causing Arcadius's cloak and all the treasures to spill out. The gold Communion goblet hit the floor, denting the rim as it hit and sounding like a dull bell. It would never look the same.

Both men tumbled and rolled on the floor. Roald lost the battle as the French blade pierced his side.

✝✝✝

Steinbiorn and Sigmund continued running, knowing they were no match for the awakening larger force of the French. Their anger mixed with fear, as they recognized they weren't going to escape alive. They had failed, but they were going to take down a few Frenchmen with them. They found the kitchen. There were two Frenchmen waiting for them.

"You French pigs!" With confidence in hand-to-hand combat, Steinbiorn thrust forward and was able to quickly subdue the first Frenchman.

Sigmund wasn't as lucky, as there were now five Frenchmen, including de la Roche, in the cramped space of the kitchen. He was hit with a fatal wound and fell to the floor, his elbow hitting first and then his head. Blood flowed from wounds on his leg and chest, making a dark puddle under him barely visible in the murky moonlight.

Steinbiorn was met by de la Roche. Steinbiorn was a good match for de la Roche, but there were now two other Frenchmen behind him. "I'm not going down alone!" Steinbiorn lunged forward, fully expecting to be cut down by de la Roche. His expectation was met.

De la Roche deflected Steinbiorn's sword with his and sidestepped. As he turned, he stabbed the Dane in the neck with his dagger. Steinbiorn died instantly as the sword cut his spinal cord just above the larynx. He fell first to his knees, then onto his side.

"Are there any others? Get torches and search the palace. Every corner!" De la Roche barked his orders.

"You. Follow me!" Edward commanded. Two men followed to find the church ware strewn around the palace floor in front of the fireplace. "Get that fire going and get me a torch!" The man who killed Roald still stood over his body. "Get me a torch!"

✝✝✝

"Where is Arcadius? Where is he?" Christos shouted out. There was no response. He retrieved the torch he had thrown at the Danes, dipped it in oil, and lit it from the embers that smoldered in the fireplace. Finally, there was light to see the remains of the calamity. Still, Arcadius was nowhere to be found.

"The cellar! The cellar!" De la Roche ran to the cellar. He wasn't the first one down the stairs. It was the only place Christos hadn't looked.

Christos was the first. Leaning his shoulder against the wall so he could go even faster, he bounded down the spiral marble stairs. "Arcadius!"

Arcadius was unconscious, blood flowing out of his side.

Christos untied him and pulled the rag from around his face and mouth and used it to staunch the bleeding in his side. "Arcadius, wake up, wake up!"

Arcadius started to stir. He was in Christos's arms.

De la Roche untied his hands. "What happened? What happened! How did you get down here?"

"Those men. From the church. The Danes. It was them. They f-f-forced me here!" Arcadius coughed. The loss of blood made him lightheaded; the cold dampness caused intense shivering. His wounds weren't fatal. "I'm s-s-sorry. There was n-n-nothing I could do. N-nothing. They were going to rip the Shroud in half. I tried, but I think they took it."

"It's okay. They didn't escape. None of them did."

"My lord, I think we have recovered everything, including the cloth." Edward appeared holding the Shroud. The men were gathering all of the other pieces. Edward bowed and handed the cloth over to de la Roche. It had been hastily and irreverently folded.

"Good work, man. You have done well." De la Roche said, still assessing the damage and potential losses. "You all have done well. Is anyone else hurt?"

More men tried to come down the stairs, but there wasn't room for all of them.

"We have two, maybe three dead. No one otherwise wounded." Edward looked around at the empty table. "We're still looking for Lazare. He had the watch."

"Are any of the invaders alive?"

"No, my lord." Edward turned to face de la Roche. "We found all of their bodies. That is everything."

"Take the bodies to the water tonight. And dump them into the Golden Horn. Do it at once. In the dark. I don't want anyone to know what happened here and what these swine may have found." De la Roche didn't want any suspicion as to the valuables he had taken into his protection. "They don't deserve a proper burial."

"Father, how bad is the wound? Will you be able to tend to Arcadius?"

"Yes, my lord. It appears he was stabbed in the side and then hit over the head." Christos looked at the welt on the side of Arcadius's hairline. "There will be a lump on his forehead, and the wound in his side doesn't appear to be fatal. It appears he was able to slow the thieves enough for the rest of us to awake and overtake them."

"Yes, you both will be rewarded." De la Roche looked around at the empty cellar. He placed the Shroud back down on the table. "At first light, reorganize this room." With adrenaline in his veins, he bolted past the few men standing behind Edward and up the stairs.

"Edward. Bring the treasures to the cellar and relock them. Post two guards in front of the gate for the rest of the evening."

De la Roche reached the top of the stairs and moved to the front of the palace. "Where are the night guards? Where are they?"

He was followed by four of his men, and they began searching. Artus found Lazare, the only one unaccounted for. "Here he is." Except for the blood that had gushed out of his neck, the guard looked like he had fallen asleep and then had his throat slit, sitting against one of the columns.

"Post two guards. If they fall asleep, they will be thrashed!" De la Roche stood over the body, then turned and went back into the palace, disgusted that the weakness of a few men could cause so much havoc and the death of two or three others. "The guards will be doubled, and there will be no more drink nor women in the palace. Get those women out of here. Now!" De la Roche was unhappy with his men and more unhappy with himself for not having organized the guard better. He would not let that be repeated.

Off the Coast of Çanakkale, Constantinople
Dusk, Thursday, June 20, AD 1204

"I grew up right there on the coast, just west of Çanakkale." Arcadius looked out over the horizon at the spit of land coming up before them. He could see farms, forest, and small fishing boats working their nets. Above the fishing boats were seagulls hoping for some scraps.

He touched his side where the wound was. It was infected but improving. It had been over a month since he was stabbed defending the Shroud. "We are so close to my homeland. Until I moved to the church to serve with you in Constantinople, I had never been outside of my hometown." Arcadius breathed in the fresh air, enjoying the warmth of the day.

They'd been traveling since dawn, and they'd already reached Çanakkale. The French were split between two ships. Most of the men were on this ship. De la Roche, the treasure, and a few of the men were on the other ship.

Father Christos was scarcely listening. He could barely keep awake from the heat of the sun and the heat of his robes.

"My father owned a few fishing boats, and we fished off the south side of the point." Arcadius kept talking, not realizing that Christos's eyes were closed. "Every afternoon, about this time after all the boats were in, we'd take a special selection to our priest and the church. He's the one that convinced me that a life with the church would be for me. My brothers were going to be fishermen. I was going to be a fisher of men." Arcadius was so proud, thinking back on his early training about Jesus and the profession of Peter and Andrew.

"When we had been out on one of our boats and had no luck, my father would always say, 'Let's try the other side of the boat. Maybe good fortune will find us there.'" Arcadius smiled. He stayed silent for a few moments. As he thought of his homeland, he wondered about the future.

Will I ever return to my homeland or to Constantinople?

He wasn't sure if he was melancholic or excited, or both, about the new adventures in front of him. The last few months in Constantinople in the middle of the crusade were the worst. Athens was sure to be better.

Christos was asleep. His hands were interlocked over his round, slightly plump belly. He snorted in his sleep.

Arcadius could see both sides of the channel . . . Çanakkale on the port side, the Gallipoli Peninsula on the starboard.

Christos awoke with a start. "Arcadius, where are we? Do you know?"

"We are just passing Çanakkale. It's where I grew up." Arcadius was crest-fallen. Christos hadn't heard any of what he had just said.

"I'm sorry I missed it. Is it a nice place to live?"

Father Christos peered out over the channel. Both sides were in view. At first, he couldn't find any city. He looked back and realized it was now behind them. They were sitting well away from the men sent to take the relics and treasures back to Athens. It was bittersweet to accompany and protect the Shroud. He would have preferred remaining in Constantinople, but the Shroud was more important. It must be protected at all costs.

Other than the sailors on the ship, there were only six of them. They played *tavli*, the Greek version of the backgammon board game imported from India. Although gambling was frowned upon, all the soldiers participated, making the whooping and hollering even louder when someone lost or won.

The rest of de la Roche's men were on the other ships. Off to port and less than one hundred feet ahead was de la Roche's larger ship. The sails were unfurled, and it was beautifully outfitted.

"Is that what I think it is?" Christos could see another galley, a Venetian displaying a gold and red flag with a winged lion holding a sword. On the deck was what looked like four life-sized bronze horse statues. "Are they from the Hippodrome?" Christos felt the shock shoot directly through his heart. "They've taken everything. How could Christians steal such treasures from other Christians? They are the symbol of Constantinople and are over a thousand years old."

Edward could see the horses as well. "Those are beautiful. The Venetians have done well for themselves. Our treasures and the hundred fifty thousand silver marks make this trip for Sir Othon a splendid haul."

"God will punish those who do not act righteously," Christos whispered to himself. Arcadius heard him. They both hoped Edward hadn't. They both had a tenuous relationship with the soldiers guarding them.

All of the soldiers were ardent Christians, and after the melee at the palace, they had begun to associate with them in a more friendly way. They did not agree about the treasures taken into their protection.

Christos would have preferred they stayed in Constantinople, but with the other factions looting the city, better to be with the enemy you know than the enemy you don't. He leaned against the railing, not willing to face the lead ship. He couldn't bear to look at what was stolen from his city—his home. *What will God's wrath wreak upon them?*

The Port of Athens, Athens, Greece
4:00 p.m., Monday, June 24, AD 1204

"It was different not being on firm ground for Sunday Mass." Father Christos looked at Arcadius, thinking of the previous day. "I was glad to conduct Mass for the men and the sailors. I hope they were able to understand my message about the eighth commandment." Christos looked out over the bow of the ship. The city of Athens was getting closer, and he could start to make out some of the buildings in the city. There were hundreds of ships in the harbor. The strong wind blew their many-colored flags, so they stood out almost perpendicular to their masts.

"I'm not sure they thought it was stealing. I don't agree with it, but I think in their minds, it was taking what was rightfully theirs. It was their payment for services rendered." Arcadius was trying to look at the future, not the past. "Besides, would you rather have the holy Shroud protected under this duke or stolen or destroyed by the Venetians . . . or by the Danes?" Arcadius thought about what those Danes did to him and what they were going to do to the nuns, not certain whether they would have killed them all or let them loose after their deeds were done.

Father Christos was still enraged that the Venetians had taken the bronze statues from the Hippodrome. Everything had been taken. Everything. The great city of Constantinople, the capital of the Roman Empire, had been raped and pillaged down to its skeleton. Father Christos started to mouth a response, but Arcadius changed the subject.

"How long do you think we'll need to remain in Athens? Someday, I think I'd like to return to Çanakkale, but first I'd like to be ordained."

Edward walked over and interrupted the conversation. "So what do you two clergymen think of this fair city of Athens?" He was one of the soldiers assigned to guard the protected treasures and the two clergymen. "I'm still not sure I trust ya, but if we've come this far, I imagine it would be hard to run off with some of that gold." His voice was deep and raspy. He had also been on the Third Crusade and was now missing the adventure of going to Jerusalem. "I was only a lad for that one twenty years ago. I'm trained and ready to fight. I still want to go to Jerusalem, but that's not gonna happen now. Worse yet, I'm stuck protectin' this."

Arcadius looked at the soldier. He had seen what fighting could do to a man and the pain they could suffer from battle wounds.

"I think we'll all be glad to get our feet on stable ground. Although I often used to go fishing with my father, I think I prefer dry land." Arcadius continued the conversation, but before he finished, the soldier turned and went back to the tavli with the others. Edward wanted to talk and laugh about battles and fighting and killing. Fishing was not for the fighter.

"So, what do you think of this city of Athens? Do you see the Acropolis up on the point there, just under the clouds?" Edward returned to the two clergy and was in a better mood. He was in good spirits and was ready to step back on dry land. "I prefer the vineyards of France. That's what you could see on the hills of our village, but this will do." He smiled, ready to partake of some Greek wine as soon as he stepped off the ship.

A strong wind continued to blow in from the port, and dark storm clouds gathered. The captain decided to anchor about a hundred yards or so in the harbor. Bringing the ship into port was never an easy task, but this time the winds made it near impossible.

When the ship was finally anchored, a dinghy arrived to transport the men and supplies back and forth into port.

"We are to quickly disembark. There's a storm brewing, and we want to get these payments to safety."

About half the booty was loaded onto the smaller boat, along with three of the soldiers. It took about thirty minutes for the first round trip.

Edward pointed out a few of the sites dotted across the city. "You may actually enjoy living in Athens. For me, I'm eager to get to Jerusalem and free the city from the Muslims. I hope it will be soon before I'm too old."

"I pray you are successful." Father Christos agreed. Jerusalem should be governed by Christians, but he was still smarting from the sacking of Constantinople and the fighting of Christians against Christians. He kept his mouth shut, not wanting to antagonize this soldier. "I, too, am happy to return to solid ground."

The dinghy arrived back at their ship, and lines were thrown to secure it. "Tie up that last line on the cleat!" the helmsman barked.

The three remaining soldiers, Father Christos, and Arcadius had finished retrieving the remaining treasures from below deck about ten minutes earlier. The harbor waters were generally calm but were now getting choppy as the squalls turned into a storm. Raindrops began falling.

"Quickly, we must go quickly. The cloth cannot get wet!" Christos complained as he spied the darkening clouds coming up from the south. "We must hurry. We don't want to lose anything on the trip into port."

Four sailors rowed the dinghy. This time it had taken longer than the previous trip because they were fighting the strengthening winds from the storm. Each minute led to even stronger winds. They finally made it to the dock, the rain pelting them from all directions. The wind came sideways, angry to receive this party with their stolen treasures. Spray blew from the tips of the waves.

Noise from ships banging against their moorings grew louder. One ship broke its mooring, and a handful of sailors went scurrying to tie it back down.

"Bring the case first. We must keep it out of the rain," Christos screamed at Arcadius and their soldier friend, in an effort to be heard above the din. It was difficult to get it onto the dock, with the dinghy jumping up and down and back and forth in the wind and the waves. "Whatever you do, don't let it fall into the water."

The dinghy crashed against the dock, and the wooden railing cracked. Though the dinghy was tied down, it was still a rough exercise to get the case up and on the dock.

One of the soldiers from the first transport trip had been waiting for them and helped Arcadius and Edward up onto the dock. The rain got worse. Arcadius and Edward followed the lead of the other soldier and brought the case to the waiting covered transport wagon.

"I think we've succeeded. The wooden case and the valise inside should have kept the cloth dry." Father Christos had trouble pulling a canvas tarp over the case. The tarp was wet and heavy, so Arcadius reached out and helped him manhandle it to fully cover the gilded wooden case from the furious rain.

Father Christos exhaled. The journey was almost complete.

Edward, Arcadius, and the soldier continued to carry the remaining relics and treasures from the dock to the waiting wagons. The sailors had been placing the treasures from the dinghy as quickly as possible onto the dock. As they unloaded the treasures, the weight in the dinghy declined, making the dinghy less and less stable. With every bump against the dock, the men in the dinghy had to regain their balance.

"Father, I didn't realize how much had been taken." Arcadius watched as a second wagon stood by to transport the rest of the stolen treasures from Constantinople. He, too, was now disgusted with the crimes the crusaders had perpetrated on the Byzantine Empire. They both looked on in horror, realizing the quantity of what was carried on de la Roche's personal ship.

"Arcadius, I will travel with the first wagon. You will come with the second. I can't let the Shroud out of my sight." Father Christos was now afraid that after this long journey, they would be separated from this most valuable reminder of Jesus and His life—and death—on earth. "You come when the loading of the second wagon is complete. Leave nothing behind."

The soldier who had helped them from the dock climbed up onto the wagon, leaving no room for Father Christos. He felt like a servant walking behind his master, as his master rode ahead of him. He was adamant, though, not to let the cloth out of his sight.

Rain soaked through his cloak, weighing him down with every step. The wagon was so full the two horses couldn't proceed very quickly in front of him. In some cases, he had to help to push. The hills in Athens made the going even slower. They were going more uphill than down.

Rain pelted more furiously than ever. Then Christos saw a glimpse of a man. Christos's face and eyes were wet so that he didn't have a clear view. There he stood, just for a second, a man in black. Then he disappeared into the fog of the cascades of rain.

Christos rubbed his eyes to clear the rain, but the man was gone.

✝✝✝

TEMPORARY QUARTERS OF OTHON DE LA ROCHE, ATHENS, GREECE
7:00 P.M., MONDAY, JUNE 24, AD 1204

"Father Christos, I am so glad you made it safely to Athens." De la Roche was in good humor now that his treasures were safe with him in Athens. Although they were in temporary quarters, they were as lavish as those of the palace in Constantinople. "Boniface will soon be naming me duke of Athens. He, on the other hand, will be named king of Thessalonica."

The politics of the day were swaying in the direction of the crusaders. The spoils were to be divided among the victors. "I would like to appoint you as keeper of the treasury and, most importantly, of the holy Shroud."

Christos did his best to hide his disdain for what was done to Constantinople. He bit his tongue and bowed, remaining silent. He remembered the pain he felt in his heart that day as the Shroud was almost taken from him.

De la Roche continued. "You and your assistant will catalog each item and determine stringent safekeeping measures for what we have received. I am considering this as payment for the services we rendered for the emperor."

Combined with the lingering heat of the day, it was unbearable to see how these crusaders stole the wealth of a once-great city.

A drop of sweat made its way down Christos's cheek and landed on his tunic. "Yes, my lord." Except for the three soldiers of de la Roche's personal guard, Christos was alone with de la Roche and was incensed that these treasures were now openly considered payment. They would never be returned to their rightful owners.

"I will pay you and your assistant a stipend that should be reasonable for you. We, of course, don't want to offend the pope in Rome. Apparently, he is displeased with some of the payment modalities that took place in Constantinople." De la Roche had just received a letter sent him from the pope about the looting that had befallen the capital of the Roman Empire and home of one of the great Christian patriarchs. "For the moment, you will keep the payments—er, ah—hidden. And if you do so, you will be safe here as long as you follow my simple instructions. My men will follow your leadership concerning their proper care and safekeeping. They are to know as little as possible of their contents."

De la Roche didn't have much leverage over the two but also didn't want to harm them, for fear of repercussions from the pope. "You may leave." De la Roche waved him off with his left hand, as if he were flicking a fly from his face. Now that the payments were in good hands, he could continue his efforts to counsel with Boniface on the political situation in Athens, Thebes, and Thessalonica and about their relations with the pope.

"One last thing. I will be returning to Constantinople in the next few weeks," de la Roche said to Christos. "I trust that while I'm away, you will inform me of any unusual requests from anyone, especially from Archbishop Michael.[7] I'm told he prefers his connections to the old Constantinople more than he does to the new Constantinople. The less he knows about these payments, the better."

The archbishop was the head of the church in Athens and was also appalled with the looting of Constantinople.

"He fears that the same might happen to his city. I will protect these treasures, but I will not let church politics lead to the surrender of my rightful payments," de la Roche continued. "When I return, I will also speak with the archbishop to advance the ordination of your assistant. I am certain he will make a great priest." De la Roche smiled. This was a perfect inducement for the both of them to remain loyal.

This was the only statement that made any sense to Christos. He wasn't comfortable sharing his true misgivings in front of de la Roche. "I—we—shall remain protectors of the Shroud until our deaths."

De la Roche waved to dismiss him a second time.

"I will inform Arcadius of the good news. He will be overjoyed." Christos bowed again, turned, and exited de la Roche's chambers. He breathed deep. *How can I be loyal to Jesus Christ and the church—Archbishop Michael, prelate of the church in Athens—and protect the holy Shroud? Did I just sell out my loyalties, my soul? And what about Arcadius? Did I just include him in my conspiracy against their new archbishop?*

---

7 Archbishop Michael II Choniates: Archbishop of the Eastern Church in Athens from AD 1175 to 1204. Defended the Acropolis from attack during the Fourth Crusade.

CHAPTER 7

The Return Home

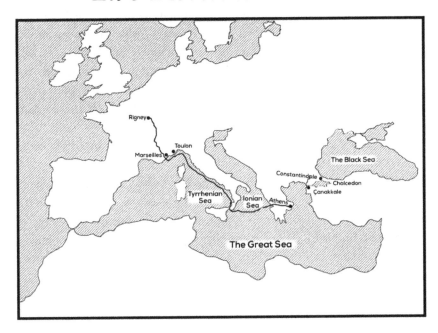

Located near the western frontier to the holy Roman Empire in Europe, Rigney, France, was the ancestral home of Duke Othon de la Roche. France was ruled by the House of France, also called the House of Capet. In AD 1004 the Burgundy region was annexed by the House of France, and the de la Roche family became a subject of the French kingdom.

ATHENS, GREECE
EARLY MORNING, MONDAY, JUNE 23, AD 1225

"Arcadius, Arcadius," Father Christos breathed in. "You have been so faithful to the church and to me these many years. I'm sorry you weren't able to return to your home in Çanakkale. How long has it been?" Father Christos breathed in and out. This time, even more labored.

"Just over twenty years. You have been a perfect mentor to me in Athens and before that in Constantinople," Arcadius responded, doing what he could to comfort his friend.

"You must now travel with the cloth and dedicate your life to it. De la Roche will be taking it with him now that he has transferred the Athens duchy to his son." Christos's breathing was very shallow.

Arcadius couldn't keep the tears back. Memories of their lives together flooded his thoughts. Remembering their time sailing from Constantinople to Athens made him smile, and he felt a salty tear reach his lip. He tried to forget the smell of war and the destruction of a once-great city, but the visions still punctuated his dreams. Athens was far from Constantinople, and this trip to France would take him farther, never to return to his family in Çanakkale.

Arcadius leaned over Father Christos. He didn't wipe the tears from his cheek, and one fell on the cushion next to Christos's ear. "Father, we will remember you always, and we pledge our . . ." Arcadius could barely get the words out. He took a deep breath. "I pledge my sacred oath to protect the cloth." Arcadius had been at Father Christos's side for decades and couldn't fathom what it would be like without him.

"Safe travels, my son." Father Christos closed his eyes and drifted off to sleep, his breathing shallow and faint.

Arcadius held his hand. It was cold and bony. He shifted the blankets to cover his friend's hands. He finally stood and looked down at Christos. The sacrament of extreme unction was complete. Arcadius continued to pray. No more words with his friend and mentor were possible. He wished and prayed this man could have control over his own life and death like Jesus, when from the cross Jesus stated, "It is finished."

The leech put a glass next to his nose and it still fogged, less and less with each passing minute. "It is only a few moments or perhaps hours now." A few minutes passed and the doctor checked again. There was no response.

Christos had passed into perpetual sleep.

They both genuflected. Arcadius recited a short prayer and genuflected again.

†††

ATHENS, GREECE
EARLY MORNING, MONDAY, JUNE 24, AD 1225

It was very early, and some of the poor sleeping in the streets hadn't yet awoken, and Arcadius's family had to step around them. A small vagrant family slept together against the wall of the inn at the wharf. The odor emanating from them, a combination of urine and sweat, was atrocious.

"Theodore, be careful not to wake this family. I have ministered to them, and they need their sleep before they start their day's labors."

Theodore had conflicting emotions. He wanted to hate their plight, yet he saw the love his father had for them, and sympathy and sadness came to him. He was the fifteen-year-old son of Arcadius and his wife Lorraine. He was often with his father as he ministered to the poor and needy.

Christos's death was expected yet still sooner than anticipated. As keepers of the cloth, he and Arcadius and his family had been scheduled this day to depart with the duke from Athens for France. With his death right before departure, Arcadius regretted not being able to preside over his friend's funeral.

"Father, can I give them a coin?" Theodore had a small change purse and took out a small coin and placed it near the head of the youngest boy in the family. Arcadius and his wife stopped while their son gave the coin to the family. "Father, why can't more be done for the poor?"

Arcadius looked over and smiled at his son. "Remember what Jesus Christ said, 'For you have the poor always with you; but me you have not always.' Regardless of how much we do, there will always be more. Is it better to give a man a fish or to teach a man to fish?" Arcadius knew there was a balance somewhere in between.

His wife, Lorraine, and Theodore continued on their way to the pier, where the final loading of the duke's personal galley was underway. Since sailing from Constantinople two decades ago, new sails had been woven for the duke's ship. They were bundled on the yardarms, with their two grand red and white stripes ready to be unfurled.

The times under the duke were good for Athens. The improvements he brought to Athens were evident in the expanded docks.

"Theodore, when I first traveled from Constantinople, I followed this grand ship but never thought I would sail on her." Arcadius pointed up at the ship a hundred yards off in the harbor. The harbor was just as filled with ships as it had been when they arrived twenty years ago.

The summer winds were minimal and there was no rain in sight. There were sailors, passengers, and traders at the port in a controlled chaos. Ships were being unloaded and others loaded.

"We will be traveling with the duke around the Italian Peninsula and then north into Marseille."

It was finally their turn to climb down into the rowboat to be ferried over to the duke's galley.

"Father, you showed me on the map where we are going. What will we do when we get there? What will I do?" Theodore asked, his mother looking up at her son. He was already taller than she was.

"My son, you will be taught in the finest schools in Burgundy. Sir Othon has promised us. You will learn French, and you'll find it is very similar to Latin."

Lorraine looked back at the city and the Acropolis. "*Au revoir Athènes, au revoir.*" She too began to learn some French words. It was these that came to mind, although she knew she would never return to see her home in Athens again. Her pride in her son shone through her loving smile. "Come, let's say it together, *au revoir.*"

✝✝✝

"Physician Guiscard." Arcadius greeted the leech accompanying the duke. "Is the duke ready for his trip home?"

The duke had severe pain in his feet and was often not able to walk. Guiscard was summoned from Paris by the duke to diagnose and care for him as his health waned. Guiscard was particularly learned in his treatment of gout, diarrhea of the urine, wasting thirst, and other common ailments that afflicted his aristocratic patients. His initial bloodletting in treating the duke made a difference, yet over time it had lost its positive effect.

"Arcadius." Doctor Guiscard gave a slight bow to Arcadius and his family as they made their way onto the deck.

They both turned to view the city. The cityscape reminded Arcadius of their initial arrival in Athens.

"He should survive the voyage well enough. My hope is that the sea air and a fish diet may assist in reducing the sweetness in his urine and the irritation of his kidneys. If I can limit his consumption of wine, I venture we might be able to mitigate his condition," Guiscard said, surveying the cityscape.

Having come of age in a fishing community, Arcadius's education in world affairs was inconsequential. Being thrust into the center of the world in Constantinople, and now in Athens, was a magnificent blessing from God.

Guiscard, on the other hand, was a highly educated French nobleman who loved reading and learning all he could. His medical training came through an apprenticeship with another doctor and reading all he could find on the human body. Treating his patients was in line with church doctrine but mostly focused on the senses of humor of his patients—the blood, the urine, and the stools. He would examine these in great detail and look for signs of imbalance. "I only hope it will also help him with his gout to minimize the suffering. The duke is a proud man and having to be hoisted onto the boat will only serve to exasperate him further."

The sailors manhandled a small crate of supplies for the doctor. The wooden box was large enough that it had to be brought onto the ship with the crane. There was one older sailor and two younger sailors manning the hoist and the lines. Guiscard's box of medical supplies had come from Paris especially for this trip.

"Careful there, son. Watch the lines. Watch the lines! You fools!" The senior sailor berated his junior. One of the lines came loose from the hoist, nearly causing the crate to fall into the water.

"Be careful with that medicine, or I'll have your heads!" the doctor shouted to the men hoisting his supply of special vinegar and other treatments intended to ease the suffering of his royal patient. The doctor moved over to the senior sailor, exasperated in their mishandling of his supplies. "The only reason for this trip and my being here is to give the duke the treatment he needs, and he doesn't need you fools ruining it before he even boards the ship! You'll need to do a much better job when we lift the duke onto the ship!"

The pain in the duke's feet was so great that walking and standing had become unbearable. The duke spent most of his time in a chair.

Satisfied his supplies were safely loaded on the ship, Guiscard returned to Arcadius. His agitation with the sailors was now diminished.

All the commotion had frightened a small rat, and it scurried away from near the sailors to a hole between the deck and the mainmast.

"I'm hoping to reduce the duke's condition with some special juices and ointments that seem to be proving themselves in Paris." Guiscard continued his conversation with Arcadius. "I've included some rare autumn crocus in my apple cider mixture, and it seems to help. But there is no cure for the duke." The doctor turned to Arcadius. "The pain in his feet is only slightly relieved by this concoction. I hope it will suffice for the trip back to his home-land, otherwise this will be a most unhappy voyage."

Arcadius knew of the suffering of the duke. The last few weeks, he had to be wheeled into the chapel, not able to walk or stand on his aching feet. Nothing relieved the pain.

Off in the distance at the pier, the duke had arrived with his entourage, who transferred him from his litter onto his chair. He winced several times but kept a smile. "Boys, just get me to my ship. Just get me to my ship."

The plan was to have him sit in the chair and hoist him into the dinghy so he wouldn't have to step down, or possibly fall down, the ramp to the dock.

"Oh my, this is going to be difficult," Arcadius said to himself, looking over the railing. Theodore also watched. Arcadius imagined hoisting the duke up to the galley deck from the rowboat would be even more challenging.

"When the duke is brought onto the ship, remember exactly how I taught you to bow," Arcadius instructed his son. He had been in the presence of the duke many times, but Theodore only once or twice. "In order to show respect, you'll need to show proper deference, and it begins with a proper bow."

"Yes father," Theodore replied, practicing his bow.

"Good. Good. I have been caring for the relics for a long time, and I wish to continue. I also hope you will take over for me when I am no longer able. And to do that, you'll need a proper bow."

After thirty minutes, the duke's wheeled chair was lowered onto the deck of the galley. Three sailors held the lines, assisted by two of the duke's attendants. The dressing down by the doctor helped to ensure the process went smoothly. As soon as the four wheels met the deck, the ship was hit by a small wave, and the chair shifted about three feet.

Guiscard was standing within reach and reached out so that the chair would not continue rolling with every wave.

"Doctor, please, my medicine. My medicine. I wish to sleep!"

The doctor, Arcadius, and his family bowed.

"I didn't get any rest last night!" The duke had been in good spirits when he left the dock, but was now in pain and in awful spirits. He gritted his teeth, causing his cheeks to tense and his brow to wrinkle. At least he was not taking his suffering out on anyone present.

The duke traveled with four attendants. Two stood behind his chair, and pushed it to his quarters in the stern. The other two remained outside the door and stood guard. The wheels squeaked loudly as he groaned from the pain. Each bump in the deck shot pain up his legs.

"Careful." The duke looked over at the doctor. "It's my right heel, my right heel this morning. It was unbearable last night."

The doctor nodded and followed the chair into the duke's quarters. He had a small bottle of his gout elixir always with him to provide as much comfort as possible. Once the duke had fallen asleep, he would refill it with the supplies just loaded onto the ship. The door closed behind them.

✝✝✝

"Theodore, show me the map you've drawn. I'd like to take another look at our route to Marseille." Arcadius and his family had been silent, watching the duke's travails to reach his quarters. There was another groan from the stern.

"Careful!" The command from the leech was loud enough to be heard from behind the doors. The duke was being transferred from his chair to the bed. Another loud groan of pain.

Theodore turned back to his parchment and unrolled it. Arcadius had

Theodore draw it from one of the duke's maps. "Father, I pray the duke's gout will subside. Otherwise, it will be a most unenjoyable trip for him." The boy had always been empathetic.

"Perhaps you should become a doctor. That way, you can care for those who are suffering," Arcadius responded, approving of his son's thoughtfulness.

"Our trek begins by hugging the coastline as we pass Corinth and then circle around the Peloponnese Peninsula and then west across the Ionian Sea." Arcadius enjoyed time with his son. It was hard for him not to be smiling when they were together. Theodore had made a very detailed map, and he and his father would enjoy following the map and their progress as they made their way around the Italian Peninsula and up to Marseille.

"Theodore, do you remember our trip to Corinth?"

"Yes, Father." Theodore paused a few minutes, remembering that Paul started the church in Corinth but was never able to return. "Do you think we'll ever return to Athens?"

Arcadius turned from watching the sailors and looked directly at Theodore. Out of the corner of his eye, he saw a small rat peeking out from the corner between the duke's chambers and the deck of the ship.

"No, my son." Arcadius's voice was low but firm. He continued to watch the rat. Theodore followed his gaze and saw it, too. "No, my son. God has new adventures for us in France, in Burgundy." Arcadius turned and watched the second ship accompanying them. It carried the duke's personal guard and some supplies. There were very few passengers on the duke's personal galley, yet he could see that the decks of the support transport were somewhat crowded. He was glad he was able to travel with some level of comfort with the duke. His trip to Athens had not been so comfortable.

✝✝✝

The Strait of Messina
Midmorning, Saturday, June 28, AD 1225

"The sea air is doing me much good." The duke turned to Arcadius. His midsection was round and added fifty pounds or so to his frame. They both stood on the bow of the ship. "My feet don't hurt as much today. I can even stand. I hope you never have what I have."

The doctor was behind them; Theodore stood to the right of Arcadius. They looked out into the Tyrrhenian Sea.

"That makes me happy. I will continue praying for improvement in your health." Arcadius was glad to see the duke in good spirits.

"I do miss my wife. She left a few months before me to arrange our home for my arrival." The duke could only think of reuniting with his wife upon his return to Rigney.

"The winds will be in our favor today. With the sails fully unfurled, this is a wonderful ship, your Grace." Arcadius turned and watched the sailors unfurl the mainsail. It had two red stripes and was brilliant in the morning sun. The wind filled the huge square sail. "With these winds, we will make great progress today."

"Paul made roughly this same trip. Do you know where he was supposed to have landed on his way to Rome?" The duke had come through Venice on his way to Constantinople. This time he traveled to the west of the Apennine Peninsula, trying to avoid any unnecessary entanglements should someone ask about the payment modalities in Constantinople. There were still many that were suspicious of anyone who had prospered from the looting and pillaging of that once-great city.

"Theodore, perhaps you could answer the duke's question." Arcadius enjoyed having his son interact with the duke, especially when he was in such good humor. When Arcadius first traveled with the duke to Athens twenty years before, he resented the taking of Constantinople's treasures. The ill will had now faded and he considered himself a friend and confidant of the duke.

He turned to the duke. "Your Grace, Theodore has become very learned in Paul's epistles."

"Yes, Father." Theodore was excited to participate. "After staying the winter on Malta, Paul landed in Puteoli, on the coast outside of Rome, and stayed there about a week until he and the Roman guards and the group of men he was traveling with marched to Rome."

Arcadius loved studying the books of Paul and had made certain Theodore knew Paul's letters inside and out.

"Someday, I wish to visit Rome. I've heard it is a most wonderful city." Theodore smiled, thinking about Rome.

"We will avoid Rome on this trip. Although Pope Innocent III has been dead almost ten years, the payment modalities from Alexios may not be fully forgotten by the papacy." The duke was not going to give up any of his hard-won payments.

"Have you checked on the relics below?" The duke asked in an offhanded way to elicit a conversation. "I have always wondered how that image was made, how it was emblazoned into the cloth." The question hung in the air for about a minute. Neither man, having been close to the Shroud for more than twenty years, could comprehend how the image, both front and back, could have been formed by the hand of man.

"I guess there are certain answers only God can know." Arcadius had thought and prayed many times about the formation of the image and always came to the same conclusion. It was an exceptional artwork made at the hand of God—not of man. It was the witness to the moment of resurrection.

The duke said what Arcadius was thinking. "I have prayed many times about this question, but God has yet to respond to my prayers."

Arcadius paused a few moments. "Your Grace, Theodore has drawn a map and has been following our progress. Would you care to review his skills?"

"Fetch your map." Theodore stepped forward. He always carried his map on his person, tucked into his tunic.

"Your Grace, I have been adding more to my map throughout the trip." Theodore's maps included exquisite drawings of the coastlines of Athens, Corinth, Mount Aetna, and Messina.

"These are remarkable, my boy." The duke smiled. "I shall have you make maps for me when we arrive in Rigney."

"Arcadius, you have trained him well."

Another few minutes passed as the three of them admired the artwork. Theodore tried to hold back his pride in his work but allowed a slight grin as he watched the duke draw his finger along their expected voyage. "My son, there are many legends of great sea dragons. You'll need to add Scylla and Charybdis here in the Strait of Messina. Perhaps also Cetus in the Tyrrhenian Sea."

Theodore's smile opened wider. He couldn't wait to learn more about these creatures. His mind raced at the thought of being in the midst of sea dragons.

"Do you know the story of Cetus?" the duke began, having learned of these myths during his years as duke of Athens. "Like Scylla and Charybdis, Cetus was a sea creature—no, a sea monster. An enormous monster. Some believe he was the same leviathan that swallowed Jonah. Now, Poseidon was God of the sea."

The duke was never happier than when telling stories to the youth. It allowed him to forget the pins and needles throbbing in his feet. The same feet that carried him to so many successful battles were now failing him.

"Cetus was a great whale, longer than this ship and possibly even wider, with a great fin that stretched up as high as the deck above the water. Possibly even higher." After many minutes of joyful storytelling, there was silence. "My boy, I'll tell you more next time. I think I've told you all for now." The duke was a truly impassioned storyteller. The tenor of his voice would go up and down, enlivening the tension and excitement of each of the fantasies.

As the duke told the fables of the three monsters, Theodore worked on his sketches. He continued after the silence commenced. The descriptions from the duke were so vivid, he eagerly began sketching immediately, starting first with Cetus. Scylla was more difficult, with six snake-like heads protruding from the body of an octopus. Charybdis was drawn as a whirlpool able to suck in whole ships that fell into its clutches.

The silence was refreshing in the midst of the sea, breezes, sun, and fresh air.

Arcadius broke the silence. "I will go and check on the cloth, Your Grace." Arcadius bowed. "We will both go."

"Theodore. Your Grace." Arcadius and Theodore bowed and backed away and then turned to go below decks.

✝✝✝

OFF THE COAST OF CORSICA
EARLY MORNING, THURSDAY, JULY 3, AD 1225

The days were filled with the duke's stories of great sea monsters and Theodore adding them to his map. The duke, Arcadius, and Theodore all enjoyed the time, which broke the monotony of being confined to the ship. Guiscard also joined them, and he had his own stories to tell, adding to the boy's education.

"Your Grace, we are approaching the Isle of Corsica," the ship's helmsman announced.

The duke was able to stand for extended periods without any pain in his feet, allowing him more energy and excitement to tell great fables to the boy. The onboard diet had done wonders for his suffering. There was hardly a moment where he felt any pins and needles in his feet.

While they were anchored off Elba, the duke had mentioned he might fancy stepping onto solid ground in Corsica as well. The lack of pain in his feet made him more ambitious.

"Shall we land? I'm afraid with this slight rain, we may not enjoy our time on the land."

It had been raining since before dawn when they left the island of Elba.

"I would like to, but with the fighting and bickering between the Pisans and the Genoans for control of the island, it may not be safe." The duke considered his choices. "Without knowing whether they are fighting or just waiting to fight, I prefer to continue on with all haste to Marseille."

"Your Grace, I, too, recommend we stay a fair distance from the coast. I also don't want to unnecessarily delay our trip to French soil and French wine." The helmsman stood at attention and awaited his orders. Over the course of the trip, the duke had become quite affable with his underlings.

"How long until we reach Marseille?" The duke turned away from the helmsman and gazed toward the shoreline. He didn't wait for a response. He was busy trying to make out the coastline through the fog and light rain. "Theodore, I'm afraid you'll not be able to capture the beauty of this island without stepping foot on it." Theodore sat behind the duke, sketching as much as he could in order to draw it onto his map later when they were no longer in sight of the island.

"Two or three days, Your Grace, depending, of course, on the winds." The helmsman stood for a minute without moving, sturdy on his sea legs as the ship groaned from a larger swell passing underneath. Having received no response, he turned and marched back to his post at the helm.

"I'm told Corsica is one of the most beautiful islands with a mix of Genoan and Pisan style architecture," the duke told Theodore, wishing they could have visited the island. It was clear this would never happen for him. "At some point in your life, I hope you'll have the opportunity to visit these beautiful isles and Rome too."

The storm didn't last too long into the morning. The days grew increasingly warmer, and the duke was getting tired of his laziness in the afternoons. He so much wanted to be back home, where he could smell the fresh air, the vineyards, and the flowers of his homeland. With the anticipation of home, his mood changed to one of exuberance. He wanted to mount a fast steed and race through the countryside, as he did as a youth learning to ride his favorite horse in the meadows of Rigney.

"I will teach you how to ride and fight in battle. You're now old enough to be able to defend yourself. I will teach you." He was starting to remember the training he gave to his own son, who was now duke of Athens, his successor. "I taught him how to ride a fast steed, defend himself in a fight and to dispatch a man with a sword. "I pray your father will allow me."

✝✝✝

THE PORT OF TOULON
EARLY EVENING, SATURDAY, JULY 5, AD 1225

The winds were very favorable, and the next two days went by quickly. The helmsman earned his pay through his navigation skills across open waters. They traversed the three hundred kilometers northwesterly across the Ligurian Sea, reaching the Provence coast within a few miles of Toulon.

"Toulon is part of Provence and governed by a fellow knight from the battle of Zara," the duke instructed.

Theodore stood next to him and sketched the coastline.

"We will be welcome to stay, but we will continue to Marseille. And from Marseille, we will travel over land directly to Rigney." The duke had never been this far west on the coast before. "The counts of Provence were friendly to the Burgundian kings. Their only enemies were the Genoans and the Saracens," the duke continued.

Theodore was listening but focused on his depictions of the coastline and the hills behind.

"The Saracens were the worst. They were Muslim pirates sailing up from Africa pillaging the coastal towns and then running off as quickly as they came. If we had been properly paid in Constantinople and not been distracted in Zara, we could have defeated many of the Muslims and possibly reduced the attacks on this coastline."

Theodore didn't fully understand the politics, yet the duke was fully involved in all of the nuances of the relationships between Greece, Constantinople, France, and Italy.

"Even England was having trouble. The English were trying to win over the Scots, and that wasn't going well. Those sons of whores were also trying to invade France and invade Burgundy. We won't let them." He looked out over the harbor and the town of Toulon.

"I always wanted to go to Jerusalem and keep that region free, but our internecine fighting destroyed Byzantium and sapped our strength and resolve to push back the enemies of Christ. After the abysmal failure of the last two crusades, I hope we can eventually build an army that will be more coordinated. There are rumors that Frederick[1] from Germany may be able to mount a new crusade."

The duke continued extolling the virtues of the Crusades to liberate the Holy Land. "But, alas, I am too old. You, Theodore, however are just coming of age. You'll need to decide whether you would fight to free the Holy Land."

Theodore understood much of what the duke spoke of, but his father was dead set against him joining any crusade, especially now that he was old enough to become a soldier. The pain and suffering his father had witnessed in Constantinople still haunted him. His father was so glad his son was born after the conclusion of the Fourth Crusade.

The duke was quiet as he watched the sailors drop anchor off the spit of land protecting Toulon. With the ship safely anchored in the harbor, the

---

1 Emperor Frederick II: Holy Roman emperor from AD 1220 to 1250. King of Germany, Sicily, and leader of the Sixth Crusade. Son of Emperor Henry VI of the Hohenstaufen Dynasty. Born AD 1194, died AD 1250.

helmsman sent the dinghy into port to purchase and trade for supplies. They had fine silks from the factories in Thebes. They were as valuable as gold and allowed the sailors to easily exchange them for food along the entire route.

The duke stayed behind, envying the men going ashore yet eagerly awaiting his entry into Marseille. He looked forward to the fresh fruit, especially the strawberries, blackberries, and raspberries. And he longed for milk and French cheese. He hadn't had French cheese since he disembarked from Venice decades earlier.

Theodore and the doctor accompanied the sailors into port.

"Your Grace, we will weigh anchor in the morning. We expect to arrive in Marseille early afternoon where you will be able to disembark," the helmsman said, making final plans for the last day of their voyage.

The duke was ecstatic. He was tempted to go into Toulon but didn't want to cause any unnecessary stir of activity.

"Well done. Well done." The duke was all smiles—very different from how he felt when he was hoisted up onto the ship. "I'm afraid we'll be parting company upon arrival. You'll be returning to Athens. I wish to spend a few weeks in Marseille gathering supplies before beginning our journey to Rigney. And I yearn to be back on a stallion—a beautiful white stallion."

"Of course, Your Grace." The helmsman stood at attention. "At your request, the men will return before dark with some fresh cheese and fresh bread. It shall be an especially enjoyable vespers this evening."

They both looked out over the harbor. The Cathedral of Toulon was under construction, the outlines of the spires visible from the ship.

"Your Grace." The helmsman bowed, turned, and departed.

The transport galley also sent a rowboat in to fetch supplies. It was full of soldiers, so there wasn't much room to return with many supplies. All the guards wanted was to get on land that night. He wondered if they'd all return back to the ship before sailing in the morning. The duke would not wait.

✝✝✝

The soldiers taking their leave in Toulon made their way to the inns, where they were able to relish a long-missed meal of local French wine, cheese, and women. They were prepared to enjoy the whole evening being away from the ship. The wine and women would keep them awake all night. Only a few of them worried about missing their transports back. Most would be content making their new lives here or anywhere in their homeland.

"Can you spare a few coins for me?" a woman pleaded, sitting at the dock, covering her face as the men came ashore from the first rowboat. She had her hand out. It resembled the dirty, gray hands the soldiers had seen of their fallen comrades. "I haven't eaten in two days and need some bread, anything." She had no strength in her voice. Her face covering fell, and the soldiers could see what she was hiding. She turned quickly so they wouldn't have to see her shame. There were two gaping holes where her nose should have been. It was a grotesque image that couldn't be unseen. One hand returned her face covering, the other stretched out again pleading for anything.

"Get away from me, you wretch!" one of the soldiers commanded. This woman had been found guilty of adultery and punished accordingly by slicing off her nose for all to see. The men ignored the woman and walked quickly past her.

Only Theodore showed pity and threw her a coin. "Please buy yourself some food." He threw a second coin. He remembered the story from John where Jesus told the prostitute, "Let any one of you who is without sin be the first to throw a stone at her." He wished Jesus had been there when the woman was convicted of her crime. Perhaps her punishment could have been avoided.

"Come, we must explore this town before we return to the ship for dinner." Guiscard didn't show any pity on the woman and grabbed Theodore's arm as they walked away from the woman. Unlike Theodore, he had no pity on those receiving a just punishment for their crimes.

✝✝✝

Guiscard and Theodore returned before dark to enjoy one of their last meals on board. It was approaching second watch, and the duke was in good spirits. After a truly French evening meal, he sat back on his chair and looked out over the horizon. The mix of bread, fresh grilled fish, soft cheese, and wine left the duke yearning to be home to enjoy the French food every day. He enjoyed this meal more than any in decades.

In the sky above, only a sliver of a moon was visible, making it dark enough to see the stars and that swath of light called the Milky Way. The doctor, Arcadius, and his wife and son were with the duke on the deck enjoying the afterglow of the French wine. The duke had the most wine, but Arcadius too enjoyed the wine more than he expected. For the duke, it was like being home. For Arcadius and his family, it was a new experience. The cheese was hard to resist. There was nothing like it in Athens or Constantinople.

"Theodore, have you seen the Milky Way before? It is a wonderful sight. To think that all those stars rotate every night around us. God's creation is truly miraculous." The duke looked over at Arcadius's son after contemplating the heavens.

"You have trained the rat well." The doctor watched as Theodore fed the rat and its family some of the cheese and a few breadcrumbs from his fingers.

Arcadius repeated the first Genesis story from memory. "Then God said, 'Let there be light' and there was light. And God saw the light, that it was good: and God divided the light from the darkness. God called the light Day, and the darkness He called Night."

Like the duke, Arcadius had to squint to see the stars. His vision had declined so that the individual stars weren't points of light. They were mostly tiny fuzzy balls.

"The Greeks believe the Milky Way came from the goddess Hera as Hermes grabbed her infant Heracles from her breast, spilling droplets of milk all across the heavens." The duke prided himself on all he learned of Greek mythology during his reign in Athens, and he enjoyed relaying his knowledge to Theodore. "When I was first married to my wife, Isabel, we would talk of the Greek fables and look out at the stars."

"Just remember, the Bible provides the only true history of the world and God's creation." Arcadius was always awed by the duke's knowledge of Greek mythology, but he couldn't let those ancient fables detract from the teachings in the Bible. Arcadius enjoyed hearing the Greek fables but loved the stories of the Bible even more.

"What are all those points of light? Did God create them too?" Theodore knew the answer, but they weren't mentioned specifically in the Bible.

The duke looked up and found Mars. "Did you know it was Aristotle who determined that Mars was farther away than the moon? He discovered that it sometimes disappeared behind the moon." The duke loved to recite scientific facts discovered by the most famous of philosophers. "You have your whole life ahead of you. What would you like to do? Be a scientist, a priest, a warrior?"

Arcadius had grown to admire the duke, but he wasn't going to allow his son to die in battle or have a leg or arm sawn off. The screams and the stench of the wounded men in the Saint Mary of Blachernae Church never left him.

"Your drawing talents would be ideal for the sciences. And you also know the Bible as well as any man." Arcadius didn't directly contradict the duke in his presence. "You have a few years to choose. There are so many opportunities available to you."

"Perhaps you could become a doctor. As a doctor your drawing skills would be very valuable." Guiscard plied his own profession, giving the boy another option to choose from.

"Perhaps the helmsman would like me to become a ship's captain. Or perhaps I simply study art and sell my paintings for a living." Theodore had learned the art of diplomacy. "Or I could travel the world visiting Rome and Corsica and then return to Athens. I could become a mapmaker."

THE HARBOR OF TOULON
SUNRISE, SUNDAY, JULY 6, AD 1225

The sun hadn't yet pierced above the horizon, but the gray light was bright enough to weigh anchor and get underway. The time in Toulon was short, yet just long enough to give Theodore his land legs and enjoy an exceptional French vespers.

Arcadius and Theodore were excited about the next leg in their journey, the next chapter in their lives. In anticipation, they had been awake for over an hour. They would be disembarking from this ship forever in less than a day.

"Your Grace, I was able to find supplies to record our journey from Marseille to Rigney. The quality of paper here is not as good as we had in Athens, but it is good enough to sketch the drawings before I apply them to parchment."

Arcadius and the duke stood together and inspected the paper acquired by Theodore.

"When I was a boy, we didn't have paper. We had heard it existed, but it hadn't quite made its way to Rigney." The duke rubbed the paper between his fingers. "I always used parchment or papyrus, but we learned about paper from the Chinese."

The duke thought further. "There are many wonders coming out of China. Now I hear there is an invention—brilliant fireworks that light up the sky." The duke didn't know what it meant but was interested in this strange culture that had brought silk to the West and helped to increase his riches from the taxes on the silk factories in Thebes. He looked down and glimpsed the rat that had accompanied them from Athens. It scurried below deck into the seam between his chambers and the deck. A rat pup scampered behind it. "We'll be leaving our little rat friend behind to accompany the helmsman back to Athens."

"Your Grace, shall we say a prayer for a safe conclusion of our journey to Marseille?" Arcadius began his prayer and solicited travel blessings from the Holy Father.

Within a few minutes of weighing anchor, the sailors unfurled the sails to catch the morning breezes. They first had to sail south past the spit of land that protected the Toulon harbor, then turn north and follow the coast to Marseille.

"It will only be a few more hours, and we'll be unloading everything." Doctor Guiscard was just as joyful as the duke. They would both be back in their homeland. Since the duke's gout had cleared up, the doctor had little to do for most of the second half of the journey. "Your Grace, the sea has been good for you. I hope your health remains, and you no longer require my services." The doctor smiled and bowed.

The duke returned the smile, his good spirits bubbling to the surface.

"I've been gone from my home a few decades, but I promise I will never leave again." The duke looked out at the coastline. "I wish to find a perfect grape to turn into the most perfect wine." Everyone smiled.

THE PORT OF MARSEILLE, FRANCE
EARLY AFTERNOON, MONDAY, AUGUST 4, AD 1225

The entry into Marseille was exciting for everyone. With the anticipation to be off the ships, unloading went much smoother than the loading had in Athens. Two small rowboats came forward to accomplish the task—one for each galley.

The duke didn't require any help disembarking, which saved an hour compared to embarking. He was the first off his galley and first on land. From the docks he was able to view the entire process. His aides accompanied him, and they stood guard as the process of transporting his men to the wharf unfolded. The rowboats could hold maybe ten men each with a little room left over for some of their gear. The entire company and all their supplies were ashore before dusk.

Three guards were stationed on each ship, and everyone else was given the evening to reacquaint themselves with French wine, French women, and French song. They were all more than happy to be among their countrymen and countrywomen to celebrate their return to their homeland. They began by trying to remember how to sing French songs. Many of the words had long ago escaped them.

The late afternoon air was warm, but at dusk there was a cool breeze coming off the water. The smell of fish and the cawing of the gulls didn't distract the men, overjoyed to be on land and about to be in the company of women.

"We shan't be traveling north for a few days, perhaps a few weeks. We'll need to arrange supplies, horses, and wagons." The duke started to get more serious about the return trip to Rigney. Theodore, Arcadius, Doctor Guiscard, and the duke stood on the docks and enjoyed the kitchen smoke from the few inns directly at the wharf. "My aides have arranged a meal for all of us at the best inn in Marseille. Unfortunately, the governor is nowhere to be found. Apparently, he has left for a week of hunting in the forest north of the city."

"I have sent word announcing my arrival in Aix to the count of Provence, Ramon Berenguer IV[2], a day's travel to the north." The duke revealed the first step of their travel plans. "Aix will be one of our first stops on our way to Rigney."

✝✝✝

It was too late in the day to begin the process of arranging transport, so camp was set up on the hills just north of the city. The first night a few men stayed on the ships, but most decided to enjoy the night on dry land—wherever their exploits with wine and women landed them.

"I am certain we will be well received when the governor returns." The duke was disappointed the governor was unable to welcome them to Marseille. Nevertheless, there would be ample time to meet and dine with each of the local noblemen along their route. He longed to hear the latest news of the pope and tell of the goings on in Athens, Thebes, and Constantinople.

"Arcadius, it is a new time in France. With the country united by King Philip II[3] and now ruled by his son, Louis the Lion[4], each of the duchies should allow us free travel through to Rigney. Although I don't expect any trouble, we shall be prepared. Our men haven't fought in over twenty years, but they know exactly what it means to fight." The duke reflected on the other politics of the day. "I'm more interested in hearing about the pope and his view of the goings on in Athens, although I imagine our news is more current than his."

The duke thought further, still concerned about his payments from Constantinople and a possible excommunication from the pope. "I hope Pope Honorius III[5] has a more lenient outlook on those participating in the Fourth Crusade."

"With Innocent III gone, the subject of the payments seems to be forgotten by Honorius. Now that you're back in France, you can rekindle your

---

2 Ramon Berenguer IV: Count of Provence from AD 1209 to AD 1245. Born AD 1198, died AD 1245.
3 King Philip II: King of France from AD 1180 to AD 1223. Born AD 1163, died AD 1223.
4 King Louis VIII, the Lion: King of France from AD 1223 to 1226. Born AD 1187, died AD 1226.
5 Pope Honorius III: Pope from 1216 to 1227. Resided in Rome. Born circa AD 1150, died AD 1227.

relationship with King Philip, and he will protect you. Plus, I'm sure your success in ruling Athens didn't go unnoticed in Paris or Rome." Arcadius patronized his benefactor, but nothing he said was untrue.

✝✝✝

The second French meal was even better than the first. Arcadius could understand some of the local language, though Theodore and his mother understood much less. After they had finished eating, Arcadius, the duke, and Guiscard left the inn and stood facing their ship. Theodore and his mother came up behind them.

"Your Grace, I look forward to enjoying many more French meals. That was wonderful," Arcadius remarked, belched, and then rubbed his stomach. "The wine is different from that of Athens. It will be a wonderful life here in our new homeland." It was new to Arcadius and his family but not for the duke and the doctor. They all laughed out loud, happily anticipating the promise of travel by land through their new home country.

"One more leg of our journey, and we'll be home." The duke, too, was glad to be free of the confines of the deck of the galley.

They made their way along the wharf by the light of a thin sliver of a moon reflecting off the waters. Their galley was a few hundred yards off. They noticed some strange lights and wisps of smoke coming from the deck.

"It looks like the men are celebrating their—" Guiscard didn't finish his sentence "Is that the helmsman?" There was someone directing buckets being loaded and hauled up from the side.

"What is going on. They're not celebrating. Is that smoke? Is that coming from—" The four of them were helpless to know what was happening, only that there was too much smoke to be from cooking.

"It's a fire in the galley!" Theodore exclaimed. He looked around for the transport that brought them to land. It was further up the dock. The two oarsmen also now observed the commotion on the stern of the ship. "They're bringing up water from the side!"

"It's fire!" They'd come all this way only to lose everything on the night they arrived in Marseille. "Fire!" Arcadius's heart leapt within him. The party was dumbstruck. They could only stand there and watch, feeling helpless, as the billows of smoke got stronger and stronger. A fire on a ship could be a disaster. Fires don't start that easily except from cooking or lanterns.

The duke and Arcadius gasped. "The cloth must not be damaged!" The duke bellowed his order, but there was no one who could obey.

Then they noticed the smoke change ever so slightly. The slight orange glow dimmed and then disappeared. The smoke changed and began to billow a new shade of gray. It had changed color from orange, then dark gray, to steamy gray, then white.

"We must get to the ship! Now!" They all started running to the dinghy moored about fifty yards away.

"It's steam," Arcadius exclaimed, still excited and hoping there was relief in sight.

More buckets were brought up from the side. Two sailors threw something into the water. They returned to the side, and they, too, threw down their buckets.

The smoke and steam became a trickle and then stopped. The helmsman went below deck. The buckets continued to be pulled up from the side. The only light now came from a few candle lanterns. There was no more smoke.

"Take us to our ship immediately!" The duke barked his command to the oarsmen who looked back and realized their charge was standing there giving them orders. "Now!"

The duke stepped onto the rowboat tied up at the dock. His two aides joined him. There was room for Arcadius and the doctor. The three others in their party had to wait for the rowboat to return. There wasn't a word spoken during the whole trip back to the ship. Their dread was etched into their faces.

The helmsman remained below deck making certain there was no further fire and no embers that could reignite. Full buckets continued being brought to the two guards and then carried below.

The duke stepped first onto the deck. The smell of smoke was everywhere. It looked like the smoke had indeed stopped, but they could see black smoke stains leading from the gangway.

"Is anyone hurt?" Doctor Guiscard was the first to speak. The cook sat on the deck, as he coughed and leaned on the railing.

"Just a bunch of smoke breathed in. Just a bunch of smoke." He managed to say in a raspy voice, barely intelligible. The doctor knelt next to him and gave him a rag to wipe his face.

"It started with the lantern," one of the guards explained.

The cook breathed in and hacked up some black phlegm. "Your Grace." Both hung their heads. They were responsible.

The duke sneered at them. "You fools." The two shuffled back, fearing what might happen next.

The duke walked down to the ship's cooking area and to the bricks that made up the onboard oven. The helmsman was there throwing buckets into the corners. "There are no more embers, but I will keep watch."

The duke sneered at the two sailors. "The boys brought in a slaughtered pig and then proceeded to knock over the lantern. They will receive lashes for their stupidity."

Arcadius followed the duke below deck, down the ship's ladder and then over to the relics. "I can't tell in the darkness what happened. The Shroud crate is wet on the bottom and blackened by the smoke and flames." Arcadius looked up, shaking his head. "Your Grace, I will be able to inspect them fully at first light."

Arcadius didn't want to do anything in the cramped quarters. The smell of smoke was everywhere. "Bring these crates up on deck. Now!" Arcadius ordered the two sailors as if ordering schoolboys. "Get them into the dry air immediately!" The smoke invaded his throat, and he coughed directly after barking his order.

The duke was relieved and watched the two men manhandle the wet crates to the deck. Due to the water, they were much heavier now than when they were dry and brought on board. He made his way back up the ladder and over to the two sailors. "Which of you is responsible for this mess?" This was the first time anyone other than his two aides had heard him in this tone of voice. "Is it you?" He smacked the first sailor with the back of his hand, who tripped on his own feet and fell to the deck. He then looked at the second man. "How about you?" The second sailor winced but did not move. The smack came but he withstood his punishment and remained standing.

"It was me, Your Grace." The duke sneered at the second sailor, breathed in, and glared directly at him. The sailor didn't move. Finally, the duke breathed in again. He broke off his glare and retreated to his cabin.

The afterglow of the wonderful French wine was gone. The whole trip could have been spoiled had this calamitous fire spread to the relics. There was absolute silence except for the lapping waves against the sides of the ship.

✝✝✝

THE PORT OF MARSEILLE, FRANCE
EARLY MORNING, TUESDAY, AUGUST 5, AD 1225

The next morning, foreboding hung in the air just like the smell of smoke. With daylight fast approaching, Arcadius, Theodore and the duke wanted to inspect the Shroud. Its wooden case was scarred with black smoke stains. Water stains were also apparent on the bottom and sides of the case.

Arcadius carefully opened the crate and saw that little to no water had seeped inside. The box in which the Shroud was stored was pulled out. It was dry except for one small corner. It had a slight smell of smoke but in the air it would quickly dissipate. The leather valise was completely dry and totally undamaged.

Arcadius smiled with relief.

The duke's smile was soon replaced by anger. "The two sailors are fools." The duke vented his frustration.

"Your Grace, if I may, I know my first instinct would be to punish the two, but I recommend a simpler path. There was no harm to the cloth. There was no harm to the leather valise and no harm to the case. Because proper precautions were taken in Athens, the Shroud survived a treacherous journey and now is destined to survive the next. I recommend we put this matter behind us and move on to the next leg of our journey." Arcadius let his words hang in the air.

The duke grunted and walked back into his quarters without saying anything. After about ten minutes, he reappeared. "I have assembled a list of supplies we will need for our travel north. We will need ten horses, three wagons, and food and drink for the weeks ahead. Make certain you get enough wine. We don't want to fall short."

The duke breathed in and smiled as he inhaled the salty sea air of the harbor one last time. He looked out over the bow of the ship. He'd enjoyed the journey from Athens, but enjoyed much more the wine of Provence and the anticipation of the journey home.

"Yes, your Grace." His two aides bowed. Aloisius was the senior from Rigney, Esmé the junior born in Athens of French parents.

"You will begin with the horses and wagons. Those will be the most difficult to acquire." The duke paused a moment. "You'll also need a place to assemble. Arrange with the captain of the guard to scout out a campsite and have him build quarters there. I have no more desire to sleep on this wretched boat another night."

Arcadius stood near the duke, awaiting his attention.

"You may go." His aides were dismissed. Finally, the duke's attention landed on Arcadius.

"Your Grace." Arcadius gave a shallow bow, almost a nod. "Your Grace," Arcadius repeated.

"I wish you, Doctor Guiscard, and your son to work to inspect the various relics and treasures. Then I wish you to oversee the unloading of the relics once camp has been set up. I wish that to be completed by the end of the day." The duke thought a bit further. He wasn't ready to accept any questions on his orders for the day. His businesslike demeanor returned, as if he were duke of Athens.

Arcadius remained quiet.

"After you have inspected everything, I wish you and your son to go into the village and find a map of the region of Provence. Then once purchased, I wish

Theodore to purchase the supplies he needs to copy that map and chronicle our journey. I am very impressed with his artistic skills and wish he would do the same for our land journey as he did for our journey through the Great Sea." The duke was in good spirits despite the near debacle of the previous night.

He waved them off as a superior giving orders to inferiors, no longer an equal as had become the norm while they were sequestered together on his galley. He was close to home and needed to lead actively. He could no longer sit back and let the helmsman and the winds dictate their progress.

Below them, on the port side, the rowboat carrying the captain of the guard and two sailors tied up to the ship. He and three of his men would be aboard in just a few minutes to receive orders. The duke and captain spoke together for several minutes. Three crossbowmen remained on the rowboat. Within a few minutes, the captain and the duke descended to the rowboat, and they were off to the wharf.

"Theodore, you have been able to catch the eye of the duke. That will be very valuable for you in this new land," Doctor Guiscard began as Arcadius and Theodore manhandled the case with the Shroud up the ladder and through the short gangway onto the deck. The smell of smoke was everywhere. "Let us help your father recheck the condition of the Shroud."

The morning sun was strong and was quite a transition from the darkness below deck. Arcadius looked up at the sun and breathed in the sea air. "Today should be a perfect day to get everything on deck to dry out."

Men's loud voices could be heard coming from the sailors. "Fools! Idiots!" The two responsible for the near fiasco were being berated by their shipmates.

Within a few minutes, the Shroud case was on the deck. "The case is only wet in the one corner. Let's hope there wasn't any smoke damage." Theodore opened the case and retrieved the leather valise. "Father, it is totally dry inside the case, no different from last night. There is also no smell of smoke. Should we air it out here on deck or not?" Theodore positioned the case, so the damp corner was in the direct sun.

"No, I think not. I don't think we want the gulls or salt sea air damaging it. We shall leave the valise on deck and let it air in the morning breeze. Let us not remove the cloth if it's not necessary."

The men were required all morning to retrieve each of the other cases brought from Athens. They were brought on deck. Only the cases nearest the blaze had any damage. Some had water damage; others were black on one side from the smoke and heat. The sun was warm enough and the air cool enough in the morning air that wisps of steam began to form from the wet area of the cloth's case.

Arcadius and Theodore inspected each case. Only those that were wet were left topside to dry out. The others were returned below deck.

Arcadius's wife, Lorraine, returned from her early morning excursion into the village. It was barely dawn when she made the short trip with two of the men. "I've brought some bread, cheese, and vegetables for us. You should smell the aromas coming from the village, especially the bakery. They are heavenly."

Theodore grabbed the loaf of bread and broke off a piece for a midmorning snack. He breathed in slowly and enjoyed every second.

Arcadius and the doctor took pieces as well. "This doesn't exist in Athens. I think we're going to enjoy Provence." They all laughed.

✝✝✝

MARSEILLE, FRANCE
MIDAFTERNOON, THURSDAY, AUGUST 7, AD 1225

The crossbowman could be seen on horseback coming along the highway for a few hundred yards to deliver a message for the duke. "Your Grace, Bishop Pierre de Montlaur,[6] bishop of Marseille, will be arriving within the hour." The crossbowman was out of breath, having ridden the last few miles as quickly as his horse could take him. "He requests you not make travel plans until you have spoken. He believes the war with the Cathars is not quite *fini.*" His horse continued breathing hard, covered in sweat from the ride.

The crossbowman took a few more breaths, then a swig of wine. Sweat dripped from his brow. "The bishop is on his return from Aix but will make haste to meet with you before you embark on your journey. He recommends you don't travel through Avignon."

"Aloisius, prepare my tent for a visitor." The duke barked the order to his aide. His mind raced. There was intrigue in the air, and the duke was anxious to find out the reason for the urgency from the bishop. He heard rumors of trouble in Languedoc but didn't realize it might affect his travel plans. "We will dine together."

✝✝✝

The duke had to wait about three hours before he was able to have his audience with the bishop. His patience wore thin and his anticipation of the import of the news from Bishop de Montlaur grew with each hour.

It was dusk. The heat of the afternoon hadn't yet subsided and his hunger was getting the best of him. His impatience overflowed a few times, but his tone didn't divulge his anger with the bishop's tardiness. It reminded him of the long waiting required just before battle.

---

6 Bishop Pierre de Montlaur: Bishop of Marseille from AD 1214 to 1229. Died AD 1229.

The bishop's carriage was seen coming around the corner of the dirt highway leading north out of Marseille. When it came to a stop thirty feet from the duke's tent, Arcadius and the captain of the guard were ready to greet the carriage and its passenger. They helped the bishop down the two steps to the ground. He was followed out of the cabin by two well-trained hounds.

"Your Grace, Duke Othon de la Roche, formerly Duke of Athens, would like to invite you to dine with him on your way into Marseille."

The bishop nodded.

Arcadius and the captain of the guard accompanied the bishop to the duke, who stood next to the entrance of his tent. The bishop's two hounds jumped down out of the carriage and followed their master.

The duke led the bishop into his modest traveling tent, while Arcadius and the captain remained outside. The tent smelled of mildew, having not been properly aired out since it was last used in Athens.

Once inside, the duke kissed the ecclesiastical ring. "Your Excellency, I'm so glad you were able to receive me and now dine with me this evening."

"Your Grace, I am honored to meet with you today, but let us move past the pleasantries."

Finally, something that made the duke smile.

"The situation in Avignon is most unstable. The pope's desire to eliminate Catharism is no small task. The pope has been waging war with those Cathars for over fifteen years, and it doesn't quite appear to be over." The bishop paused and watched Aloisius pour wine into his cup. A mosquito alighted on the back of his hand, and the bishop smashed and killed it. "Those Gnostics are a pesky bunch. They refer to themselves as good Christians, but their unorthodox Christianity needs to be squashed like a bug.

"As you will be traveling north, I would recommend you take a more easterly route, first through Aix, then through Manosque and Sisteron. From there, you should be quite a distance from any potential fighting. It may delay you only one or two days but will guarantee you're not involved in any of the hostilities. As you've just arrived from so far away and so long ago, it wouldn't be right for your homeland to detain you anymore. I also recommend you meet with Archbishop Raimond Audibert[7] in Aix." The bishop took a scrap of meat and fed it to his dogs, white Talbot hounds. They must have weighed about sixty pounds each, both fat and spoiled. This breed was especially good for hunting, but these dogs were in no condition to run long distances to support the hunt.

---

7 Archbishop Raimond Audibert: Archbishop of Aix from AD 1223 to 1251. Died AD 1252.

"Your Excellency, your words are most valuable to me. We will heed your warning and do our best to stay clear of the fighting. My only wish now is to return home to grow wine and enjoy the company of my family. Bloodshed is now for the younger in our faith." The duke continued with pleasantries then became more serious.

"Your Most Reverend Pierre. Tell me what you can about the pope and his predilections toward Constantinople. Pope Innocent III[8] was disappointed in the battles, as was I, between Christians in Zara and then in Constantinople. And now, with Honorius III, how does he stand relative to Athens, Venice, and Constantinople? We were so disappointed when Jerusalem was lost to the Muslims led by Al Kamil[9] only a few short years ago." The duke paused and stared at the bishop's eyes to perceive any possible intimation of his thoughts.

The bishop had met many royal personages and knew how to keep his emotions and opinions to himself, especially concerning the Albigensian Crusade. "Just like the pope in Rome, in Aix today, we are more worried about the Cathar heretics. Their dualism beliefs of God as the force of good and Demiurge as the force of evil are contrary to those of the pope and of all Christianity. Gnosticism is not part of our Christian doctrine."

"Interesting that Gnosticism continues to appear. Apostle Paul had to fight to keep the faith pure among the early converts, and now Pope Honorius and Innocent before him must do the same. Even in Athens there were two faiths preaching primarily the same thing. The Great Schism, from two hundred years before, left two churches between Athens and Rome. I fear there may never be reconciliation between them." The duke was ready to talk further on the subject. He was keen to learn more about the political situation engulfing his homeland. Athens was now far away and the concern of his son. His concern was in Rigney.

The bishop continued to speak of the challenges faced by the church in France. "I know you have just arrived from Athens, but here in Provence and in neighboring Languedoc, we have other challenges. The Albigensians, the Cathars, continue to try to separate from the true faith, that of the pope and Jesus Christ as is found in the Bible. There is only one God. There aren't two— one good and one evil. It is nonsense and is nowhere found in the Gospels."

The duke pressed the bishop for another hour, each enjoying the local wine.

---

8 Pope Innocent III: Pope from AD 1198 to 1216. Resided in Rome during the Fourth Crusade.
9 Al Kamil: Muslim ruler and fourth Ayyubid sultan of Egypt from AD 1218 to AD 1238. He defeated the Fifth Crusade. Born circa AD 1177, died AD 1238.

"Your Grace, I have bored you enough with talk of the problems facing us in the south of France. We are happy you were able to arrive safely but recommend you make your way to Rigney using a more easterly route. The battles with the Cathars are not yet over."

The duke was quiet for a few moments, realizing he had been gone way too long. The politics of his homeland had indeed changed. The duke was going to enjoy learning all he could about the new France. His first encounter with the bishop was better than he ever expected.

✝✝✝

MARSEILLE, FRANCE
MORNING, THURSDAY, AUGUST 7, AD 1225

"Arcadius, let us pray before we leave on the last leg of our homeward journey." The duke stood outside of his tent.

Arcadius, stood with his wife and Theodore, the doctor, and the captain. He breathed in the clean morning air of Provence. There was no salty sea air—only the fresh air of the forest.

"Bring the cloth. I wish you to say a prayer for our safe journey home."

Arcadius and Theodore retrieved the valise from the first wagon. Theodore and Lorraine would be riding on this wagon, Arcadius, on horseback. They returned within a few minutes with the valise. Arcadius took the cloth out. It had been folded so that the gray, bearded face of Jesus could be seen.

The duke genuflected and knelt before it. A raven overhead cawed at the assembly of the three wagons breaking the silence.

"In Nomine Patris et Filii et Spiritus Sancti. We pray today to Saint Denis, patron saint of France . . ." Arcadius prayed, thinking of Saint Denis and his intercessions for the needy. In his new home, he hoped that together with his son, they would be able to spread the word of God and of His Son. It had been so long since he had thought of his desire to be ordained. "Jesus, be with us, just as your bearded image is with us as we embark on this last leg of our journey. In the name of Jesus Christ, amen."

The duke was slow to rise. He remained another few minutes deep in prayer.

Two horses neighed in anticipation of their upcoming travel.

"Arcadius, it is unfortunate, but we won't be able to pray again in the presence of our bearded man until we understand the political climate. It's been twenty years, but as you know, Pope Innocent was never pleased with the methods of payments taken from Alexios." The duke strode over to his horse, and Arcadius and Theodore followed. "When we arrive in Aix, I hope to speak with the archbishop there to understand further any repercussions we will need to be on the watch for. I'll need to see if Honorius III is differently inclined than Innocent III. Bishop de Montlaur was unable to provide any insight."

Even after twenty years, the duke was not going to risk excommunication by revealing the treasures he had in his possession.

✝✝✝

Cathédrale Saint-Sauveur d'Aix-en-Provence, Aix, France
Morning, Saturday, August 9, AD 1225

"Go into the cathedral and inform the archbishop that the duke of Athens would like an audience with him this afternoon." The duke was very specific in his instructions to Aloisius. "We must speak at his earliest convenience."

The archbishop was overseeing the never-ending renovations and improvements. With the city of Aix becoming the capital of the province, the cathedral grew in significance, requiring its building to grow with it. Two new wings for the transept were proposed and just needed the right funding to proceed. Construction had been progressing for years, but without more funds, it would potentially need to be put on hold.

The archbishop had been meeting with stonemasons all morning and was glad to meet with someone not looking to be paid. Perhaps there could be money from his new interlocutor. "How may I be of service?"

"Your Excellency, the former duke of Athens, Othon de la Roche, has just arrived from Athens by way of Marseille and would enjoy the courtesy of your company this afternoon." Aloisius bowed, kissed the archbishop's ring, and awaited a response. The archbishop smiled. The duke would make a perfect supporter of the cost of the renovations.

"Unfortunately, I cannot meet this afternoon. I am available tomorrow immediately after morning Mass. I can't work on this building then, so I will be glad for the change in topic," the archbishop smiled. "We can meet here in my chambers."

The duke and his entourage enjoyed Sunday morning Mass the next day. The Mass reminded him of masses when he was a child. They were so different from those in Athens. The Athenian churches had round, gilded Roman arches, filled with the aroma of incense. Here, the incense was barely noticed.

"Go in peace, glorifying the Lord by your life. *Ite missa est.*" The archbishop concluded the Sunday morning Mass as always with the traditional directive to go forth and be sent. Parishioners whispered in response, "*Deo Gratias.*"

It had been many weeks since any of the duke's small troupe had been present at a formal Mass. Each was glad to begin a return to a more normal worship routine, after having spent the last few weeks on a ship away from formal Mass.

The duke's party included himself, Arcadius and his family, Doctor Guiscard, and the captain of the guard. They were slow to rise.

The archbishop remained busy greeting and dismissing parishioners. They waited until the sanctuary had cleared before making their way to greet the archbishop.

"Your Excellency, how good it was to hear your homily and Mass. It has been many weeks since we've been to a formal Mass. Arcadius has been guiding us during our voyage, but your service in this beautiful church was splendid." The duke knelt and kissed the ecclesiastical ring.

"Your Grace, I am so glad we will be able to spend a few minutes together." The archbishop and duke both walked together to the archbishop's chambers. The chambers were larger than the duke expected.

The duke's party followed behind, out of earshot. A table was set up for a party of four: the archbishop, the duke, Arcadius, and the archbishop's aide. Lunch consisted of local cheese, sausage, bread, and wine. Freshly picked plums, grapes, and apples were in season and concluded the meal. Conversation was pleasant but of no import to the duke's objective.

With lunch finished and pleasantries complete, the duke began his inquiries. "Your Excellency, I return to my home country after many years— decades in fact—only to find there is strife and division here as well." The duke thought it best to begin with the most current issues facing the church in Provence, even though his objective was to understand the pope's feelings regarding payments received in Constantinople. He wished to be absolved of possible wrongdoing. Others had been excommunicated for less, and his payment was surreptitiously accompanying him on his return home. They were rightfully his, and he would do all in his power to keep the current pope from taking them.

The archbishop repeated similar messages the duke had heard a few days before from the bishop of Marseille. The discussion of the Cathars and the fight against them begun by Innocent III, and fought now by Pope Honorius III, lasted over an hour. "No one can foresee how this will end. It is clear the Cathars will not be able to continue. As Gnostics, they cannot think they have special knowledge known only to them. Jesus's message is open to all who wish to receive it. The pope, and all of France, for that matter, consider them heretics. He is inclined to offer leniency if they convert back to a right thinking of God. Otherwise, I believe his wishes are to wipe them out." The archbishop let his words hang in the air a few moments. It was a clear signal that deviation from church dogma would not be tolerated by this pope, nor France or the French king.

"Even though we wish we could regain the Holy Land, divisions within the church with these Gnostics are making that near impossible. It is even slowing the funding for the renovations and completion of this wonderful cathedral." The archbishop landed a hint as to the predicament he found himself in.

Finally, the duke had an opening to speak about the situation in the Holy Land and in Constantinople. "After the tragic loss of the Holy Land to Al Kamil, do you foresee another Crusade? I've spent much of my life sacrificing for this noble cause, but now find myself too old to participate directly as I once did." The archbishop sensed his opening.

The duke thought of the pain in his feet that had subsided since embarking on their journey from Athens.

"There were many crimes committed in the name of Jesus in the Fourth Crusade . . . the fighting with Zara, then with the Christians in Constantinople. I know that the last pope, Pope Innocent III, disagreed with the way the payments were taken to fund the Crusade. He was disappointed there was little progress in freeing the Holy Land. In any case, I am certain this pope could be convinced to overlook many of those crimes given the right inducements. A word from a well-placed archbishop could easily cause the pope to look the other way." The archbishop had learned the art of not-so-subtle subtlety and continued to use it to his advantage.

The duke also understood the message and used that message to his advantage.

The conversation continued for another hour, both men feeling like they had gained what they needed. The archbishop received a very generous gift of silver from the duke. He didn't object—and he didn't ask—that it may have come from dubious sources as payment for the services provided during the Fourth Crusade.

In return, the archbishop would make certain to advocate for the duke in case he was ever called upon. The archbishop also provided a letter penned to Bishop Jean I. Allegrin of Besançon,[10] the home of the bishop overseeing the region of Burgundy containing Rigney. The letter introduced the duke to Bishop Allegrin and informed him of the archbishop's special relationship with the duke and the pope. The letter also included a special request concerning Arcadius.

---

10 Bishop Jean I: Allegrin bishop of Besançon from AD 1225 to 1227. Born circa AD 1180, died AD 1237.

✝✝✝

"Arcadius, you have been very loyal all these years to me and to the payments. I wish to repay you for all you have done. I would like to think that the relics we brought back and especially the holy Shroud have been instrumental in our good fortunes. It's been two months since we've returned. I'd like to pray on the cloth." The duke stood from his red velvet cushioned chair in the chapel. He no longer suffered from his gout, but on occasion, had trouble moving about the palace. Being home and leading a much less stressful life had reduced the flare-ups.

"Please go down to the treasury and bring the cloth. I wish to see it and display it for you and your family. Make certain to return with them." The duke smiled, trying to hold back his joy. He handed Arcadius the key to the palace treasury room from around his neck.

"Your Grace." Arcadius bowed, and he and Theodore turned and made their way to the treasury. Arcadius was overjoyed to pray with the duke and the cloth. He would pray that his son now seriously consider a future in the priesthood.

He had only once been inside the treasury. It was when they first arrived at Rigney to stow the relics in the duke's possession. Talk of the treasures had been kept to a minimum. Not only was the duke never one to brandish his gains, but he worried about word of the payments making their way to the pope.

Arcadius and Theodore returned after about five minutes. Theodore held the leather valise protecting the cloth.

The duke and his wife, Isabel,[11] were both seated. No one else was present, not even any of the household staff, adjutants, or family attendants. The duke was very careful about limiting knowledge of his possession of the cloth. Only these five were ever made aware of it, for fear it would be confiscated, stolen, or worse.

"With your permission, Your Grace." Arcadius bowed and unfastened the buckle on the valise and slid the cloth out. Arcadius's wife stood, and the three of them began to unfurl it. Arcadius held the head and face of Christ, his wife the front of the legs, his son the half with the image of Christ's back. Arcadius was surprised to notice a slight smoky scent coming from the cloth. After the calamity at the port in Marseille, he thought it might be a good time to air it out over the next few days.

---

11 Isabel: Wife of Duke Othon de la Roche.

"You have done well for me protecting this cloth. Now I wish to repay you for your loyalty. When I spoke with the archbishop in Aix, he provided a special dispensation for you to become ordained, if you so choose, even though you're married. The church does require priests be celibate, but in your case, the church is willing to make an exception. He has communicated that to me and provided me a letter stating exactly that." The duke had finally made good on his promise to Arcadius two decades before. His sense of satisfaction and pride in his friend was as broad as his smile.

Arcadius was ecstatic. "That's wonderful news. I had long ago abandoned hope of ever becoming ordained. It has been so long. I didn't expect this, especially after the death of Father Christos."

"There is one requirement, however. It is a very simple one." The duke became a bit more serious but was still smiling. "You must remain here and continue to care for the relics and, especially, this cloth." Both Arcadius and the duke smiled at each other.

Arcadius quoted from one of his most favorite verses in the Old Testament, from Ruth, "Where you go, I will go, and where you stay, I will stay. Your people will be my people and your God my God. Where you die, I will die, and there I will be buried." Arcadius punctuated the last five words. He had been living this verse with the duke for over twenty years and would continue for another twenty.

CHAPTER 8

The Collegiate Church of Saint Mary, Lirey, France

The Hundred Years' War between England and the continent continued on and off. The Truce of Leulinghem, signed in AD 1389, provided a short hiatus, as each side licked their wounds and endeavored to build support and finances to recommence hostilities. Saint Mary's Church in Lirey, France, a tiny village about 170 miles from Rigney, was built by Geoffrey I de Charny,[1] descendant of Duke Othon de la Roche, to house and display the holy Shroud after a grant of land by King Philip VI[2] in AD 1343. It was apart from the main fighting, but not by a large distance.

---

1 Geoffrey I de Charny: Married Jeanne de Vergy, descendant of Duke Othon de la Roche. Known for his books on chivalry. Appointed by King Philip VI royal counselor and bearer of the sacred battle standard of France, the Oriflamme. Died in battle in Poitiers clutching the Oriflamme. Born circa AD 1306, died AD 1356.
2 King Philip VI: Born AD 1293, died AD 1350.

Saint Mary's Church, Lirey, France
Noon, Friday, January 8, AD 1390

One hundred fifty years had passed since the holy Shroud was brought to middle Europe. Father Arcadius's son, Theodore, decided not to enter the priesthood. He became an artist and remained close to his family and to the de la Roche family. Many of his paintings can be found at Chateau de la Roche.

As generations passed, children would enter the priesthood. Others would stay close to the Rigney de la Roche line. They believed they had a duty to continue the protection of the holy Shroud. Six generations later, through the close family ties to the de Charny family, Rafael Onfroi, a direct descendant of the Arcadius family, was ordained in the Roman Catholic Church and assigned to the Collegiate Church in Lirey.

When King Philip VI granted the land for the Collegiate Church of Saint Mary in Lirey to house the Shroud and other relics, Onfroi's uncle became the protector. When Onfroi's uncle passed away, Father Rafael Onfroi inherited the duty to protect the holy Shroud and was appointed to the leadership of the Lirey Church.

†††

Father Onfroi locked the treasury room, located under the altar of Saint Mary's Church, and put the key back underneath his frock. Outside, the weather was a biting cold, but it was even colder and damper in the dark room. The leather cord holding the key around his neck was long enough so that he only had to bow slightly to be able to unlock the church treasury without having to remove it from around his neck. He kept the key tied around his neck, and it never left his possession.

Next to the key was a simple, carved wooden cross hanging around his neck, given to him by his mother on the occasion of his ordination. There was also a pilgrimage medal given to him by Sir Geoffrey[3] over twenty-five years ago on the same leather cord as his cross. The medal had an image of Jesus's face from the Shroud and an empty cross on the reverse. Sir Geoffrey was the inheritor and protector of the Shroud, going back to Duke Othon de la Roche, his forebear of over five generations. Sir Geoffrey placed his solemn trust in Father Onfroi to care for and protect the Shroud. There was only one higher duty for Father Onfroi—to God.

The day's exhibitions were exceedingly busy, with over one hundred participants praying to the Shroud, offering payments, and being dispensed

---

3 Geoffrey II de Charny: Descendant of Duke Othon de la Roche, son of Geoffrey I de Charny. Died AD 1398.

indulgences for themselves and for their deceased relatives. The exhibitions continued even though Bishop Pierre d'Arcis of Troyes[4] claimed the Shroud was a fake. D'Arcis claimed it was a sacrilege for it to be offered for veneration. He had even appealed to the pope to decide the matter once and for all.

At Onfroi's urging, today's monies were to be received to help defray the costs of the repairs to the Cathedral of Saint Peter and Saint Paul in Troyes—d'Arcis's Cathedral—that had recently sustained damage from the collapse of one of the enclosing arches of its clerestory. Father Onfroi had also been the assistant to Geoffrey for many years—more than he could count—and was considered Geoffrey's confidant and counsel. Although he hadn't left Lirey to minister to the dying and wounded fighting against the English in Flanders, at Saint Mary's Church in Lirey he had the privilege of ministering to those seeking indulgences for their loved ones in purgatory.

Three men rode up on beautifully adorned horses. A carriage followed behind them, displaying the flag of the Vatican emissary. A man stepped out of the carriage, making certain his cloak was drawn tight to stave off the stinging cold of the January day. "Father, I am Deacon Vauquelin. These are my men. I wish to deliver a letter to Sir Geoffrey. It is from Pope Clement.[5] I also wish to inform him a similar letter was delivered to Bishop Pierre d'Arcis of Troyes." The official messenger from the pope stood outside the treasury and displayed the letter.

Father Onfroi locked the gate to the treasury room and put the key back under his tunic. He turned and looked at the man and the letter. Onfroi had only seen one other letter with the pope's seal. Just as other letters from the pontiff, this one was sealed with a leaden bulla attached to the parchment with a gold-colored ribbon.

"I will take you to him immediately. I trust your journey was uneventful."

The messenger didn't respond. He stayed aloof in his silence.

There were three additional men in the messenger's entourage. Each dismounted and tended their horses. Steam came out of the horses' nostrils as they exhaled and relaxed after a long ride in the bitter cold.

Just as Jesus would, Onfroi displayed extreme deference to the man from the Vatican. *Those that are first shall be last* . . . He had learned long ago there were two types of people: the arrogant who enjoyed flaunting their rank and the humble who realized they could get along just as well without their rank. Onfroi had suffered his fair share of pompous people around Sir Geoffrey.

4 Bishop Pierre d'Arcis: Bishop of Troyes from AD 1377 to 1395. Died AD 1395
5 Pope Clement VII of Avignon: Pope from AD 1378 to 1394. Resided in Avignon as anti-pope.

"Sir Geoffrey can be found in his chambers here in Lirey. He's been here all week while the exhibitions have been taking place." Father Onfroi tried to make small talk, but the papal messenger would give no more than a simple yes or no in reply. The four men had no interests outside of completing their mission so they could return quickly to their duties and privileges in Avignon for the pope.

Followed by the three other riders, they proceeded to the small annex building where Sir Geoffrey had his chambers while in Lirey. The hint of his arrogance became a full-fledged banner of pride as they walked.

Inside the annex, two servant women cleaned the floors of the entryway. The heavy planking was already exposed, with the rush mat having just been rolled up and put outside. Each woman had a bucket and a coarse hand brush, and they worked on their hands and knees scrubbing the wooden planks. When the father and the messengers arrived, the women stood, backed toward the far wall, and bowed.

"Your Grace, a letter from the pope has arrived. I believe it concerns the Shroud. I present messenger Deacon Vauquelin." Father Onfroi stood to the side and provided a clear path for the messenger to face Sir Geoffrey.

"Deacon Vauquelin." Onfroi bowed slightly and gracefully motioned his arm for the papal messenger to step forward.

The deacon advanced and stood about six feet in front of Sir Geoffrey. "From His Holiness in Avignon, Pope Clement VII." The messenger took two small paces forward, stretched out his hand holding the letter, bowed, and waited, statuesque, until it was taken from him. As he stepped forward, his perfumed scent confessed his family's wealth.

Sir Geoffrey took the letter and inspected the bulla. It was a leaden seal with the images of Saint Paul and Saint Peter on the one side and the name of Clement VII on the reverse. The bulla wasn't perfectly round, but the insignia was authentic as being from the pope.

Geoffrey pulled a knife from his desk and then, without tearing the parchment, he carefully cut through the sealing wax. The writing was in Latin and easily legible.

Father Onfroi looked on, wondering if they would have to discontinue the exhibitions of the Shroud. He felt the edge of the pilgrimage medal inside his frock. As he had done hundreds of times before, he traced the outlines of Jesus's face on one side and the smoother rectangle of the empty cross on the reverse.

Geoffrey held the letter to the light that came in through a small glass window. It took a few minutes to read the letter, and then Sir Geoffrey began to smile. "Onfroi, we have succeeded. We have been given permission to continue the exhibitions!" Geoffrey's glee was effervescent. "Thirty-four years ago, my father exhibited the Shroud and was threatened with excommunication. Now I exhibit the Shroud, and it is the Troyes' bishop who is threatened. His Holiness has given us permission. You and I were just boys when my father first displayed the Shroud, and now we can make this relic available for all to see. Bishop d'Arcis is also ordered to keep silent concerning his opinions on the Shroud under threat of excommunication." Geoffrey emphasized *opinions*.

Geoffrey smiled and looked up at Onfroi, who smiled back with an even larger smile. "My lord, that's wonderful news."

Sir Geoffrey could finally put his battle with Bishop Pierre d'Arcis behind him. The Shroud was not an icon or a painted image, as d'Arcis claimed. It was confirmed by Pope Clement VII of Avignon as the true burial Shroud of Jesus Christ.

"Deacon, you and your men will join us for celebration on this wondrous news from His Holiness." Geoffrey looked for his writing implements. "Onfroi, fetch us some fresh parchment and the sealing wax. We must thank His Holiness immediately."

The messenger bowed and remained at attention.

Father Onfroi found a fresh parchment right from a compartment inside the writing table next to where Sir Geoffrey had been sitting.

"Onfroi, make preparations. We will have a celebration of this stupendous news. Make accommodations for Vauquelin and his men in the guest house. They will be staying a few days."

Vauquelin wasn't happy at this statement. The expression on his face didn't change. He would not be able to turn down this invitation from the son of Geoffrey de Charny, hero of the Hundred Years' War. Instead of returning the next day, they would be away from the comforts of Avignon for another few days.

Father Onfroi was gifted with wonderful, artistic penmanship and became the scribe for Geoffrey as he dictated his letter. Though the letter was only one page, it took an hour to write. The politics of writing a letter to the pope was not lost on Sir Geoffrey. "Done. Now let me sign and seal it. Where is my signet ring?" Geoffrey's ring reflected the coat of arms of his father, made up of three shields, two on top and one centered below.

The scent of lavender, chamomile, and basil wafted into Sr Geoffrey's chambers from the entryway, mixed with the perfume of Vauquelin. The servants finished cleaning the floor and replacing the rush floor mat, adding dried herbs to keep the bugs away.

"When she inherited the Shroud from my great-great-grandfather—four greats—over one hundred fifty years ago, my mother, Jeanne de Vergy,[6] had always wanted to host exhibitions of the Shroud but was prevented at every turn. Now we have fully completed her wishes. With this papal bull, we can do so." Geoffrey was euphoric. "Her dying wish to me was to find a way to exhibit this relic for all of France."

✝✝✝

SAINT MARY'S CHURCH, LIREY, FRANCE
AFTERNOON, FRIDAY, JANUARY 8, AD 1390

"There is no one guarding the Shroud or the church, neither at night nor during the day." Godwin was gleeful. "There will be no one to stop us. All we'll need is the key, and that is in possession of the priest. Once we've stolen the Shroud, we'll be paid handsomely when we bring it to King Richard II."[7] Godwin and his two compatriots had been spying on the church in Lirey since the day before. With the Truce of Leulinghem in force, the need for them to remain in northern France had passed. They could return home.

Originally from Surrey, England, the three Englishmen were dressed in cloaks that disguised their true origins. For fear of being recognized as English, they had left their horses in the forest outside of Lirey, about a mile away from the church. They sat through the exhibition and paid their indulgences. The Lirey Church had nothing to deter them from breaking into the church and taking all they could carry, including the holy Shroud. At the conclusion of the exhibition, the three of them stayed in the church and watched Father Onfroi as he and two acolytes returned the Shroud to the locked treasury. After Onfroi returned, the three men got up and made their way out of the church. After the exhibition the three walked about 100 yards into the forest, having said nothing to anyone for fear of being discovered.

"Do we have permission from the king?" Lyman was the first to break the silence. He, too, wanted to be paid but mostly wanted to make a difference. After fifteen years away from their homes across the channel, he didn't want to return with nothing to show for his efforts. "We were promised more money, and with the Truce from Leulinghem, that'll never happen. I want to return home with fame and fortune."

"I, too, have nothing to go back to. I lost three fingers and my ear when I earned this knighthood, and I'm not going to suffer in squalor just because

---

6 Jeanne de Vergy: Wife of Sir Geoffrey I de Charny and mother of Sir Geoffrey II de Charny. Died AD 1428.

7 King Richard II: Known as Richard of Bordeaux. King of England from AD 1377 to 1399. Born AD 1367, died AD 1400.

the king wants a truce." Godwin rubbed the stub that was his ear. It still felt raw, even six months after the injury. "It was the three of us that saved Arundel's life in the battle of Margate."

"I hate fighting from ships. I want to fight hand to hand, face to face in an open field, not the crowded spaces of a galley. I want to see the life of the man drain out of his eyes. I want to smell his fear as I approach." Godwin longed for the next battle. He was a sergeant, the same rank as Lyman before being knighted. He had been fighting for many years, ever since he was old enough to handle a sword.

The three men continued spying on the church. They kept their cover in the thick trees, a few hundred yards from the church. They had a clear view of the church's entry.

"I don't see those four men who remained after the service. They were dressed like they were from some place important—maybe Avignon." Percival was the youngest with rank of archer. He had joined the fight against the French only a year before, going against the wishes of his uncles.

"We'll return tomorrow to learn more about the protection to the Shroud. If there's no one guarding the church, we'll easily be able to take what we want and be on our way." Lyman began walking back to their horses. All three of them had fought hard at Margate, and they were in no mood not to get paid.

Percival wasn't so sure. "Robbing from the church. We should take from the rich French merchants and landowners but not from the church." Before Percival became a page, his uncle wanted him to become a priest in the church. Instead, he joined the fight against the French. His uncle was a priest and detested the killing and the constant battles between the English and the French. Percival could remember his words exactly, "Such useless killing just so the king can have his glory."

"You will do it! I demand it! Or you are worthless to me." Godwin grabbed Percival's cloak and pulled him toward him. With the other hand, he pressed against the pommel of his dagger. Godwin had to resist taking his dagger and stabbing the insubordinate right then and there. He looked directly at him and snarled. It was the third time he had to reprimand this man since the truce. The next time he would kill him. His glare made it clear he had no choice in the matter. Godwin finally threw him back and then glared over at Lyman. He didn't want to do this alone. He needed the help of the two of them, but he would do it alone if he had to.

Lyman remained silent, in no mood for a standoff with Godwin. He also didn't want to return home without compensation. This was the only way for them to get paid their due. Lyman would help Godwin steal the Shroud for the king. They all walked in silence until they reached their horses.

Godwin mounted his horse and began riding off. He breathed in the fresh cold air. It helped to calm him. He wouldn't tolerate any resistance from these subordinates.

Percival looked at Lyman, both tired of the arrogance of their senior. They slowly mounted their steeds and followed Godwin. "This war must come to an end. I and, before me, my father fought for far too long, and nothing has been achieved. Yet I believe France is in the wrong. My father died in the fighting in Pontvallain, and it accomplished nothing. Nothing! Stealing the Shroud would only inflame old wounds, but if the earl instructs us to do so, I will." He looked away and galloped off to catch up to Godwin. Without instruction, Percival's horse simply followed the horse ahead of him.

They rode for an hour to a small clearing where they had rested the night before. Lyman was able to restart the fire from some embers still glowing from the morning. They each had some bread and dried meat.

"It is Father Onfroi. He has the key. He can open the treasury for us." Godwin was ready to act. Robbing the Shroud on a Sunday would not work. There would be too many parishioners milling about that might be willing to resist. "We'll need to come back Tuesday or Wednesday in the evening. We'll abduct Onfroi and then steal his key."

Lyman stoked the fire. It was a bitter cold night, and snow began to fall. The air had the sweet scent of ozone mixed with smoke from the fire. The mead combined with the fire only partially kept them warm. "We should ride to within a few hundred yards and then walk the rest quietly by foot. We don't want them to know we're coming."

✝✝✝

LIREY, FRANCE
LATE AFTERNOON, TUESDAY, JANUARY 12, AD 1390

Just like their first visit to the church, after the exhibition the three Englishmen lingered, as if to be praying. They needed to keep their eyes on Father Onfroi to see what he did with the Shroud after the exhibition. They also needed to know where to find him later that evening when they were to steal the Shroud.

After the exhibition, Father Onfroi conversed with Sir Geoffrey about their evening meal. The two often ate together when Sir Geoffrey was visiting Lirey and the Shroud. The afternoon exhibition was over, and there was a good collection of funds for the church.

"Your Lordship, I would like to recommend we send some of the funds collected today to Bishop d'Arcis of Troyes. He may consider it an olive branch, especially since the collapse of the nave." Father Onfroi and the Lirey church were not part of d'Arcis's diocese. Nevertheless, he felt there was no need for continued bad blood between Lord Geoffrey and the bishop in Troyes.

"We shall discuss this over our evening meal together. Perhaps you're right. The Troyes cathedral is in serious need of repair." Sir Geoffrey made his way back to his temporary quarters, looking forward to a meal and some wine with his friend and spiritual guide. "I have heard that not only did the nave collapse, but the beautiful rose window has fallen out of the clerestory. I pray something like that doesn't happen to our church.

"The deacon and his men will be joining us. I will enjoy hearing more news from Avignon." Sir Geoffrey was glad he was able to keep Vauquelin and his men a few extra days. Tonight would be their last night here. He enjoyed hearing about goings on in the world outside of Lirey. "I would like to hear more about the Avignon pope's stance on the Truce of Leulinghem and the relations with the church in Rome."

✝✝✝

The meal was simple, and the discussion did have its benefits. Father Onfroi enjoyed the mead, as did all the men from Avignon. The mead, combined with news of Pope Clement VII of Avignon and his rivalry with Pope Boniface IX[8] in Rome, made for lively conversation. Apparently, the schism would continue for a few more years. It was the opinion of all the men that the newly installed Roman Pope Boniface was not going to repair the split. Certainly, the almost hundred-year line of Avignon popes wasn't going to align quickly with the pope in Rome.

"Pope Urban[9] was crazy." Geoffrey took another swig of mead. "Everyone was glad when he made his way to the Lord. I guess we'll never know whether he died from the fall from his mule or from poison from his friends in Rome." They all smiled. "Boniface is illegitimate without the support of the French cardinals. After the Roman cardinals erred in their selection of Urban, they should have demurred and supported Clement in Avignon. He is the rightful pope, and without the support of the French cardinals, the Roman pope cannot be deemed legitimate."

Everyone agreed. There would be no military action to mend the schism.

---

8 Pope Boniface IX: Pope in Rome from AD 1389 to 1404. Born circa AD 1350, died AD 1404.
9 Pope Urban VI: Pope in Rome from AD 1378 to 1389. Born circa AD 1318, died AD 1389.

The French and English were out of money and momentarily devoid of ambition. "Perhaps with the truce with England, the young King Charles VI of France[10] can exert more influence over some of the Italian states to sway them from their errant ways in supporting Boniface." Father Onfroi knew enough of the politics to give an opinion without saying too much.

The discussion continued for another hour. Onfroi stood, a little unsteady on his feet from the mead. He bid farewell and made his way back to his home in the rectory just opposite the church. The papal emissary and his men did the same, and they walked to their temporary quarters located next door to the rectory. The sound of the five was muffled as a light snow fell silently to the ground. The moon couldn't be seen, but its light through the clouds helped light their path.

✝✝✝

"There they are, and all a bit contented from too much wine." Godwin could see that everyone had too much to drink. They stood at the edge of the wood. "The priest will be easy to persuade to hand over the key." He emphasized the word *persuade* and smiled as he said it. "We'll wait until things have settled down in the guest quarters and in the rectory."

After a few minutes, they could see smoke billowing from the chimneys of the rectory as Father Onfroi stoked the fire to keep himself warm throughout the night. No such smoke came from the guest quarters. They were sufficiently inebriated that they would sleep the night through the cold.

They waited another few minutes until the lights from the rectory candles were finally snuffed. "It won't be long now. Percival, you and Lyman go in the back door, and I'll go in the front," Godwin instructed.

Lyman and Percival crept silently to the door. The bar across the door was easy to raise from outside, and they inched their way to where Onfroi was sleeping.

Godwin grew frustrated in his attempt to open the front door. Instead of risking noise at that time of night, he gave up and ran around to the back door, which was open. Percival and Lyman had their quarry. Lyman reached his arm around Onfroi's neck.

Onfroi was still struggling when Godwin approached. "You will take us to the treasury."

Percival and Lyman each took one of Onfroi's arms. Lyman pressed his dagger against the man's neck, keeping him quiet.

Adrenaline overtook the effects of the mead Onfroi had consumed, and

---

10 King Charles VI of France: Known as the Beloved, later the Mad from AD 1380 to AD1 422. Born AD 1368, died AD 1422.

he was now wide awake. He could feel the cold in his hands and the blood rushing to his head.

The four of them marched out the door and across the way to the church.

"Open it." Lyman looked directly at Onfroi, and could see the fear and dread in the preacher's eyes.

Onfroi tried to resist, but Lyman increased the pressure of the dagger against his throat, daring him to slice his neck through. Lyman smiled, enjoying the adrenaline rushing through his body. The joy of winning in hand-to-hand combat came back to him, remembering the feeling of watching the life drain from his adversary.

"Don't kill him. We need him." Percival didn't want to be part of killing a priest. That would surely send him and his compatriots to an eternity of hell and damnation.

"Easy, Priest, easy." Lyman removed the dagger from the priest's neck and jabbed it against the man's ribs. "Take out your key and open the door."

Onfroi stiffened his side where he felt the dagger pressing against his ribcage. He feared what would happen next after he handed over the key. Onfroi removed the key from under his frock.

✝✝✝

A man in black watched through the light snowfall. He moved inside the guest quarters and whispered to the sleeping emissary. "Wake up. Wake up."

The papal emissary didn't want to move but could feel the urge of his bladder. It was full of mead and wine from dinner. In the dark, the man groaned, unable to find the chamber pot. He stood up and pulled on his boots and tunic, yet not fully dressing. As he moved outside the rear of the guest quarters and next to a tree, he watched the snow come down. Relieving himself, he watched the steam rise from the dark puddle in front of him. Just as he finished, he heard a slight commotion from the direction of the church.

He walked around the corner of the quarters and glanced in the direction of the noise. "Why is the door open?" Looking more closely, he could see lights and shadows flickering from inside.

He ran back inside the guest quarters. "Wake up, wake up. Something's wrong," Vauquelin whispered to his guards.

They woke with a start, yet still foggy from the mead. One of them grabbed his head. The other wanted to clean his mouth out.

"Get your sword. There's something wrong!" Vauquelin said in a hushed, imperative tone. "Come out the back door. Hurry. Now!"

Vauquelin moved out the back door and waited for his three men. Each was ready. Their training had included some hand-to-hand fighting, but their purpose was more for show rather than for physical combat.

✝✝✝

Onfroi led the three men to the treasury in the cellar of the church. The iron gate was formidable unless there was a key. All of the church's treasures were kept there, including two silver Communion chalices, a silver bread tray, and several candlesticks. There was also a locked strongbox filled with coins from the exhibitions.

Lyman attempted to lift it, but it was heavier than he expected. "We won't be able to run very fast with this case." Lyman grinned thinking of what he could do with that much money. Their prize though was in a decorated case. It, too, had a lock. "Give me the keys."

Onfroi wasn't moving fast enough. Godwin wanted to be out of there with their loot mounted on their horses. Onfroi took the keys from his neck, but before he could hand them over, Godwin grabbed them and ripped them from his neck. The leather cord didn't break, causing Onfroi to lurch forward toward Godwin. Godwin yanked at them again, and this time, the cord broke.

"No." Onfroi resisted, but he was no match for the three of them.

Lyman punched the squirming priest, and he fell to the floor unconscious. "We don't need him anymore." Lyman kicked him in his stomach to make certain he was out and wouldn't follow them. He considered killing him but, looking at Percival, decided against it.

Godwin opened the case and pulled out the Shroud. It was wrapped in a red silk cloth inside a leather valise. "I'll carry the Shroud. You take what you can carry." He slipped the Shroud inside his tunic, leaving his hands free. He decided to carry nothing else. The other two would carry the money. He had the prize he was looking for. He would present it personally to the king.

Lyman put the church ware into a sack and threw coins in on top. Percival took the candlesticks and threw coins in his sack as well. Each had twenty pounds of church treasure in their sacks.

✝✝✝

Vauquelin and his guards entered the church. The candlelight and voices coming from below confirmed his suspicions. "We'll wait for them to come out of the cellar." Deacon Vauquelin and the papal guards made their way to the treasury, knowing they needed to protect at all costs that most valuable relic.

Lyman appeared first, his bag of loot slung over his shoulder and held by one hand with a torch held in the other. He wasn't expecting the thrust into his abdomen. His grunt surprised Percival and Godwin, who were right behind him, and they watched their friend fall to the floor. As Lyman fell, he thought of the faces of the men he had stabbed. There was no pain or anguish. There was no pity for himself or any of the men he killed. His life simply ended there on the cold floor. He didn't die a hero. Instead, he died a common thief. Meaningless.

The torch was the only source of light inside the church, casting shadows everywhere. Percival lost his hand as Vauquelin's sword came down on it and sliced right through.

Thud. Blood spurted out of his wrist where his hand used to be. Fear was in his eyes as a prayer came to his mind asking for forgiveness. Regret in participating in this failed theft filled his last thoughts. He dropped the sack, stood up straight, and let the papal guard pierce his chest. It was the first man the guard had ever killed.

"You won't take me alive!" Godwin shouted, standing behind his fallen friends. He took out his sword and held it in one hand, his dagger in the other.

Vauquelin thrust first, but it was deflected. From the other side of the cellar threshold, one of the papal guards swung down and knocked the dagger out of Godwin's hand. With only two fingers, Godwin's grip was nowhere near strong enough to keep hold of the dagger against the force of the guard's sword. The torch had fallen facing Godwin such that he was fully lit, while Vauquelin and his men were in darkness. Vauquelin swung again and again, but each thrust was fully defended.

During the commotion, Onfroi awoke, his head pounding from the blow that left him unconscious. He grabbed his side and found no blood, just pain from Lyman's kick. Hearing the commotion, and without thinking, Onfroi bounded up the stairs and thrusted his body into the back of Godwin, pushing him into Vauquelin's reach. With Godwin suddenly exposed, the papal messenger landed a successful thrust to Godwin's side, and Godwin fell back down the stairs taking Onfroi with him. Onfroi hit his head on one of the steps, and he again fell unconscious.

There was no way for anyone to succeed coming up a set of stairs and fighting off more than one defender. Godwin slumped dead on his back as his body slid to the bottom of the stairs behind Onfroi, his head landing at the feet of the unconscious Father Onfroi. A pool of blood flowed out his side into a puddle on the first step, then dripped down to the floor as more and more of his life spilled out.

CHAPTER 9

Margaret de Charny, Lirey, France

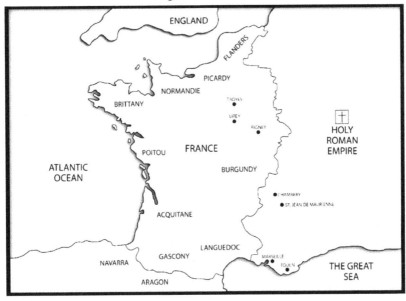

The Shroud was passed down through many generations from Duke Othon de la Roche to the de Charny family, when de la Roche's great-great-granddaughter, Jeanne de Vergy, married Geoffrey I de Charny. Geoffrey I founded a collegiate church in Lirey near Troyes, with permission from King Philip VI,[1] to house and protect the Shroud. Disagreements festered over the ownership and came to a head with Margaret de Charny,[2] Geoffrey I de Charny's granddaughter.

---

1 King Philip VI: Reigned over France AD 1328 to AD 1350. Born AD 1293, died AD 1350.
2 Margaret de Charny: Geoffrey II de Charny's daughter. Became Countess de la Roche, second wife to Humbert de Villersexel. Died AD 1460.

Chateau de la Roche, Rigney, France
Midmorning, Friday, July 6, AD 1418

"**M**adam, there are reports again of English marauders raiding just south of Nancy." Louis came in with the morning meal. As always, it was served on a silver tray. Blueberries were in season, and a bowl filled to the brim was presented along with some cold sausage, bread, and warm broth. It was cool inside the residence, and her tabby female cat, Chausette, named for the white sock-like fur on all four paws, kept Margaret's lap warm.

Although she had only married the month before, her new husband, Humbert de Villersexel, count of de la Roche and lord of Saint Hippolyte sur Doubs,[3] was not present. They had barely consummated their marriage when he rode off to his palace in Saint Hippolyte sur Doubs to make preparations to receive the valuables from Rigney.

For both, theirs was a marriage of convenience. Margaret was tired of her loneliness. Her first marriage had not been satisfying, and with her husband's early demise, she was left alone managing their estate and properties. She would have preferred marrying her longtime friend, Louis, her butler and confidant, but he was already happily married with children of his own.

"Louis, I don't fancy traveling to Humbert, but I guess I must to keep up appearances. How nice it would be to go back to our teenage years when the world was so much simpler. We wouldn't have to care about property, war, or the church." She had always had a love for him, especially in her teens when they lived like twins. In her station, it would never have been possible. Margaret de Charny was the daughter of a line of great and chivalrous knights. Louis was a commoner from a family always in her family's employ.

Her thoughts drifted back to that magical time of freedom and carelessness. "Remember when we rode out through the forest and picnicked near that stream? It was such a beautiful sunny spring day." She smiled. It was her first kiss. She knew Louis had had the same feelings for her, but it would have been scandalous for her to explore those thoughts. Afterward, she had to rein in her love for her friend so he could be by her side for as long as possible. "I was always afraid my father would find out about us and kick you and your family out of the household." She sighed. A pang of sadness hit her. "He would have never understood."

She went back to reading her Bible. She was reading the story of Jesus and the transformation of water into wine at the wedding in Cana.

Louis said nothing, thinking back to those times as well. A smile came to his face.

---

3 Humbert de Villersexel: Count of de la Roche, lord of Saint Hippolyte sur Doubs. Born AD 1385, died AD 1437.

Margaret looked up from her Bible. It was a worn leather-covered edition of the four Gospels given to her by her father. It was originally commissioned by her great-grandfather, Geoffrey I de Charny, when he completed his third book on chivalry. "I am so tired of these marauders. Every day there is another report and another report. When will this war end?"

The raids out of the north had continued for almost thirty years. Her scorn for the English started to overflow. She steeled herself and focused back on her reading. "Jesus says to turn the other cheek, but I don't believe I can do that when we've been fighting them for over eighty years. For the life of me, I don't know why the English continue their efforts against us. We will never let them rule France." She looked out into the garden and watched a pair of fawns meander past her rose bushes, take a bite of the grass, and then bolt off into the wood after their mother.

"Of course, ma'am." She could no longer remember when Louis's calming voice had not been with them.

"Louis, we shall ride in fifteen minutes. Make certain everything is ready." The plan was to ride first to Lirey, retrieve the Shroud from the Saint Mary Church, retreat south to Saint Hippolyte sur Doubs, and then travel farther south if necessary. "The Shroud has been in our family for two hundred years. Ever since Duke Othon de la Roche brought it in payment from Constantinople."

Louis already knew this fact. He fully understood why they were going to reclaim the Shroud and bring it to Saint Hippolyte sur Doubs.

Margaret's cat leapt from her lap and ran to the corner of the room. A small mouse scampered toward a crack in the floorboards but wasn't fast enough to escape the speed of the cat. She had it in her mouth.

"Chausette, good girl." The mouse wriggled, but Chausette was not going to let go. The cat adjusted her grip as the wriggling continued. Margaret took another berry, and the mouse fell limp hanging from Chausette's mouth. Chausette dropped the mouse, turned and looked at her owner, and then back to her quarry, with her full attention evident in the focus of her tensed ears. "Louis don't let her eat that now. I'm sure she'll have enough to eat in our new home."

Louis thumped his foot against the floor. Chausette scampered off, leaving her lifeless prize.

"Ma'am, everything is loaded." Louis stood at attention. The small caravan included three carriages, fourteen horsemen, and twenty in the guard.

"We shall go." Margaret stood and looked back at her home one more time, not certain whether she would be able to return. She didn't finish the blueberries. The dead mouse was left on the floor for the staff to remove.

†††

Saint Mary's Church, Lirey, France
Early Afternoon, Friday, July 6, AD 1418

"The countess is approaching." Raphael came into the sanctuary where Dean Lucas was cleaning the wax from the candle stand from Mass the previous day.

"We must get their full assurances the Shroud will be returned once these interminable hostilities cease." Dean Lucas was adamant about the return of the Shroud. "That Shroud was a bequest from Geoffrey I de Charny and sanctioned by King Philip the VI as well as Pope Clement VII of Avignon[4]. It was the reason why this church was consecrated. We have been commissioned by the pope to protect the Shroud of our Lord." Dean Lucas stood and felt like this was the lesser of two evils. Risk the Shroud being destroyed by the marauding English, or hand it off to this countess and possibly never have it returned. "With the papacy of Pope Benedict XIII[5] in Avignon having been quashed, this countess must assure its safe return."

†††

"Dean Lucas, the countess de la Roche." The captain of the guard entered the church and announced the arrival of the countess. She was the last to enter, behind her escorts, and wore a flowing silk gown with a bonnet covering her hair. She held her Chausette in her arms.

With her marriage to her new husband, Humbert, she became the Countess de la Roche, but she preferred *de Charny* because of the notoriety it engendered from her grandfather's heroism. He had earned recognition and respect from his fighting of the English. After all, Geoffrey I de Charny was named *porte-oriflamme*, bearer of the sacred royal battle standard of France, by King Philip VI.

The dean turned and stood before the captain and the countess. To their sides were two additional guards. Their purpose was to provide a show of force. With or without the approval of the dean, the Shroud would be leaving with the countess.

The blood vessel on Dean Lucas's forehead bulged. He said nothing.

"Dean." The countess moved forward, directly faced the dean, nodded to him while looking down on him. She was taller than him by over ten inches. He did not bow.

---

4 Pope Clement VII of Avignon: Antipope from AD 1378 to AD 1394. Born AD 1342, died AD 1394.

5 Pope Benedict XIII of Avignon: Antipope from AD 1394 to 1423. Born AD 1328, died AD 1423

"We don't know when this war with England will end, but both this church and I request your assurances that it will be returned once the English have been removed from our lands." Dean Lucas now spoke not from a position of physical power but from his political power derived from the papacy and the archbishopric in Paris. He could feel the hair on the back of his neck rise. The only trust was in his lack of trust in this woman.

"There shall be no assurance!" Margaret spoke, emphasizing each word and each syllable. Her stern voice caused the cat to tense. She had to hold tight to keep her from jumping free. Realizing it made no sense to make enemies of the church, she kept the emotion from her voice.

This dean, although not bishop, was well connected to the king and someday may become elevated to one.

"I understand your concerns. Our purpose is to keep this relic of our Lord and Savior safe and out of the hands of the English. This church is a lovely setting for this cloth, and I do hope it will one day be able to return." The duchess was skilled in saying many words without saying anything.

Dean Lucas again did not bow his head. He waited a few seconds, then finally turned and waved his arm to where the case holding the Shroud was located.

"The key." The captain of the guard made the request, although it was a clear command to the dean.

Dean Lucas paused, then removed it from his neck and handed it to the captain, who then handed it to the soldier standing behind and to his left. He nodded, and the two men proceeded forward to the case. Within a minute, the case and the leather valise were opened, and the two men removed the cloth from its red silk pouch.

"Bring it here."

All eyes were on the two men.

The captain wanted to verify it was the Shroud. They had seen it several times during previous exhibitions here at this church.

The cloth was folded to display the dark and distorted face of Jesus.

"Your Grace." The captain was satisfied but awaited the blessing from the countess.

She nodded in approval, not looking away from the dean, saying nothing.

The two men returned to the case and replaced the cloth back into its pouch, then into the case. One of the soldiers locked the case, and the two men lifted it and proceeded out of the sanctuary to the awaiting wagon. A slight rain began to drip on them as they placed the case into the covered wagon.

†††

CASTLE OF VARAMBON, AIN, AUVERGNE-RHÔNE-ALPS, FRANCE
EARLY EVENING, THURSDAY, JUNE 4, AD 1457

"Louis, I have spent almost forty years keeping the Shroud safe." She reminisced back to that day in the Lirey Church. Margaret, almost eighty years old now, stood from her writing table, fuming from the letter she had received. The pope had fulfilled his threat.

At her age, she was unsteady on her feet. Louis was only a bit steadier. He tried to reach out, but she was able to steady herself in time without falling back into her chair. As she stood, she watched the trees full of leaves sway in the summer breezes.

"After so many years protecting this cloth and dedicating my life to spreading the word of Jesus, that Parisian archbishop dares to excommunicate me. I will never return this Shroud to Lirey. Those fools can think they can have my connection to the church removed. I will not stand for this. After all, it was my forefather who brought that cloth, protected the cloth, and then loaned it to Lirey! How dare they!"

Louis remained quiet, holding a silver tray with a fresh goblet of wine.

"I've been protecting this cloth from the English for forty years, and they want to steal it from my hands!" She emphasized the words *forty years*.

"Yes, Ma'am." Louis had been with the family all his life. The two had grown up together—born only a few years apart—although he grew up in the kitchen, and she ate from the kitchen.

Louis's son Ethan, now forty-one, stood behind him. He would be taking his place soon.

"Ma'am, I always enjoyed being with you when the cloth was exhibited to those many throngs. It brought you such joy. You have been a remarkable evangelist and proponent for Jesus and Christianity."

"I have written a letter to my stepbrother Charles.[6] Please make certain it gets into his hands as soon as possible. He will be able to assist with these supposed men of the cloth in Lirey." She had only now started to calm down. She handed the letter over and with it her anger. The letter would settle this matter once and for all. A smile came over her face when she realized what she had said. "They are not men of my cloth!" She grabbed the goblet and took a long swallow, ignoring the fruity taste of the Burgundian wine. She was already on her third glass. It was the local wine that kept her youthful.

---

6 Charles de Noyers: Half-brother to Margaret de Charny.

Margaret looked down at the case that had been at her side for almost forty years. "Ethan, go get two more of the staff. I would like to look on the Shroud."

Ethan returned with his wife and her sister. Her family had been with the Villersexel service staff for as long as Louis's family had been with the de Charny family. Pregnant with their first child, Ethan's wife, Gabriel, was his younger by ten years.

Ethan retrieved the valise, and the two women removed the cloth and began to unfold it. Just as they fully unfurled it, her baby gave a quick kick against her rib cage. Gabriel put her hand to the side of her bulging belly. She was due in a few weeks.

"Your baby is kicking like John kicked Elizabeth when Mary visited her before Jesus's birth." The bitterness in Margaret's heart had now calmed as she and everyone gazed on the cloth. The light of the candles flickered onto the image. It seemed to come to life. As the three held the cloth, Margaret moved them closer to the windows where the brilliant orange light of dusk streamed in.

"Look here, these marks on his back. They are from the scourging." She tried to count them, but there were too many. "I count over thirty, but there are many more. The agony he suffered for us, and this was only the beginning."

Gabriel was kicked again. She looked away, praying her son or daughter would never have to suffer like Jesus did.

Margaret moved to the face. "He had beautiful long hair." Some of the images were so clear that anyone who looked upon the cloth could imagine everything about Jesus's moments. "The one side of his face seems beaten, and this blood on his head must be from the crown of thorns." She looked closely at the capital E in the center of his forehead. "No man could have painted this. It is truly a supernatural work. That idiot thought this was a fraud. How he dared!"

She'd viewed the image so many times, and each time, her sympathy for the man in the image grew stronger. "That bishop of Troyes thought this a fake over seventy years ago, but he was so wrong." She touched the side of her face, wincing at the pain of the imagined blow. "The pain this man suffered. How dare they." She thought of the Roman soldiers whipping and beating the Son of God. She could feel each snap of the whip.

"How dare they." This time she whispered those three words, although it wasn't clear to Ethan whether she meant the Roman soldiers that tortured Jesus, the naysayers about the truth of the cloth, or those clerics in Paris that had just excommunicated her.

Silence overcame the sounds from the slight breezes outside. The muscles in her jaw tightened as her bitterness toward the archbishop and the Lirey Church came welling up within her.

✝✝✝

CASTLE OF VARAMBON, AIN, AUVERGNE-RHÔNE-ALPS, FRANCE
LATE AFTERNOON, WEDNESDAY, DECEMBER 10, AD 1459

Margaret had barely left her estate for the last two years. She was no longer allowed in the church—any church. "Ethan, please bring your wife and son. I wish to see them. He so reminds me of Louis."

Louis had passed away just two weeks before, but she couldn't forget him. He had been with her for her whole life. He was more of a loving husband than Humbert, who was now gone over twenty years, or her first husband, Jean de Baufremont,[7] who had been gone almost fifty years. Now she was alone, truly alone. Her fate was in the hands of her stepbrother, Charles, and Duke Louis I of Savoy.[8]

Jesus was in her heart while her mortal family faded away . . . her first husband, her second husband, and now Louis. Throughout her life Louis and the cloth had been her only constants.

"Yes, Ma'am." Ethan stoked the fire and added a few logs to start it roaring again. It had begun snowing a few hours before, and his wife and son had just returned from playing outside. He retreated from the fire, leaving Margaret to enjoy the crackling blaze.

Margaret's dog had replaced her cats and was splayed out in front of the fire, enjoying the warmth from the hearth.

His son Louis, named after his grandfather, came in and set up the checkerboard to play with Margaret.

Margaret was distracted but played anyway. Her brother Charles was deliberating with the Parisian archbishop, the duke of Savoy, and others to get his sister's excommunication lifted. It was never right that there should have been an excommunication, but storming in with her guard contingent to attempt recovery of the Shroud from the Lirey deacon didn't go over well. The dean had more power in Paris than Margaret expected. Even forty years later, she bristled every time she thought of that little man in the Lirey Church.

She moved her arm to pick up her cup of tea. Her failing sight caused her to bump the handle, and the tea spilled. "Oh, dear. Now I've made a mess."

Gabriel quickly moved to wipe up the spilled tea. She returned to the fire while Ethan looked on to the checkers game being played by the countess and young Louis.

She treated him as if he were her own son. "You have learned the strategy

7 Jean de Baufremont: First husband to Margaret de Charny. Died AD 1415.
8 Duke Louis I: Duke of Savoy from AD 1440 to 1465. He received the Shroud from Margaret de Charney. Born AD 1413, died AD 1465.

of checkers very well. Next year I will teach you how to play chess. You are certainly smart enough to master its strategy."

Louis looked up and smiled. He replaced all the pieces to give the countess another chance to test his skills. "Plan your enterprises cautiously and carry them out boldly."

Margaret repeated one of the sayings from her grandfather—one of many that helped guide her life. She hoped young Louis would learn and live by each and every one of the many rules of chivalry, just as she had. She sat down and played the next game with Louis.

As they played, Ethan heard the distinct sound of clopping of hooves in the snow. No one was expected at the castle until the next day, but Charles was riding as quickly as possible to give his stepsister the news. Margaret didn't quite hear; her hearing being diminished due to her age.

"Madame, it is your brother Charles." Ethan looked out the window over the courtyard. "He is a day early from Paris and Lirey. I pray he brings good news."

Margaret wasn't sure whether to smile or to worry. She did so want to be reinstated into the church before she died.

"I win," Louis proclaimed.

Margaret didn't react, but instead was apprehensive about the prospective news from her stepbrother.

†††

Within less than a minute, Charles had made his way up the stairs and into the sitting room.

"Margaret, I bring good news." He was beaming, happy to bring her good news. The muscles in his cheeks were so cold he had to rub them to show his smile. Facing Margaret, he stood in front of the fire like a triumphant general from a hard-fought battle. Steam rose from the wet cloak on his back.

Her health was starting to fail, so she didn't rise when he entered the room.

The melting snow dripped from his cloak. He removed it and handed it to Ethan. "If you pay a stipend to the Lirey canons, they will now recognize you are in rightful possession of the Shroud. Your excommunication will be lifted. After all, it was your father, Geoffrey, who gave them the Shroud. You have won, Margaret. You have won." Charles handed her a document with the seal of Saint Mary's of Lirey on it. His hands were still cold, so he walked back to stand in front of the fire.

"This accord documents that your father, Geoffrey II de Charny, Lord of

Savoisy and Lord of Lirey, had given the Shroud to the Lirey church and that they transferred it to you for your services to protect it from the English."

"It's a bribe to the church in Lirey." Margaret sneered. "I protected that cloth all these years while those English rampaged through our country." She stabbed the air with her crooked forefinger. She wasn't happy. After a moment, she took a deep breath. "If this cloth belonged to them, they should be paying me for the protection services I gave that cloth. But they're not. I'm supposed to pay them?"

"Margaret, you get to keep possession of the cloth, and then with your bequest, it goes to the Savoys. You get to keep the cloth. They have agreed to that." Charles pleaded his case, surprised Margaret was not happy with the status of the excommunication and the cloth. "You get to be reinstated into the church and get to keep the cloth." Charles reemphasized the result, but Margaret's expression didn't change.

Ethan and his wife stood to the side of the fire, afraid to get pulled into the conversation. They wished they could retrieve their son, but they were grateful he seemed to ignore the conversation, replacing the checkers for their next game.

Several minutes passed. Margaret looked at Louis and then down at the checkerboard. The pieces were all aligned and ready to play again, but she wasn't ready for any more battles over the cloth or battles on the checkerboard. "Louis, I'm sorry, let me sit with Charles. Perhaps you can take this and play with your mother." She finally smiled as she realized the excommunication was lifted. The elation in her face was evident at thoughts of returning to church and the comfort of worship. Perhaps she would take her first Communion in Lirey. That little dean may still be there. She smiled even more broadly.

CHAPTER 10

The Shroud in Chambéry, France

Situated in the Alps, Chambéry was the capital of Savoy from AD 1295 to AD 1563, on the crossroads of Burgundy, France, Switzerland, and Italy, about 160 miles northeast from Turin, Italy. As the kingdom of France grew in power, expanding from the west, Chambéry was too exposed, and the capital was moved eastward to Turin.

SAINTE-CHAPELLE CHURCH, CHAMBÉRY, FRANCE
AFTER MIDNIGHT, WEDNESDAY, DECEMBER 4, AD 1532

"We must get in. We must!" Father Valentin shouted. Everyone had the same thoughts, but they couldn't make any progress. "Get the keys!" The iron grille encased the niche where the Shroud case was stored and locked with four separate keys. It had been held there between exhibitions since it was received from Margaret de Charny upon her death. Now it was in danger of being destroyed—1,500 years of history could be destroyed in one all-encompassing fire. Valentin would give his life if he had to, if only there was a way to trade it for the safety of the Shroud.

"That won't work," Simone interjected. The pain in his hands was incapacitating. He had been deacon, just like Liam, at the Sainte-Chapelle Church in Chambéry for eight years, and they had never had a fire. He tried to pull on the iron grille, but the heat from the fire had superheated the grille, and Simone burned his palms and fingers when he grabbed on. Smoke filled his lungs, causing him to cough.

"Liam, quickly, go get Pussod. He should be able to pry the grille open." The heat was unbearable, but no one was going to leave without the Shroud. Father Valentin also began coughing.

Small fires were common in churches, but he had never experienced one this big. The silver ornamentation on top of the Shroud case began to melt.

"The case is starting to smoke." Simone tried to find something, anything, to open the grille. The grille meant to protect its contents was now a poised weapon to inflict its destruction.

"Get water!" Father Valentin shouted, coughing again. His shout was raspy, and he could feel the smoke in his lungs.

Buckets of water were only able to slow the flames. They ran and got more water, but it was only enough to slow the battle, not to win it. The flames continued. Steam mixed with the smoke.

Pussod heard a loud banging but couldn't quite understand where it was coming from. He noticed a man outside his window. No one ever banged on his door. Locksmiths were never needed that late at night. The man was dressed in black and slipped behind the corner opposite his home.

Pussod was now awake and saw a strange glow in the sky coming from the direction of the palace. "That's strange." Pussod rotated his body, so his legs were now exposed to the cold in the room. "Is the palace on fire?" He could feel the cold on his knees below his braies, the boxer-like underwear he wore with his undertunic in bed.

"What if it is the Sainte-Chapelle?" Pussod now sat on the side of the bed, his brain accelerating and shaking off the fogginess of sleep.

The bells in Tower Yolande, connected to the chapel, began to ring out, slowly at first and then faster, signaling the urgency of the situation.

✝✝✝

Liam's heart pounded in his chest as he knocked as loudly as he could with the side of his fist. The pounding was just as loud as those from minutes before. He had run from the church to the locksmith's home. "Pussod, Pussod. Wake up. Come quickly." His heart beat so heavily he could feel it in his burned hands. They were throbbing from having tried to help Simone open the grille.

The man in black looked on and then disappeared around the corner.

Pussod was already awake and fully dressed. He had thrown on his clothes as fast as he could. His blouse was on backward, and he couldn't button it. He left it and threw a cloak over his shoulders. "I'm here." Pussod ran out the door within seconds of Liam's banging.

"How are you ready?" Liam was confused. "Pussod, the Sainte-Chapelle, the Shroud. We need something to pry open the grille, or the Shroud will be destroyed." Liam could barely talk. He had ingested too much smoke. His breathing was loud and fast. "You need to bring your tools quickly."

Within seconds, both were racing to the palace. Pussod carried a saw, a large hammer, and a ten-pound iron wedge. Liam carried a long iron stake. Within a minute, they were close enough to where the orange glow had resolved into distinct smoke and flames, gushing out of what was the roof of the church.

When Pussod and Liam arrived, the roof was already mostly caved in and much of the smoke escaped through the roof. Only another minute and the roof over the Shroud would cave in.

A line of townspeople formed a bucket brigade, fetching water from the river a few hundred feet away, and passing the buckets from person to person.

The rear entrance to the church was open, and Pussod and Liam both ran through the choir and behind the altar. Pussod saw the silver clad case partially covered, with some of the silver having melted and other parts deformed, with the wood underneath partially smoldering. He took the rod from Liam and pressed it between the locks and tried to pry the grille open, but two of the locks were too strong. Immediately he wielded his hammer on the locks. One gave way in short order, but the last one would not surrender its protection of its charge. After a few swings, he positioned his wedge directly against the last lock. Two more swings of the hammer succeeded, and it too gave way.

"Out of my way!" As soon as the last lock was freed, Father Valentin reached in and, using his frock as an insulator, grabbed the case and pulled it out of the niche. It was still smoking, the ornate silver decorations badly damaged.

"Out of my way." Valentin now had the case in both hands. He ignored the pain and ran with the case to get outside as quickly as possible. He would do anything to save this precious relic of Jesus Christ.

Simone and Pussod followed, Liam ran past to get a bucket—anything to staunch the smoldering and save what might be left of the cloth.

They were finally outside. Valentin put the case down. It was lighter than he thought it would be. Adrenaline coursed through his veins but his coughing took over, and he was unable to open the case.

Liam took a small bucket from the line and doused the case with water. Smoke and hissing emanated from the case. A second bucket from Pussod quashed the hissing and brought the smoke to a small trickle.

Simone took over, desperately trying to open the case and not giving up. He fumbled around and was stymied by the smoke in his eyes and the burns on his hands. Anguish that the Shroud might be lost overtook him.

Pussod began to help. Finally, working together, they opened the case. Wisps of smoke emerged from inside, but the contents were mostly intact. Pussod removed the red silk pouch that contained the Shroud.

"Liam, water. More water!" Valentin wheezed. His speech was raspy and barely intelligible. Valentin now used his hands to stop the smoldering advancing inside the red silk pouch. He pressed his palms down on each of the embers and snuffed them out. He wasn't going to let pain defeat him. He did his best not to bleed on the cloth from the wounds on his hands from the burns. Liam returned and gently poured water on the spot in the corner where the heat was the strongest. The wisps of smoke finally quashed.

"Liam, more water, just in case." Valentin used the sleeve on the back of his wrist to wipe his brow. Simone breathed in and coughed deeply but focused on his elation at the survival of the cloth. He and Valentin smiled at each other causing them both to cough again. Pussod stood up, breathing heavily and coughing up smoky phlegm. Valentin and Simone dunked their hands into the bucket to soften the pain.

There was a crash behind them as another portion of the roof caved in, directly above where the Shroud had rested only moments before. The four men turned their heads to see a billow of sparks and smoke accelerate skyward. They leaned back, glad they weren't still in the church. Pussod was a hero for arriving as quickly as he did.

"Liam, unfold the cloth," Pussod instructed, reaching to assist. They carefully unfolded the fourteen-foot-long damaged cloth.

Simone and Valentin were exhausted but needed to see the extent of the damage. Its full extent was hard to assess in the dim light, but there was damage. Thankfully, the lifelike images of the bruised body weren't burnt, although they were concerned the water used to staunch the smoldering might leave a stain. There were at least eight holes where the silver gilding had melted and dripped through the case and burned through the folded cloth. The cloth appeared to have simply smoldered but had not caught fire. Thankfully, the folds, silk pouch, and case had deprived the flames of oxygen, minimizing the damage.

A crowd gathered. Some worked to extinguish the fire in the church. Others stood and observed. Most formed a bucket line.

Chambéry was the capital of Savoy, and the duke and his family were in residence when the fire started. They, too, were awoken by the calamity. The duchess and her two sons joined the line, while Duke Charles III of Savoy[1] directed where the water was to be thrown. Because of the distance from the river, most of the buckets were only about half full by the time they reached the church. The water was thrown onto several hotspots but wasn't enough to mitigate damage to the church and its decorations. The duke's chapel sustained heavy damage from the fire.

Another crash. This time it was the stained-glass windows depicting the passion of Christ. The largest image in the middle illustrated the Shroud inside the tomb with the three women peering in, but it was now gone.

"Liam, Simone, refold the cloth, and we'll bring it to my quarters." The pain in Father Valentin's hands from the burns pulsated as the adrenaline wore off. "We don't want to damage it further."

Liam and Simone coughed intermittently, trying to expel the smoke and dust from their lungs. Their hands and arms stung with sharp pains from their burns. Pussod stepped in and saw Simone's and Liam's hands were useless from the burns.

"Pussod, thanks to your efforts, the Shroud was saved," Valentin said, coughing again.

Pussod looked beyond the bucket line and saw a man dressed in black. The man surveyed the activities but did not assist in the bucket line or firefighting.

"Father, do you see that man?" The man ducked behind the corner and disappeared. Pussod nodded in the direction. "That man, dressed in black. Did you see him? I believe he is the one who woke me right before Liam rapped on my door. Why did he do it?" Pussod spoke to himself now, trying to unravel what had happened. "I think he saved us precious seconds before the roof caved in."

Neither Valentin nor the others heard him over the noise from the fire and people on the bucket brigade.

The man dressed in black was gone among the shadows.

The bucket brigade continued for another hour to douse the remaining hotspots and extinguish the sources of flame and smoke. The talk of the townspeople and those on the line concerned the Shroud.

---

1 Duke Charles III: Most Serene Duke of Savoy from AD 1504 to 1553. Born AD 1486, died AD 1553.

The duke relinquished his task of directing the water and hurriedly approached Father Valentin and the others as they inspected the damage.

Father Valentin stood. "I'm sorry, Your Grace. We tried to get there sooner."

Duke Charles knelt before the cloth to pray.

✝✝✝

POOR CLARES CONVENT, CHAMBÉRY, FRANCE
EARLY MORNING, THURSDAY, APRIL 16, AD 1534

"Sister Mary Robert, please check and confirm that the tables are properly set up and ready to display the cloth." Pacing back and forth, Reverend Mother Abbesse Louise de Vargin[2] let her nervousness infect everyone else. Her rapid-fire orders sent the sisters in all directions around the convent.

The Poor Clares Sisters had been chosen only a few months earlier to repair the damage to the Shroud caused by the fire two years before. They would be working on the most valuable relic in man's possession.

Mother Louise hoped and prayed they were worthy. "Sister Mary Clarence, go find out when the entourage will arrive. They are supposed to be here in less than fifteen minutes."

"Sister Mary Lucia, go with Mary Robert. She may need your help." Mother Louise reconsidered. "No, stay here. I need you here in case I need something."

Sister Mary Lucia was typically calm, but now she wished she was accompanying Mary Robert. The nervousness and indecisiveness of Mother Louise was like an expectant father waiting for his wife to give birth.

Mother Louise paced back and forth. It would be the first time such nobility would be counting on her and her small convent to perform such a momentous task as the repair of the burial cloth of Jesus Christ.

She addressed Mary Lucia. "How is your sewing? Do you have confidence in your sewing? Everyone says you're the best sewer in the convent. Is it true? Are you the best?"

"Yes, Mother Louise. Yes." What else could she say? "My mother taught me to repair clothing, and her father taught her. Our family has been tailor for the nobility in Vercelli for several generations. I am very familiar with all types of cloth and all types of—"

The captain of the guard interrupted them and announced the arrival of Duke Charles III, Most Serene Duke of Savoy, and the papal representative, Monseigneur the Legate.[3] "It is time."

---

2 Reverend Mother Abbesse Louise de Vargin: Reverend mother of the Poor Clares Sisters Convent, Chambéry, France.

3 Monseigneur the Legate: Representative of the pope. Mentioned in the "Report of the Poor Clare Nuns", Chambéry, 1534. No name was given.

Sister Mary Lucia bowed.

Mother Louise glanced over at the captain of the guard and then made her way out of her quarters. She disliked interruptions even more so when she was nervous. There were no more preparations that could be done. *Was that Father Marius?* Mother Louise saw him and looked over at Sister Mary Lucia. Mother Louise gave her a terse glare.

Father Marius stood immediately behind the bishop of Belley, Bishop Philippe.[4] Marius had been relocated to another church after the affair with Mary Lucia. After six years, even wayward priests were forgiven.

Mother Louise did everything in her power to keep the sisters chaste, but all too often, something happens. *Was he now under the tutelage of the bishop?*

Mother Louise, followed by Sister Mary Lucia, entered the nave and stood ready to receive the delegation bringing the damaged cloth. The procession of carriages had stopped outside the narthex to form a line. In front was Monseigneur the Legate, followed by His Highness, Monsieur Bishop Philippe, also known as Messire the Suffragan. Other dignitaries, canons, ecclesiastics, and nobility lined up behind them.

"Your Excellency." Bishop Philippe removed the Shroud from its new temporary case carried inside the carriage of the monseigneur. The original silver-clad case was no longer usable. The fire had melted the silver and molten silver burned through the wooden case and damaged the Shroud. A new case was being crafted but would not be complete until after the repairs were made. The Shroud was folded inside a new red silk pouch.

He bowed, removed the silk pouch from its temporary case, and handed it to the monseigneur. At that moment, the church bells rang out announcing the arrival of this most holy relic.

The monseigneur raised the pouch above his head, lowered it to chest level, and proceeded into the church. Inside, the procession moved to a viewing table that ran down the middle of the nave covered with clean white cloths. When the monseigneur reached the center of the table, he gently laid the pouch down. "Bishop Philippe."

The bishop bowed and proceeded to remove the Shroud from the red silk pouch. He laid the folded cloth on the center of the table and nodded to Mother Louise. Behind him stood Father Marius. Mother Louise nodded to the bishop. She glanced at the priest, suppressing her disgust toward him.

Mother Louise and Sister Mary Lucia proceeded to unfold the cloth and laid it out on the table. Its full length stretched to both ends of the makeshift

---

4 Bishop Philippe de la Chambre: Bishop of Belley, AD 1530–1536. Also known as Messire the Suffragan. Mentioned in the "Report of the Poor Clare Nuns," Chambéry, AD 1534.

table. The formal viewing and handover would take place here. The repairs would take place in the choir.

The two men inspected the cloth, in awe of the image yet pained at the damage the fire had wrought. Mother Louise and Sister Mary Lucia tried to remain focused on the two men but were drawn to the image. The men lamented over the extent of the damage; the women lamented over the extent of the needed repairs. "Bishop, I wish to inform you and the monseigneur that all of the Poor Clares Sisters have prayed unceasingly since your notification of the pending repair, and we will continue our vigil night and day until our work is complete. We pray for the steady hands of Sister Mary Lucia and her sisters as they undertake this momentous task."

"Now we shall ask the remaining dignitaries and nobility to verify this cloth is one and the same cloth, the burial Shroud of Jesus, and they will testify to such." The monseigneur and bishop stepped back and made way for the procession of eleven dignitaries to examine and inspect the cloth. Each was saddened and awestruck to see the damage inflicted by the fire. Two apostolic notaries accompanied them and recorded each one's name and their testimony as to the authenticity of the cloth. This process required just under thirty minutes.

"Now we shall ask the remaining gentlemen, ecclesiastics, and prelates to inspect the cloth and verify its authenticity," the monseigneur announced as the last nobility retraced his steps back to the nave. Eighteen more men made their way to the cloth and inspected it. Each was similarly disheartened but verified the cloth was the cloth known as the Shroud of Jesus.

✝✝✝

Father Marius caught the eye of Sister Mary Lucia. She looked away, doing all she could to suppress those feelings she had years ago. There were pleasant memories to be sure. The picnics at the lake. The warm sun on her legs. He was the only man she ever loved—the only man who would ever comb his fingers through her hair. But those fond memories only led to heartache. She couldn't see her son. She would never see her son. There was a void in her heart caused by this man. She had yet to forgive him. But now, she felt both hate and love welling up. *Lord, please. No. No!*

Father Marius had also suppressed those feelings. He didn't know if there was a child, although he suspected. There must have been. How else would they have found out? *Was it a boy or a girl?*

"Bishop, are you satisfied this is the cloth having been previously in possession of the Sainte-Chapelle Church in Chambéry." The monseigneur handed a letter stating as such to be signed and sealed by the bishop. The signing required only a moment, but the two remained to view the image one last time, mesmerized by what it symbolized.

"Reverend Mother, please remove the Shroud and display it in the choir." Bishop Philippe gave the order, and the two refolded the cloth.

Sister Mary Lucia picked up the folded cloth and placed it on the outstretched arms of the Reverend Mother, who then proceeded out of the sanctuary and into the choir. Mother Louise placed the cloth on the center of the table, and the two of them again unfolded the Shroud. Sisters Mary Robert and Mary Clarence lit two large candelabras to provide additional light in the dark choir room.

The bishop and the monseigneur followed them into the choir. "We will repair fourteen triangular holes on the cloth by sewing in fourteen pieces on the burnt areas." The bishop spoke explicitly. "Another four areas at each end of the cloth will also be repaired. This totals twenty-two separate repair locations."

Father Marius, the bishop's assistant, wrote down his exact specifications of the repair. There were fourteen main holes and four areas at each end of the Shroud where the cloth had been damaged by the molten silver.

"Mother Louise, you are now to name the sisters who will be charged with repairing the cloth." The monseigneur signaled to the notaries.

"Sister Mary Robert, Sister Mary Clarence, and I will be assisting Sister Mary Lucia in making the repairs. We will be the only ones to touch the cloth."

"If anyone other than the named four persons shall come into contact with and touch the Shroud, the punishment will be major excommunication," the monseigneur directed in a booming voice. He wanted everyone in the room to hear the punishment for any mishandling of the cloth. The bishop emphasized the word *major* to make clear that any infringement on this rule would mean absolute exclusion from the church and from any social interactions with members of the church. "No one may touch the cloth."

A crowd formed inside the church after the Shroud was moved to the choir. Although they could not see the Shroud—except for those who were being pressed against the grille to the choir—it was an honor and privilege just to be in its presence.

✝✝✝

Their eyes met again. *Stop looking at him. I can't. I can't.*

The hearts of Father Marius and Sister Mary Lucia were eternally bound. Sister Mary Lucia was unable to will that bond to break.

✝✝✝

The preacher to His Highness, Duke Charles III of Savoy, turned to the people squeezing against the grille and began a short Mass. Once his homily was complete, he turned to the three sisters and Mother Louise, whereupon they recited the Confiteor. "I confess to Almighty God, to Blessed Mary, ever Virgin . . ."

Having said it so many times, Mother Louise normally lost track of the words but not this time. As always, but especially this time, Mother Louise found special meaning when she came to the words *mea culpa, mea culpa, mea máxima culpa.* Now being next to the death wrap of her Lord and Redeemer, the words meant much more. She would be responsible for the holiest of relics, and in all her being, she wanted to live up to the work she and her sisters were charged with.

". . . pray for me, to the Lord our God." When the Confiteor was complete, she looked over at Mary Lucia, her eyes closed, and imagined her praying the same supplication as well. *Please, Lord, give me steady hands to make these repairs.*

The crowd listened to every word as the sisters recited the Confiteor, though the people had heard the words hundreds, if not thousands, of times before. Each one of them repeated the words under their breath.

The preacher continued, ". . . I absolve you from your sins in the name of the Father and of the Son and of the Holy Spirit." The preacher paused. The air was getting thick with all the people causing the temperature, humidity, and smell in the small space to become uncomfortable. "Amen." The scented perfumes from the dignitaries were not enough to cover the caustic odor of sweat.

A few hours passed and the bishop ordered the choir to be emptied. Once emptied, the protection of the Shroud was left in the hands of the guards. There was a break for the midday meal. After their meal and now having seen the damage, Mother Louise and the sisters spent the afternoon making final preparations for the work ahead.

"We have completed the third ironing of the Holland cloth, and we are ready to bring it to the choir." Sister Mary Lucia looked at Mother Louise and then at the other sisters. The Holland cloth would be sewn onto the back of the Shroud. The two sisters put down their smoothing irons, and both, in unison, wiped their brows. Ironing was hot and hard work. The day before, the Holland cloth had been cleaned twice and, after each cleaning, was fully ironed and folded. The sisters were determined to remove every crease out of the linen cloth. It had to be perfect. Similarly, a white cotton cloth cover had been prepared to keep a wood-framed cloth work surface and the Holland cloth unsullied as it was transported to the choir.

Sister Mary Robert handed Mary Lucia the folded Holland Cloth. It was still warm from the ironing. She held it as if holding a precious tray of fine cakes to be presented to His Highness. Sisters Mary Robert and Mary Clarence each picked up one end of the fifteen-foot-long work surface. Mother Louise carried a small basket of sewing implements made up of scraps of cloth, needles, thread, and scissors. They were ready.

Mother Louise walked with confidence, leading the way out of the dining hall and to the choir at the back of the Sainte-Chapelle Church. Her nervousness from before had vanished. "Guard, make a path so we can enter," Mother Louise commanded. The crowds inside and outside the church had grown even larger while they were gone, and they now needed help to make their way back to the choir. Inside the choir were six guards to make certain no one came into contact with the Shroud. Outside, six additional guards allowed only a certain few to enter.

"Make way, make way." The guard boomed, and slowly the people made a path. Two other guards joined in to push the crowds back.

Sister Mary Lucia didn't move until everyone had backed off far enough so that there was no chance anyone would get close enough to even touch the Holland cloth, against which the Shroud would be sewn. Sisters Mary Robert and Mary Clarence made certain the cloth work surface was not sullied by coming into contact with anyone in the throng.

Two of the six guards in the choir began lighting more candles to provide as much light as possible. The air thickened while the guards moved to push the throng back away from the grille, but this effort failed. They simply wouldn't move, and with so many people standing behind the gate, those in front were not able to move back. There were only so many people who could catch a glimpse of the Shroud and the repairs, yet everyone pushed forward. The choir was already crowded enough without allowing more through the gate to observe and possibly slow the repairs.

"You may unwrap the work surface," Mother Louise directed her two underlings.

The work surface was laid out on two separate tables running parallel to the table with the Shroud. They then unfolded the Holland cloth. Sister Lucia handed out needles and thread, and all four worked to baste the Holland cloth to the work surface.

Mother Louise began reciting the convent's work prayer, "Creator God, thank you for providing us with the gift to share our talents." The other three sisters repeated along with her, all in unison. "Make us faithful stewards of your creation to enhance the human dignity of our global family." The basting of the Holland cloth to the work surface required twenty recitations. "We ask this in the name of Jesus, who lives and reigns with you, and the Holy Spirit now and forever. Amen."

It was now time to transfer the Shroud and baste it to the Holland cloth. All four women circled the Shroud, with Mother Louise and Sister Mary Lucia on each end and Sisters Mary Robert and Mary Clarence in the middle. Each of them genuflected and said a silent prayer. Mother Louise nodded, and they reached down and picked up the Shroud and carefully placed it over the outstretched Holland cloth.

"Creator God, thank you . . ." The prayers soothed their pains as they were so close to the tortured image and the blood of Christ. They were also afraid any mistake would lead to permanent damage to the Shroud.

"His Highness the Duke of Savoy," the sergeant at arms announced, causing a new ruckus from the entryway to the choir. The people hoping to catch a glimpse of the Shroud tried to make a path but couldn't easily step back. The guards leading the entourage pushed against the men and women, and slowly a corridor formed. Somehow, they pressed even harder against each other, and the duke and ten other dignitaries were able to enter the choir to inspect the relic.

There was little room for anyone to move and give His Highness and the other dignitaries their proper distance. The room was filled with the smell of the people and the scent of the candles.

Messire Audinet, the chamberlain of the High Highness, broke the silence. "Your Highness, Mother Louise will be directing the repairs."

"Tell me if you have any concerns about your pending work. Do you feel you are capable of making the repairs?"

Mother Louise answered His Highness with a simple small bow by nodding in the affirmative. This same question was repeated word for word to each of the sisters about to handle the Shroud. Each repeated their bows. Once the interrogations were complete, His Highness stepped back to observe the work.

During the interviews Marius had his first chance to move closer to Mary Lucia. He brushed against her, and she turned and glared at him. He had gone too far and backed off. He hoped perhaps an opportunity would present itself so he could speak with her in private.

"The colors must match. We will need to dye the Holland cloth and the repair swatches. The colors must be exact." Bishop Philippe was adamant.

What Mother Louise thought would go quickly would now be delayed by ensuring the repair cloths and the Holland cloth would exactly match the color of the faded herringbone weave of the Shroud.

"Sister Mary Robert, are you versed in dying cloth?"

Mother Louise nodded and signaled her permission for Sister Mary Robert to respond.

"I have experience. My father was a tailor, and as a youth, I worked with him, cutting, stitching, sewing, and dying cloths of all kinds." Sister Mary Robert looked down, feigning deference to her position. "This may require several successive attempts to make certain the colors match exactly, Your Excellency."

†††

Sister Mary Lucia still glared at Marius. There was no forgiveness in her eyes. He shouldn't have brushed up against her.

†††

The bishop was about to respond when the duke approached. "Is there a question I can help to resolve?" There was complete silence in the room. No one moved. It was the first time the duke had intervened in the goings on.

Sister Mary Robert's heart began beating much quicker. Having both the duke and the bishop together was completely unnerving. A fly landed on the duke's lapel. It was only noticed by Sister Mary Robert. It flitted around but didn't leave the duke. There was a small stain on his jacket, imperceptible unless looking closely. Perhaps it was some honey from breakfast. The fly found it and made numerous attempts to feed on it.

†††

Sister Mary Lucia stood near the bottom of the cloth near Jesus's feet. She kept her eyes focused on the feet to avoid Marius's eyes. The blood and the twisted feet indicated how the nails pierced each foot. Her mind flashed from her love and hate for Marius to the pain Jesus suffered. She had to take a breath and look away. She fought back the tears.

†††

"We have decided the backing cloth and the repair cloths will be exactly dyed to match the color of the Shroud cloth, Your Highness." The bishop was the only one to speak in the presence of the duke. Even Mother Louise remained silent. "This may require a few additional days but will be necessary to make certain the repaired cloth is a perfect reconstruction of the original."

The bishop awaited a response from His Highness. There was none.

"Your Highness, we shall proceed accordingly. I will approve the color matching, but if you would also like to view the dyes prior to them being stitched into the cloth . . ."

✝✝✝

Father Marius looked longingly over at Sister Mary Lucia, but she didn't—and wouldn't—return a glance. The heartache still burned within her.

✝✝✝

"Carry on." The duke was satisfied and returned to his chair.

It began to rain, and the humidity inside the choir increased to an intolerable level. Mary Lucia could feel sweat beading on her forehead.

The duke grew drowsy as heat radiated in the room, and he fell asleep in his chair.

The sisters continued their work, wiping their brows every so often to make certain their sweat would not drip onto the Shroud. The fly returned for a second meal from the duke's lapel.

The Holland cloth was removed from the work surface. Different batches of dyed cloth were brought forward for three days until the bishop approved. The Holland cloth was dyed with this last batch and then basted onto the work surface. The Shroud was placed on top of the Holland cloth.

"Bring the cloth into the sunlight where we can fully test the match." The bishop was adamant that the colors match both in the dim light of the choir and in the bright light of the sun. The room was cleared so the cloth could be brought outside. Another clean cotton cloth was placed over the wooden frame, with the Holland cloth and the Shroud underneath. Within minutes, the four sisters carried the frame outside into the sun where the temporary cotton cover was removed, and the bishop was able to inspect the color match.

After a thorough inspection of the entire length of the Holland cloth, the bishop called out, "The match is perfect. The repairs may proceed."

The repair work continued for two weeks. Each stitch, each cut, and each repair was checked and rechecked. Finally, after toiling for days and days in the confined space of the choir, with everyone looking on, Sisters Mary Robert and Mary Lucia were able to step away and inspect each of their repairs.

Mother Louise followed each of the sisters and inspected the same repairs, going over each stitch and each patch before inviting the bishop to inspect their work.

The Shroud was made whole again.

✝✝✝

Every day Sister Mary Lucia focused on her work, but he was there. He was always there. He was like a fly trying to feed off a scrap of food. She couldn't turn without seeing him. She did everything she could to keep her eyes down so they would not meet his.

✝✝✝

"Mother Louise, have you completed your repairs?" the bishop of Belley asked in a loud, formal voice.

"Yes, we have." The sisters and Mother Louise bowed to His Excellency and stepped back from the cloth.

Bishop Philippe then repeated the process and inspected the exact same route each of the sisters had taken. Each of these inspections required over thirty minutes. The bishop looked up and faced the duke. "Your Highness, the repairs are complete." Bishop Philippe extended his arm for the duke to inspect the repairs.

The duke stepped up to the Shroud and inspected the cloth. He viewed each of the patches and the Holland cloth just as the others had done. "They have done a remarkable job. The color matches perfectly, and the patches are in perfect order. I commend the sisters for their excellent work."

Others were allowed to enter the choir and inspect the repairs. After another hour, everyone was ushered out of the choir and into the nave of the church.

The sisters laid out the red silk cover and rolled the Shroud inside. A gold-colored cloth was placed over the rolled cloth and, bowing their heads the entire time, Mother Louise and Sister Mary Lucia picked it up and handed it over to the bishop and the suffragan, his assistant bishop.

A path was made by the guards inside the nave and Bishop Philippe and the suffragan carried the cloth through the nave. At the other end of the nave, standing inside the double-door entry to the church, the duke received the bishops. The duke turned and led the bishops out of the church. Behind the bishops the assemblage of dignitaries followed the cloth as it was carried in silence to the chateau of the duke of Savoy.

Each of the dignitaries lit a candle, and all the bells of the town began to ring out. As the Shroud was carried down the steps, the crowds began singing *Jésus nostra Redemptio.*[5]

---

5 Jésus nostra Redemptio: Jesus our Redemption.

†††

When the procession had passed, Sisters Mary Robert and Mary Lucia walked back to their quarters for some bread and broth. "We have been working on that cloth for two weeks. It's so nice to be outside and breathe in that fresh air. It is like a new day is dawning." Sister Mary Robert was relaxed and able to enjoy the early evening air.

"The pain our Lord and Savior suffered for us," Sister Mary Lucia began in a whisper, revealing the weight on her heart. "Several times I have been brought almost to nausea. I am in awe at being so close to something that once draped the body of our Savior, and yet I am sickened by what He suffered. I could barely hold back my tears."

Thoughts of her own baby and where he was now came to her. She didn't even know his name. She could feel a tear forming in her eye. She hadn't seen him in six years. He was taken away by Mother Louise before he could even suckle at her breast. *I only held him an instant. I chose the name Zachael for him. I have no idea what his name is today. My poor Zachael.*

"Be quiet. We cannot be caught talking like this." Sister Mary Robert interrupted her, looking around to see if anyone could hear them. "You mustn't talk like that. You mustn't."

"But I must. I am often almost in tears. It's the most horrible thing I've ever experienced. I can't imagine what His mother Mary suffered seeing her son tortured, wounded, and then murdered." *Only Mother Louise knows what happened. My son was from Father Marius. He was the father.* The memories of losing Zachael brought tears to her eyes again.

"Be quiet!" Sister Mary Robert whispered with an adamant voice. "Be quiet. We cannot talk like that. Stop that crying!"

"But how did Mary, mother of Jesus, bear to see her son suffer like that?" *I hope my son never goes through something like that. Never. Please, God, I pray to you. Please!* "I have a hole in my heart when I see the cloth." It was not only for the risen Christ but also for her son. He had been ripped from her arms. *Zachael. Zachael.* She whispered his name, but the hole only got wider. The tears flowed more rapidly. "Zachael." *I don't care if Mary Robert finds out. She must suspect anyway.*

"Who? Stop. You must stop." Sister Mary Robert was at a loss. "What is wrong with you today?"

CHAPTER 11

The Shroud in Turin, Italy

In AD 1563, Turin was made capital of the Duchy of Savoy by Duke Emmanuel Philibert,[1] duke of Savoy, moving the capital from Chambéry, Savoy for lack of trust in the neighboring French. The Shroud was displayed regularly, but constant use led to problems. It needed to be repaired.

CARDINAL'S CHAMBERS, MILAN
MIDMORNING, WEDNESDAY, JULY 18, AD 1578

"Your Eminence, I beseech thee. You can't simply walk from Milan to Chambéry." Cardinal Charles Borromeo's assistant, Petruccio, moved to remove the breakfast tray. "That's very far. Even if you could walk twenty miles per day, it would take you a month to reach Chambéry."

"This reformation from thirty years ago is gaining traction, and we must

---

1 Duke Emmanuel Philibert: Duke of Savoy, AD 1553–1580. He recovered the Savoy state from the French and made Italian the official language. Moved the capital to Turin. Born AD 1528, died AD 1580.

continue to demonstrate that we are not swayed by their heresy against the church." Cardinal Charles Borromeo[2] remained adamant, thumbing through the pages of the book he held. "How dare that man. Ninety-five theses and a German translation of the Bible. How he dared. We should dig that man up and burn his body and throw the ashes in the river, just like this book."

It was a translation one of his parishioners brought to him after Sunday Mass. "Look, this one was printed just four years ago. With the printing press, there must be hundreds, maybe thousands, of these abominations." Borromeo threw the book into the fire. "This is written in German! Latin is the language of the Bible. Latin!"

"Your Eminence," Petruccio interjected but to little effect.

"Next, we will be conducting Mass in German. The pope is the vicar of Christ on earth, and through him, he has appointed us each as priests. We are the means by which the masses reach God. They cannot go directly to Him. Never! The Roman Catholic Church is the ultimate interpreter of Scripture. Not some backwater priest."

Petruccio waited another minute or so. "Let's focus back on the plague."

Borromeo looked up from the fire where the Luther Bible was burning and faced his assistant. "The Roman Catholic Church is based on the Latin Bible, and a Latin Mass is the church. If we want to make changes, we must make them from within. Not just separate, and definitely not in German!"

"It's taken over a year—almost two years—for this plague to run its course. With it gone, we can now begin to celebrate Mass inside the church instead of on its doorsteps. If you're gone for a month, we'll be having Mass without you for a long time. Do you believe that is wise?"

The plague had killed hundreds a day. It started with a fever and headaches and often progressed to abdominal cramps and enlarged lymph nodes. Almost 25,000 people in Milan and in the surrounding community had been wiped out . . . nearly sixty percent of the population. Agriculture and commerce collapsed.

"There are so many orphans and families with nothing who must be cared for. You can't be allowed to be gone that long. The city needs you."

Borromeo thought a few moments. "If we don't show how much we're willing to sacrifice for God, then how can we ask our congregation to sacrifice? This is a battle against those Calvinists and those Lutherans. We have done well to wipe out the practice of solicitation of indulgences, but we must continue our diligence. There are some things that must never be changed. Verily, this walk will be symbolic of what we of the Roman Catholic Church can achieve."

---

2 Cardinal Charles Borromeo: Archbishop of Milan from AD 1564 to 1584 and a leading antagonist against the Protestant Reformation. Born AD 1538, died AD 1584.

Borromeo was tall and thin with penetrating eyes. He led a simple life outside of the church, sleeping on straw with a diet of bread and water. He only dressed in magnificent finery when leading Mass. The counter-reformation was taking hold and many of the ninety-five theses were being addressed. Borromeo pushed hard to make certain priests were properly trained. The Catholic Church was changing.

"Petruccio, I want you to write to Duke Emmanuel Philibert to inform him we have prayed each and every day at each Mass to the Shroud to break this plague, and our prayers have been answered. We will be walking to Chambéry, and we would like to give our blessings for the gift of the Shroud for what it has done against the plague here in Milan."

Petruccio nodded. He wasn't able to convince his superior otherwise. Although Borromeo was only forty years old, his health had suffered due to his scant diet and his unending work with the poor and the sick. "The church in Milan will support you fully in your walk to Chambéry. I will make certain of it."

"This Sunday, we shall have our last Mass on the steps and announce that the plague has been broken. We will, from thence forward, celebrate Mass from inside our church."

✝✝✝

CARDINAL'S CHAMBERS, MILAN
LATE AFTERNOON, SUNDAY, AUGUST 13, AD 1578

"Your Eminence, a letter from Duke Emmanuel Philibert." Petruccio handed Cardinal Charles Borromeo the letter. The cardinal broke the seal and unrolled it.

"His Highness agrees with my sacrifice but will be moving the Shroud to Turin 'to reduce the distance required for His Excellency on this most valuable walk.'" The cardinal smiled and whispered a few words of prayer to himself. "His Highness has heard of the intrepid work we have done here in Milan in supporting the poor during the crisis." The cardinal reread the letter. "'You are to be commended for the generous gifts you made to the Milanese people, the risks you took to feed them and to minister to them during this protracted plague. All of Milan is grateful. Your services to the Milanese saved countless lives.'" Borromeo reiterated the words from His Highness.

"I shall pen a letter for you to set a date for your arrival in Turin." Petruccio was relieved the distance he and His Excellency would be walking would be much shorter. "Perhaps the exercise and fresh air will help to improve your health. We will only need about seven days to walk to Turin, just less than the distance Jesus needed to walk from Galilee to Jerusalem, much less than walking to Chambéry."

✝✝✝

The Shroud had been laid out for Duke Emmanuel Philibert and Cardinal Borromeo.

"Your Highness," Borromeo began. "The church wishes to thank you for organizing this week of celebration. We can celebrate the many blessings Milan and Turin have received through God and the Shroud."

The duke and Borromeo inspected the Shroud and the repairs from over forty-five years ago. "God blessed us with the work of the Poor Clares Sisters. They did a remarkable job to repair and protect this divine cloth for us for all millennia."

"I commissioned the royal artisans to construct this table just for the purpose of displaying this magnificent cloth." Duke Emmanuel Philibert had seen the cloth many times before but had only spent a few minutes marveling at this miraculous relic of Jesus. "My intention is to move the cloth permanently to Turin. Chambéry is too close to the French border, and, besides, it will be easier for you to come visit." He smiled. "It was moved to Chambéry eighty years ago, but after the fire, I wish to build a new cathedral in its honor. I will be counting on your support with the pope.

"The Borromeo family is one of the most powerful in all of Italy, and you have a very close ear to Pope Gregory.[3] Your Eminence and His Holiness will have made many changes in the world, and there are many more you will make." The duke continued speaking while Borromeo kneeled in awe of the Shroud.

Borromeo said a short prayer under his breath at each of Christ's wounds captured in the image. The distorted feet, the bloodied wrists, the pierced rib, the distended shoulders, blood on the head and the disfigured face each gave witness to the suffering Christ endured for all mankind.

"My wishes are also to keep the Shroud in Savoyard hands and not have it fall to the Spanish or the French. When the duke of Athens brought the Shroud from Constantinople, he brought it as a prize in payment for his efforts during the Fourth Crusade. He and his family kept it hidden for many decades when, finally, it was made available for viewing in Lirey. When my predecessor purchased it from the de Charny family, his intention was to make it available for all to see. It naturally needed to be moved to an important location, and it has now finally made its way to Turin, the new

---

3 Pope Gregory XIII: Pope from AD 1572 to 1585. Died AD 1585.

capital of Savoy, where I will protect and care for it. We can't have it suffer the risk of fire damage ever again."

Borromeo looked up and glanced in the duke's direction, then back at the repairs made by the Poor Clares Sisters. "Truly, this image was divinely created. It represents the conquering of Jesus over life and death on earth. It must be properly venerated and available for all Catholicism to see." Borromeo purposely didn't say Christianity since the Lutherans and the Calvinists were heretics and must be brought back into the fold. Borromeo was also in a bargaining mood. No sense in providing a favor without asking for one in return. Each of them was focused on thoughts of Jesus Christ and his suffering during the passion. Neither one of them took note of the slight bulge along the top edge of the cloth and what it portended.

"Your Highness, I, too, would like your help and support." Borromeo looked at the cloth, still in awe of the nature of the image and all it reflected from the stories in the Gospels. "In God's name, I will do everything in my power to bring those heretics back to the Roman Catholic Church. At the Council of Trent, we instituted many reforms, which will require much effort to bring about. Although I am adamantly opposed to Luther splitting off from the church, I do believe he highlighted many aspects of the church needing to be corrected. I need your continued support in promoting these changes within the church."

The duke nodded his assent. He was certain Borromeo would be able to bring about many of the necessary reforms for the church to thrive. The cardinal lingered another five minutes, then sat down and went into deep contemplation and prayer.

"Our sacrifices are nothing compared to what Jesus died for. He went through unspeakable pain—the crown of thorns rammed into his scalp, the whipping, the nails through his wrists and feet, the slow, agonizing death on the cross." Borromeo spoke out loud, but it was mostly to himself. He finally looked up.

The duke marveled at the image of Jesus's face. "This cloth documents all that he suffered. What if he wasn't punished, if he wasn't crucified? Would Christianity have still emerged? If Christ had simply died of old age, like Confucius or perhaps like Muhammed being poisoned by his contemporaries?" The duke looked at his friend and began contemplating the questions posed by the cardinal. "Would you or I be here today, being a faithful believer and follower of Jesus Christ?"

Saint John the Baptist Cathedral, Turin
Noon, Sunday, October 12, AD 1578

"Today is going to be a most beautiful day," Cardinal Charles Borromeo said, handing his crozier to his assistant, Petruccio. "It is already a perfect day. We will truly be in the presence of Jesus Christ today." The mood in the cathedral was never so buoyant.

"It was very crowded during Mass today. Father Arcanzola gave a perfect homily. He reminded me of you before you became bishop, Your Eminence. His inflection, everything." Petruccio smiled and helped Cardinal Borromeo remove his red robe to relax for a few minutes before the procession to the Piazza del Castello. The smell of smoke from the fireplace lingered in the room even as the fire was just a few small embers.

"You should not patronize me, but once in a while, it's okay—especially on a day like today!"

"It was good to have the other prelates here." Borromeo's excitement permeated the room. "The archbishop of Turin, Gerolamo della Rovere and of Savoy,[4] and my old friend, the archbishop Cipriano Pallavicino of Genoa.[5] This will be a great day for the Catholic Church and us. I will forgive having Bishop Domenico della Rovere.[6] He was a good friend of Pope Pius V, but I never felt he acted strongly enough to implement all the reforms from the Council of Trent.[7] Sometimes it seemed he tried to work against me, especially concerning the formal training for transitional deacons." Borromeo sighed. "That is for another time. Not for today. Today, we will celebrate where we agree, not argue over where we disagree.

"Send in Father Calandrini." Petruccio walked to the door of the cardinal's chambers, opened the door, and nodded to the man standing in the hallway.

"Father, you may come in now." Father Calandrini had worked closely with Petruccio, but to be called on a Sunday, right before the exhibition, only meant bad news.

"Your Eminence." Calandrini walked to the cardinal, knelt, and kissed the ring on the outstretched hand before standing.

"Today is a day for celebration and high spirits, don't you think?"

Calandrini nodded.

---

4 Archbishop Gerolamo della Rovere: Archbishop of Turin from AD 1564 to 1592.Elevated to Cardinal AD 1586. Born AD 1530, died AD 1592.

5 Archbishop Cipriano Pallavicino: Archbishop of Genoa from AD 1568 to 1585. Apostolic Nuncio to Naples, Italy, AD 1566. Born AD 1509, died AD 1585

6 Bishop Domenico della Rovere: Bishop of Asti, Italy, from AD 1569 to 1587. Born AD 1518, died AD 1587

7 Council of Trent: Held between AD 1545 and 1563 to address key issues of the Reformation.

"How familiar are you with the Council of Trent?" The encounter was kept short. The cardinal didn't want this unfortunate management of his shepherds to ruin his high spirits.

Calandrini nodded again, not responding verbally to the discussion. The less said, the better. He knew his situation was precarious.

"I would like you to read the decree from the council again, and we will meet tomorrow to determine how we will need to rectify your behavior and your situation. I suggest you also read and pray on First Corinthians, chapter seven."

Borromeo looked at the man in front of him. Calandrini was taller, by about two inches, and thinner. He had been on his staff for several years. Borromeo was also thin, eating a very basic diet and avoiding the cuisine and wine of his homeland. He looked into the priest's eyes. The man's fate was in his hands.

"You may go." Petruccio opened the door and kept his eyes on Calandrini as he turned and exited the cardinal's chambers. They could now return to preparing for the exhibition, the first of its kind. He hoped there would be many more.

"Petruccio, how much do you think this problem is due to that German, or is it simply original sin? Cannot man's temptations be overcome by faith?"

"Your Eminence, it is time. I shall answer your question when we return." Petruccio stepped away from his senior as they both finished straightening the cardinal's cassock. Petruccio put the brush down, satisfied he had removed every fleck of dust and hair from the cassock.

Next, Borromeo picked up his robe and draped it over his shoulders.

Archbishop della Rovere entered Borromeo's chambers and nodded.

The cardinal retrieved his crozier, and the two of them walked slowly to the cathedral.

Petruccio followed the two men about two steps behind.

The Shroud was ready, and it was being displayed by the priest and other dignitaries from Turin.

Borromeo stopped and turned to his longtime friend and confidant. "Petruccio, if you'd like, you can also help to carry the Shroud. It will be a short walk, but it may be something you'd like to participate in with the other younger prelates in the church." The cardinal and Petruccio smiled. Petruccio was two years older than the cardinal.

The crowds were gathered outside the cathedral. All of Turin and Savoy had turned out. The duke's royal guard lined the streets to keep back the throngs and to provide a view for as many as possible to this holiest of relics. The six church functionaries would lead the way with the Shroud in their hands.

Next came the other prelates. These would be followed side by side by Archbishops Gerolamo and Cipriano. Then came Cardinal Borromeo, followed by Petruccio. The duke of Savoy would follow on his horse twenty yards behind Borromeo. He would be escorted by his personal guard troop, made up of twenty men decked out in their finest uniforms. The beautiful red, white, and blue colors of the Savoy flag stood out against the black of the guard's stallions.

Two acolytes opened the massive doors to the cathedral, and the Shroud became visible to the throngs lining the streets.

Not yet in sight of the crowd, Borromeo leaned back toward Petruccio. "Did you hear that? A deafening silence. First, there was the din of the throngs talking and carrying on and then the booming silence." Borromeo whispered so as not to interrupt the solemnity of the moment.

The duke was mounted on his horse ahead of his family's gilded carriage. His white stallion and the black stallions of his personal guard stood at the ready, his men trying to hold them quiet, but it wasn't possible against the sudden silence of the crowd. Their neighing was the only thing that could be heard as the Shroud was marched out of the cathedral and onto the street.

The younger prelates held the Shroud along the long edge, each doing their best to keep it level and off the ground. Father Arcanzola held one end, directly over the image and blood of the feet.

Borromeo stepped out onto the last stair and looked out. The noise from the crowd began to slowly reemerge. The archbishops were about ten yards ahead of him. They turned and faced him, as did all the other prelates of the church in front of them. Another minute passed, and Borromeo held out his crozier in his left hand and extended his right hand. The crowd again went silent. This was his only duty for the procession.

Off to his right, about twenty yards down the boulevard, was a man standing against one of the trees. He was dressed in black in a way that didn't fit into the day's event. This man didn't participate like the others. He was expressionless and oblivious to the pomp and circumstance.

Borromeo glanced at him and then back to the throng. He genuflected. "In Nomine Patris, et Filii, et Spiritus Sancti, amen." Everyone in the throng did the same. Some went further and touched their knee to the ground and repeated this most Catholic of phrases.

Borromeo paused another minute, waiting for the throng to be silent again. He lowered his crozier and right arm and looked down to proceed down the steps. The prelates in front of him turned and began their march down the wide boulevard. Once Borromeo reached street level, he was no longer able to see the mysterious man dressed all in black. He contemplated sending Petruccio after him, but the thought faded from his consciousness once they reached the piazza.

The procession to the Piazza del Castello required about thirty minutes. There the duke had built a raised platform to display the Shroud. As the procession passed, the throngs were allowed to close in behind them. On the dais were seats for all the prelates, the archbishops, and Borromeo. Petruccio stood behind the chair of Borromeo. Next to him was the throne chair for the duke of Savoy. The autumn weather was perfect—not too hot, not too cold—for the three hours required for the throng to pass and view the Shroud.

On the way up the stairs of the platform, the Shroud was stretched a bit as each of the prelates took the twelve steps to the display area. No one heard the sound, but it was clear something had happened. No one noticed the corner of the Shroud—the corner held by Father Arcanzola—tore, just slightly. It had been handled so many times the corner finally gave way. Arcanzola grabbed a larger portion of the corner, bundling it up in his hand.

Once the entourage was on the dais, the senior prelates, cardinals, archbishops, and bishops moved forward and took over holding the cloth in front of the mass of people. There were tens of thousands of onlookers. No one wanted to move from their positions, yet each was in constant motion, shuffling one step to the left or right and craning their necks to try to get a better view of the miraculous image.

Cardinal Borromeo took over the central position. His right hand held the Shroud just above Jesus's face, his left hand over the back of Jesus's head.

Three bishops stood on Borromeo's right, three on his left. After about thirty minutes the senior prelates were relieved by another seven priests and church dignitaries.

After about two hours, Borromeo again noticed the man dressed in black. He didn't approach the Shroud but instead focused his gaze on the cardinal and the duke.

"Petruccio, that man, do you see him? The one in black. Do you see him?" Borromeo nodded in the man's direction. Petruccio saw him. No one else took any notice. They were listening intently to a conversation between the duke and duchess on the dais sitting to his right. Something about the negotiations to increase the holdings of the Savoyard state in southern France.

"Yes, Your Eminence." Petruccio saw him too. He just didn't fit in. "Shall I go find him and have him meet you?"

"Yes, but don't scare him off." Borromeo whispered directly into Petruccio's ear to be certain he heard him over the din of the crowd. "Tell him His Eminence would like to meet Tuesday evening at dusk."

At that moment, the man disappeared into the crowd. Borromeo and Petruccio continued their oversight of the procession, but they also continued their scan of the throngs to see if the man would appear again. He was nowhere to be found.

Petruccio looked over at the Shroud. He saw the result of the wear on the cloth from the many exhibitions and now from this one. The top edge where the Shroud was held was distorted. The threads were wider, and light could be seen coming through in an uneven pattern. The edge of the Shroud began to fray. It looked like the top edge was also a slightly darker color.

Immediately disturbed by what he saw, Petruccio wondered whether there was other damage caused by the frequent exhibitions or if it had been weakened by the heat of the Chambéry fire.

How could this gift from God last for millennia into the future?

Saint John the Baptist Cathedral, Turin
Early Afternoon, October 12, AD 1578

"We must leave. Immediately. If we want to keep this child—our child— we must." With the exhibition under way, no one was nearby to notice that Sister Junipera had entered the quarters of one of the male priests.

"But where will we go? Where?" Sister Junipera felt the slight lump in her belly. She had already begun to love the child, even though she was barely showing the results of her liaisons with her love, Father Calandrini. She always wanted to be a nun. She loved the church and all she was able to do through the church, but now her love for this man changed all that.

"I am to meet with Borromeo tomorrow, and if we stay, he will send me to Milan to separate us forever." Although no one was around, Calandrini spoke softly. He reached out and put his hand on Junipera's shoulder. "And you will have the child taken away from you. They will take me away immediately without any chance for me to ever see you again.

"I suggest we escape to Geneva. The new church forming there will take us in. If not there, we can go to Germany. The Luther sect allows marriage of their priests." Calandrini had been formulating his thoughts ever since he found out about his impending fatherhood. Now it was time to turn those thoughts into a plan. He could no longer work on the staff of Cardinal Borromeo. "I have been thinking through the options, and it is only a few weeks' travel between here and Geneva. If we leave now, the weather won't be too harsh."

"What will we do for food? For clothing? For the baby?" Junipera feared the unknown, the loss of certainty serving as a nun.

"If Borromeo was going to walk to Chambéry, we can walk to Geneva. We can make it." Calandrini tried to comfort his lover and soon-to-be wife. "They will marry us there. We can both work for the church, or if not at least worship. The Calvinists are strong there, and we can be together."

"I don't just want to worship. I want to be part of the church. I want to help the poor." In that instant, Junipera realized her life was no longer going to be as she had hoped.

"My brother has money. His silk trading business is doing well. He'll loan us the money. I don't want to leave the church, but I won't leave you. I won't leave our baby." Calandrini could see a plan coming together. He had baptized many children, and he wanted a child of his own but couldn't rectify that with his commitment to the church. His dreams had come true, though not in the way he expected—fleeing from the church abandoning his vows. "My brother will help us. If we have to, if I can't be part of the church, I will work for him." Calandrini peered into Junipera's eyes. "I will sacrifice everything for you and the baby."

✝✝✝

Saint John the Baptist Cathedral, Turin
Dawn, Sunday, June 13, AD 1582

It had been four years since the exhibition of the Shroud after his walk to Turin and celebration. Borromeo returned to view the Shroud but took the carriage this time. "I don't know what today is. This new calendar has me completely confused. Will today be Sunday or Wednesday?" Borromeo chided Petruccio. "His Holiness is about to change things in a big way. Apparently, Sunday won't be Sunday anymore."

Borromeo enjoyed the moment. He understood the reasoning behind the calendar change but continued chiding his assistant. "How could a calendar be off? Don't the sun, moon, and stars rotate around the Earth? Copernicus said the earth rotates around the sun, and now Gregory wants to change the calendar. He wants to switch to the new calendar in October. Perhaps next, we will learn to fly."

"It's not clear to me either, Your Eminence." Petruccio had no idea how the calendar worked. He had become a priest through the favors Borromeo bestowed on him. Borromeo would never have let him become a priest without first rigorously studying, as if he had been to the seminary. He had given Petruccio many things to read, and Petruccio had learned from them and was able to connect all of the critical doctrinal concepts. With his years being the assistant to Cardinal Borromeo, he was well versed enough to be a man of the cloth.

"With the Shroud now permanently residing in Turin, it won't be difficult for us to come and view it." The cardinal was already thinking past this visit to his next opportunity to be in this presence of God. "When we came four years earlier and viewed the cloth with the duke of Savoy, it was plain to see how much He sacrificed for us and yet what little we sacrifice. The whip marks and the blood stains show Jesus's martyrdom for us." The cardinal looked down at his silk robe and the gilded teacup he had just drunk from. "What do you think? Should we give all this up to flaunt our piety? Should we ask the rich to give it up? Will that help the masses? Or should we work to evangelize and educate?"

Petruccio waited a moment and then responded. "You have already given up all finery, except when it comes to official functions." As Borromeo advanced in age, he often used his assistant as a sounding board. Petruccio enjoyed the finery but knew his friend was right. To serve the poor, to encourage them into the church, riches—especially of the church—couldn't be flaunted.

"Should I give up all my—and the church's—riches to pass through the eye of the needle to live through eternity with God in heaven?"

Borromeo was tired after their trip from Milan. He sighed. "I thought Turin would be closer to Milan, but a four-day carriage ride is still a four-day carriage ride." The carriage ride required only a few days less than walking but was much more comfortable, although sitting in his coach wasn't all that comfortable. "When we walked here four years ago, I was a lot younger than I am today, yet I feel more exhausted now than before."

Borromeo sat in a comfortable, cushioned chair upon their arrival, glad to be out of the confines of the carriage. "I'm glad you recommended we arrive two days early. I needed the rest."

There was a knock at the door. "Your Eminence, we are ready." It was Father Arcanzola. He was assigned the unenviable task of summoning the prelates. Neither of them were ever punctual, and regardless of the pleadings of Arcanzola, they would only come when they were good and ready.

Cardinal Paleotto, Archbishop of Bologna, was even worse than Borromeo. Paleotto arrived a few days earlier than Borromeo, since his trip required two weeks, but this didn't make him early for anything else.

Along with His Eminence, Cardinal Gabriele Paleotto,[8] his cousin Alfonso[9] was also present. Their pilgrimage would be rewarded with three viewings of the Shroud.

"Alfonso, you may never be able to see again what Jesus Christ suffered for us. This Shroud proves the truth of the apostles' writings of Jesus's death." Cardinal Paleotto thought of the days ahead of them. "You shall accompany me, and I suggest you take detailed notes so you will always remember."

"Yes, my cousin." Alfonso had grown up with his cousin and used the honorific *His Eminence* only when they were in public. On this trip, they would be in private much of the time, so he was simply *my cousin* or *Gabriele*. "The Shroud is the most significant evidence of the resurrection other than the writings in the Bible. Where those stories were written, the Shroud is physical evidence—a witness to the resurrection."

Father Arcanzola knocked on their door. "I cry your mercy, Your Eminence, we are ready."

Within a few minutes, they all gathered in the showing room of the palace. The display table had been set up and the Shroud rolled out.

Alfonso was in awe of the size and lifelikeness of the image. Alfonso examined the Shroud closely. "The quality of the linen is quite fine and the weave extraordinary." He continued to examine each and every inch. "How would Joseph of Arimathea have come up with a cloth on such short notice? He would have had to have purchased what was available. There was only so much time. And Jesus was a simple man. No one would have wanted to bury Him in a royal cloth. He was a carpenter and a poor man who eschewed wealth of any kind, living off the gifts He received from His followers. He was even buried in the tomb of His friend. His family didn't own a tomb that could be made available to Him."

Cardinal Paleotto had never thought about the composition of the cloth. He was just awestruck by the image. "My cousin, you may be correct." He wanted to spend time meditating to himself, but his cousin was palpably galvanized by what he saw. He also didn't want to discourage his cousin from his observations. "You'll need to memorize and write down everything you see. Write down everything—your initial impressions, thoughts, everything. You may never get a chance to view it again."

---

8 Cardinal Gabriele Paleotto: Archbishop of Bologna from AD 1566 to 1597. Argued for the devotional role of holy images, including the Shroud. Important figure in the Council of Trent. Candidate for the papacy in AD 1590. Born AD 1522, died AD 1597.

9 Alfonso Paleotto: Archbishop of Bologna and Corinth from AD 1591 to 1610. Cousin to Cardinal Gabriele Paleotto, successor to him in AD 1597 as archbishop of Bologna. Author of the first printed book on the Shroud in AD 1598. Born AD 1531, died AD 1610.

Alfonso nodded. He did not meditate like the others, instead taking it all in in a scientific manner.

Alfonso was only able to take in so much that first viewing. Although it lasted about an hour, it raised questions that would take weeks and months to answer. Maybe they would never be answered. A renewed study of the Bible and the passion would have to be undertaken to corroborate what he observed here with what was in the Gospels. "Your Eminence, tomorrow when we return, I wish to review in detail the hands and the wrists. The book of John records Jesus's words, when he appeared in the locked room, as, 'See my hands.' But these marks are in the wrists."

"Yes, I noticed that also. Tonight we can review Scripture and your notes." His Eminence was not worried about minor inconsistencies. "This cloth had survived the fire and fifteen hundred years. Perhaps there is a difference in the definition of a hand or wrist in the original Greek. There is always an explanation."

"We were blessed that the fire in Chambéry did limited damage. What a loss it would have been for Christianity had this relic been totally destroyed in that fire." Alfonso's thoughts swirled between the marks and the patches made by the Poor Clares Sisters over fifty years ago. "The color of each of those patches matches the cloth perfectly. We are blessed that the images of the body were undisturbed."

Neither of them took special note of the imperceptibly darker edge where the hands of fifteen centuries held the cloth. Nor did they notice the one edge didn't lay flat like the rest of the cloth. Their focus was on the center of the cloth—the image. One edge had acquired a few bulges as moisture and handling led to threads being pulled and stretched and creased.

✝✝✝

The second day's viewing took place in the morning. They were only able to view the Shroud undisturbed for a few short minutes. Many others also attended and crowded the room.

"You may remain as long as you wish, Alfonso, as I have some conversations with Cardinal Borromeo to attend to."

Alfonso memorized every detail of the hands and the apparent wounds. The nails did not pierce the back of the hands but the wrists. The blood flowed down the arms. "This is strange," Alfonso whispered to himself. "The flow of the blood. Is it from while he was on the cross or postmortem?"

They were all ushered out of the viewing room, and Alfonso ran back to his quarters. He had brought paper and ink with him, and he began writing his direct recollections. "It appears on the holy Shroud that the wound is seen at the joint between the arm and the hand, the part anatomists call the carpus, leaving the backs of the hands without wounds." Once he finished his writings, he began drawing. He used charcoal for the image and red ink for the blood.

✝✝✝

For Alfonso, the third day of viewing was a disappointment. His Eminence and Cardinal Borromeo were allowed a private viewing, but only for the first hour. Their entourage, including Alfonso, was not allowed into the room during this time. This permitted the two cardinals to sit in meditation and prayer while they were in the presence of the image of Jesus Christ.

It was only later that Alfonso was afforded entry, but the number of people meditating made it difficult for him to observe and catalog his findings. His excitement became an agitation to the other guests and dignitaries. He needed to be able to observe each and every square inch, which was not possible with all the others in attendance. He did spend some time—albeit at a distance—and noticed the hands had no thumbs. *Where were the thumbs?*

"I'm sorry you weren't able to spend as much time as you would have liked, but this Shroud is a precious gift from God, and many, many people want to revere it and confess their sins," Cardinal Paleotto said as the two of them walked together back to their chambers. It had been a long day, and they were both in need of some rest. "Let us make a plan to complete your study of the Shroud. You have already made some extraordinary findings, including the observations about the wounds on the wrists and the missing thumbs, as well as your questions about how the image was made."

"Someday I'll return and complete my drawings. How ideal it would be to have a life-size copy of this image. Then it could be studied in detail." Alfonso stood up from his drawing. "Perhaps we can petition the pope for an exclusive viewing of this holy relic."

✝✝✝

SAINT PHILIP NERI CHURCH, TURIN
MIDDAY, TUESDAY, OCTOBER 16, AD 1694

Over one hundred and fifty years had passed since the Poor Clares Sisters had made their repairs. The Shroud had been exhibited countless times, always with people using their bare hands to grasp the same edge and resulting in visible wear and tear.

"Father, Father, please don't. Please. We can't use black thread on the patch. The thread must match the color of the linen. We can't use black." The black threaded repairs would stand out against the tan brown of the linen. Sisters Cornelia and Louisa were adamant, but so was he. The more they pleaded, the more implacable he became.

"Duke Victor[10] gave me full authority on this, and I will do it my way." He would not sway. Even though they were right, he was not accustomed to being contradicted by anyone, let alone these women. *These sisters. What did they know about something as important as the Shroud? I will not be spoken to like this!*

Father Valfrè[11] was a member of the Oratory of Saint Philip Neri. As a member of the Oratory, Valfrè and his brother Oratorians were bound together by a bond of charity. The sisters were part of the convent attached to the Saint Philip Neri Church.

The sisters continued whispering among themselves but couldn't come up with anything to make him change his mind.

Father Valfrè was exceedingly kind to the poor, but to his underlings, he was a tyrant.

They finally relented. Since the regular exhibition of the Shroud in Lirey beginning almost two hundred years before, and the Poor Clares Sisters' repairs fifty years later, the Shroud had begun to show its wear. There were candlewax droppings, wine drip stains, and one of the Poor Clares Sisters' repairs had started to come undone. Worst of all, the edge where the Shroud was handled was frayed and unraveling. Father Valfrè's task was to repair the problematic patch and the unraveling edge by weaving in linen and cotton thread that matched the color of the Shroud.

"Sister Cornelia, we have the next batch of thread for the reweave." Sister Beatrice entered the room, holding three skeins of thread. There was over a thousand feet of thread coiled up between the three of them. This was their third attempt at matching the thread color to the threads in the Shroud. The last two tries were both too yellow. This time they used a slightly more diluted solution of the dye with a small dose of madder added. The dried madder dye added a touch of red, yielding a good match to the tan brown of the Shroud.

"Bring it here," Sister Cornelia said, waving her arm for Sister Beatrice to bring the newly dyed thread. Sisters Louisa and Cornelia were both over

---

10 Duke Victor Amadeus II of Savoy: Duke of Savoy, AD 1675–1730. Born AD 1666, died AD 1732.

11 Blessed Sebastian Valfrè: Catholic priest and a member of the Oratory of Saint Philip Neri and known as the Apostle of Turin. Born AD 1679, died AD 1710.

sixty years old. Sister Louisa had the best vision but limited dexterity in her fingers. Sister Cornelia, the most senior, was just the opposite. She had no arthritis, but her near vision was failing. Sister Beatrice was the youngest, but her sewing skills weren't of the quality required to assist in the repairs to the Shroud. The three of them walked over to the table where Father Valfrè had just finished his prayers and was about to begin working.

As usual, Valfrè had to wipe the tears from his eyes. His praying at the Shroud always led to tears. The thoughts of Jesus suffering—the wounds, the distorted hands, the blood at the feet—left him with a hole in the pit of his stomach that couldn't be filled.

"This is very close, very close." She compared the three coils several times at several points along the length of the Shroud. In each case, the colors matched exactly. "The last two attempts were too yellow. These look perfect. Father, would you like to have a look?"

Father Valfrè examined the sample thread and then compared it against the Shroud. He repeated the comparisons at the same locations as Sister Cornelia. "Sister Cornelia, you have trained the sisters well in the art of thread dying. Yes, I think this is perfect. Yes, you may begin the reweaving of the edges."

Sisters Cornelia and Louisa were members of the Saint Philip Neri Convent, primarily known for their thread spinning, embroidery, and sewing. Besides their sewing skills, they cared for unwed mothers who made their babies available for adoption.

"I may be only partially available to help today." Sister Beatrice made her announcement, preferring to work on the Shroud instead of helping the women and mothers. "We have taken in a newly pregnant young woman who has been badly beaten and thrown to the street. I will need to care for her until she has healed enough to care for herself. We hope the baby will survive. We'll know in a day or so."

With the acceptance of this batch of thread, Sister Beatrice would now be free to tend to the newly arrived woman and her soon-to-be-born child. There was nothing more she liked than to care for a woman in her direst of need. As a nun, she was not permitted to have children, so she treated each of the women and children as one of her own. "The healing of this woman will require just as much care as this cloth."

"I heard she was bloody and beaten from head to toe. Has she confided in you as to who the perpetrator was?" Sister Cornelia gritted her teeth when she thought of all the girls she'd treated over the years for the same crime. "I pray for their forgiveness, but it is the hardest praying I can do. It goes against every fiber in my body. I only hope the baby survives."

Sister Louisa was the most skilled at reweaving, and she and Sister Cornelia had been practicing their skills on a separate cloth. In the convent, Sister Cornelia was the teacher of dying skills, whereas Sister Louisa was the teacher of sewing and clothing repair.

"Father Valfrè, Sister Louisa will begin her work as soon as you have completed your patches. She and I will first remove the existing threads and then begin replacing them with the new." Sister Louisa rubbed her hands in anticipation of the upcoming pain in her knuckles the detailed work would generate. "We'll remove about three inches from the edge and then begin the reweaving."

"Shall we work to replicate the exact weave, or should we introduce a slightly different weave to strengthen the edges overall?" Sister Cornelia had become adept at asking a question as opposed to suggesting her preferred solution. In that way, Valfrè would claim to have made the decision, but each time the chosen decision was the direction she would have otherwise advocated for. She was disappointed she was not able to sway Valfrè to a more sensible approach than using the black thread on the patches.

"We shall use a different weave. The weave will need to be much stronger so that the Shroud can continue to be exhibited as necessary." Valfrè helped the sisters choose an appropriate weave—not the three over one herringbone style currently in the Shroud but a much stronger one. Their decision was to help the Shroud last for millennia to come. Sister Cornelia smiled. It was what she knew was best.

The work was painstaking and began each morning after an hour of group prayer at the foot of the Shroud. Sister Cornelia's first try had to be removed and replaced by Sister Louisa's. It was not of a quality needed for this repair, so she was no longer part of the hands-on work. Only Sister Louisa would be allowed to make the final repairs.

Sister Cornelia's role became one of keeping the candles lit and providing supplies and sewing implements while Sister Louisa arduously wove each thread. In between caring for the pregnant woman, Sister Beatrice kept the fire going and stayed away from the cloth so that charcoal from the fire wouldn't contaminate the work. Every half hour or so, Sister Louisa would stand and warm her hands in front of the fire. The heat helped to soothe the pain in her arthritic fingers. She had tried using leeches to numb the pain and reduce the inflammation, but the last time, for some reason, the bleeding wouldn't stop. She couldn't use leeches now because she did not want to take the chance of getting blood anywhere near the cloth.

For two weeks, Valfrè supervised the sisters directly until the midday meal and prayer. Afterward he supervised feeding the poor outside the church, only returning after they had all been fed. "Sister Louisa, you have made great progress," Valfrè said as the first inch of repair along the fourteen-foot length of the Shroud was complete.

"When our work is done, it will be a work to be proud of," was all Sister Cornelia could say. She would be prouder if the black thread were replaced.

On the third day after reweaving began, with little fanfare, the archbishop and the duke arrived. "Your Eminence, Your Grace," Valfrè uttered as soon as he saw them.

Sisters Louisa and Cornelia stood and bowed, then backed away from the cloth. When they stood, the current thread was woven through to about the top of Jesus's head and was left dangling off the table, with the bronze needle almost touching the floor. Sister Louisa instinctively left her leather thimble on top of the cloth. Sister Cornelia noticed it, stepped forward and snatched it, bowed, and returned, standing between Sisters Louisa and Beatrice. Behind her frock, Sister Louisa rubbed her hands together. The pain in her fingers had not ceased from the day before. She had worked too long, and her knuckles had not yet recovered. She feared the pain would be with her every day for the next two weeks of the repair work.

Father Valfrè bowed and remained next to the table where the Shroud was being worked on. The duke and archbishop said nothing as they leaned over the cloth inspecting the progress and quality of the repairs.

The duke straightened up, not averting his gaze from the cloth. "I notice you've chosen a slightly different weave. I'm not sure I like it." The duke made no comment on the black threads. His focus was on the edge repairs.

"Yes, Your Grace. I chose this particular weave because of the strength it provides. As we shall continue to exhibit the cloth, it needs to be very strong to withstand further damage. I assure you that when the repairs are complete, it will not be noticeable and will allow the Shroud to be exhibited many times without the need for repeated repairs." Father Valfrè was used to getting his way with his superiors.

Sister Cornelia smiled, happy her idea was presented as the proper solution.

"I agree with Father Valfrè, Your Grace. This will strengthen the Shroud." Archbishop Michele Antonio Vibò[12] concurred with his underling.

"Hmmm." The duke had learned early on to let the experts make the decisions. He preferred to set the strategy and let others implement it. "I trust

---

12 Archbishop Michele Antonio Vibò: Archbishop of Turin from AD 1690 to 1713. Born AD 1630, died AD 1713.

your judgment. Alert me when the work is complete. Good day." He didn't wait for a response and hurried out of the room.

The archbishop nodded to Father Valfrè and then followed the duke.

"I'm surprised he made no comment about the black thread. Perhaps he didn't notice it," Sister Cornelia whispered to Sister Louisa. She still smarted from the decision to keep the black thread.

CHAPTER 12

The Story of STURP

Several hundred years passed. Several world wars were foisted on the world and modern science had come of its own. The Shroud had fallen into obscurity—almost. In AD 1978, STURP (Shroud of Turin Research Project) was formed, by scientists primarily from the Los Alamos National Laboratory in New Mexico, to scientifically research the authenticity of the Shroud and make conclusions about how the image was made. They had solved some of the world's biggest challenges, and now the Shroud piqued their curiosity.

KENT LABORATORY, UNIVERSITY OF CHICAGO, CHICAGO, ILLINOIS
LATE AFTERNOON, THURSDAY, OCTOBER 26, AD 1949

"Professor Libby,[1] Professor Libby," Georgia McGinnis ran to catch up with Professor Willard Libby. "Professor, I was wondering if it's possible to be an assistant with you in the winter quarter?" She was a first-year master's student in physical chemistry at the University of Chicago, hoping to

---

1 Professor Willard Libby: Professor of University of Chicago's Institute for Nuclear Studies. Born AD 1908, died AD 1980

work toward her doctorate. World War II had been over for a few years now, and with resistance, more women began to study for their postgraduate degrees.

"I may have need of some help, but the money isn't good. I was impressed with the draft of your master's thesis on using nuclear energy to build electric power plants. We are working on some interesting projects coming up in the new year. We'll be dating a few woolly mammoths as well as developing a method to verify the calibration of the whole process." Professor Libby always had a smile on his face, especially when he thought about all the things he could do to determine the ages of objects containing organic material. "Walk with me to my office, and we can talk. I'd like to learn more about you."

McGinnis also smiled. She had high hopes to work on a project that tied modern science with archaeology. "I just finished reading one of your articles in *Physical Review* magazine. I think it was from June 1946 on radiocarbon dating. I am fascinated about the cosmic process generating the carbon-14 in the atmosphere and how carbon-14 decays over time."

McGinnis tried to act smart, but she had more questions than answers. "If carbon-14 decays into nitrogen with a half-life of about 5,700 years, how accurate would it be for artifacts that might be 50,000 years old?"

"For a master's student, that's a great question. That's exactly what we need to investigate this coming winter, and that is, how can we better calibrate our radiocarbon dating. You see, we assume that cosmic rays impinge on the atmosphere at a constant rate over the last tens of thousands of years. But what if that isn't the case? What if ten thousand years ago the remains of a supernova caused a peak in the cosmic rays hitting the earth's atmosphere?"

McGinnis was fascinated by the question.

"That would tend to change the ratio of carbon-14 atoms to carbon-12 and potentially invalidate all our findings."

Libby assumed Georgia understood that it was the ratio of the remaining undecayed carbon-14 atoms to carbon-12 atoms that could be used to determine the age of the specimen. Libby decided to test her. "Miss McGinnis, tell me, how does this process work?"

Georgia didn't expect to be tested right then and there, even though she had just read Libby's paper the night before. "As I understand it, it goes like this. Since, after death, organic material stops ingesting new carbon atoms, the ratio of carbon-14 to carbon-12 at the moment of death is constant and equal to whatever's in the environment. However, over time, carbon-14 decays at a known rate, whereas carbon-12 does not decay. As the number of carbon-14 atoms decays into nitrogen, this leaves a higher and higher proportion of carbon-12 in the specimen. The age of the specimen is directly correlated to this ratio of carbon-14 to carbon-12 atoms."

"So, tell me, what could be some of the errors that could creep in?" Professor Libby now wanted to test whether Georgia truly had a grasp on the methodology. "Of course, other than what I just mentioned."

Georgia had no clue, and her look of puzzlement was obvious. She saw a smile come over Libby's face. He enjoyed asking a question to trip up his students, especially the ones he liked. He did it to his kids, too, and they loved being intrigued by the challenge. "Remember this, Miss McGinnis. Asking why something might be wrong leads to knowledge but also leads to evidence that the scientific method might be very right."

Georgia was silent. Her mind went blank. She knew she could figure out the answer but was never confident when asked extemporaneous questions.

"Okay, never mind. As you can imagine, there are many other considerations that might go into the error profile of this method." Professor Libby continued. "One thing we're considering is using the core of very old redwood trees to confirm decay over time. Since the rings on the outside of the tree are thousands of years older than those on the inside, we can possibly use that knowledge to calibrate our dating methods against these rings." Libby stopped walking and gazed through the window out over the courtyard. It was another beautiful cold October day in Chicago. The leaves had fallen, the sky was clear and blue. They had just made it up the stairs to the floor where his office was. He turned to Georgia. "So, does this sound like something you could contribute to?"

Libby smiled, knowing he had her hooked. "You would be the first woman on our team and there would be challenges."

"Yes, absolutely. When can I start?" Other than this last question, Libby didn't ask Georgia many questions. She tried to hold back a smile but was unsuccessful. Georgia had clinched the job and was excited to begin working on something that could change the way we observe the world.

†††

KENT LABORATORY, UNIVERSITY OF CHICAGO, CHICAGO, ILLINOIS
8:00 A.M., MONDAY, JANUARY 19, AD 1950

"I did some research on your question and came up with the following sources of erroneous results, so I want to see what you think." Georgia handed Libby a list of four items. It had been three months since Professor Libby had offered her a position on his team for the winter quarter. This was her first day.

"First a lack of the constancy of carbon-14 being generated in the atmosphere from all sources, including past atomic tests and astronomical activity, such as supernovae." Georgia pointed out that she remembered Libby's question to her months before.

"This one is a challenge because it seems that the generation of carbon-14 in the atmosphere changes with the season. I'm wondering if this is due to the average temperature and expansion of the upper atmosphere." Georgia saw that Professor Libby was enjoying his first day with his new intern. She knew he was interested in new thought experiments, especially if his students and interns could challenge his thinking. "I'm also wondering if there is a difference regionally. For example, do the cosmic rays hitting the northern hemisphere match the rate in the southern hemisphere?

"Second, inaccuracies in the knowledge of the exact decay rate of carbon-14. This is a small one but nevertheless for completeness should be included. Third, inaccuracy in the measurement of carbon-14 and carbon-12 by the mass spectrometer. I always wondered how accurate this could be." Georgia had memorized her list but referred to her notes just to make certain she had it right.

Professor Libby smiled at this one. This was where he was working at the moment. "This error and your previous one are especially important as the age of the specimen approaches maybe ten times the half-life of carbon-14. What do you think? Do you think carbon dating could be reasonably accurate up to maybe fifty thousand years?" He asked the question pointing out to her that he also remembered her question.

"Given that the half-life of carbon-14 is about 5,700 years, the amount of carbon-14 in a sample would be incredibly small. Unless there was a huge sample or the mass spectrometer was amazingly accurate, it would not be appropriate to use carbon-14 dating to measure an organic substance approaching fifty thousand years." Georgia surprised him with an answer.

"Very cogent, very cogent." Libby smiled, glad he had her now on his team. "And worse yet, carbon-14 dating is destructive, so the larger the sample required, the more of the sample is destroyed. This may not be ideal for small organic archaeological specimens."

Georgia continued with her list. "My fourth and potentially fifth source go in a different direction and don't relate to carbon-14 directly but more about the process." She returned to her list. "Improperly prepared samples. For example, there could be contamination on the specimen from more recent handling or contamination from other organic sources not tied to the specimen."

"You could also get contamination by a tree growing its roots into the artifact or mold or mildew not being properly cleaned from the sample." Libby gave a few additional details. "Good work. That's a pretty good list." He had a handful of other sources of contamination, and he was sure these would be a big area of contention as this technique became more mature.

"I have a fifth source," Georgia held back her smile, proud of being able to show off her knowledge with her new mentor. "But it's not an error in the measurement as much as it is in the validity of the sample. I didn't put this on my list, but it is something to consider." Georgia waited a minute and then gave her last source of error, "Fraudulent samples. I could imagine there would be some subterfuge in providing samples. Or it could be that the sample was just taken incorrectly. With many artifacts, they are agglomerations of many pieces that may have been brought together at different times for fraudulent or other reasons."

"Go on." Libby was now curious.

"Well, for instance, counterfeit books are often made to appear legitimate by gluing in the first page of an original book." Georgia wasn't doing a good job of explaining. "I mean, often the age of old books is determined by the age of the inside cover. If the inside cover had been stolen and cut out from an original book and glued into a fraudulent book, then the age of the fraudulent book would be deemed older than it was."

"These are all good reasons for erroneous—or maybe the term is not erroneous—but rather less than accurate measurement of the true age of the specimen." Professor Libby was a good judge of character, and he knew he made the right choice with Georgia. "This is exactly the kind of thinking I like in my interns. Good work. We'll never know where carbon-14 dating will take us. It may be used in the most mundane of ways but could also be used in the most spectacular of scientific queries."

†††

RAMADA INN, ALBUQUERQUE, NEW MEXICO
MIDMORNING, WEDNESDAY, MARCH 23, AD 1977

"As much as I want the analysis to show that the age of the Shroud of Turin is just under two thousand years, what if we find something different?" Even though she had never seen the Shroud, Claire Fontaine believed it was the true burial cloth of her Savior and Redeemer, Jesus Christ. "It is very heartening for what can now be done in science that could never have been done before. Take, for example, the findings from Dr. Frei here in this article.[2] He is a Swiss criminologist and an expert in the study of pollens for forensic research."

They stood outside the hotel conference room waiting for the meeting to adjourn. Inside the conference room were ten scientists, each with a scientific specialty. Their knowledge could lead to accurate dating of the Shroud of Turin as well as to an understanding of the mechanism that caused the image.

"His findings are fascinating. For him to determine the sources of the pollen spores, he must have an extensive library of all the spores around the

---

2 Professor Max Frei-Sulzer: Botanist, professor, Zurich University.

world," Karen Cunningham interrupted. She was fascinated by the value of pure scientific research. She was a PhD candidate studying under Dr. Donald[3] and Dr. Joan Janney[4] at the Los Alamos Laboratory. "So much can be invested in the capture of data, and yet it only has consequence after it has been assembled and codified. Years and years of work had to go into gathering and studying all those samples of pollen."

"Who would have thought that collecting pollen samples over many years from around the world would lead to such strong proof that the Shroud is real—that it was in Jerusalem and eastern and western Turkey." Claire Fontaine, also a PhD candidate studying under the Janneys, was more interested in the new radiocarbon testing methods—an area in which she was becoming an expert. "One piece of data—pollen in this case—is interesting, but exhaustively collecting pollen from around the world, that's priceless."

"Before she had me, my mother worked with the first scientists on radiocarbon dating, which is a completely different field, but they had to test hundreds of samples to validate their process. Growing up, I remember her telling stories of how she met Professor Libby." Karen looked down at her watch. "I have a faded picture of her, Georgia McGinnis, and Libby himself standing with the rest of his team over one of their first carbon-dated artifacts . . . a woolly mammoth. They tested everything they could get their hands on to validate the dating and results of radiocarbon testing."

"God gave us the craving to satisfy our curiosity, and with that, we've been able to determine a method to use what's in the air—carbon—to determine the ages of valuable archaeological finds." Claire's thesis was to advance Libby's work further. It would provide additional proof that the decay rate of carbon-14 could be used to accurately determine the age of archaeological artifacts. "This method was developed by Libby after the war and is now ready for the next big test to determine the age of the Shroud of Turin. Is it two thousand years old or is it an invention of medieval times?"

"Think of cats, monkeys. Curiosity spans all animals, especially the young as they explore and learn more about their world. Just like our children. They are the true scientists." Karen Cunningham, PhD student and Claire's best friend, considered when she'd have kids, wondering if she should wait until after her thesis was approved.

"Still, this dimension of the pollens in the proof of the Shroud being the true burial cloth is very hard to refute by the deniers." Claire put down

---

3 Dr. Donald Janney: Los Alamos National Laboratory image analysis. Member of the 1978 STURP team.
4 Dr. Joan Janney: Los Alamos National Laboratory technical support. Member of the 1978 STURP team.

the magazine containing Dr. Max Frei's article on the pollens found on the Shroud. "His work showed they originated from plants only found in Israel and Turkey and proves that the Shroud was in those areas. How would a medieval forger know to spread these specific pollens on the cloth?"

✝✝✝

The door to the meeting room finally opened, and the participants began to emerge. Dr. Donald Janney and his wife, Joan, finally exited and walked over to Karen and Claire. The Janneys were both ecstatic. Joan Janney summed up the meeting. "We are going to formally petition the pope to allow us to use radiocarbon dating to date the Shroud. The work from Dr. Frei is considered groundbreaking, and we expect it will allow us to date the cloth to the beginning of the first millennium."

"Be wary of being so biased. We are going to try to accurately date the cloth. We'll let the findings speak for themselves." Dr. Donald corrected his wife, something that was not often possible.

"We are proposing a series of over twenty different types of analyses, including microscopy, infrared spectrometry, and radiocarbon dating. This will be the most comprehensive scientific examination of the Shroud." Dr. Joan Janney could hardly hold back her excitement. "We will have conclusive proof that this cloth is the true burial cloth of Jesus Christ." Joan smiled back at her husband, ignoring his admonition of needing to be neutral in their opinions when conducting their research.

"Dear, we must be open-minded. We can't let confirmation bias creep into our analyses, regardless of how much we want it to be true." Dr. Donald Janney agreed with his wife, but for the sake of appearance and for Shroud deniers, they had to maintain scientific neutrality.

✝✝✝

THE HALL OF VISITING PRINCES, TURIN ROYAL PALACE, TURIN, ITALY
EARLY MORNING, MONDAY, OCTOBER 9, AD 1978

"I wonder who our next pope will be. It's tragic that Pope John Paul[5] died after reigning only thirty days," Dr. Janney whispered to his wife. They weren't part of the group that had transported the Shroud into the Hall of Visiting Princes the day before.

The work hadn't yet begun, but everyone was present. The whole assembly of the STURP—Shroud of Turin Research Project—was present, including a

---

5 Pope John Paul I: Pope from August 26, 1978, to September 28, 1978. Born AD 1912, died AD 1978.

handful of international scholars. They stood in front of the entrance to the hall, a beautifully decorated room covered in artwork and wooden wall coverings. It was a markedly different venue than the Ramada Inn eighteen months before.

"I hope the naming of the new pope won't affect our work."

"Shh. Here comes Archbishop Anastasio Ballestrero.[6] Hopefully, he'll allow us in." Joan was impatient. She had already had too much coffee, and then they had arrived early. Plus, Italian coffee was so good, yet so much stronger than American. She wanted another cup, but she was also already shaking.

"Ladies and gentlemen, welcome. We are so glad to have you during this momentous investigation into the study of our most precious relic of Jesus Christ." The archbishop spoke for another twenty minutes. His English was impeccable, though he had a strong Italian accent.

The tension in the room was palpable. Everyone was anxious to learn the results of the investigation. The ceremony was more important to the archbishop than the results of the study. After all, the church had been around for two thousand years, and it would be around another two thousand, regardless of the results of any scientific findings concerning the Shroud.

"Regardless of the outcome of your work, I am reminded of John 20:29: 'Thomas, because thou hast seen me, thou hast believed: blessed are they that have not seen, and yet have believed." Ballestrero liked to conclude all his speeches with a message for his audience.

The thrust of his speech ignored the risks to him and the church. If the Shroud turned out to be a fake, he and the church had a lot to lose. With any investigation, there was always risk of damage to the relic. With any investigation, there was the risk that the outcomes would jeopardize the authenticity of the relic and embarrass the church. With any investigation, there was always the risk of fraud, deceit, and hidden agendas to take advantage of the situation for personal gain.

Ballestrero and the church assumed a lot at risk by allowing this battery of scientific tests. Nevertheless, Ballestrero was instrumental in gaining permission for the test to take place. He finally concluded, "If the Shroud is proven to date back to Jesus's crucifixion, it doesn't mean that we should believe. We should believe whether we've seen or not."

Finally he nodded to Father Giuseppe Rossi. They removed the key from his neck and opened the doors to the magnificent Hall of Visiting Princes. The windows were covered to control the light levels in the room. There on

---

6 Archbishop Anastasio Ballestrero: Archbishop of Turin, Italy, from AD 1977 to 1989. Born AD 1913, died AD 1998.

one side of the floor, with the Shroud fastened to it, stood the table that was normally used for exhibitions. "I have here a signed document stating that this cloth being displayed here is the authentic cloth. It is signed by His Eminence, Archbishop of Turin, Anastasio Ballestrero."

Once work on the Shroud began, it would be transferred to a steel table on the other side of the floor and held in place by magnets to avoid damaging or corrupting the Shroud. The steel table was to be covered in gold Mylar developed by NASA so that oxidation from the steel wouldn't contaminate the cloth.

Dr. Joan gasped as she entered the room that held the Shroud. "It's bigger than I expected." It was difficult for everyone to enter with the two oversized tables, the equipment, and the number of people. As soon as they crossed into the hall, both doctors saw the image and stopped in amazement. They could not believe they were realizing one of their life's seminal moments.

"It's way bigger," Dr. Donald agreed with her. "Do you realize there are maybe only a few hundred or thousand people total who have had the honor of being this close to this image of the moment of resurrection? John and Peter saw it at the tomb. Depending on your version of Shroud history, possibly Joseph of Arimathea, King Abgar of Edessa, archbishops, Roman emperors, dukes, kings, and popes. It's a short list of prominent religious and political figures over the last two thousand years, and we are now a part of that list."

"It is truly a shame we won't be able to do the radiocarbon dating, but I understand the concern. The methodology is too new and requires too large of a swatch for it to be sensible," Joan Janney lamented. Running a test would require samples to be cut from the Shroud. As she took in the magnificence of the cloth in front of her, she could not accept being responsible for anything that would harm this invaluable relic. Radiocarbon dating was not approved for this round of analysis.

"Father Rossi will review the ground rules. You have the next five days to complete your investigations." The archbishop made his announcement and reiterated this was the most valuable relic in all of Christianity. "With the recent death of Pope John Paul and the interregnum we now experience, I expect the utmost of reverence to be paid to the Shroud, the Catholic Church, and of course to our Savior and Redeemer, Jesus Christ."

"Remember, this isn't simply a test subject that can be dishonored." Father Rossi read through the agreed procedures, but no one listened. They whispered among themselves; in awe of the solemn responsibility they were about to undertake.

"This is a miraculous cloth containing a miraculous image, which includes traces of blood from the Divine." There was a pause as Father Rossi looked around the room. Rossi was the assistant to Archbishop Ballestrero. He regained everyone's attention with his silence. It was clear that nothing could happen until he gave his last permission.

"You may begin." The whispering returned and broadened to a boisterous buzz before some semblance of order started to emerge.

The study protocol and schedule for each team had been agreed upon in advance. Each team that wasn't part of the initial data gathering was to remain against the walls and out of the way.

Father Rossi stepped back, maintaining a watchful eye. After a few moments the din faded into the background as everyone began to focus on their prescribed tasks. Dr. Donald Janney turned to his wife, "This is truly a momentous occasion for all Christianity and for all humanity. What we learn from our investigations and analysis will help the faithful—and faithless—around the world. If the Shroud is a medieval fake, it will be important to make that known. Given the state of scientific method and tools today, we may not be able to prove it one way or another, and that will also be a message for all the world." His wife turned to him and smiled. The excitement in her eyes reminded him of the same look as they exchanged vows years before.

✝✝✝

THE HALL OF VISITING PRINCES, THE ROYAL PALACE, TURIN, ITALY
EARLY MORNING, FRIDAY, OCTOBER 13, AD 1978

The work proceeded for 120 hours straight. With jet lag and lack of sleep, none of the team of scientists knew what time it was. Their biological clocks were ignored as they worked and rested intermittently on and off for five full days. Sleeping on the hardwood floors of the Hall of Visiting Princes was painful, but after the second day, it had become routine. After the third day, the snoring, flatulence, and body odor didn't stop anyone from sleeping or working. They collected dust, new pollen samples, and Shroud blood, along with other data for analysis. And with their unfettered access to the Shroud, they took images of the linen at all levels of magnification and varying wavelengths.

"I am so exhausted. I don't think I've worked that intensely and slept that little since before my dissertation defense," Dr. Donald said to his wife, Dr. Joan Janney. Even with such exhaustion, he didn't want to leave the hall.

They both took one last look at the Shroud. "We may never be in the presence of God like this ever again."

"We will head to the airport this afternoon after the scheduled lunch with the archbishop, and you'll be able to sleep on the plane back to the US," his wife responded.

They exited the hall and made their way back to the bus that would return them to their hotel. Over the course of the five days, they had only once left the presence of the Shroud to shower and change clothes.

Donald looked back at his wife. "We are the ones who may provide the rest of the world with scientific certainty that God was here on earth in the form of a man and that he miraculously rose from the dead. We can't prove that he appeared to Thomas or the others or the two on their walk to Emmaus. But we will prove—" he looked at Barrie Schwortz,[7] one of several non-Christians in the expedition, "prove or disprove that this cloth captured His image at the moment of resurrection. With the selection of a new pope starting tomorrow, we will provide a new path to our understanding of Jesus's time here on earth."

He paused again and looked at everyone. They were all exhausted.

✝✝✝

ARCHBISHOP BALLESTRERO'S CHAMBERS, THE ROYAL PALACE, TURIN, ITALY, EVENING, TUESDAY, OCTOBER 11, AD 1988

"Your Eminence?" Father Rossi looked in on Archbishop Ballestrero. His door was open. Having worked with Ballestrero many years, he simply walked in and sat down.

"I am rereading some of the results from the STURP report. Regardless of what this radiocarbon testing indicates, I'll need to be prepared for the questions that will follow."

Rossi had a copy of the report in his hands as well. "I particularly like the finding that says, 'We can conclude for now that the Shroud image is that of a real human form of a scourged, crucified man. It is not the product of an artist.'"

"It's been five years—"

"Seven," Rossi interjected, glad to have been part of such an important scientific inquiry.

"It's been seven years since the STURP report was published, and as I reread it, new meaning and new questions continue to come from it." Ballestrero emphasized *seven*, knowing he needed to have the facts straight if asked by the press. "It says, 'The basic problem from a scientific point of view is that some explanations, which might be tenable from a chemical point of view, are precluded by physics. Contrariwise, certain physical explanations, which may be attractive, are completely precluded by the chemistry.'"[8]

Ballestrero would have liked to have had conclusive proof of how the im-

---

7 Barrie Schwortz: Official documenting photographer of the STURP research team.

8 Excerpted from a summary of STURP's conclusions provided as a press release at the final meeting of STURP, September 4, 2021, https://www.Shroud.com/78conclu.htm.

age was made but was more than satisfied with the thoroughness of the report and the presentation of their findings. He hoped the next round of analysis would take man's understanding of the miraculous image even further. More importantly, he hoped the Shroud and the results would help Christians and non-Christians all over the world.

"This cloth remains an enigma even when the best scientists keep trying to understand its construction. It's either an incredibly well-done fake or a recording of the most significant, miraculous event in the history of man." Ballestrero wanted the report to prove the authenticity of the cloth but was open to whatever would result.

He stood and walked over to the window. On the street, he noticed a man dressed in black, looking up at him. The man didn't move. They both stared at each other. For some reason, the internal conflict he had in his mind dissipated into a warm sense of calm. The man turned and walked away.

✝✝✝

BRITISH MUSEUM, LONDON, ENGLAND, AND THE ROYAL PALACE, TURIN, ITALY, AFTERNOON, THURSDAY, OCTOBER 13, AD 1988

The chalkboard said it all. "1260–1390!" Dr. Michael Tite,[9] Professor Edward Hall,[10] and Dr. Robert Hedges[11] announced their conclusions at the British Museum concurrent with the announcement in Turin by Archbishop Ballestrero of the same. The results of carbon dating were devastating for all researchers of the Shroud of Turin. It was a blow to the heart of all Shroud scientists. Anyone studying the Shroud had to reevaluate their beliefs as to its authenticity. The archbishop contracted with three separate laboratories to determine the age of samples taken from the Shroud and they were in concurrence.

"1325," Archbishop Ballestrero announced. "1325." This second time repeated in a more sullen voice. "We have used three separate laboratories to determine the age of the Shroud cloth, and they have each determined an age ranging between AD 1260 and AD 1390. This is the time believed to be when it was located in Lirey, France. During this time, it is believed the de Charny family of Rigney gave possession of the Shroud over to the small church in Lirey, France, built specially to house the Shroud.

The noise in the room was deafening. No one expected this age. Upon

---

9 Professor Michael Tite: Director of the Oxford University Research Laboratory for Archaeology and the History of Art.

10 Professor Edward Hall: Research Laboratory for Archaeology and the History of Art Laboratory, Oxford University.

11 Professor Robert Hedges: Deputy Director of the Laboratory of Archaeology and the History of Art, Oxford University.

the conclusion of the archbishop's remarks, reporters ran from the room to post their stories.

The archbishop didn't remain long to answer questions. It was an utter disappointment. He retired to his chambers, exhausted. The results were in such contradiction to his expectations that he couldn't keep his mind from racing. He was drained and realized this result would be his downfall. He would be cast aside from the church for having led the scientific analysis found to dispel the authenticity of the most valuable relic of Christianity.

The headline in London's Sunday *Times* read, "Official: The Turin Shroud is a Fake"

"Your Eminence, I'm sorry to bring you this news, but I am only following your wishes. It seems all the major news outlets have the same message." Father Rossi tried to calm his friend and mentor. "I suggest that after all this noise quiets down, we can investigate how this date is in such contradiction with all the other studies." A pile of seven different newspapers showed the same general headline: the Shroud is a fake created around AD 1325.

"I am sorry. I have let you down. I have let everyone down," Ballestrero lamented. "I was certain that after all the evidence from all the different scientists that this was going to produce, once and for all, conclusive evidence that this Shroud was the authentic burial cloth of Jesus Christ. At the very least that it dated from the first century."

After a moment, Ballestrero continued. "I will wait a few months, then I will resign my post as archbishop. I can't imagine His Holiness will want to have me as one of his subjects." Ballestrero sighed. "I don't know what will become of you. I wish for you to accompany me in retirement, but I'm not sure you would want that."

"The Lord himself goes before you and will be with you; he will never leave you nor forsake you." Father Rossi recalled the verse from Deuteronomy. "I will never leave you nor forsake you." His longtime friend and mentor had just been dealt a ruinous defeat. The comforting words of Moses showed that his mentor was not alone.

Ballestrero finished the verse, "Do not be afraid; do not be discouraged." He smiled at the words from Deuteronomy. He found them to be some of the most powerful words of comfort in the Old Testament. It was the only bright spot in the day. The love Rossi showed to him eased his mind after the sad events of the morning.

"No, Brother Rossi, I will let you contemplate your alternatives. I will help you find another more valuable posting."

CHAPTER 13

The Turin Fire

The story of the Shroud did not end with the 1988 radiocarbon testing. The radiocarbon testing was not the final word. Not everyone believed the radiocarbon dating was valid. The Shroud continued to be venerated, albeit to a much lesser extent. There were still believers of its authenticity—radiocarbon dating be damned. Over years and decades, the validity of the dating came into question.

The Shroud remained stored in the Cathedral of Saint John the Baptist in Turin. The cathedral was built at the end of the seventeenth century—over three centuries before—by Charles Emmanuel[1] II, duke of Savoy, to house and protect the Shroud. Safeguards continued to advance, but eventually they were too good. When fire broke out, instead of protecting the Shroud they hampered its rescue.

THE ROYAL PALACE, TURIN
ABOUT 8:00 P.M., FRIDAY, APRIL 10, AD 1997

*T*he first drag on a fresh cigarette blunted the adrenaline that was only now subsiding. "It's not often we get to serve the UN Secretary

---

1 Duke Charles Emmanuel II: Duke of Savoy, AD 1638–1675. Born AD 1634, died AD 1675.

General.[2] I wonder what the big hubbub is all about." Emilio looked over at his prospective late evening conquest.

Both of them enjoyed the fresh air outside the Swiss Hall of the Turin Royal Palace. With all the candles burning inside the palace, it was getting pretty stuffy. "It doesn't really matter as long as they're paying." They both laughed.

"That kitchen is hot. The fans are never strong enough. Even in this spring weather, it's not cool enough in there." Emilio lit up another cigarette. His sweat was finally starting to slow. He moved his shoulder to unstick his shirt from his back. It was the first time all night where he was able to take a break from the heat and the constant running back and forth between the chafing dishes and the dining room.

Giana took a last drag on her cigarette and threw the butt into the drainage stones behind the hedgerow. "We need to go in. They will need their plates from the sixth course cleared." She stretched up on her toes and kissed the taller Emilio on his cheek. It was the second cigarette she had enjoyed during their short break.

Emilio still had a few drags left on his MS—the most popular cigarette brand in Italy. It burned his throat a bit more than the American brands. He was proud to be an Italian and smoking Italian. He waited for Giana to disappear inside. They had worked together many times, and at the end of the night, they would frequently end up having a few glasses of white wine and much more.

He turned and made his way in. Giana was no longer in sight. He cavalierly flicked his cigarette into the ashtray. It missed and fell on the floor and rolled under the door. He didn't care that it was still lit and smoking.

✝✝✝

SAINT JOHN THE BAPTIST CATHEDRAL, TURIN
ABOUT 11:00 P.M., FRIDAY, APRIL 11, AD 1997

"Dinner was excellent this evening. I could eat pasta every day of the week." Guido Principe kissed his wife and moved into the bedroom. He started to take off his shirt and pants. Guido and his wife lived in a modest home only a few blocks away from the Turin palace.

"But I feed you pasta every night, Guido." His wife, Giovanetta, followed him into the bedroom. "I know exactly what you like. A little pasta, a little sauce, and a lot of prosecco."

---

2 Kofi Annan: Secretary-General of the United Nations from AD 1997 to 2006. Born AD 1938, died AD 2018.

They had barely hit the bed before they fell asleep. "Guido, wake up, wake up."

There was a shadow of a man outside their bedroom window.

Guido wasn't sure if someone had been calling him or if it had been a dream. But he was certain there was a man in black next to his window. The man remained there only until he saw Guido up and awake.

I'm never going to get back to sleep tonight. He frowned and furled his brow. The shadow of the streetlamp lifted, and the light came streaming into the bedroom. His wife was snoring, so he nudged her. After a moment, when she didn't roll over, he nudged her again. She didn't roll over, and she didn't stop snoring. Guido noticed a new color of light coming in from the window—an unusual orange that flickered between darker and lighter shades.

Guido got up and looked out their window. "Giovanetta, wake up." Now he was much more adamant. He never thought he would see something like this, but he knew exactly what it was. "The phone, the phone!" Down below, walking away from the window, was a man dressed in black.

Guido ran to the phone and dialed 1-1-2, the Italian emergency number. "Hallo, Hallo." The orange light danced across the rooftops. Finally the operator came on the line. "There is a fire. A fire. A fire at the palace, maybe the chapel of the Shroud." Guido took a fast breath. "I can't tell where it is, but it's definitely a fire, and it's getting stronger. Hurry. Hurry!"

✝✝✝

SAINT JOHN THE BAPTIST CATHEDRAL, TURIN
1:15 A.M., SATURDAY, APRIL 12, AD 1997

A squad of eight firefighters entered the cathedral and ran immediately to the Shroud. The Shroud had been positioned behind the altar since the restorations had begun in the Guarini Chapel, directly adjacent to Saint John the Baptist Cathedral. They looked on without knowing what to do.

Squad leader Mario Trematore[3] was the first to enter. He knew it would be tough to break through the one-and-a-half-inch thick glass without some help. This was his church and his Shroud, and he was responsible for fighting fire in this church.

Bang. "Glass is already falling on the case!" More glass sprinkled down and made a high-pitched percussive sound. A twelve-inch triangular wedge of glass from the roof landed on the case safeguarding the casket holding the Shroud. *Bang.* Another piece fell to the floor.

---

3 Mario Trematore: Fireman, Turin, Italy. Rescued the Shroud during the fire of AD 1997 in Saint John the Baptist Cathedral.

"Make way!" Trematore boomed. "Make way!" He had brought the sledgehammer and prayed it would help to free the Shroud from its protective case. The first blow glanced off the outer layer of protective glass. He'd only used a sledgehammer a few times before.

His first blow was a test. He didn't want to hit it too hard and damage the silver-plated casket that held the most valuable of all relics. He didn't care what the nine-year-old radiocarbon dating said. This was the Shroud of Turin, and it was real. The blow was not aimed quite right. "Give me more room."

He swung again. *Thud.* This time a solid strike, but the bulletproof glass didn't budge. Not even a mark. He reached back and swung again with his whole body behind it, resulting in a crack of the glass.

The other firemen looked on and gave verbal support. Again. Again. More strikes, and finally, the outer protective glass started to move. He continued striking the glass until the crack widened and the glass started to give way.

Sirens and horns blared in the background, while debris crashed all around them. Their anxiety intensified. They were losing their confidence that they could save the Shroud in time.

The booms echoed through the sanctuary. *Bang.* More glass fell from above. "*Attenti! Attenti!*" Everyone had to scream to be heard. After innumerable blows, the outer glass cracked into layers of spider-web shards. Holes formed where the hammer struck. Finally, the glass cracked all the way along the bottom. "*Attenti!*" Mario reached out and pulled the outer glass down, and it came crashing to the floor.

Mario wiped his brow. Fake or not, he was not going to let this fire destroy the Shroud.

A glass box protected the silver-plated casket and provided another layer of protection. Mario inhaled smoke as he took one more deep breath and struck the glass box. The smoke got thicker. There were only a few inches between the glass wall and the silver. Large shards of glass and masonry blanketed the top of the glass box protecting the silver casket. More shards from the roof continued to fall. Mario coughed and smokey phlegm came up.

"Careful, Careful!" The squad leader didn't want to damage the precious contents behind the glass. One shard hit his arm and glanced off his thick protective jacket and went unnoticed. Mario grabbed the hammer different-ly now trying shortened and quicker blows. *Thud. Thud. Thud!* The booms echoed throughout the cathedral. The light in the church flickered between orange and black as the flames burst forth and then were hidden by the smoke. The next blow finally broke through the glass. The head of the sledgehammer penetrated about two inches, but the glass didn't give way.

Mario aimed about four inches to the left and broke through again after two swings. Another six inches to the left, two more swings, and he broke through again. Again and again he swung. Was the hole large enough? Mario put the hammer down and leaned it against his leg.

"Help me pull this glass away! Tutti!" All those present joined the rescue. Two of Mario's squad helped pull the remaining shards out of the way of the casket so it could be removed. The glass was strong enough to stop a bullet but not strong enough to hinder the faith represented in this sacred casket.

"Wait. Enough!" Mario threw the hammer to the floor and reached in to grab the casket. It was about one foot high, one foot deep, and four feet long. The squad looked on in awe at the elaborate silver plating. It wasn't something they would ever have thought they would be this close to.

Mario grabbed the casket and raised it onto his shoulder. "Out of the way. Out of the way!"

Everyone in the squad surrounded him and placed a hand on the casket. It would not be allowed to fall. A seal with a thin, red ribbon ran down the center and around the width. From the top of the casket, it resembled a beautiful red cross against the silver décor. The décor sparkled in the makeshift lights.

Each man present would have given his life to save this relic. Though the scientists thought they had disproven the authenticity of the Shroud, it belonged to the valiant firefighters. Clouded in smoke, Mario's squad still had faith that it was the true burial cloth of Jesus.

✝✝✝

CHAPEL OF THE HOLY SHROUD, TURIN
EARLY MORNING, FRIDAY, APRIL 19, AD 1997

"In an old building like this, I'll bet the wiring is at least fifty years old." Massimo and his assistant Luca walked around the back of the chapel where the Shroud was stored. Massimo was Turin's chief fire inspector and Luca his new assistant fire inspector. It was the first time they had worked together.

They stepped carefully so as not to trip on the debris. Pieces of glass, stone, ceiling tiles, and charred wood lay all over the floor.

"Some of the wiring is probably even older. When was electricity invented?" Massimo smiled.

"I'm amazed the Shroud wasn't damaged. How blessed we are," Luca commented, following Massimo as they walked through the wreckage. There was a beautiful painting completely burned on one corner, charred on the rest.

"I was involved in a murder case that turned out not to be murder," Massimo started to relate one of his last investigations. "It turned out it was old wiring, old junction boxes, and old circuit breakers. Actually, they weren't circuit breakers. They were fuses." Massimo stepped over the glass shards and smashed panes of bulletproof glass. "This reminds me of what I read about the fire in the 1500s. The Shroud was locked behind a gate, and no one could break through. Finally, the Chambéry blacksmith was able to pry open the gate so the Shroud could be removed.

"I read that the US Constitution is safeguarded by a system that automatically lowers it down many floors so it can't be damaged by smoke, fire, or water. At night it descends on an elevator into a vault below the floor." Luca was proud of his knowledge of the system.

"In these old buildings, there might be catacombs below the display cases. Who knows what you'll find down there." Massimo made his way from the temporary location where Fireman Mario Trematore saved the Shroud to some of the cables that had been set up for the renovations. "You see, this is what should never be done. These high amperage tools, which make renovation easy, are an accident waiting to happen. They can put out spikes and currents these old cables just weren't ready for."

Luca knelt next to him and pulled up the extension cord. It was singed, almost beyond recognition. He and Massimo followed it back to the source. "Nothing unusual here. The thing so challenging with an electrical fire, actually any fire, is that everything, including almost all of the evidence, goes up with the fire." Luca sighed. "I just hope we can find the cause of this one. If it turns out to be arson, that arsonist wouldn't last long in prison.

"Turinese don't like anyone who would deface a church, much less someone who would deface our most prized relic. Nobody believes that radiocarbon dating crap. There is no way anyone could believe that the image on the Shroud was painted."

Massimo tapped Luca on his forearm. "In an old building like this, a good mechanical joint can loosen up over fifty years' time. Copper can oxidize and then with just too much amperage, it can heat up and start a fire inside the wall."

"The world isn't going to want to hear that the Italians can't do some simple fire detective work." Massimo sighed, realizing they may not ever determine the cause. He also realized he would be personally blamed if they couldn't find the source of the fire. "My money is on exactly that. An electrical fire behind the walls caused by running modern construction machines on old cable. The problem is that with all this destruction, it won't be safe for us to inspect everywhere to find the source, whether it was electrical or not."

Luca entered the remains of the Swiss Hall. Everything was charred or burned. It was here that the chafing dishes for the UN Secretary-General's affair in the Royal Palace were held. The chafing dishes kept each dish of the six-course meal warm so everyone could be served at exactly the same time, regardless of when the food came out of the kitchen.

"I was hoping the caterers were returning in the morning after the meal to do their final cleanup, but that is not the case. All of the dishes, warming trays, and chafing dishes were removed prior to the start of the fire." Luca was disappointed that this was not going to go well to find the cause of the fire, especially if it was electrical in nature.

"Look at how many dishes were heated on the one extension cord. The caterer's report claims they had eight chafing dishes in this room set up on four folding tables." Massimo could easily see that this, too, could overload the old wiring and cause a hidden fire behind the walls.

"A fire behind the walls could burn for hours before it made its presence known. Look here." Luca pointed to the outlet for the chafing dishes. He got down on his knees. "We'll need to determine how much amperage one of these dishes requires. I'll bet it's more than the circuit allows, and there were eight of them."

"Four amps." Massimo knew. "Four amps. That's about 32 amps on one circuit designed for fifteen or twenty. This is definitely one option."

"Since the reconstruction has been underway for over seven years, it is unlikely something changed in the electrical reconstruction usage that would cause the circuits to overheat." Massimo could see that the chafing dishes were a possible flash point of the fire. "Let's keep looking."

"Agreed. There's still a lot more to see." Luca stood up and began looking elsewhere.

"The caterers should follow specific electrical standards when they cater events in these historic buildings. We should make that recommendation as part of our report." Massimo made a note on his notepad.

"Massimo, we should review exactly what the construction schedule was for the week leading up to the night of the fire. Were they doing anything differently that day? Did anyone stay late to finish their tasks? Let's hope the project leader has good records of exactly the work being performed."

"Let us hope his notes didn't burn up in the fire." Massimo picked up a cigarette butt and put it in a bag for evidence. "This butt didn't cause the fire, but we'll need to make certain we check for others." This cigarette butt was singed on the side that faced up but still white on the other side, indicating the used butt was a victim of the fire, not the cause. On the unsinged side was a smudge of lipstick. "A wayward cigarette butt may be option number three."

"The same applies here as well. This room has always been used for warming stations prior to serving the food." Luca interjected a similar thought about the catering. "Why was last night any different from previous events? There are eight warming stations. Let's review their report as well."

✝✝✝

It took months to finish the investigation, with several teams researching the source of the fire. After six months there was no conclusive report, as each team found differing causes. One team believed it was arson, and another team found no chemical accelerants to support that theory. Another team concluded overheated circuits ignited flammable chemicals used in the reconstruction process. Others had other conclusions.

But they all agreed that the fire hazard warning system was inadequate and that the damage would have been significantly less had it been fully up to code.

CHAPTER 14

Is Not Seeing Not Believing?

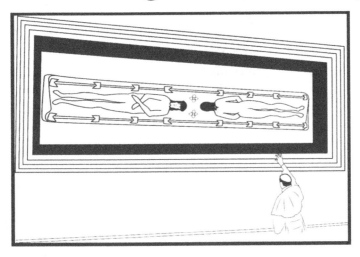

The papacy was hesitant to make a statement on the authenticity of the Shroud, generally declaring a hiatus on further testing of the cloth. Whether a work of art fabricated by the hand of man or as a witness to the resurrection, it would serve as a focal point to contemplate the suffering of Jesus during the passion.

SAINT JOHN THE BAPTIST CATHEDRAL, TURIN, ITALY
AFTERNOON, SUNDAY, MAY 24, AD 1998

"**P**urple is a perfect color for the display," the pope's photographer, Matteo, whispered to his assistant, Mia.

The Shroud was displayed in an enormous partially gilded frame and mounted on a purple velvet background.

The pope reached out toward the Shroud and prayed, taking in the suffering of Christ and the sacrifice he made for all men. It was the first time he had meditated at the Shroud since the fire the year before.

"After all the controversy surrounding the authenticity of this cloth, I think His Holiness does believe it is truly the burial cloth of Jesus. Even from this distance, I don't know how an artist from the thirteenth or fourteenth century could have ever painted or produced this image. It's just too realistic, and out of this world." Matteo and Mia stood about forty feet away from the pope and off to the side. The pope had directed his entourage not to disturb him during his meditations.

For over ten minutes, the pope lingered in silence in front of the Shroud. He approached it, reached out and held the frame, and prayed his thanksgiving that it had not been destroyed.

Mia and Matteo continued to observe. Matteo took a telephoto shot of the pope looking directly at the wounds in the hands.

"Do you think further testing will ever conclusively prove that this is real or a fraud?" Mia asked, trying not to disturb Matteo as he photographed the pope.

"I wonder if those people who are not believers would become believers if the Shroud was determined to be authentic and dated from the first century? Would those same people not believe if the Shroud is determined to be false? If people have faith, do they need the Shroud to make their faith stronger? Isn't faith either yes or no? Do people have half-faith, and with an authentic Shroud would that faith be strengthened to three-quarters? Without the Shroud, would that faith be weakened to one-quarter?" Matteo's questions hung in the air.

"Your Holiness, it is a magnificent image. Regardless of other findings, I have faith in Jesus, and I have faith this is the true burial cloth of Jesus," Cardinal Bishop Angelo Sodano[1] said to the pope, belying his over fifty years as diplomat for the Holy See, Pope John Paul II. "Even if it is a forgery, it is a magnificent forgery, capturing the true suffering of Jesus and all that He did for us on those fateful days of His passion."

"As Catholics, we don't need tangible proof that Christ died for our sins, that He was resurrected, and that He is with God and all the saints." The cardinal straightened his robe. "We have faith. What more do we need?"

Pope John Paul II[2] was still silent. Finally, as he and a few others gathered, he broke the subdued tones. "This is an image of God's love as well as of human sin. It attests to the tremendous human capacity for causing pain and death to one's fellow man and stands as an icon of suffering of the innocent in every age."

The pope lingered in silence in front of the Shroud for another ten minutes. He approached it, grasped the frame, and stood continuing his meditations. He prayed again, thanking God for the suffering of Jesus Christ to free

---

1 Cardinal Bishop Angelo Sodano: Cardinal since AD 1991. Dean of the College of Cardinals and Cardinal Secretary of State for His Holiness, Cardinal Bishop of the Suburbicarian See of Albano, Italy.
2 Pope John Paul II: Pope from AD 1978 to 2005. Born 1920, died 2005.

all men from their sins. When he was done, he opened his eyes. They were slightly moist, as he envisioned the incredible pain Jesus suffered for him and for everyone.

Matteo attempted to capture an image of the pope's hand on the frame and on the hands of Jesus. It wasn't quite the shot he was looking for, but the camera clicked, nevertheless. "Maybe we can do some effects after the fact."

The pope turned to Sodano. "Perhaps we should allow some further testing on the cloth. Since it is not a matter of faith, it is not for the church to decide. We must entrust scientists with the task of continuing to investigate the questions connected with this sheet. What do you think?"

Sodano nodded his agreement and the two of them proceeded out of the hall.

✝✝✝

LOS ALAMOS, NEW MEXICO
MIDMORNING, WEDNESDAY, OCTOBER 24, AD 2004

"When I published this paper, I knew it was going to cause a brouhaha," Raymond Rogers[3] said, using one of his favorite words. "After the 1260 to 1390 announcement that the Shroud was a medieval fake, my research adds a new page to the vetting of the Shroud as the authentic burial cloth of Jesus Christ. Just as important as Dr. Frei's pollen study, this analysis will be something that all of Christianity and all of humanity will positively embrace."

Ray Rogers, chemist and Shroud researcher, sat with Dan McKay, radio host and interviewer. They both wore headphones and sat in front of bulbous foamy microphones. Behind the soundproof glass stood a team of producers and editors broadcasting the audio out over the airwaves. Rogers was one of the original STURP research team and had continued performing additional research to determine the authenticity of the Shroud. Twenty-five years after the STURP project, he continued to bring new scientific findings to the world.

"So how does this differ from what the radiocarbon dating derived as the date of the Shroud?" The radio interview proceeded, touching on all the key points for and against the authenticity of the Shroud.

"That research was a major blow to the dating of the Shroud and set us back many decades. The perceptions about the authenticity of the burial cloth may never recover. I believe there were several flaws in their research, but today I want to talk about a separate line of research, which adds to the mounting evidence that the Shroud is the true witness to the moment

---

3 Raymond Rogers: Director of Chemical Research for the Shroud of Turin Research Project (STURP). Born AD 1927, died AD 2005.

of Jesus's resurrection." Rogers was careful how he proceeded with his argumentation. He had practiced with his wife to make certain it would be easily understood by a nonscientist.

"The method described in my paper differs markedly from the radiocarbon dating. It uses a chemical analysis of the provided samples and indicates the results of the radiocarbon testing were wrong. I don't doubt radiocarbon testing, but I do doubt the sampling process. When the three radiocarbon laboratories in Arizona, Oxford, and Zurich ran their tests, there was something wrong with the samples. They were either contaminated, not properly treated, or not properly selected. GIGO: garbage in, garbage out. Even the inventor of radiocarbon dating, Professor Libby from the University of Chicago, brought forward these potential areas of inaccuracy of his dating process."

"How do you come to this conclusion?" Collin McKay[4] had been following the analysis of the Shroud and knew his Christian listeners would be keenly interested in any new news. He was a Shroud advocate, although he hadn't yet heard a fully conclusive argument refuting the radiocarbon dating.

"Today, I want to speak about another test. I have run a separate analysis using a different methodology. My analysis looks at vanillin and lignin as well as the dyes in the Shroud. These are two organic chemicals found in all plant fibers. You see, the samples analyzed by the three labs, I believe, show a unique coating with a yellow-brown plant gum. I believe this plant gum was applied either by the Poor Clares Sisters or Father Valfrè to match the colors of the repairs to the original Shroud material."

"Are you saying you may have found plant gum on the Shroud? I thought the STURP team found no such thing?" McKay played the antagonist in the discussion.

"That's a good question. As you may recall, I was one of the STURP team members and our examination at the time did determine that the image was not made by hand. No paint, dye, or other colorants were found." Rogers breathed in, certain he could clarify the question. "We must be careful not to conflate the cloth containing the image with the cloth taken as a sample for the radiocarbon testing. They are two very different things. The image is in the center of the Shroud. The radiocarbon samples were taken near a corner of the Shroud."

"Okay, that makes sense. And I guess it wouldn't make sense to take a sample from the image itself," McKay said, trying to add to the reasoning behind the question. "I would imagine the pope wouldn't allow that, especially if it were a destructive test."

4 Collin McKay: Radio interviewer, KNKT Albuquerque, New Mexico.

"Correct. My conjecture is that Father Valfrè or possibly the Poor Clares Sisters or possibly someone else—we may never know—repaired the cloth in the corner directly where the radiocarbon samples were taken." Ray Rogers continued his discourse.

"Father Valfrè or someone else using a French weave, also known as an invisible weave, wove in new threads to strengthen the top edge used to hold the Shroud during centuries of exhibitions. I hypothesize that the samples taken for the radiocarbon dating were not wholly made up of the original cloth. They were made of thread, possibly a mix of linen and cotton, from the fifteenth or sixteenth century, mixed in with the original fabric woven into the Shroud during one of these repair processes." Rogers realized he was getting a bit scientific. Exactly what his wife warned him about. "I apologize for the scientific details, but I think they're important. The radiocarbon dated samples couldn't provide a date from the beginning of the first millennium because they were rewoven in the 1530s by the Poor Clares Sisters or, more likely, by Father Valfrè in the late 1600s when they repaired the cloth." Rogers hoped he was able to explain this critical hypothesis so the audience would fully understand.

"The radiocarbon dating is one to three hundred years prior to their repairs? How is that possible?" McKay pushed back a bit, certain Rogers would be able to explain his conclusions.

"Before I answer that, let's understand the age of the actual Shroud cloth based on my new methodology and research. Vanillin is a component of lignin, two chemicals found in all cloth. However as a cloth ages, vanillin decays out of the cloth and over time disappears completely from the sample. This is the case for a correct sample of the original cloth. There's no vanillin in the lignin. Had I been present at the radiocarbon dating announcement at the British Museum, these are the six words I would have written on the chalkboard: there's no vanillin in the lignin."

"How significant is this result?" McKay played up to Roger's ego.

"It is extremely significant." Rogers enjoyed the question. "Radiocarbon dating is just one chemical method to date an archaeological artifact. It has many flaws, and I'm sure that over time the flaws in the radiocarbon testing will come to light." This was a direct jab at the three labs and their results. "Testing for vanillin in the lignin is also a chemical test, just that it is searching for the relative amounts of vanillin. And it is a simpler process to test."

"In your paper, you mention that the temperature at which the Shroud was stored could affect the decay rate of the vanillin. How would that affect your age estimates?"

"Exactly. If the cloth were stored at twenty-five degrees Celsius, ninety-five percent of the vanillin would be lost after 1,319 years. This is the same as about seventy-seven degrees Fahrenheit. At twenty degrees Celsius, it would take about 3,095 years. Given that there is no vanillin in the sample, the age of the specimen must be at least 1,300 years old, if not older. It couldn't be just 600 years old as the radiocarbon dating suggested."

"With this study have you invalidated the radiocarbon dating?" McKay wanted Rogers to come to a firm conclusion.

"Yes. Exactly. There is something wrong in the radiocarbon dating, and my belief is that the errors in the result will be found out." Rogers was glad he was able to make a definitive statement as to his opinion concerning the radiocarbon testing.

"One thing I always have trouble with science is that they can never prove a positive. It can only prove a negative." McKay reached back into his science classes from years before. "That is, in your case you can only prove the Shroud is at least 1,300 years old—much older than the radiocarbon testing would have us believe—but you can't prove it is the authentic burial Shroud of Jesus Christ."

"Yes, I don't think we'll ever be able to prove the Shroud's authenticity. We will only be able to show with a high probability that it dates to the first century and that all indications are that it is of a crucified man from that era and that the imaging process was not known at that time, nor known even today. It was miraculously generated." Rogers restated what his wife had told him almost word for word if this question came up.

"Now to your question of the two hundred year difference in the radiocarbon dating to the date of the Poor Clares's repairs. I'm not sure I have a good answer there. My unsupported opinion is that there was some contamination across their samples. Most likely, the samples taken were the repaired edge of the Shroud, where there was a mix of new and old fibers and where the Shroud was most handled during its exhibitions. This left behind sweat and oils from their hands on that particular spot. In addition, radiocarbon dating was only in its infancy when the original test was conducted. The technology is now much more mature as is my recommendation to Pope John Paul II, the Catholic Church, and Archbishop Giovanni Saldarini[5] of Turin. He's the person responsible for the Shroud, the official custodian. I recommend a second, more careful, radiocarbon test of the Shroud be undertaken."

---

5 Archbishop Giovanni Saldarini of Turin: Archbishop of Turin from AD 1984 to 1999. Born AD 1924, died AD 2011

"Would the fire of 1532 have made a difference, or even the recent fire in Turin, in your vanillin results?" McKay rephrased the question. "Would either of these events—generating excessive heat and smoke and carbon—would either of these events have contaminated the Shroud and affected the accuracy of the vanillin-lignin dating?"

"Highly unlikely, since linen is not a good conductor of heat. The fire, in comparison to two thousand years, these fires lasted only an instant. And the damage was highly localized to where the silver melted and then burned through the cloth. By the way, this is the same thing, that is, the loss of vanillin. The loss of vanillin is what we see with other old linen cloths that have been tested in this way. For example, the lignin of the Dead Sea Scrolls indicates no vanillin either."

"Dr. Rogers we're out of time but if I may summarize your conclusions. First, you found no vanillin in the lignin, meaning that the cloth is at least 1,300 years old, much older than that found through the 1988 radiocarbon dating.

"Second, that the corner where the radiocarbon samples were taken may have either been corrupted with other threads from the time of the repair and/or the sample was not properly cleaned to remove grime and oils from the centuries of exhibitions, specifically using that corner to hold the Shroud."

"That is exactly correct. If we were to invalidate the results of the radiocarbon testing, all the other tests, which we didn't even talk about, all point to a dating of the Shroud somewhere near the first century." Ray Rogers made his last plug to nudge listeners to doubt the validity of the radiocarbon testing.

"There you have it, ladies and gentlemen. Another dimension in the controversy surrounding the Shroud. The brouhaha continues. This is Collin McKay of KNKT, Albuquerque."

✝✝✝

Los Alamos, New Mexico
Noon, Wednesday, October 24, AD 2004

"With that, I disagree. Whether the Shroud is authentic or not should have nothing to do with a true Christian's faith. I can't remember exactly what Jesus said to doubting Thomas. Something like, 'Not seeing and believing is much more important than seeing and then believing.'" McKay and Rogers were both done with their lunch and waited for the waitress to clear the table and bring them some coffee.

"The question is, how does the Shroud, whether true or false, affect your faith?" McKay continued his questioning, as if they were still on air.

Rogers realized he was getting too impassioned. He lowered his volume and slowed the pace of his response to McKay. He had already had enough excitement for the day. "Should it make a difference? Is your faith stronger because there is proof of Jesus's miraculous resurrection? Or is it just something interesting further confirming a faith that is already confirmed?"

"My only point is that there are those who need to see, like the Missourians—the show-me state—they need to be shown. They don't just take things for granted," Rogers continued. "There are others who have faith without seeing."

"But—" McKay tried to interject.

"However there are nonbelievers—and there are more and more of them every day—who may come freely to faith with a proven, valid burial cloth of Jesus. How many people were once believers but have lost their way? How many came back after the awful events of nine eleven and have again fallen away?" Rogers emphasized his words, except this time with disappointment in his tone. "How many of them will have children who will have never been touched by the love and knowledge of Jesus Christ? How many will not know that He suffered unbearably on the cross, took on our sins, died for us, and then came back, resurrected like He said He would?"

"Are you saying the Shroud is a way to evangelize non-Christians?" McKay felt like he was interviewing again.

"No. Well yes. I am saying there are many ways to convert non-Christians. Perhaps an authentic Shroud could be one of them." Rogers was enlivened by the discussion. He was a chemist and a Christian, and part of his faith was to evangelize nonbelievers.

"I tend to agree with you, but that doesn't mean we need the Shroud for the believer. Don't we need it for the fallen believer or the never-believer? If a nonbeliever or a doubter could be swayed through the Shroud to follow Jesus Christ, then couldn't it be a valuable tool in Jesus's commission for Christians to bring more believers closer to Christ?" McKay had learned early in his career that by posing his opinion in the form of a question, it didn't fully give away his stance on the question.

The waitress cleared the table behind McKay and listened in on the arguments both men gave. She put her hand to the cross hanging around her neck.

"Yes, I would agree, but I would permit that if it were billed as a controversial work of art that might be the true burial cloth of Jesus Christ. This is what its perception is today by many nonbelievers." Rogers leaned in. "There will always be believers of the Shroud regardless of the science, and there will always be disbelievers regardless of the science."

"Even many Christians have the perception that it is simply a work of art, a work of forgery, and not the authentic burial cloth of Jesus." McKay pushed his point, even though he wasn't 100 percent convinced of its legitimacy. "And yet they believe."

"If it is not the true burial cloth but, instead, a work of art, it will not bring nonbelievers to Christ. I'm sorry I can't abide by that argument. Rogers spoke softly to drive his final point home. "However if it is truly the burial cloth of Jesus, it is one of the most important relics known to man. It provides proof of the most consequential event in human history—the resurrection of Jesus Christ. Perhaps it would be better to call it the resurrection cloth. As a simple burial Shroud, it would simply show his blood and other fluids from his body. As the Resurrection Shroud, it provides an enduring witness of the most important event in human history."

> Then Jesus told him, "Because you have seen me, you have believed; blessed are those who have not seen and yet have believed.". . . But these are written that you may believe that Jesus is the Messiah, the Son of God, and that by believing you may have life in his name. (John 20:29, 31 NIV)

EPILOGUE

Can we ever discern the truth? There is my truth and your truth, but can we ever discern the true truth?

*W*here does the story go from here? Will there be other tests? In 2013 Padua University repeated the radiocarbon testing, and their results yielded an age between 280 BC and AD 220. Many scientists felt these results were tainted because of the Christian bias of the researchers. Will there be other results that will contradict these? Were these, or any other tests, simply reflecting confirmation bias, or were they truly unbiased, providing a definitive rebuttal to the controversial 1988 radiocarbon dating results? The pollen testing, the chemical testing, the matching with the Sudarium, and now the new radiocarbon testing all speak scientifically to its authenticity.

The original radiocarbon testing speaks against it. New data surrounding the tests have mostly debunked the validity of the radiocarbon dating. There were many errors in their testing: they didn't follow the agreed sampling, they communicated between themselves, which they agreed not to do, and they may have fudged the statistics surrounding their results. Recent data has come to light that all of the sample results have systematic statistical bias. This bias wasn't made public. It means that there is an unexplained error that could potentially invalidate their findings. They may have even covered up the way they calculated the validation statistics of their results.

The naysayers stick with their alleged facts: there was no mention of the Shroud before the 1300s, that is, the Dark Ages. The radiocarbon dating is always referenced as being the true date of the Shroud, bolstering the date above and that de Charny was a charlatan, having commissioned the cloth to be painted. Will the church allow further testing, and will new tests and new methods confirm or deny the authenticity of the Shroud? Will any new evidence reduce the controversy of whether it is the true burial cloth of Jesus, or will it just lead to more discord? Only God knows how this story will unfold.

I hope I have provided a plausible history of the resurrection Shroud—how it traveled from Jerusalem, from Golgotha, to Turin, and all the stops in between. It is important for man to be able to see and believe, but as Jesus taught us, it is blessed to believe and not see.

I'm sure over the years, new evidence will come to light that may change some of the elements of this story. I look forward to learning about them and will hope to incorporate them into my story. If you find anything that might be incorrect or implausible, please reach out to me through my website, GuyPowell.com.

In the meantime, I will be publishing a supplement on the Sudarium, the Face Cloth of Oviedo, the Crown of Thorns, and the True Cross. Stay tuned.

More and more evidence has been collected pointing to the authenticity of the Shroud. No one will ever know, but the evidence continues to mount.

Sign up here for more information. www.GuyPowell.com/Shroud.

ORDER INFORMATION

REDEMPTION
P R E S S

To order additional copies of this book, please visit
www.redemption-press.com.
Also available at Christian bookstores and Barnes and Noble.

FIND OUT MORE (GUYPOWELL.COM)

NEW BOOKS ON THEIR WAY FROM GUY POWELL

If you liked this book, stayed tuned for more. This is the first in a series of books on valuable relics of Jesus. Books planned or in process include *The Sudarium, The Crown of Thorns, The Holy Grail,* and others.

THE SHROUD OF TURIN

View and listen to some great videos recorded by the author interviewing some of the most well-known experts, researchers, and scientists studying the Shroud and other invaluable relics.

Visit guypowell.com and sign up to receive the latest news on the Shroud of Turin and Guy Powell.

Https://www.guypowell.com

CPSIA information can be obtained
at www.ICGtesting.com
Printed in the USA
BVHW081938280623
666449BV00008B/364